Private '

'In a sense, the real heroine is not s(
that part within a mile's radius of Liv
. . . conveys with great freshness th
ugly quality, its capacity for absorbi_
for re-inventing itself in the process' Ruth Pavey, *Independent*

'McNeil has a poet's eye for the warehouses, caffs and galleries of
newly gentrified Clerkenwell . . . It is a singular pleasure to read
McNeil's prose. She has an extraordinary feel for language and on
every page she surprises the reader with arresting turns of phrase
. . . *Private View* is a delight to read' Philip Ells, *Canada Post*

'Haunting absences lie at the elusive centre of this memorable new
novel . . . McNeil casts a . . . sharp and evocative eye on twenty-
first-century London . . . a memorable piece of reportage from the
psychic spaces of the way we live now' Phil Baker, *TLS*

'A strong, clear-headed writer brings freshness and vibrancy to [her]
characters . . . complicated, nuanced and crackling with
cosmopolitanism' T. F. Rigelhof, *Globe & Mail* (Canada)

Nights in a Foreign Country

'A superb collection of 14 zesty short stories – sensual, razor-sharp –
set in Canada, Britain, France and central America. Start reading it at
the airport and you will miss your flight'
Michael Thompson-Noel, *Financial Times*

'Her language is lyrical and tightly controlled, her characters almost
overwhelmingly vivid' *Observer*

'Nights on tropical bare mountains, doomed romance and sharp
observation combine powerfully with a taste for exotic metaphor in
Jean McNeil's highly assured debut collection of short stories'
Mary Colson, *Sunday Times*

'By turns sinister and sensual, heartfelt and anguished . . . McNeil's
vignettes summon an exhilarating sense of nights spent whiling away
the small hours on the bohemian wild side . . . Subtly crafted
narratives are delivered with control and accomplishment'
Timur Moon, *Daily Express*

Jean McNeil was born in 1968 and grew up on Cape Breton Island, Nova Scotia. She has lived in London since 1991 and has spent long periods in Latin America. She is the author of one novel, *Hunting Down Home*, and one volume of stories, *Nights in a Foreign Country*, as well as the *Rough Guide to Costa Rica*. She works as an editor and researcher at the Latin America Bureau in London.

By Jean McNeil

Private View
Nights in a Foreign Country
Hunting Down Home

private view

JEAN MⁱⁿⁿNEIL

PHOENIX

A PHOENIX PAPERBACK

First published in Great Britain in 2002
by Weidenfeld & Nicolson
A Phoenix House Book
This paperback edition published in 2003
by Phoenix,
an imprint of Orion Books Ltd,
Orion House, 5 Upper St Martin's Lane,
London WC2H 9EA

A CIP catalogue record for this book
is available from the British Library.

ISBN 0 75381 691 1

Printed and bound in Great Britain by
Clays Ltd, St Ives plc

The battle to conquer pure sensation will always be fought in the heart of the city.

FERNANDO PESSOA, *The Book of Disquiet*

For Diego Ferrari

THE AQUARIUM

This is a moment from before she knew him, a moment like many others, which they both inhabited but have no memory of, in the way that so many moments of our lives wash off us like rain.

She has been back only a month. She walks through Chinatown, bathed in triangles of neon red and gold. Faces stream by her, like the imprisoned angelfish that swim gaudily through tanks in the restaurants that line each side of the street, eyes bulging, mouths searching for crumbs of food, while all around them diners feast on the flesh of one of their relatives.

He sits only three blocks away, on a stool at Bar Italia. They will not meet, at least not tonight. Three blocks is enough, in this city, to decide your destiny.

He asks for a café latte from the barman, who looks about twenty-eight but is already losing his hair. The cardiac arrest-strength coffee fails to revive him; he puts his arms down on the counter and lays his head down on his left arm, as bored children do.

Italian cable television roars from the dark end of the bar. Improbably blonde women newsreaders announce late snowstorms and impenetrable political clashes between small men wearing good suits. For a second the gurgle and hiss of the cappuccino machine drowns out the snowstorm blanketing Torino, the heated squabble of politics.

He sits like this for half an hour, watching the procession of faces from the street, caught in the mirror lining the bar. People swim by in the night, just like the fish in the tanks of the

Chinese restaurants. Some meander by the window, looking at him out of the corners of their eyes. Others seem to be on patrol, moving swiftly, with a purpose.

Hers is one of the faces that passes by the window. Not everyone who passes is beautiful, but in almost every face he sees something of the abrasive symmetry of beauty. He looks at each face with equal interest, wondering about the passions behind its features, what would happen if that face were to become part of his life. It's not that he is looking for love, only that he is trying to capture that specific moment, the one before desire becomes memory.

one

BREATHLESS

After the private view everyone crowded the Barley Mow on Curtain Road, standing outside on a carpet of broken bottles and pint glasses artists had smashed, mostly deliberately. Furious minicab drivers tried to plough through the crowd but it only sidled closer. The cab's wide-eyed occupants looked at the crowd with terror, as if it were one of the riot mobs taking to the streets that month in Indonesia and not a group of artists bent on getting pissed.

Conrad was in a corner talking to a group of people she had never seen before. She stayed where she was, partly because of Conrad's tendency for lacing introductions with social epitaphs: 'This is Alex. She hasn't had a show in a year. She doesn't know many people.'

She did recognize a few people, mainly by reputation: the 'twin brothers' (they weren't even brothers) who got a Turner Prize nomination last year for reconstructing Guernica using matchsticks, the sour-faced woman who did the 'inside out' installations, where she took everything inside a house and deposited it on the pavement in the same configuration.

Around one in the morning Conrad looked pointedly in her direction and rolled his eyes – the signal he was ready to go.

'So did you meet anyone tonight?' he asked as they walked home together up the Hackney Road.

'Basia.'

'Who?'

'You know, the woman who's auditioning for the role of Fucked-Up Artist.'

3

'Oh, God,' he groaned. '*Basia*.'

She had been standing near the scaffolding watching the mini-cab drivers turn puce as they were set upon once more by the art mob, when she turned around to find a small woman beside her. She struggled to recognize the woman, whose dark hair was done in pigtails, although her face suggested she was too old for the Pippi Longstocking look. The woman came closer. There was a strange fixed look in her eye.

'I'm angry. And twisted. People don't like me. They find me hard work. But I'm just screwy. I haven't had an easy life, you know.'

'I'm sure you haven't.'

The woman looked her square in the eye. 'But I'm a genius, actually.'

This was too much. 'How do you know you're a genius?'

The woman leaned – no, tipped – closer to her. 'Believe me, I *know*.'

Basia didn't look that deranged, she decided. She was well-dressed and wore subtle, well-applied make-up. She was a good artist, apparently. Alex had heard Rachel pay her the highest compliment in her universe: 'She knows her stuff.'

Before she could move away Basia gave her a hard, cunning look. 'I can barely stand to listen to these twats talking about the *art world*. How can you?'

That was enough. 'I'm standing here listening to you. I guess that makes you one of those twats.'

'Gruelling.' Conrad stopped to light a cigarette in front of the strip club on the corner. He cupped his hand around his feeble lighter. Behind him the bouncers lurked, thick men dressed in tuxedos with faces like those wide-jowled fish; what were they called? Grouper, mahi-mahi? Businessmen from the City skyscrapers down the road tripped out of black cabs and into the club's gaping mouth.

'You're just fresh meat, that's all,' Conrad went on. 'She tries to catch you out, get you to betray yourself and everyone else. Never tell her *anything*.' He shook his head. 'But you should see her work. The work will blow you away.'

'So it doesn't matter if you're a narcissistic madwoman, as long as you make good art?'

He sighed. 'Sometimes that's just the way it is. All kinds of people you wouldn't want to know personally you end up respecting as artists, or writers. Being nice doesn't seem to be a prerequisite for talent. It's not very fair.'

'So we should just excuse Basia's flawed personality because it's being pressed into service for the greater glory of Art.'

'I'm sorry you got stuck with Basia. I think everyone's afraid to talk to you, that's why you get the head cases.'

'Afraid? What are they afraid of?'

'They're worried you might start talking about what happened.'

'Why would I do that?'

'I don't know. People are paranoid. They don't want to discuss it, I guess. Maybe they think it could have been them. You know what I think?' Conrad gave her his I'm-going-to-be-frank look. 'I don't think artists are particularly sympathetic people.'

This was quite something to say, considering Conrad was an artist. So was she, or she had been. By this point they were standing in front of their flat. Conrad put the key in the door and they went inside.

That was the winter she was dragged from private view to private view by Conrad, like a mascot. He was a coward like that: she had never known him to go anywhere alone, or even to spend much time by himself. She suspected he was frightened by his own company. To others he seemed concrete, one of those distinct personalities who had made a career out of being himself. But if he was left on his own for more than two hours Conrad's idea of himself fizzed away in a cloud of smoke.

At that point she had been living with him for nine months, or rather they shared his flat, a sub-loft: a big space but not up to Clerkenwell new media tycoon standards. It was on the first floor of what used to be a timber merchant's offices near the Hackney Road. The decor reflected Conrad's obsession with emptiness: bare floorboards studded here and there with the odd non-functional white object, a desk with complicated silver lamps spidering from its surfaces, a bookshelf made of cool Norwegian pine.

The space itself was early Victorian, with tall windows and filigree patterns of woodwork ringing the ceiling. The slope in the kitchen was reflected in the lopsided omelettes and tilting cakes that came out of the oven. Subsidence. Conrad wouldn't even let her say the word. It terrified him probably more than any other word in the English language, as it carried a £20,000 price tag. Alex swallowed the word but it surfaced in her dreams, when she dreamt that the whole city was listing, like a crippled ocean liner.

They lived in an area style magazines called 'up and coming'. Before she left to go travelling, she had gone to Conrad's flat once or twice. Then it had been marooned between empty warehouses whose signs had been blasted from the brickwork, leaving ghostly brick-dust outlines: Bakelys Ironworks; T.W. Martin & Sons Upholstery. Now the warehouses were £200,000 flats and shiny, cavernous restaurants, and the view from Conrad's window was punctured by the giant stork forms of cranes tilting above Spitalfields, Canary Wharf, Blackfriars.

Over and over again, she was told how lucky she was to be surrounded by bathroom fixture warehouses, looming malevolent housing estates, the scruffy grocers of indeterminate nationality. AFRO WORLD, WICKED LADY, KINKY LADY, POLLY'S CORNER screamed the shopfronts – and they were just the shoe wholesalers. They were close to the City, and to the old East End and its streets, their names a strangely thrilling mix of commodities and philosophers: Swedenborg Gardens, Rope Walk, Elf Row, Glasshouse Street.

London: she thought of it as a winter city, garlanded by history, for all its centuries it had been stuffed with art and aristocrats and most of all, the seething poor. The greatest city in the world. She would never live anywhere else.

Still, it was difficult not to feel that buried somewhere within the triumph of these thoughts was a rehearsal of future leavings.

That night they were off to the flat of one of Conrad's rich 'friends' – otherwise known as people who bought his work. This was one of the perks of Conrad's recent semi-success: he now had a gallerist and several private collectors interested in his work, but somehow he still hadn't broken through to the stratosphere of Turner Prize nominations, of shows in Paris, in Berlin.

They would see Oliver Fielding, one of the many new technology instant millionaires; Tania Rusk, a merchant banker and her husband Jason Stonehouse, the venture capitalist. Tony Slade and Justin Mawksley were known collectors with their own design business – they were the ones responsible for the Motorola ad with a woman about to be eaten by a crocodile making her last mobile call to her hairdresser.

Jack Flaunt and Faustino Caballero were fashion designers who had hit it big by designing the so-called utility wear that had made up much of the uniform of under-thirty-fives for the last few years. They bought a couple of small paintings from Conrad, and put the children of some Brazilian oligarchs onto his work. The funds from this sale allowed Conrad to re-do their kitchen in dark grey steel, with an industrial-strength oven and unfinished surfaces. It was called a 'galley kitchen' and that's exactly how she thought of it, like being moored in some hip trawler which had floated up from the Thames.

Conrad's new friends were all only twenty-six or twenty-eight – younger than her and even younger than Conrad. The rich friends had a uniform picture of artists, which she supposed she fitted: bohemian, slouchy, charmingly uncon-cerned with making money, perhaps thinking herself morally superior because of this. They were all perfectly civil to her, but it was obvious to everyone she didn't really fit in. She was not a habitué of that permanent departure lounge they all seemed to be living in, sipping aggressive cocktails, talking in those vague droning voices which never sounded of shock or passion.

But when they went to the private views in their area it was a different crowd: *their* crowd, and therefore more real; people Conrad had gone to art school with, a proper London art school that had been credited with sparking entire movements in British art.

Conrad seemed to know everyone, and everyone him. Although in that mean Darwinian way, this had something to do with his looks. Lanky and slightly Teutonic, he was blessed with cheekbones that supported his skin like masts do sails, wheat-coloured hair and exquisite Armagnac eyes – Alex had borrowed this adjective from a bartender lover of Conrad's. She wasn't sure exactly what colour Armagnac was, or how it might differ from, say, Calvados, but it was true: his eyes were amazingly fine.

She looked across the living room, which was typical of the spaces she found herself in lately: prairie-wide, stalked by windows and the resolute darkness of a London winter night outside. She looked past the edgy furniture to where Conrad was leaning one hand on the wall, towering above a delicate-looking woman wearing pink kitten heels. She was looking up at him in a rapt, disbelieving way, most likely wondering from where this heron of a man had swooped down.

She had seen even determined women who deal with men on a resolutely asexual basis be taken apart by Conrad's eyes. His eyes found a thread inside them and slowly started to unwind it until the spool was empty and the determined women only a mass of tangled string. He had this look which he could turn on or off like a tap: desirous but unfocussed, his caramel eyes were melting, dripping down – he was taller than almost everyone – onto the face of whoever he was talking to.

The woman lit a cigarette and smoked it nervously. Alex wondered if she would meet this woman later that night, stumbling out of the bathroom, or quietly trying to close the door without waking anyone up. It used to be that nearly every night she would bump into one of these stuttering girls or thin intelligent men in the corridors of their darkened flat. Conrad was one of those rare men to whom women and men responded equally, and he himself seemed to make little distinction between the genders.

But that night they went home alone, just the two of them.

'Who was that woman you were talking to?' she said.

'Who?'

'The one with the pink shoes.'

'Didn't clock the shoes.'

Men never noticed these things. 'The one with the blond hair and the big green ring on her finger.'

'Oh, her. She's the wife of a banker. One of Tania's friends. They live in Berlin.'

'Funny her husband didn't come to rescue her from your clutches.'

'Oh, him. Men in leather trousers – ech. Why do Germans always swathe themselves in leather when they're trying to look hip? It must be their Nazi biker past.'

Conrad felt he could be xenophobic toward Germans because his own family came from there, although several generations back. They had emigrated to Canada, where Conrad had grown up. He hated being mistaken for a German and made sure people knew where he stood vis-à-vis history, which he refused to let rest, calling Lufthansa 'Luftwaffe' and decrying the universal bad taste with which Germans seemed to be afflicted, especially in footwear. 'I mean sandals, fine. I even have a pair of Birkenstocks.' Conrad would say. 'But sandals worn with white sports socks?'

When they were home she took up her usual position on the stairwell leading from their flat to the derelict loft upstairs. There, through a narrow rectangular window, she could see the skyscrapers of the City bunched together like glass-stalked flowers. Above them identical Magritte clouds trooped across the sky.

Standing there at night, staring at the City, was the only way she could feel close to it, the breathless city they were living in, where everything seemed lived in double-time, a headlong rush in which she all but had to remind herself to breathe.

Only a few blocks away, in the buildings lining Bishopsgate, global petroleum prices were set, currency was speculated upon, wealth extracted from the furthest reaches of the globe by green digits and men hanging off telephones. The nightly newscasts were like News of the Future: anti-capitalist demonstrations, GM foods crossing the species barrier, gene selecting for your baby, trafficking in women by Albanian mafias, illegal immigrants thrown overboard alive from ships – the twenty-first century collides with dark ages. It was as if the present had been obliterated, and they were living in an undifferentiated slew of past and future.

'Alex? What are you doing up there?' Conrad's voice drifted from the living room.

'Nothing, just looking.'

'I don't know what there is to see,' he sighed.

At night the city was cool and silver, like one of Conrad's drawings in silverpoint and graphite. She tried not to be threatened by it, to think of it as a money-garrison, increasingly an encampment of the super-rich. Although this was exactly what was happening in their area, the bankers moving in, inch by inch, like subversives, until one morning she woke up and half the cars parked in their road were Jaguars.

Outside, moored above the City skyscrapers, was a London sky: one half clear, the other dark with cloud. *Breathe in*, she instructed herself silently. *Breathe out*.

two

WINTER

The women at work had those old-fashioned names, Harriet or Phillipa, but shortened to something monosyllabic and androgynous: Hat, Phil. According to their weekend adventure anecdotes, they seemed to drink just as much as the boys.

On Monday morning they were all in the kitchen, reporting back on the weekend's escapades.

'We went to Creme Palace. It was raunchy.'

'You know, that film about the future robot wars—'

'They had sex in the *toilet*?'

'Cool.'

Alex, at thirty-one, was ancient by the agency's standards. Andrew, the accountant, turned to her, worried she was feeling left out. They were sweet like that, they always tried to show interest, even though they probably thought she should have a couple of kids by now. That was another thing she noticed about the generation only a few years behind her: they were kind, but surprisingly socially conservative. But for the safari shirts and rucksacks their values were stuck in 1955.

'What did you do on the weekend, Alex?' Andrew asked.

'Conrad and I went to a couple of private views.'

'Wow,' they chorused. 'Cool.'

'Did you see anyone?' Hattie meant anyone famous. 'Like that art terrorist guy who presents that programme on Channel 4 – what is it?'

'Where they turn people's homes into installations,' Prakesh added.

'No.'

'Oh, too bad.'

They drifted off to take up their places in front of the giant Macintosh computers, where they would spend the better part of their working lives. At the moment, work was an advertising and communications agency. It was an environmentally-friendly, socially-aware workplace. They wouldn't do Shell, for instance, or take any government jobs.

'We're a *friendly* company.' Michael, the Director, told everyone this when they were hired. Recruits were left to figure out what this meant for themselves. She supposed it meant not connected to the merciless working world out there of skirt-wearing women, Christmas bonuses, video-conferencing and industrial tribunals.

She was now an account director, supposedly responsible for the 'visual content' of campaigns, although Michael had originally hired her as a research executive, and this was still how she spent much of her time.

They worked exclusively with charities. During the day she laboured over statistics of the progress of the AIDS virus in the population of southern Africa (1 in 4 adults under 35 infected), the murder rate in Kingston, Jamaica (the highest in the world) or the number of people officially disappeared by the Chilean dictatorship (3, 182), trying to fit these numbers to images and words that would jerk sympathy out of the average materialist.

At lunchtime she put on her coat and walked among the shops of Covent Garden, into French Connection or Marks and Spencer's – taunting lunchtime refuges where she would browse but buy nothing. It was unusual for Michael's kind of company to have offices in Covent Garden, given its extortionate rents. This was only one of several mysteries that surrounded Michael.

He was Irish, very cultivated, sophisticated and handsome in a Liam Neeson kind of way. He was easy to work for, but kept himself to himself. For example, no-one knew if he was gay or straight; they knew he wasn't married and he lived in Maida Vale. They all trooped over to his flat the previous year for a

Guy Fawkes Night party. It was expensive, tasteful, and stocked with friends who they all agreed might have come from Rent-a-Friend: well-dressed, well-behaved people displaying a requisite element of quirkiness but who seemed slightly uncomfortable. When they dissected the evening in the office the next day they all remarked that they seemed to know Michael much better than his so-called friends.

'What's that?' Michael pointed to the corner of the office where a white papier mâché figure stood on four uncertain legs.

'Hattie made that last night,' Alex explained. 'It's going to be the Art and Design Scapegoat. When things go wrong, we can blame him.'

Michael shook his head. She almost expected him to say, 'kids', even though he was only five years older than her. He looked at her then, long and strange. She wondered if he was going to ask her, 'what are you doing here?'

She had never spoken that much with Michael. Only once, when he heard where she had been, he suddenly took an interest in her.

'I've never been to Central America,' he said. 'Did you like it?'

'Very much. It's a very complex society.' She always came out with things like that – *a very complex society*. If Conrad were there he'd say, 'I hear they're looking for a lecturer in social anthropology at the LSE.'

'I should go sometime,' Michael said, his tongue hesitating as it often did on the 'o's. She thought he tried to cover up his Irish accent. Sometimes he came out sounding American. 'It's done you a world of good.'

She nodded, although she wondered where the phrase had come from, who would think such a thing really existed: a world of good.

Now Michael was walking toward her across the office with those long, confident strides of his. He had that look on his face she dreaded, as if he had just had a brilliant idea. She could almost see the lightbulb suspended above his head.

'There's someone I want you to meet.'

13

His tanned forearm locked over hers and he literally shepherded her out of her cubicle and across the grey prairie of open-plan desks. They came to a halt in front of one of them. In it, a small dark-haired woman sat with her back to them.

'Erica, there's someone I'd like you to meet.'

The woman turned around. She had a small face, rather dark-skinned, with large brown eyes.

'Erica has just joined us from Stride Fallon Stride.' Michael named a rival agency that had succeeded in wrestling the Alzheimer's Association account from them the year before. 'She's going to be handling some of the new accounts, just as a trial.'

'Hello.'

'Hi, pleased to meet you.' Erica spoke with an American accent.

'Erica needs to start at the top.' Michael turned to her. 'Alexandra is the best.' She thought, the best what? Best minion? Best wage slave?

'Erica will be working with you.'

'Great.' She continued smiling, even though her face was getting sore from being kept in a jolly rictus for at least five minutes.

'What's the project?' she asked Michael when they were safely out of earshot.

'It's—'

'Michael! Line Two.'

'Catch you later,' he said.

She decided to ask the design team about Erica. They always knew everything at least twenty-four hours before she did, possibly because Stuart, the art director, was rumoured to be having an affair with Michael's PA.

'Not much,' Hattie shrugged. 'Except Michael must think it's some coup, hiring her from SFS. She got married a month ago, that's all we know on the personal front. Although that's more than we know about Mr Mystery,' Hattie said, referring to their inscrutable boss. 'Maybe he doesn't have much of a life. I hope he gets one. It's pathetic, at his age.'

Get a life. She heard people say this all the time. They seemed to know what it meant: a life. It was clear to her, although perhaps it wasn't the best way to do it, that a life is what you accept to live. A life can be something very small, something very strange. A life can be anything.

At six o'clock she put on her coat. It had been dark for nearly three hours. On the streets renegade bits of tinsel and the skeletons of Christmas trees attested to that darkest of season: early January.

Another bathysphere winter in London, she thought. Damp submersible nights spent plunging into the ground in lifts, worming through the bowels of the city in the glistening canisters of the underground, rising in another part of town. Each time she made one of these sudden surfacings she felt her bones protest, as if she really had decompressed too quickly.

Winter was a reassuring season. The city sucked her into its shiny routine of dinner, friends, private views, drinks, bars, restaurants, films, concerts. She didn't have a chance to stop and think: what am I doing with my life? Do I have a life?

She had been back in London for a year and a half, but it seemed less. Time was moving strangely, folding in on itself, then opening out, like a jacob's ladder. She went to sleep on Sunday only to wake up to find it was Tuesday, but she doesn't remember living through Monday. When people at work asked her what she did at the weekend she couldn't remember a thing.

Each night at home, she tried to work. She went to the little studio she set up in Conrad's flat and sat behind her drawing table. The window looked out onto bank towers and a couple of four- or five-storey modern council flats – an unrelenting urban view without so much as a tree or a wedge of green. Although could see the spire of Shoreditch church: a stout white spout, graceful and undemanding.

She stared at the buildings in front of her, imagining the random movements of City workers, envying them, even, for the inexorable routine of mortgage-commute-office-bullying-borderline alcoholism in which – if you believed the news-papers – they were all caught up. But day after day the page remained blank, her drawing pens and paper untouched.

Before, she had been driven. She needed to work. That was the best way to describe it: not a choice, or a desire, but a need. Now the need was gone and in its place was a kind of expectant silence, not unlike the silence before thunder or an explosion, when you half sense what is coming, because the air seems drained of sound, as if the coming detonation has sucked out everything in advance.

In London, if you don't keep producing, you are quickly forgotten. No painting meant no shows, no collectors, no source of income. She did what she had to do. No artist would be proud of it. She got a job. This was how, nearly a year ago, she found herself at Michael's company.

They sat around the pine-finished conference table Michael had spent a fortune on.

'I want you all to be aware that we are about to branch out.' Michael threw his arms wide on either side of his body.

'Branch out?' Stuart repeated. She could tell he thought this was a rather American thing to say.

'Both geographically and in terms of subject matter. I want us to represent overseas companies and concerns who find it impossible to get a toe-hold in the collective consciousness.'

Michael was always saying that: the collective consciousness. She could only presume this was a misreading of Jung, and that what he meant was the majority *Sun*-reading, ITV-watching public.

All through Michael's speech she watched Erica. Her face remained studiously neutral. She had the kind of face in which you could still see her as a child. She made this distinction because she thought the majority of people – Conrad was one of them – were impossible to imagine ever having been anything other than adults.

Her olive skin was thrown into strange relief by hair the colour of muscovado sugar, which she wore tied back from her face. She stuttered with energy, although not of the nervous kind; rather it was that go forward, creative energy that employers so admire.

She approached Alex as they filed out of the meeting.

'I thought your presentation yesterday was very good.' Erica was referring to the day before, when they had all attended her briefing of a potential client about their campaign, which was to be a series of public advertisements about climate change. She had been explaining how natural disasters reinforced local inequalities, or some similarly obvious equation. 'You just look so relaxed up there in front of people.'

There was something unusual about the way Erica looked at people: instead of gazing in that manner of taking a survey, a quick impression, Erica lanced her with her eyes, imprinted her glances, individually landing on the skin, nose, eyes, mouth.

'I don't mind being up in front of people.'

'I think that's a real skill,' Erica said, smiling warmly. 'I was thinking, would you like to go for a drink after work?'

'Sure.'

'I don't know where to go, though.'

'I do,' Alex said. 'I've gone upmarket lately. Now I go to wine bars,' she laughed. Stuart, Hattie and the rest went to pubs, but she had defected to sip mediocre Merlot and eat tough olives in low-lit places that played a steady diet of Chet Baker.

'That sounds okay,' Erica said.

'So,' Alex ventured, as soon as they were out of the office. 'I understand you've just got married.'

Erica's eyes widened in surprise. 'How did you know that?'

'The Art and Design team. They know everything.'

'But I haven't told anyone.'

'You must have said something.'

'I wouldn't.'

'Perhaps it was on your CV, or your application.'

'I know it isn't. I don't even think of myself as being married. I hate the term *wife*.'

She had heard this before. As soon as people got married they felt they could complain about it.

'Why did you get married then?'

'Oh, who knows? My husband wanted to. My mother was happy for once.' Erica shrugged. The whole subject seemed to cause her pain. 'In the eyes of society I'm married off now and the next thing I should want to do is have children.'

'But you don't?'

'My husband wants to, but—' Erica looked out the window. She smiled at something she seemed to see there. 'It just doesn't seem to be a priority with me. I don't know why he's so desperate.'

Unlike so many newly-weds, Erica had none of that sated, stable air about her. She didn't have the look of someone who had just embarked on a big, gleaming cruise ship. Secretly that was how Alex thought of the married state: suddenly there are all sorts of things to explore which previously seemed uninteresting, like state rooms, table tennis, deck chairs, a swimming pool. After they had finished exploring these distractions the couple in question begin to populate all the cabins, to name their captain and their chef. Eventually the cruise ship sails into the horizon with their name plastered on its side.

Still, she wondered if it might be exciting to be embarking on a future with someone else, a future that has some shape, some basic seaworthiness.

Just then, Michael came in the bar. She had never seen Michael in there before; as far as they knew he didn't drink. He looked around distractedly, as if he were there to meet someone who hadn't yet arrived. His eye landed on them, or rather on Erica's back, and he smiled. He approached the table.

'Well, hello there,' he said in a faux-hearty Coach voice which conveyed the message that it was good to see members of the team socialising. She hated it when Michael said that: the team. As if it was passion and commitment that bound them together and not the chain-gang clink-clink of salaries and mortgages.

'Right, see you then,' Michael drifted out of the bar, without meeting anyone. As he left Chet Baker sang, *I fall in love too easily. I fall in love too fast.*

They raised their eyebrows in unison. 'Michael's a bit of an enigma.' Alex sighed. 'We think he's gay.'

'Why?'

'I don't know, because he's so furtive, maybe. Not that the two are in any way related, of course.'

Erica shook her head. 'I don't think he's gay. And anyway, who cares?'

'Of course, it's just idle speculation by bored employees.' Alex was embarrassed. Maybe Erica thought her reactionary. 'No doubt his heart is in the right place, though,' she said, to change the subject. 'He could be making a lot more money if he were prepared to sell out to the big commercial accounts.'

'He won't do them at all?'

'He turned down a food multinational because they buy cocoa from plantations in West Africa that use slave labour, he won't do Ford because they're part of an oil lobby, he refuses to even think about clothing retail if they use underpaid labour, which is almost everyone—'

Erica smiled. 'Where did he get such a conscience?'

'I think he worked for an Irish development agency for a long time. He got a job in advertising when he came to London to get enough money together to buy a house, and I think he found he liked it – I'm sure no-one was more surprised than Michael – so he decided to combine advertising with being a decent human being.'

'You seem to know him really well.'

'Nobody knows him well,' Alex shrugged. 'These are just things I've picked up as I've gone along.'

'How long have you worked for him?'

'Not long. Nine months, I think – No. *God*. It's been a year now.'

Erica laughed. 'Don't sound so shocked.'

'It is shocking, how time passes, without it taking any notice of you.'

'What did you do before?' Erica asked.

'I'm a painter. A painter who can't paint.' She tried to mop up the hurt that had soaked her voice.

'Why not?'

'If I knew I wouldn't be working here.'

'You're a good account director, I hear.'

Alex shrugged and smiled, as if to say, thanks, but it's not what's important to me.

They walked to the Tube together, passing the increasingly expensive shops that lined the streets. It wasn't that late, but it was dark – it had been dark for hours, possibly for ever. That was January in London: a darkness in which you had to make your own light.

'You sound like you've spent a long time in the States,' she ventured.

Erica nodded. 'I went to school and university there.'

'Which part?'

'Virginia. The north, not the south. The south is hicksville. We lived hear D.C. Well, here we are.' They had arrived at the Tube.

'Well, I'm going this way—'

'And I'm going this way. Bye,' Erica called. 'See you tomorrow.'

'Bye.'

She stood there for the briefest moment, watching her go through the turnstiles. The truth was, she didn't take the Tube home and had only walked Erica there out of politeness.

Just before she turned to leave, Erica's face had shut down, very slightly, like the drawing across of a shutter which said: just because we have shared certain thoughts, thoughts you could even call intimate, don't think that I owe you anything next time.

So she knew from the beginning that in spite of whatever confidences they might have shared, she knew no more about Erica, really, and that the next time she saw her they would have to start all over again.

*

She keeps them in a deep drawer, a slippery slew of unsorted photographs. She sifts through these glossed slices of memory until she comes to the one she is looking for.

It isn't a very good picture; he is slightly out of focus, his face hidden underneath a straw cowboy hat he must have picked up in some farmer's market. She can just make out that his squinting eyes are brown, that his skin is quite dark, really, for an Englishman.

Behind him is a sea of purple mountains; beyond them a ridge of volcanoes puncture the sky with their serrated molar tops. Next to him, only half in the shot, is a Maya woman with an elaborate head-dress. In Xela the women pile woven materials on their heads, arranged in folds and fringed with pompoms; even then they are so small they only reach Ben's shoulder.

Most of their pictures are like this: typical couple-travelling-on-their-own photographs: one of him, then her. Only one shows them shoved hastily together, snapped by a friendly passing tourist or one of their bus-seat companions on the long journeys over mountains and through griddled lowland fields.

Instead of each other they turned their cameras on the landscape, which was so outlandishly beautiful that it became surreal, the colours out of kilter. Fields were so green they looked magenta, and the volcanoes were the purple of bruises. The country invited them to think in names for colours they had learned in art school: cerulean, carmine, cobalt, viridian. They took rolls and rolls of film, sealed them in plastic bags and put them in refrigerators the few times they stayed in places with electricity. When they opened the bags they could smell the chemicals of the film, images held captive in their brew.

They spent no more than two weeks in Xela. Later, she would forget the days and the dates. Her memory would only return slowly, not unlike watching a photograph develop: fluid, stop, fixer; the outlines first, then the detail, finally the colour.

At times what happened has the slowed-down, hazy quality of dreams. Only later do details sharpen, as if emerging from a smudged lens only recently cleaned. Later she realized that the dream-like quality of it was the mind's way of protecting itself, as if it were smearing a layer of gelatin around each individual thought. Otherwise they would be too sharp; they might puncture something irreparable.

She came home to winter in London, the mackerel city, grey ribbed by black, brownstone and lead. During that time she thought about nothing; memory refused to infiltrate the incessant stream of present in which she lived. Even so, a reservoir of delayed thought was filling and filling. Like a child growing, it was unstoppable. She never knew thoughts could be like that – fecund, insistent.

Snapshot. There they are, in Xela, the morning they arrived. Coloured stencils hang over empty cobblestoned streets, flapping in the wind. She made a promise to herself then, that she would be less governed by fear, more adventurous. That she would try to find beauty in things.

And it was beautiful. The rain in Xela, falling in metal curtains. The clouds in Xela, moving across the sky like grey-suited dictators. Ben in Xela—

She stared at his face, covered in the knit of shadows thrown by his hat. She had once been to university with him, slept beside him, travelled with him.

She blinked, his face swimming against the darkened blind of her eyelids.

22

three

MAN SET ON FIRE

Conrad launched himself into the kitchen and started to peel an apple. She watched the rind tumble from its surface, rolling into buttery coils in his deft painter's hands.

Everything Conrad did he performed with a combination of thrust and grace. He had the bigness, the essential confidence, of someone who was raised in North America. He went to the gym regularly and was the only man she had ever met who could count calories. He owned more shoes than she did, with his five pairs of trainers (at her last count; they had probably multiplied) three Doc Martens, and ankle boots from some smart men's clothier in Soho.

'So, are you coming?' He asked, his mouth full of apple.

'Where?'

'To the opening.'

She sighed.

'Oh, come on.'

'I don't think I can take another encounter with Basia.'

'She won't be there. It's the new gallery in Hoxton, you know, the one that in a few years will be seen as the vanguard for all the big-name commercial galleries moving east and pushing up house prices and making rich people actually travel east of Holborn.'

'Who's going to be there?'

'The usual. A lot of self-serving artists and buyers with more money than you or I could ever imagine. Hmm,' Conrad leapt around the kitchen, apple falling out of his mouth. He often talked with his mouth open. She wondered if this were a North

American habit as well. 'I'm thinking of buying some ceramics for the flat. What do you think? I mean some real ceramics. Art pieces.'

'Don't you think they'll clutter your aesthetic?'

Conrad's decor was all desert landscapes dotted by potted cacti, cushions in adobe shades thrown in a deliberately casual way across a butterscotch-hued leather sofa. The interior design books lined up on the shelves had titles like *Casa Mexicana, Tuscan Villas, Estancias of Argentina, Feng Shui for Bathrooms*. The entire flat looked like it was decorated by the set designer on one of those films where Michael Douglas gets seduced by rapacious women.

'Come on, Alex,' Conrad wheedled. 'Why don't you want to come? Everyone will be there.'

'That's why I don't want to come.'

Conrad scowled. 'You are so anti-social.'

'Next time.' She knew he was less disappointed by her not going than by having to go without an escort.

Conrad went to the private view and she went out to see a film and then get a Vietnamese takeaway. She arrived home at ten o'clock to find a party in progress.

'Alex. What's up?' said people she didn't know. 'How's the job? I heard you work in advertising. That is so cool.'

She picked her way through clumps of individuals, trying not to knock over Conrad's prized designer lamp.

'—that Scottish painter. The bloke who paints those domestic violence scenes; women with bruises, black eyes. It's really political—'

'—Oh *politics*—'

'He was takin' the mickey, know what I mean?' This was unmistakeably Stewart, talking in squirty estuarine. 'He wanted to give the shit to me for 1,000 baht more than it was worth, yeah? So I said, listen mate, I'm not taking any of this shit, and the geezer pulled a gun, yeah? A *piece*, as they say in America.'

She found Conrad in the kitchen, making pink-coloured cocktails.

'Stewart's telling the story of how he was almost shot in Thailand again. I guess he doesn't realise there are repercussions to trying to cheat an impoverished national of a country with no gun laws out of money.'

'Hmm,' Conrad said.

'I don't know what you see in these people.'

Conrad was shaking his silver cocktail mixer. 'They're artists, just like you and me.'

'If they're just like you and me, why don't they talk sense?'

He shrugged. 'They're pretty smart. Dougal won the Warrington Prize last year and Lou's an art critic.'

'This might be news to you, Conrad, but someone's professional profile does not equal their merit as a character.'

Conrad brought the cocktail mixer to an abrupt halt. 'I guess I'm just not as demanding as you are.'

He turned and leant against the counter. In his hands were two candy-floss pink cocktails in which bright little wedges of lime floated. They were really quite pretty.

'I just don't see how everything has to be meaningful all the time,' he said. 'What's wrong with frivolity? How else are we going to distract ourselves from the inevitabilities of life? Not too many people would be up to your standards of rigorousness, Alex. I wonder if even you're up to your standards.'

'What does that mean?'

'You make life hard on yourself.'

'Oh, now I understand. I can't believe I've missed it all these years. The point is to make things as easy for oneself as possible.'

Conrad left the kitchen. She watched him lurch through the crowd, cocktail shaker in hand, pouring drinks like a priest possessed of a singular dazzling vacuity administering communion.

She stood on the threshold of the living room, spooning noodles from her Drunken Fish into her mouth, watching his guests flit about the living room. They looked like fluttering angelfish, this one striped, that one turquoise and pink, their narrow mouths opening and closing, sipping at words.

'Absence?' she heard someone say.

'*Absinthe*. That French drink. It's banned.'

She finished her takeaway and slid it into the bin. The skeleton of the fish looked up at her from the top of the pile, his hollow eye a mute reprimand.

Absence was one of those banned substances in their house. Conrad had stopped talking about Ben months ago. If she even ventured the topic he moved away quickly, evading her with that catlike way he had. For Conrad, Ben's name had become like an artifact, something to be taken out and dusted once in a while, admired for the pure symmetry of its beauty, then put back into a glassed cabinet to be protected from the sun and hum of life.

Conrad drifted back into the kitchen and dived into the refrigerator. 'Why don't you get out there and talk to people? You know, I bet you're one of those dark, saturnine women at weddings,' his muffled voice came from inside the fridge. 'The very slightly older woman who is disgusted by the whole thing, who wears black dresses and looks slightly vampish. The woman who gets dirty looks from the mother of the bride and her friends.'

'The woman who will never be married.'

He closed the fridge. 'Listen, could you get some more beer? There's a tenner in my coat pocket.'

She took the chance to escape. Outside the air was still crisp, the penetrating damp of an English winter. As she walked up the street she passed a placard with that day's *Evening Standard* headline. MAN SET ON FIRE IN LONDON STREET.

Red lozenges of buses tore up and down the road, streaming rubbish in their wake. She spied on her neighbours as she walked, glimpsing the walls of people's living rooms above the shutters they kept perpetually drawn across the windows. Many were painted a deep, hungry red.

Just before the off-license she saw a bunch of flowers tied to a lamp post. It was the third she had seen that week. They were affixed to park railings, bus shelters, or just lay on the ground. Sometimes she stopped to read the notes attached to them, even though rain often erased the message. Others she could just make out amid weather damage: *Wilson, 18, who's Tragic Death was by a Drunk Driver. Forever Beautiful.*

She was sure she had never seen them until recently. It seemed that overnight London had been garlanded with wilting momentos to victims of random thuggery or car accidents.

She took the stairs to the flat slowly, expecting to open the door into a trickle of dissolute party leftovers. But the door was locked. No light seeped from under the frame. From behind the door came the buzzing silence of a flat recently vacated by people.

They must have decamped to the pub, she thought as she turned the key. She opened the door and reached for the light switch. As soon as her hand was on it, she thought she felt someone's fingers close over hers.

She snatched it back. 'Conrad?'

Someone was in the flat, still. Although what she felt was more abstract than a presence, more like a solid block of air. An image skittered across her optic nerve – an impression, hologramic and insubstantial – of a brown-eyed man. Then the smell hit her: wool or felt. An oily, animal smell. For a second, she felt afraid.

She went to turn the light on again. In the second between darkness and the flare of light, she saw a pillar in the middle of the living room, a shimmering column of white stone. But there was no pillar in their flat, even before Conrad had the far wall knocked out to make the space more open-plan. She knew because he had showed her the architect's drawings.

The light came on. Behind her she heard Conrad's unmistakable hyperactive step on the stairs.

'What are you doing loitering by the door?' he said. 'You scared the hell out of me.'

'I felt something. Just when I opened the door. Something really strange. And a smell—'

'What did you smell?'

'Mud, mainly. Wool, or felt. Like wet felt.' She paused. 'There was someone here, when I opened the door. I'm sure of it.'

'What? Someone in the flat?'

'More like a presence than a person. It was more a – a *fume* of a person.' She sat down. She realised her heart was pounding. 'I feel really unsettled.'

He didn't say anything immediately. He went to sit on the sofa, lowering himself into its folds slowly, a troubled look on his face. 'I suppose I should have told you.'

'Told me what?'

'That's the problem, I don't know what to say.' He threw up his hands. 'I've felt something a couple of times. Once I even saw—'

'Hang on. What do you mean some*thing*?'

'Once I came home and opened the door and there was a man staring at me. I thought I was being burgled at first, but then I noticed he didn't look like any man I'd ever seen before. He was really thin. Gaunt, actually. And his eyes were so vivid, like they were lit by torches.'

'What did you do?'

'I blinked. I held my eyes closed and told myself that I was hallucinating, that when I opened my eyes I would realise the flat was empty, that it had been empty all along.'

'And?'

'And I opened my eyes and there was nothing.'

'So what's your conclusion? It was a hallucination?'

He shook his head slowly. 'I wish it was, but I don't think so.' He picked up his shoulders and dropped them in a sudden seismic shrug. 'I don't really know what it was.'

'Are you saying it's a ghost? Because I don't believe in ghosts.'

'Neither do I,' Conrad said quickly. 'But I wonder though, if they exist, do they believe in us?'

For a long time afterward she thought about the vision she had seen, the quick impression that had skittered across some previously unknown chamber of her mind. His brilliant brown eyes, his sad beard, the strange clothes he wore, his estuarine smell.

Who was he? If he really were a ghost – she allowed herself for the moment to gloss over the fact she didn't believe in them – he could be anyone. London was the great transit lounge of history. Centuries of products, slave-paid, exotic fruits and animals, muskets, adventurers had passed within a mile of their flat, through the sludge river, then the long reedy estuary, finally spit out into the North Sea.

She thought of all the men who passed through Gravesend like pre-ghosts, destined never to return. They ended farming big leaf tobacco in Belize, killed by torqued snakes, or eaten by tigers in Rajasthan, or drowned by typhoons in the South China Sea. So many men and women on their way to remote deaths, finished off by a killing tropics lassitude. This had almost been her fate, too.

At night she stared into the sky from their living room, watching the waxing and waning of the winter moon, looking like a milky jewel pinned to a piece of velvet. The floorboards echoed the rumble of a train leaving Liverpool Street Station, heading for Essex. The trains passed close enough to see their cargo of wan commuters.

London must look like that from space, she figured: a burst of light, all of them in the middle of it, strangers in a brightly-lit building. And from it, long orange ribbons unravelling; night trains leaving the city, disappearing into a tapestry of black.

*

Quick – a breath. Then gulp. Her tongue flaps against the roof of her mouth and sticks there. It is coated in fur, so dry it has hardened and fuzzed.

Above her the sunlight shimmers through an aquarium surface. She is coming up from a deep place where she has been submerged. Rising fast, shot up like a bubble.

As she breaks the surface light comes, first as a chink underneath her mind's door. Then, slowly, the door opens. It flows in; a sideways, askew light, travelling through her left eye to her right, flooding her mind.

In that same instant she becomes aware of an insistent but foggy pain somewhere behind her eyes. Then, like a maddening video installation she had once seen, where twenty television screens fizzed into and out of static, she fades out again.

Next attempt at consciousness.

A lace curtain of sky. Green – too much green, like a world swathed in brocade. The insistent metallic chattering of some machine, a pinball arcade. The pain was still there, but it had retreated like an animal to lick its wounds.

She sat up. Stars formed entire constellations in her eyes. She felt herself passing out again – blood-drain and nausea. She tried to remember where she had been. A vague sense that she had been flying, or spinning, then caught by trees, forced itself into her mind, but stubbornly refused to cohere into memory.

She saw that the lace curtain was actually trees, their leaves

30

filigreeing into a solid canvas of sky. She breathed with relief. It was all a nightmare. That's right. She would wake up any second. She was in London, looking at the paintings of her friend Yves, whose work was all about forests and leaves, painting them over and over again, in dozens of different colours and sizes until he arrived at his own understanding of that crucial treaty, the one struck between light and dark.

four

YOU FEEL TOO MUCH

Rachel greeted them at the gallery door, or rather, greeted Conrad. Because she was no longer an artist, at these events she was just an extension of Conrad, Alex knew, more his mascot than a person in her own right.

Rachel was wearing an orange miniskirt with mauve sheer tights. On her feet were snakeskin pumps. In her spare time Rachel designed textiles with bright patterns and enamelled colours that looked Indian. She wore these fabrics all together, often pairing her orange miniskirt with a leopard-skin transparent shirt, a wine-coloured velvet cardigan thrown over it, and a turquoise scarf round her neck. Other times she wore orange and silver vests with little mirrors sewn into them.

'Why does Rachel insist upon wearing all that crap?' Alex had overheard one of Rachel's so-called friends bitching at an art opening. 'She looks like a bloody third-world bazaar.' But she respected Rachel's refusal to wear the art world uniform of the moment, the tight military-beige shirt and black combat trousers.

'*Conrad*,' Rachel breathed. 'I'm *so* nervous.'

Conrad gave her the indulgent smile he reserved for a very few friends. 'You're always nervous. You're nervousness itself.'

It was true: Rachel was one of those spidery people. Every-thing about her was limbs, extensions, nerves, like a touch-sensitive keyboard – the pressure from one finger could light up a web of feelings.

Rachel and Conrad had known each other forever; she forgot how they met and maybe they themselves had even forgotten; it was one of those meetings lost in the spliff haze of art school.

Rachel was the only performance artist among Conrad's friends, and one of the few left in the art world at all. In general, performance art was Out. Conrad didn't know why she persisted. 'She's never going to make it with that work. She should just concentrate on sculpture, or installation – and even that's hard.'

'Maybe she likes what she does,' she speculated.

'Sure, sure,' Conrad said quickly. 'But if she's not going to make it, what's the point?'

Everything she had heard about Rachel, from Conrad, from conversations overheard at dinner parties or private views, from Rachel herself, all the anecdotes, stories – and she was the sort of person who naturally spawned stories – impressed upon her more than anything how one person could do so much. The last twenty years of Rachel's life seemed to have been a single breath of non-stop creativity.

The height of her notoriety had been three years before, at the time of what Rachel called her Love show. She had been out of the country and had missed it, but people still talked about it.

'We went in there expecting hell on wheels,' Conrad had told her. 'Really thought she was going to put us through the metaphorical grinder. It's hard to appreciate how ruthless Rachel's art used to be. So the show was a real surprise.'

For the Love show Rachel had put a pile of possessions: clothes, shoes, books, on a stage. A sparse winter landscape was projected on a white background, a photograph she later revealed had been taken near Auschwitz – Rachel had discovered only a year before the presence of a Jewish grandmother in the family.

The shoes, clothes and books had belonged to Rachel's family, some of them to the mysterious Jewish grandmother, and some of them to Rachel herself.

She came onto the stage, dressed in black, and began to put

all these possessions, one by one, in boxes. She sealed the boxes with the shoes, clothes and books with giant white tape. On the tape was written, in large red block capitals, LOVE. She gave each of the boxes away to a random member of the audience, who sat there, stunned, with a box sealed with Love tape on his or her lap.

'She was putting her house in order,' Conrad reminisced. 'She was packing away things of herself and her past that she didn't need anymore. But she wasn't doing it with regret or disappointment. It was a hugely generous thing. Everyone was very moved. Some people who got boxes even cried.'

Rachel called the show Packing Up, but everyone came to call it the Love show. Near the end of the run she sold off her extra rolls of the Love tape. After the final performance she was approached by someone who knew someone with an exclusive design shop and for six months Rachel and this man went into partnership manufacturing the Love tape and selling it to card shops. She made enough to live on for three years.

'The Love show was a fluke,' Rachel said. 'I thought it would be panned as sentimental. And at that time no-one was interested in performance art. They still aren't.'

Nevertheless, she kept at it. Rachel had the perfect face and body for an actress, or a performance artist. Only five years before, perhaps, she had been quite beautiful, but now, in her late thirties, her face had settled for being strong in a very English way: a wide plain for a forehead, a narrow bridged nose ending in a slightly bulbous point. Her lower lip dropped winningly, as if it existed only to tremble, like Jane Birkin's. Although she had such dramatic features, Alex had seen Rachel look surprisingly plain. She looked her best when she wore strong make-up: dark eyeshadow, heavy mascara, eyeliner and red lipstick. On most women this would look garish, but Rachel's face absorbed the definition like a sponge.

The show was called You Feel Too Much. She seemed to be continuing the theme she had started with her previous show, Beyond Desire; the one before that, Conrad' s favourite, had been You're Not Even British, for which she infiltrated the immigration hall in Heathrow and secretly videotaped officers interrogating Africans.

That show had been shut down by the police once word of it got out. 'If it had ever got out to the press it would have made Rachel an Art Star overnight,' Conrad lamented.

The You Feel Too Much show was a departure for Rachel. It was more an installation than a performance piece. At the far side of the gallery she had built a minimalist funeral parlour: a hanging purple curtain, trimmed with gold, a wrought iron pedestal on which cards of condolence rested. On them Rachel had pasted headlines taken from papers like *The Sun* and the *Mirror* detailing car accidents and disappearances: *Family of Four Killed in Bank Holiday Tragedy. Lindsay Last Seen Near Reservoir.*

'Her theory is that we've all been anaesthetized against feeling by media culture and excessive choice,' Conrad explained as they made their way around the gallery. 'We're living in a sensationalist culture which uses death as just another commodity. Because we have no community no-one knows how to grieve, until it's somebody famous and then the teddy bears and flowers burst out in hives of sentimentality – or at least that's the way Rachel sees it.'

They talked – or rather Conrad talked – to a few people she had met at similar functions. The same faces seemed to circulate endlessly, turning up intact and unchanged in different parts of London, in Bethnal Green and in Chelsea, in Deptford and St John's Wood.

There was Dietrich, the unusually sunny German painter of what could only be described as bursts of light, like sunspots or light storms; next to him was Mariela, a taciturn Spanish import who was supposedly Miró's great-niece but whose monochrome canvases lacked any of his playfulness. Standing a couple of feet away was Jared, a painter from Texas, who made a point of wearing his cowboy boots and Stetson hat everywhere in case people were in any doubt as to his origins. Talking to Rachel was the tiny Irish photographer whose pictures were taken leaning out of high-rises at dangerous angles. His last series, 29th Floor, was shot from the top of Guy's Hospital, to which he had to be admitted a short time later, after he tried to jump.

As usual, being a private view, everyone ignored the actual work on show, choosing to drink warm beer and talk about their careers instead. As was often the case, she ended up being the only person actually looking at the work. At one end of the room was a tiny painting she had missed on their first tour of the gallery. The canvas was completely black, but a sentence had been painted in little red capitals: DEAD.

She stood in front of it for awhile, absorbing the word, *dead*. A lead ball, its neat symmetry of vowels bookended by ds. There was little in the word to suggest the real meaning of it: the crunch of bones, the liquidity of intestines, the damage, the hurt.

She felt a hand on her shoulder. 'Are you going to be all right with this?' It was Conrad.

'I was just thinking, this show could be distressing to some people. Don't you think Rachel should have some kind of disclaimer outside?'

'This is Art, Alex, not a community project.'

After the show Rachel gave them a lift home. The city streets were dark and slicked by a recent bout of rain. Conrad sat in the front seat beside Rachel. She sat in the back, her head butting between them, like a child with its parents.

'Did I tell you I'm going to Italy to see my father?' Rachel said. Rachel's father was a successful sixties pop art painter. 'He even painted the Beatles.' Conrad had told her, struggling to sound unimpressed.

They whipped around a corner a little too fast, the wheels slipping on the wet asphalt. Rachel had learned to drive in Italy, Conrad had told her, but she had missed the significance of this until now.

'I'll see my sister,' Rachel continued. 'Anna lives with an ageing novelist. She's his second wife and he's used her to have a second round of babies with, as far as I can see. A brood mare with a bohemian pedigree and lovely blonde hair. Anna's very *willowy*.' Rachel scowled.

'What does your mother do?' Alex inquired.

'She used to be a sculptor. A good one too. Then she turned into a wife and mother. She still potters away, though. Literally.'

'What's your brother up to these days?' Conrad asked.

'Screwing over poor countries. Of course, he calls them *emerging markets*.' Rachel whipped the car around a tight corner, nearly slaughtering a surprised pedestrian on a zebra crossing. 'My brother's a fund manager,' she explained.

That would make him the rebel in Rachel's family, Alex thought.

They streaked though the streets of their area – dark, brooding streets that until very recently had been empty at night. Now twenty-year-olds clogged its corners on the way to some club or other, the girls dressed out of 1976, tottering in high heels worn with pencil-thin trousers which flared at the bottom, a band of little Lauren Huttons.

They rounded a final corner in the direction of their flat and passed another yellow placard. It stood with its feet apart at the junction, facing motorists. INCIDENT, it read. APPEAL FOR WITNESSES. Serious Assault. Have you seen anything? She had seen another of these placards only the week before; that one announced that a man had been shot at dawn at the junction of Kingsland Road and Ball's Pond Road.

'Everyone hated me in college, Alex,' Rachel spoke to her reflection in the rear-view mirror. 'You wouldn't believe how much. Before I learned to be more careful they would say, "So, what are you up to this weekend?" They'd all be going to slum it in Brick Lane. And I would say, "Oh, I'm going to Italy to visit my Dad. He's lecturing in Florence." Or I would mention that Lucian Freud had come over for dinner on Saturday night.' Rachel laughed. 'So stupid. Even my tutors thought I was such a name-dropper they deliberately gave me crap marks. I had to become a performance artist instead of a painter, just to get away from my father's reputation.'

'Do you see them much, your family?'

'Not really. They live in Italy most of the year now. I could visit them more often, I suppose. But when you're there it's so Boho you'd positively want to scream. Like the latest starving British painter in residence, wandering around in his second-hand black suit in the full Italian sun. Then the local aristocrats come for lunch and park their Ferraris in the driveway. My father marches everyone around on a tour, from the studio to the gardens to pointing out the material for the curtains, for which he *absolutely scoured the markets of Marrakech*.' Rachel shivered. 'Then they all pretend to be Edwardians and play croquet on the lawn. It's like being caught in a permanent *Room with a View*.'

Conrad laughed. 'I've never heard that one before.'

'I'm amazed by how you describe your family,' Alex said. 'I could never have that much distance on my family. It was all so intense.'

Rachel shifted gear jerkily. 'You've got to have a sense of humour when you're surrounded by people who take them-selves so seriously.'

They came to a skidding stop at a traffic light. Alex could see Rachel's face in the rear-view mirror, its determined, slightly disappointed expression illuminated by the red light.

'Another thing my family has shown me,' Rachel said, 'is that it doesn't matter how passionate and rebellious you start out. Whatever you do, if you become successful and fêted and rich, then eventually your wife takes up ceramics or cooking or animal husbandry. You buy a pile in the countryside and start growing organic vegetables. It even happens to rock stars.'

'*Especially* to rock stars,' Conrad said.

'But you don't want anything to do with all that?' she asked.

The light changed and they charged through the intersection. 'Oh, I'll inherit it all eventually.' Rachel smiled. 'I'm the only one in the family who needs it. Anna's got her novelist, and my brother's got his funds, or whatever. That's why I can afford to rubbish it now. One day it will all be mine.'

*

Rachel dropped them at their flat. Once inside Conrad dived straight for the refrigerator and took out a beer.

'Did you ever sleep with Rachel?' she asked.

'Christ no,' Conrad scowled. 'Well, maybe once, but years ago. When we were young and idealistic.' He took a swig of beer. 'I wonder if being idealistic is ever going to come into fashion again.'

'You were idealistic?' She smiled.

'I must have been, about art anyway. Art was my escape route. It was different for Rachel of course. For her it was the most natural thing to do, like following your father into the demolition business. She was drinking warm beer at private views by the time she was seven years old.' He paused and looked at the floor. An unhappy look settled on his face.

'What's the matter?'

He didn't answer straight away. 'I don't know. Something about Rachel. We go back so far together. I'm realising we're getting older, and we're still caught in irony, and it's a trap. Like the way Rachel rubbishes her family, which is really about how hurt she is by their coldness, by the fact they haven't come to see her in London since they moved to Italy four years ago. We just whitewash what we really feel with irony.'

'I think irony comes out of having more breathing space than we've ever had before. We're not hard up against ourselves, like this.' She put her open palm in front of her face, inches away from her nose. 'For the first time in our history we're not worrying about hunger or invasion, so we have the luxury of not having to take ourselves very seriously.'

Conrad frowned. 'But those things are even more likely than they ever were. That's what I don't understand, this false sense of security. I feel like it's lulling us into a fatal complacency.'

'What do you think is going to happen?'

He shrugged. 'Could be anything. The Iraqis with their not-so-secret nuclear arsenal. We're making them into the Germans of the 1920s and thirties. International sanctions, pariahdom, we're killing their children. That's bound to end badly. Or the Chinese. They've always wanted to take over the world. They're the biggest fucking nation on earth and they don't have our liberal hang-ups or commitment to human rights. And they spit and blow their nose in the street. Maybe one day they'll decide they'd like to blow their nose in Vienna, or London.'

'Do you really think about that, someone taking over the world?'

'I just think about change. I hate change. Even though I know I should be grateful. We're in more control of our lives now than at any point in history. We've never been so free.'

'Free to douse people with petrol and set them on fire.'

'Oh, come on,' he groaned. 'Talk about me being obsessed. They're isolated incidents.'

'That's five this year. When are you going to think it's a problem?'

She had seen the item on the nine o'clock news. The man was black, and he had been walking home late at night outside Oxford. A car full of white kids had stopped, pretended to ask for directions, then tackled him. One of them went to the boot of the car and took out the spare can of petrol. 'He was very lucky,' said the doctor, who they interviewed in the lobby of the hospital. The camera light reflected off his glasses so you couldn't see his eyes. 'He has only thirty per cent burns. It could have been much more serious.'

'Ever since you came back you've been obsessed with these events,' Conrad went on. 'I'm trying to tell you about things in the world that frighten me, and believe me, they're not random events of the kind you're fixated on. They're not my personal obsessions, or compulsions. I don't have to put myself through some traumatic event over and over so I can assuage myself of some guilt that it's ridiculous to feel in the first place.'

'You think I feel guilty.'

'I don't know what you feel,' he sighed. 'I just think the dead are dead, and that's a shame, but we can't do anything about it. Our responsibility is to look after the living.'

'I find that hard,' her voice came out like a whisper. 'Because if no-one remembers you, then you never existed.'

Conrad sighed. 'But you're moving on, right?'

'Yes,' she said. 'I'm moving on.'

She mounts the stairs to the top deck of the 243 bus. Someone is smoking a joint. The smell curls inside her nostrils.

The joint-smoker is talking on his mobile phone. 'Can you hear me? Yeah? I said did you fill you' tank w' petrol?'

She wondered where she was expected to be moving to. It wasn't the breaking-and-setting-up-camp kind of moving on that nomads and hunter-gatherers had done for ninety-nine per cent of the history of humanity, but rather the onwards and upwards trudge affluent westerners of her age were expected to make: accumulating savings, keeping an eye on the property market, buying a flat and then one day a car.

She knew Conrad wasn't referring to this consumerist hike. He wanted her to distance herself emotionally from her past, from an accidental happening in her life which made no sense to anyone – and least of all to her – but which had given her a kind of new life.

Here she is, moving on in her new life: crawling up the Kingsland Road on a filthy London bus with someone smoking a joint and talking rubbish on their mobile phone.

The grass smoke gets thicker. She looks around for a window to open, but it's one of those new, hermetically sealed buses. Everything these days – trains, lifts, buses, cars – are built shut tight, like little canisters. She longed for the old British Rail trains and their sash windows, where you opened the door yourself by sticking your hand out the window and turning the handle, and not obeying those little beeps.

'—I dunno,' the joint-smoker is still going strong, ten minutes later. 'Might'a been yesterday.'

She is feeling quite stoned. She stumbles down the stairs and out of the bus.

At home she switches on the TV. On BBC 1 is *Gardening Grotto*, on BBC 2, *Victorian Gardens*. ITV has *DIY for Dummies*. Channel 4 is showing *Mediterranean Dinner Parties*. She switches the TV off.

Outside it has begun to rain, the slow, cold rain of an English winter. She likes how the rain seems to elongate moments, the dreary sensuality of these wet evenings. But is it enough, she wonders, this rain, to cool a man's skin, to extinguish the fire.

There was a hollow echo to her breathing, as if she were inside an empty drum. A thin gurgling stream of fluid forced itself through her throat. She coughed and spat, gulping for breath. Was this what it felt like to die? Choking on your own fluid, shredding oxygen as it tried to infiltrate your lungs.

In another minute her breathing had stabilized, and she was able to lift her head. She found she was looking out of a smudged car window. If she swiveled her eye to the right she could see only a gauzy mass of shadow. No matter how she turned her head the shadow refused to budge.

She brought a dirt-stained hand up to her face, her fourth and fifth fingers askew (she would come to realize they, along with her arm, were broken) and, dodging the shooting pains that ricocheted through her arm, felt that her eye was still there, in its socket.

Directly in front of where she lay was a newspaper-sized sheet of what looked to be white metal. She looked up again and saw more of these pieces strung, in strips or in tatters, hanging from the branches of the trees like sinister Christmas decorations.

She shook her head again to try to dislodge the fug on her eye; she caught a glimpse of metal on her wrist: her watch. The glass had shattered in a spider-web pattern. Through it she saw nine-thirty, or nine-twenty. She moved her wrist and the watch hands skittered around, spinning to twelve-thirty, then to five p.m.

With some effort she bent her neck – three different registers of pain, wrapping around each other like a helix, assailed her from its muscles – and peered into the sky. She would have to learn to tell the time from the sun. It hung mid-way in the slope of the sky; late afternoon, she guessed.

With her good eye she inspected her legs. They looked more like two tree trunks, streaked with bark and muck. A quick vision tore its way through her mind: of leaves razoring her, her legs skinned by branches. She was sockless and shoeless, her trousers untidily cut off at the knee, the leg of one flapping behind her like a sail in the doldrums.

She sat up, levering her body into a sitting position in increments of agony, then tipping herself forward so she could come to rest on her knees. She became aware of a throbbing pain in her left ankle. It faded slowly, as if the pain had to fight to make its way through her body.

She lost her balance and tipped over, landing on her broken right arm. The pain was unlike anything she had ever felt before. It shredded each nerve individually, picking them apart like faulty embroidery. Red spots danced dervishly in her head, and she passed out again.

five

HEAT

'Hey, we've got that video from the States.' Stuart, the art director, yelled over his partition. They were expecting a tape detailing the types of environmental destruction the firm's new client was fighting against.

They sat down to watch the video in a darkened, stuffy room. Erica was on her right, Stuart on her left. The screen stuttered into an image of a crude gash ripped in the rainforest. The camera panned out to show the forest dotted with hulks of amphibious equipment that looked like they had been left behind from the set of some *Star Wars* film.

The river was the colour of red mud. The video panned in on the water to show silver fish floating, belly-up. Then the image shifted to show a black blob erupting from the ground, like a small geyser. The men in the video, hard hats on their heads, their faces streaked by brown grime, all cheered.

She stood. Everyone else was still glued to the television screen. Erica looked up as she left.

In the bathroom she splashed cold water on her face. Erica found her there, leaning over the sink.

'Are you okay?'

'Yes. Fine.'

Erica peered at her. 'Your eyes are all bloodshot.'

Alex raised her face to the mirror to find that little red webs had colonized the whites of her eyes. 'Jesus. Where did they come from?'

'Do you want to go to the doctor?'

She closed her eyes. 'I'll wait a bit. Maybe they'll go away.'

By the afternoon the red webs had faded, but her face hadn't regained its colour. Her skin was sallow, nearly yellow.

Erica appeared at her door. 'Listen, I was thinking, would you like to go out to dinner? I mean, when you're feeling better.'

'Sure.'

On Thursday they walked down a street close to the office, looking for a restaurant. There were three or four, all called Trattoria something.

'I guess it's Italian, Italian or Italian.'

The joke was feeble but Erica smiled gamely. They chose the place that looked the most authentically kitsch, with lace curtains of the windows and the tricolore on the sign outside. Indeed it was run by a real Italian family, who brought them watery red wine and enormous slushy pizzas.

'So what happened on Monday?' Erica began, her voice pitched carefully between concern and I-don't-want-to-pry. 'I couldn't help noticing you weren't well.'

'It just makes me sick, how people just go into a landscape like that and rip it to shreds. Especially a rainforest.'

'Have you spent much time in rainforests?'

She nodded. 'I spent most of a winter and a spring in Central America.'

Erica smiled. 'I grew up in Guatemala. I don't remember very much of it now, though. It's strange, I was there until I was fourteen. Maybe my memory is fading.'

'You must remember lots of things.'

'I do, but they're all a child's memories: more sensory impression than anything. I remember the dust of the dry season and the constant battle to keep insects from the food. Screens on everything. Then in the rainy season nothing would ever dry. We had to seal all the food tight in plastic containers, put rice in the salt, pound the caked sugar. I thought all things tended toward solidity, because in that climate if you leave anything out for even half an hour it turns damp. I even thought dead people were like that, that bodies would settle and congeal in bunches like bags of sugar.'

46

She nodded. 'H-e-a-t,' she pronounced the letters as individual words. 'It sounds like something delicious, but you know it will ultimately wound you.'

Erica smiled. 'I've never heard it put like that.'

'Why did you leave?'

Erica waited a minute before speaking. She seemed to be considering her answers more carefully now, like the first time they went out together. 'My father had to leave. We all had to leave.'

'Do you mean you're political exiles?'

She nodded. 'More or less.'

'Where are your parents now?'

'My mother lives in the States. My father's dead.'

'Oh, I'm so sorry.'

'That's all right,' she said impassively. 'I try not to think about it that much. I think I've filed his death in the back of my head, for future inspection. It's so strange – like having to forget that the person ever existed.' She paused. 'What I think now about my father was that I don't remember a time when he wasn't tired. He had these eyes, I think you call them raccoon eyes.' She demonstrated by lifting up her hands and putting her fingers into o's and placing them across the bridge of her nose.

'Dark circles.'

Erica nodded. 'He had a lot of responsibility. He was always under pressure. We never saw him much – he would come home at night and look at us as we slept.'

'Us?'

'Carlos and I. My brother.'

'Where is he?'

Erica shrugged. 'Who knows. He decided to divorce us when my father announced that we were leaving. He didn't want to come, so he stayed. I think he works as an actor or an impersonator. Something really weird. All I know is, we went to the States, and he stayed there. It's been six years since we've heard from him.'

'Don't you wonder about him?'

She could see Erica squaring something within herself, as if she had to quietly move pieces of furniture or other large objects in order to negotiate an answer to her question.

'I miss the Carlos I knew as a boy. I wonder what happened to him. He changed so much, when he became a teenager. I wouldn't really know him now. I'm not even sure I'd recognise him.' She swallowed. 'Maybe I'm just used to it, to not knowing. I like it, in a way, that I don't know where my brother is. I think it means there is space for wondering in my mind. I think, for me, he represents the necessary mystery in life.'

'You think life has to have mystery?'

'I think life would be very dull without it, don't you?'

She considered the question for a second. 'I'm not sure I find mystery as interesting as most people do.'

Erica looked at her quizzically. 'So, tell me about this guy you live with.' There was something forced in her tone, as if she wasn't used to, or didn't believe in, girlish commiserations.

'Oh, Conrad. I don't live with him that way. I've known him for years. He's an artist. He oscillates between being a normal, thoughtful person and as camp as tents and portable stoves.'

Erica laughed. 'Is he gay then?'

'Sometimes yes, sometimes no. I think he's made a practical decision to increase his options by being attracted to both sexes. He has a lot of lovers but I'm not sure if he's ever been in love.'

'He sounds interesting.'

'He is.' She laughed. 'Far more interesting than me. If you met him, you'd be Conrad's friend, not mine.'

'You sound suspicious of him.'

She was a little shocked, that Erica, nearly a stranger, would perceive something she hadn't even admitted to herself.

'The only thing I'm suspicious of is that he resists feeling anything very deeply, even though I know he can. Somehow I think of this as a *sin*. Which is odd, because I never think in those terms: sin, redemption.'

'If you're not religious you have to have your own notion of sin.'

'He's changing, though. He's becoming more thoughtful. If

Conrad would allow himself to feel and think like I know he can, he'd be devastating. He's very good looking.' she added, for clarification.

'So you're not going to let me meet him, then?' Erica raised her eyebrows. 'I might fall in love with him.'

'Well, I figure you might be safe. You've just got married.' Some quality she hadn't seen in her before peeked out at her from the depths of Erica's eyes, as if that were the place it lived, normally hidden – a practical creature, perhaps a little cruel. 'Just having got married is no guarantee you're not going to fall in love.'

'I always thought that was the purpose of marriage, to say, I'm not going to look anymore.'

'That's what most people think.'

'But they're fooling themselves.'

Erica shrugged her comment away. 'Maybe your friend is just getting older.' She said this as if it were obvious, as if she had figured it all out in advance, like a particularly facile crossword. 'Some people improve with age.'

'I think it's more that his generosity is winning out. That's his great secret: he's a kind person, even generous.'

She remembered the night Conrad had offered her a place to live. This was when no-one else wanted to talk to her for fear she would burst into tears, or be otherwise disagreeable or embarrassing. They had met in the café and gone to a private view together and he had said, 'I need a flatmate. Why don't you move in?'

It was such a simple invitation, but heroic, for her, in comparison to the frightened evasions of her parents and the people she used to think of as friends. Later she would understand that Conrad had lived enough to know that death was part of life. He knew that death really was that black and casual: it happens, shrugs its shoulders, then walks away into whatever lair it inhabits.

'Well,' Erica said. 'I guess I should make a move.'

' "Make a move". You've been here long enough to talk like an English person.' She smiled to show this wasn't a criticism.

'God, don't people say that in the States?' Erica laughed. 'I don't know which dialect I'm speaking anymore. Sometimes I think of them as mutually unintelligible. Do you know when I first came here it took me three months to work out what people were saying?'

She walked Erica to the Tube, then caught the bus home, nearly breaking her ankle on the stairs to the upper deck, as usual, as the driver whipped around a corner.

The bus wound through the medieval streets of the City: Ropemaker, Threadneedle, Bread, Wood, and Milk Streets, Garlick Lane. It was after closing time and the streets were empty but for a few windswept figures. In each building a security guard sat alone at his desk, surrounded by the flicker of monitors and the City's antique, forbidding aura.

Usually she used these long bus rides to think about work. That night, though, she thought of Erica, of how she was light and flexible – no, *pliant* was the word. Her deftness was rooted in some essential confidence: she didn't seem to have suffered from the self-esteem crises that plague most women.

She was not immediately beautiful, rather one of those people whose grace became apparent when examined in motion: thinking, walking, sitting. She wore expensive clothes, cashmere and silk, soft fabrics that invited touch. She managed to be elegant without looking conservative.

None of the people Alex worked with ever invited her for a drink to talk about serious, personal things. They went to the pub to talk about football scores and the latest brand of trainers or whether twenty-eight was too old to go on rave holidays in Cyprus. Erica had responded to her questions with a startling truth and intimacy, but always holding something in reserve. Her air of mystery sat so awkwardly against her essential warmth, her openness. Alex was unused to this kind of puzzling complexity, after so long in the art world, where most people played themselves like a role they had decided to take on.

Erica made her feel like an incontinent self, lacking caution, inhibition, strategy. This was the trick Alex had never managed to perfect: to hold herself back, somehow give the impression that a dramatic internal monologue was taking place inside her. Like ripples on the surface of water where a deadly current lay underneath, she would show only the most superficial signs of the depths of emotion she was capable of feeling.

'I don't know if to even think about going back to my country or not. Is it even my country? I left when I was fourteen,' Erica had said. 'Should I go back to the States? But the States is only the place where my father dies – died,' she corrected herself, a rare slip in her otherwise flawless English. 'My mother lives in one of those retirement communities in Florida. Boca Raton – do you know it? Well, think of old people living in glorified mobile homes and playing golf all day while alligators occasionally devour their dogs.'

Alex tried to picture it but couldn't. She had never seen a retirement community, other than the pre-fab ground-level flats that lined the roads in their area.

'I'm here in England – in London, I should say, because of my husband. Apart from that I don't have any real ties to this country.'

'What about friends?'

Erica shrugged. 'Only friends I've made through work, my last two jobs. Two women and a man. But we don't see each other that often. It's not the same as when you've gone to university in a country, gone to school, lived your whole life in a peer group.'

'I don't know anyone from school,' Alex admitted. 'And only one or two people from art school.' She modified her statement, lest Erica think her a social outcast. 'Of course, I know a lot of people, still, from those years. But they aren't my real friends.'

'Who are your friends then?'

'I'm closest to Conrad, but—' She hesitated. 'I used to have more friends.'

'What happened?'

Good question. What had happened?

She had come back, gone to the same openings she had always gone to, saw the same faces floating in the sea of artists.

She couldn't work up enough interest to talk to people she had once spent whole evenings with, in pubs, in galleries. Instead she chose to walk the city alone, mapping its secrets. She let telephone calls and notes of concern go unanswered.

Slowly, without even trying, the people she had thought were her friends retreated into the background like a shadowy Greek chorus, leaving her alone on the stage. Alone, except for Conrad, who was himself turning into a peripheral character, like one of those pages or knights in Shakespearean plays who are forever coming on stage only to announce some catastrophic event, followed by their own departure.

'What about your work?' Erica had inquired. 'Why did you give up on art?'

'I'm not convinced it was very good. It lacked commitment. I can see that now.'

She didn't know why she said that. Of all the criticisms she had received for her work – that it was spooky, self-indulgent – lack of commitment had never been one of them.

'What was it about?'

'Nightmares. No, dreams. Well, my dreams were usually nightmares. It's hard to describe, but basically I used dreams as a starting point, and made drawings and paintings out of them.'

'Were your dreams always such a good source of inspiration?'

'I used to have the most vivid dreams, full of demons and narrow escapes and kissing unlikely people. But they were just a starting point. The real topic was the subconscious.'

'I can never remember my dreams.'

'Neither could I, so I used to wake myself up at four-thirty or five every morning, the deepest point of REM sleep, when your dreams are at their most outlandish. I would put my alarm clock on and write down my dreams. When I could stay awake. Sometimes I just fell asleep with the pen in my hand. I had the worst ink stains on my sheets.'

'But you don't make anything now?' Erica asked.

'I tried. But nothing – nothing happened. All those years, in

52

art school and after, I had been so driven, so focused. And then it evaporated, almost overnight. It took me awhile to figure it out. I kept producing for awhile, then I realised all my work was coming out white.'

'White?'

'As in blank. Up until then, I loved colour. My drawings might have been black and white, but the single thing my tutors at art college agreed on was that I had a sophisticated use of hue and shade, as they put it. So, to lose that—' She stared into the window. 'White is the colour of depression. For most people it's black, of course. But for an artist white is the negation of colour, of everything you've learned and loved.

'When everything went white I tried writing. People remember the Christmas card piece I did, which got a good mention in *Time Out*. I hung white cards exactly the way some people display their Christmas cards, straddled on pieces of string across the kitchen hearth. You had to stand on a chair to reach the cards. Inside I wrote messages in faint pencil. Just phrases. Whatever came to mind.'

'What did they say?'

'Things like, *Missing you. Hope the remaining children are well. We heard you survived the wreck. Where are you?*'

'Messages to the void,' Conrad had called them. He found them creepy. She had tried to explain to him, saying, 'They're just memories.' 'Whose memories?' he had insisted. 'Memories of what? They seem more like provocations to me. Why don't you try to say something about how we're living?'

'What, paint a block of holiday flats, or those cabins they have on the beach in Essex,' she retorted. 'Or obese women living in council flats in Birmingham. Working-class grotesque. Fey comments on the drab miniature that is English life. I don't think so. It just doesn't move me.'

Across from her Erica was sunk in thought. Erica traced the rim of her wine glass with her index finger, listening. She did this often, Alex noticed. It was a compelling gesture, at once sensual and exact. 'It sounds interesting to me. I like those unanswerable questions. Why don't you start making work like that again?'

'I feel I have nothing to say. I can't engage with life like that any more. I was never very good anyway,' she shrugged, 'as an artist.'

'It sounds like you might not have given yourself a chance.'

'It's over, now. I don't want to think about it much, I don't want to be haunted by my own work. It's like re-reading your diary years after the fact. Grisly.'

Erica had fixed her with that warm gaze and said, 'You're unusual.'

Alex said nothing, just waited for her to explain. Erica held her gaze and smiled. 'You speak frankly. You're not protecting yourself, throwing up little verbal smokescreens.'

With that kind of flattery it was hard not to like Erica. Although really, she distrusted flatterers, and was usually unable to return the compliment.

She thought again of her sympathetic nodding, the warm look in Erica's dark eyes, turned down low but intense, like coffee kept hot on a blue gas flame. But there was something subtly professional in it, like how a therapist or a doctor would look at you.

At the same time Erica reminded her of the kind of person she had once aspired to be: difficult, impenetrable, with sharp edges on which, if you were not careful, you could cut yourself. These people were always loved because they insisted upon it, made you work for it, and the legions of masochists that made up the rest of humanity duly obliged.

The bus disgorged her on her street. Conrad wasn't in. She flicked on the television: *Newsnight.* The screen showed an aerial view of what looked like ragged ribbons scattered over a hillside. *These are queues of refugees. They have been driven out of their villages by Serb paramilitaries,* a grim voice intoned. It was the first anniversary of the invasion of Kosovo by Serbia. She clicked the television off.

six

PATHS NOT TAKEN

She sat in one of the old world cafés in South End Green, eating an overpriced croissant. Across the road the Royal Free Hospital listed like a crippled battleship. She was steeling her nerves before entering its fishy corridors and laminated light to receive another round of X-rays. She had already had about twice her lifetime's allowance of radiation, she calculated.

She had been coming here once a month for nearly a year. She wondered what the twenty-first-century torture chamber would throw at her today. As usual, the neurologist sat her in a threadbare office lit by a single fluorescent strip, and as usual he said he had 'found no physiological causal factors'. Each time this happened she watched his face, sallowed by the phosphorous light, and felt a queasy mixture of relief and alarm.

'What's the matter, then?' she would ask. Then he would launch into a layman's description of the workings of the brain. She could see it pained him not to use the expensive words he had struggled through medical school to employ, words like *contusion, hippocampus, haematoma*; words she discovered in her own cheap time, reading books on neurology at the library. She discovered she had a taste for the ancient tang of Greek medical language, and wished she had mastered it.

'It works like this.' The neurologist launched into another explanation, holding a grapefruit-sized model of a brain in his hands, turning it over and over as he spoke. 'When new information enters the brain, it comes in the shape of nerve cell activity. This is what we call an impression, or an apprehension. It only lasts for seconds, sometimes less. Most of it doesn't get stored. It just goes—' he fluttered his fingers in the air.

'Evaporates,' she said.

'But if the information is worth storing, then we keep it in certain areas of the brain. The patterns of nerve cells in which the information came in the first place persist, so it can be retrieved at any time. But to do this, some of the nerve cell connections have to be strengthened, sometimes at the expense of weaker nerve connections. That's why some memories are more persistent than others.'

'And this – strengthening and weakening, is it permanent?'

'It seems to be, although changes in the brain might take weeks or even months to really harden.'

She had heard this before: the brain was exactly what it looked like, a piece of plasticene. It was moulded by experience, and like a piece of dough inexpertly kneaded it had fissures. Under stress, fault lines formed along the lines of least resistance; fissures in consciousness, like cracks in the earth's crust.

'It's important to remember that we are very good at forgetting. When our ability to forget fails us, and memories become persistent, we call it trauma.' He finished. Then he said, 'why don't you try therapy?'

'But I don't need therapy,' she protested.

He gave her a long cool look that told her people who thought they were traumatised usually weren't, and those who protested were the ones who needed the most help.

'All right,' she said. 'I'll give it a go.'

She found herself in the therapist ghetto of Tufnell Park. In London therapists seemed to congregate in specific areas: East Finchley, Stoke Newington, Tufnell Park – places where until recently the kind of weepy Victorian houses needed for a consultancy could be found for a reasonable price.

She had her sessions in a room at the back of the house, facing a wet garden, surrounded by objects she felt sure had been chosen for their comfort value: a wall hanging made of wheat chaff expertly woven into braids, mutedly cheery paintings of flowers and, as always, the little clock ticking softly, placed where the client could see the pound signs passing.

With her, they passed mostly in silence. She was paying good money for someone to sit in a room with her in nearly complete silence occasionally punctuated by the therapist's looks of pointed concern.

She looked down at her hands. Outside, birdsong drowned out the ticking of the clock.

'I keep thinking of turning back time,' she said, finally. 'I want to arrive back at that point where everything changed, and just take another course of action. Take another bus to another town, stay a week longer in the lowlands.'

The therapist nodded. 'You seem to be thinking about the paths not taken.'

She went around for days with that phrase dangling in her mind, leering like an ugly puppet: *Paths not taken.*

They were all trapped in a maze, a real one – just like the puzzles made from hedges where the Elizabethan court had entertained themselves. As in a sinister fairy tale, little girls can't find their way out and die of dehydration, their inert bodies are found only inches away from the camouflaged door.

In those first few months back in London she tried to retrace her steps in that impenetrable green maze, to unwind her trajectory, turn this way and that. She spent those months sitting in Soho coffee shops, watching random faces fizz in and out of view, trying to read the sentences of light the neon restaurant signs drew on glistening cars as they slid by.

She went by herself to exhibits in museums. At the British Museum she stood for an hour in front of Lindow Man, the stone-age man who had been embalmed in a Danish bog for millennia, staring at his graphite skin, its sheeny leather folds. The Rosetta Stone exhibit told her how a Frenchman named Champollion had laboured to decipher its three hieroglyphic languages. She recognized in its cryptographic tanglings the deliberate, willful opacity of her life in those months. Her days had the same shape as the Coptic symbols, their parabolic meaningless swirls.

There was no record, on stone or paper, of the deals she made with herself during her time in the forest, of things she had never thought of before, like how the future could be something contingent, something that might not happen.

Now she was back in the future, which had miraculously become her present. She ought to have been happy. She got work, met men who pursued her vaguely, desultorily. If they didn't get her, someone else would come along. Eventually, she realised that was the problem: her interactions lacked the passion she built between herself and herself during those days she was lost. Somehow passion had become necessary to her in a way it had never been before.

All around her people were victims of mysterious depressions. The newspapers threatened her with a steady diet of stories about people caught in compulsive shopping disorders, epidemics of alcoholism among young women, and the imminent possibility of meteors striking Earth. Meanwhile, she walks the streets of London with the impression she is clutching something organic but which is in decomposition, like fruit.

She was back in the real world, looking forwards, looking back, strung by that essential tension of the question, what next? Stepping delicately toward the future, dodging the crumbling edges of the yaw of memory which had opened like a sinkhole beneath her feet.

She didn't know how long she spent in this wandering state, only that it was more than a few months. This was before she got the job with Michael's company and she was slipping from one temping DTP job to the other, keying words, changing point size and fonts and making decisions about typefaces – Bodoni Black or Helvetica Ultra Bold? – drifting from one silent office full of strangers to another.

At night she went home to a bottle of red wine, consumed hastily and guiltily, and whatever food she could muster the energy to cook. Conrad was out: Conrad was always out, she was beginning to realise.

Her own voice boomed through her head until it was not hers at all, rather some overlord who had taken up residence inside her and whose job it was to tell her to do things: get dressed, get the bus, go home.

Worse, she found she couldn't read. A random word – anything from *blue* to *antediluvian* – might leap out from the pages of a book and bite her on the lip, causing her to burst into tears. She wouldn't know why that word provoked a reaction.

Raw and dizzy, she walked the streets. She came to know the city intimately during these lonely weekend mappings, discovering William Blake's tombstone in Bunhill Fields near the Barbican, and the small streets of Spitalfields and their shuttered Shaker houses. She found her way though the London maze of Closes, Parks, Groves, Rows, Walks, Passages, Yards, Mews, Crescents, Lawns, Ways and Greens. Even if so many of her turnings were blocked by construction sites, by piles of rubble from recent demolitions or vans delivering loft-sized pieces of furniture.

She struggled to remember the city she had moved to eight years earlier, to attend art school. She could only recall a sense of threat, as if she had come to live in the centre of a bull's-eye. She had imagined it as a military target on Iraqi maps or in the backrooms of pubs in Ulster, the A–Z open on a table sprayed with detonators.

Those were the years of being hustled off the underground with the words SECURITY ALERT booming from the tannoy, looking leerily at empty plastic bags. Then, London seemed a violent city and its violence was completely arbitrary: the 68 bus, the Tube, a quick drink in a pub, walking down the street – the long tentacle of evil could reach out and suction itself onto her at any given moment.

Now the Peace Accords had been signed, a truce had been called. Carrier bags lost their menace, and pavement litter bins reappeared after years of exile. White vans were no longer full of young men with shaven heads wearing bomber jackets, on their way to detonate Canary Wharf.

'I just can't believe you actually went around thinking every white Ford Transit van was full of IRA sleepers,' Conrad said one night when they were recalling the terrorism years.

'I used to have to leave the Tube sometimes, simply because someone had left a plastic bag behind in the carriage. I'd run up the escalators and out of the station and stand there with my heart pounding.'

He shook his head. 'You were paranoid.'

'I thought it was what I deserved, on some level. To be blown up.'

'I hope your therapist can work that one out for you,' he said, meanly.

But she decided one of the paths not taken would be therapy. She put a stop to her expensive hours of silence in the consoling North London house. Experience would be better rehabilitation; it would wash over her and like the ceaseless coming and going of a tide it would erode the edges and jutting promontories inside her. She would get a job, drink beer, go for curries in Brick Lane. She would listen to Conrad and his friends talk about anything at all, and this would heal her. That was how, more than a year ago now, she found herself working for Michael's company, living in Conrad's flat, accompanying him to private views; a mute companion, an afterthought.

It was spring now, and England was soft and green, like a lettuce. This was her favourite time of year; in spring she always felt unsettled, addled, wanting more. She waited for the hunger to return – the hunger to feel, to live, even to love. But a shapeless spectre hovered on the rim of her future, ruining the view.

She couldn't look at it, couldn't even guess what it might be. Perhaps this was just another failure of imagination, she thought, like her inability to see past the dark luxurious curve of the path not taken.

*

The first night stretched itself over her mind thin and tight, a membrane through which she can see nothing but hear everything. Without her eyes, or the moon, or a torch, she was defenseless and foetal, gripped in the arms of a liquid forest.

Leaves rustled around her ankles and she sprang away. It was a snake, she was sure, one of those pit-vipers with the heat-sensor placed squarely between its eyes. She considered climbing a tree, but she'd be no safer. The eyelash viper lived there.

In the end she couldn't stand up any longer. It must have been about midnight: five and a half hours of darkness to go. She wedged herself inside a piece of metal whose sharded edges tore the skin from her calves. Its inner casing was covered in a spidery web of wires and electric cables that branched everywhere like veins and ended in tattered shreds. She had seen a leg like this, only today. She was walking in circles, not even realising it, to try to quell the hunger ransacking her innards, when her forehead bumped against what she thought was a branch. She looked up to see a tattered ganglion of veins dripping from a severed leg. It hung upside down from its ankle, like a torso-less trapezist.

She was surprised to find she had no reaction to it; the leg was no more horrifying than a broken child's toy. She brushed the blood from her forehead and kept going, walking increasingly elliptical circles, like a deranged moon orbiting a shattered earth.

seven

MISSING

The man came barrelling out of the bathroom and straight into her.

'Oh. Hi.' He jumped back as if he had been hit. She could see him thinking, bloody hell. A woman.

'Hi.'

'Who are you?' he said.

'Who are you?'

'Ciaran,' Conrad called from his bedroom. 'This is Alex. She lives here.'

'Oh, right.' Ciaran offered a still-soapy hand. 'Pleased to meet you.'

When Ciaran had been given coffee and, she suspected, Conrad's spiel about no commitment expected or given, he left. She had seen this many times before. He handled the women differently, but with the men there was a pattern.

The men he brought home were usually Celts; Alex secretly called them Dial-a-Redhead. She wondered what Conrad saw in these Scots and Irishmen, although they could be passably cute, with their nervous male energy, their like of what they call good craic.

She came into the kitchen to find him reading the news-paper, a steaming pot of coffee parked on the table. Outside thunderheads had moored themselves in the sky. One of them swallowed the sun and the morning was dark.

She flicked on the light.

'Do you have to seduce everyone? Is there anyone in the world you draw the line at?' She found herself saying this without even thinking. She could hear the anger serrating the edges of her words.

He tossed her a cruel little look. 'You, maybe.'

'Since when? Since you had me once?'

He attempted a smile. 'I believe it was more than once.'

'What is it you see in these Rent-a-Celts?'

His face gathered itself up into folds, like a crumpled piece of paper. He put his newspaper down with a crack. 'You are so condescending.'

'You don't think of them as individuals. You just like the seduction. Then you get bored with them.' She was surprised at the black wave of anger washing inside her stomach.

'So what if I get bored? Everyone is boring eventually. Maybe I'm just faster to admit it. You don't want to see that kind of honesty. It's too bare for you, too obvious. You want everything to be tangled up in meaning.'

'I just think we owe it to each other to consider each other, to really think about the person,' she said. 'Otherwise we're just consuming people.'

'God,' he screwed up his face in disgust. 'Why do you think anonymous sex has to be usurious? Women want everything to be forever, which is just a mask for control.'

She'd heard this before. 'Women are sponges,' Conrad had said to her once. 'They suck you up. Everything becomes about their precious emotions and their progeny. Once they've reproduced they figure they occupy the moral high ground and you don't exist any more.'

'That's just regular misogyny,' she had retorted at the time. 'I expect better from you.'

Now he glowered at her from across the table. 'Have you ever just run your finger down someone's back and thought: I love this back. I love this sensation. You don't think bodies are important?'

'I refuse to think about people like dismembered body parts.'

'I don't believe you. You've never seen a stranger's body and wanted it? The feel of a body,' he persisted. 'The slope of its limbs, the textures of its skin, you don't find any delight in that?'

'I don't think so.'

He said nothing for a minute. Outside, rain streamed down the kitchen window. When he spoke again his voice was quiet, even pleading.

'You might not understand this, but I'm not promiscuous. I just want to live. To really *live*.'

'For you *really living* means having a lot of sex. It's different for me.'

'What does it mean for you then?'

'I don't know.'

'Exactly. You're moralising without offering any kind of alternative. You feel you can disapprove, just because my kind of love isn't going to lead to the formation of a family unit which can then be manipulated by society, sentimenta-lised and forced to fork out four hundred quid apiece for a holiday in Majorca in August because that's the only time you can go because of the bloodsucking brats you've brought into the world.' He paused. 'You have no idea what true experience is. Pure, undiluted. It's empty, bruising. You come out purified.'

'But I don't want sex to be a car crash,' she said.

'What do you want it to be, *reassuring*?'

For Conrad sex seemed to be a journey to self-discovery, reached through an explosive, momentary thrill. For her that kind of sex was like cocaine; it felt passably all right while you were on it, but afterward it left a hole. No, that's not right: a wound.

'You want to understand things all the time,' Conrad sighed. 'All you'll have at the end of your life is moments of your own exquisite, superior moral understanding instead of moments of joy.'

'Which is what you have? *Moments of joy* with people whose name you can't remember the next morning?'

'You think only things that are permanent have meaning.'

'It's just that your kind of experience is meaningless to me.' Her voice was quiet. The fight had left her. 'I couldn't access the heart of anything that I knew was going to be so temporary it would never enter my life again, if I know even while it's happening that it will be just a memory.'

'That's just unrealistic, Alex,' he dismissed her with a wave of his hand. 'Nothing is forever.' He looked sad, as if he felt the meaning of his words. 'I wish you weren't so fixated on memory. We *have* to forget, you know. Can you imagine what it would be like if you remembered everything? Memory can be just a constant dull pain, reminding us of people who are dead; each time we think of them we remember we'll never see them again.' He lowered his eyes. 'Believe me, I know of what I speak.'

'I read about this man in Russia who had no memory at all,' she said. 'He couldn't remember what he had done last year or yesterday or even the moment before, when he had been spooning coffee into his cup, or looking at the sun. The sensation of everything he felt disappeared as soon as it was experienced. His life was like a car passing through a series of traffic lights – red, yellow, green – at high speed.'

She pictured being the man: moments coming at him, singular, like bullets, until they made contact with his skin. Then they evaporated.

'What happened to him?'

'He went mad.'

Outside, the thunder had cleared away. The sun was still trapped behind the wall of cloud in the west. Flutes of light filled the sky in a pleated pattern. Chestnut and cherry trees gleamed in the strange metal light, their blossoms littering the pavement like confetti.

Conrad levered himself up from the chair. 'Time to go to work.'

'You don't work.'

'Oh, right, I forgot. I'm an artist, an overgrown child still fixated on inflicting egotistical displays of creativity on a passive audience. Time to go to *play*.'

She went jogging in the dishevelled local park. On all the trees were white posters, secured by a piece of yellowing tape wrapped around the trunk.

MISSING: Gordon. A friendly, happy border collie. Rachel and Joanna miss him terribly. Have you seen him? The dog's rough furry features were photocopied in black and white. His grey tongue was hanging out a little and his eyes were bright. The ink was bleeding a little from when it rained. Gordon the border collie was leaking down the page. She wondered what had happened to him.

＊

She didn't know how long she lay there – it could have been three hours or a whole day, maybe even two. She could have stayed there forever, her back against the soft mulch, wrapped in a wet blanket of humidity and pain.

The wind picked up and sheared the canopy trees, making them careen about like besotted teenagers at a heart-throb concert. Just as she was getting up the courage to try to sit up again, she heard a thump, not more than three feet away from her inert body.

She tried to raise her head, but it was like picking up a bag of concrete. Shears of pain unravelled themselves through her neck and upper back. She managed to swivel her eye until she saw the offending object. It was a bag, sitting primly on the forest floor. Letters cohered out of the haze in her eye: JANSPORT.

That afternoon several things made the same journey toward gravity: a shoe, another bag, a clump of wires – they all sat mutely, almost apologetically, on the forest floor. But the sinister piñata was ruined when a sudden wind dislodged a large piece of metal and it fell next to her, grazing her right leg. She decided to move away.

She would have to walk, broken ankle or not. She found a strip of cloth, possibly from her own trousers, and wrapped it around her ankle tightly, passing it underneath the arch in her foot. Then she went scouring for a shoe, crawling, her injured ankle held high off the ground behind her, just like an exercise she used to do at the gym to build her upper arms and shave her thighs.

Her hands took the full weight of her body, sinking into the woody mulch. After dragging herself across the forest floor for only fifty metres or so, she was exhausted. Just as she was about to rest, she felt her palm land on an object, squishing it further into the ground. She released her arms and sat back on her haunches, angling her head toward the ground so she could see.

It was a man's shoe, crushed but intact, a kind of brogue – the comfortable yet serious shoes worn by academic men. She had a flash of a family standing on a tarmac – the father carrying a rucksack, wearing jeans and a light brown safari shirt. Two women, one of them the daughter, both blonde, wearing tennis shoes. She rubbed the image this way and that, but it would not cohere.

There was something underneath her shin. She sprang up, despite her broken ankle. Poking up from the muck like a lost treasure from another age was a woman's shoe. She put it on her good foot – a perfect fit. Only much later did she realise it was her own.

eight

DAMAGE

In April it became winter again. A snowstorm made the Easter lilies shiver and the buds on the plane trees shrank back in shock. Thick snowflakes fell against a darkened sky. In an instant Londoners reverted, as if following an old code, to that winter world of hard-set faces in wet coats, aggressive umbrellas, a sooty woollen smell.

'What's happening to the weather?' A legion of scientists from gleaming laboratories in better-funded countries, journalists and weathermen try to explain. In the end they all say, we just don't know.

Someone grabbed her shoulder as she came out of the bathroom.

She turned around. It was Erica. 'Did you hear?'

'Hear what?'

'We've got the entire Rainbow account.' Rainbow was the biggest environmental campaigning organisation in Europe. 'We're going to do their ads for the run-up to the climate change summit.'

'Nobody told me.'

'It was only announced last night.'

'Then how did you hear about it?'

'I happened to be working late,' Erica explained. 'Michael told me. He just found out himself.'

'The summit's quite soon, isn't it?'

'December.'

'I can't believe we landed that. Rainbow's huge.'

Erica nodded. 'And we're tiny.'

'It just doesn't make sense.'

'Do you want to talk about it over dinner?' Erica suggested.

'All right.'

'Tomorrow. After work.'

Conrad was bent over the stove, prodding something with a spatula. 'So what are you doing tonight?'

'Going for dinner.'

Conrad's eyebrows shot up. 'Anybody interesting?'

'Just a work colleague.'

'You're going to dinner with a *colleague?*'

'What's so awful about that?'

He turned and gave her the long scrutinising look of a sculptor, or carpenter: someone who took raw materials and changed them through shape. She wondered if that's what he wanted to do to her, or if it was just pity. 'So what are you going to talk about?'

'We've got a new campaign. For an environmental organisation. It's about climate change.'

'Oh.' He rolled his eyes.

She wanted to say: this is serious. Out there, forests are burning. Fish are vanishing from oceans. Cloud banks are migrating north in search of cool.

Meanwhile they roam their flat, suspended there at night among their machines – computers, dishwasher, video. The machines hum like life-support systems in darkened hospital corridors, accompanying them through the night.

Erica was already there when she arrived. She sat framed in the restaurant's large, mirror-like window like a still life, dressed in a black jumper; the white collars of her shirt sat around her neck like a halo. Her hair was brushed back, her dark face concentrated as she read the menu. Beside her sat a vase of enormous trumpeting lilies. There, framed in the window and the night reflected on her face, she had the quality of a thought, a sketch, an unspoken dream.

70

The restaurant was low-lit, full of couples huddled over candles. On the tables were small white dishes with a slick of olive oil in the bottom, a basket of complicated bread and round terrines of sea salt crystals and pungent multicoloured peppercorns.

They sat with a candle between them, moody glasses of red wine parked in front of them like chess pieces they might move on an invisible gamesboard.

'So what does your husband do?' she began.

'He works for the government.'

She waited for more. When Erica wasn't forthcoming she pressed on. 'What does he do for them?'

'I'm not sure I understand it,' she smiled apologetically. 'Something to do with policy.'

Erica didn't strike her as the sort of woman who wouldn't understand the detail of her husband's job. 'Doesn't he talk about his work?'

'We're really independent,' Erica explained. 'I know that's not fashionable now, but we have a kind of 1950s marriage – not that I stay at home and cook dinner,' she added hastily. 'We both want the same thing, to use our marriage as a base. We take trips away, side-trips if you like, but we view our relationship as a home.'

'You take side-trips? Where? Into other people?'

'Not necessarily,' she frowned. 'Although there might be room for that. I'm not sure. We haven't tested it yet.'

'It doesn't frighten you, that he might meet someone?'

'You know, women are always saying that, "aren't you worried about your man having affairs." But I might meet someone, too. I might have an affair. Nobody seems to consider that.'

'But you're not looking for it, to have an affair?'

Erica didn't answer straight away. 'I just don't believe that there is one person, however lovely they may be, who is going to give me everything I need. I need various people. I just wish I could find a practical way of doing this that didn't hurt people's feelings,' Erica finished on a pained note.

71

'Doesn't that mean you'll have to lie?'

Erica gave her a careful look. 'I think lies are necessary, sometimes.'

She frowned. 'Do you feel comfortable lying?'

'Not lying. Just not telling the truth. Not feeling as if I have to.' A worried look flooded her eyes as she spoke, as if she realised the seriousness of what she was saying, its possible meanings.

From the first second she had met Erica, she could see there was something veiled and willful about her. She suspected many women were like this. She also knew she wasn't one of them.

'Do you ever think you'll find the right person?' Erica asked her.

'I did. Although I didn't have a chance to get that far.'

Erica's eyes betrayed a glimmer of surprise. She didn't suppose Erica had considered what it would be like if her options for love were taken away from her, suddenly and without permission.

'What happened?'

She took a breath. 'I had an accident, just over a year ago—'

'What kind of accident?'

She waved her hand. 'I'll tell you some other time. But the result was, although it took me a long time to realise it—' she smiled, '—the result was, I can't remember certain things.'

'What things?'

'Initially, I couldn't remember anything, from about two weeks before the accident. It's not uncommon, as a problem.' She didn't know if she were reassuring Erica or herself. 'It's called retrograde amnesia. When you have a severe blow to the head, or trauma, it wipes out memories of what happened just before. Most people recover their memory, usually in the first year after whatever has happened.'

'But you haven't.'

'Not yet.' She smiled in that way she had learned to do, apologetically, on behalf of her faulty consciousness. 'The neurologist says there are parts of memory that aren't able to

72

resuscitate themselves. After the first year, any memories you haven't recovered are probably lost.'

'What can't you remember?'

'Just the two weeks before the accident and the accident itself.'

It wasn't a lie but it seemed the right thing to do – as Erica said, not to lie, exactly, just not to tell the complete truth.

'Is it brain damage?' Erica frowned.

She shook her head. 'All I had was a concussion. They treated that there. And when I came back—'

'Came back from where?'

'From travelling.'

She realised she hadn't spelled out the details, the circumstance. Normally she was a good storyteller, but this story came out in reluctant fragments.

'Were you hurt?'

'Other than broken bones, no.' She could feel a dull ache starting up; her ankle, her jaw, her arm, but most of all her ribs, two of which still lay askew. 'There's not much we can do about ribs,' the doctor had told her cheerfully.

Erica stared into her wine glass. 'I'm sorry if I've brought up a difficult subject for you. I can see you don't want to think about it.'

No, she didn't want to think about it. She could so easily forget it, shoving it to the back of her life like the luggage she stored in Conrad's loft. Although she understood that cutting off from her past put her in a false position; either she denied it ever happened, or she could obsess about it, seek the approval that it never gave her. To do this she had to face the fact that – for awhile at least – life never wanted her there, inside it; it had even demanded that she leave.

But other times, inevitably, those days are vividly, shimmeringly alive. They thrust themselves into her present, reminding her she is not only an A–B in the databases of credit card companies and of supermarkets, a foot-soldier in the army of consumers: buys wine, organic food, takes two foreign holidays a year, uses the bus to conserve the environment, researches natural disasters and societal disintegration on the Internet. She is not going to be reduced to her consumer profile, the data used by a thousand call centres who harass her each evening, wanting her to support the Hampstead Theatre, take out a different type of savings account, get a mortgage.

If she thinks about her life now, then the sixteen days on her own couldn't have been less like a dream. It was real, so real she can still feel the soft mulch of the rainforest floor beneath her feet, she can feel thirst burning its way into her lungs.

Nothing will ever be so real again. It is her life now that feels like a waking dream. She is merely another somnambulist walking toward egg whisks in John Lewis, mail-ordering futons, taking package holidays, buying her life from a catalogue.

She sat up and looked around the restaurant. They were one of the last islands of diners in a sea of empty tables.

'I'm sorry. We've talked about me the whole time.'

'That's all right,' Erica smiled. 'Last time it was me.'

They paid the bill and left. When she arrived home Conrad was nowhere to be seen.

She climbed in bed under two duvets. In that cold April, although the daffodils were peeking from the edges of the park, she could not get warm. She curled herself up in a ball and fell asleep with the radio on. At five a.m. she was woken by a mellifluous woman's voice reading the news.

'The body of a Catholic woman has been found in a bog on the borders of Armagh.' The woman's beautiful voice made it sound almost reassuring, as if this was the only possible outcome.

She looked out her window into a dark London sky. She tried to imagine what it would feel like to be shot, lying alone in a bog. The cold sponge of the ground on her nose. Or maybe she had lain face up, counting the stars until they extinguished themselves. Perhaps she was dead before she fell. She supposed it varied from person to person, how long it took to die after being shot.

It was dawn before she could get back to sleep.

*

In the morning she is fine. In the morning she is believable. She thinks: I exist.

By the afternoon she has evaporated. She is a figment of her own imagination. This realisation sends her tumbling into long tortuous sleeps. Aided by the heat, she sleeps all afternoon.

When she wakes up hunger is there to greet her. The hunger pains are nothing like that pre-lunch chattering of a stomach. This is a wild yowling hunger that causes her stomach to constrict like a snake, curling itself tighter and tighter. She wonders what will happen when it lashes out.

She goes to sleep in this hunger delirium, thinking about her stomach, about snakes, how she read, in one of those books about the conquistadors that she made herself read before travelling, that jungle snakes are often arboreal, and strike at the throat. This is why the boots, torso armour and iron helmets worn by the Spanish conquistadors didn't help them as they hacked through the jungle: there was a chink, an area of exposed skin, on the neck.

She awoke around four or four-thirty. The heat of day was already draining from the forest, and dark collected in cobalt pools. She became aware of a raging thirst growing to a roar inside her throat. A stream trickled not far away. She lurched in the direction of the sound, and found water the colour of dark beer. It was half stagnant and sure to be full of parasites. She knew she shouldn't drink from it, but she had no choice.

Sitting beside the stream, she noticed the strange quality of the late afternoon silence in the forest: not so much silence as a place that had been drained of sound, sieved like water from vegetables. She had always believed the jungle to be a place of eerie screeching sounds, chirrs, sudden cries of alarm. It was, but only at night.

Then, at what must have been five o'clock, or five-thirty, it started. Like a soundtrack turned on at first low, then medium volume, it tuned up: the nocturnal orchestra of the rainforest. She put her arms around her legs and gathered her body up. She wanted to make herself small, an invisible spectator in the auditorium of night.

nine

SIEGE MENTALITY

'Morning, Conrad.'

'Hmm?' A watery membrane covered his eyes: this was Conrad in the morning: a toad-Garbo look, glossed eyes stranded between his cheekbones, amphibian and glamorous at once. His hair stood straight up on his head. He rubbed his eyes with his fists, like a child.

'What are you doing tonight?'

'There's opera on Radio 3, *Live from the Met*, Verdi. Thank Christ, a break from Wagner.'

'What happened to KISS FM?' She used to come home to find him dancing in the living room to some hardcore Saturday night mix.

'KISS is for teenagers.' He lurched toward the coffee maker. 'What are you up to?'

'Going out with Rachel. That show you didn't want to see.'

Conrad shuddered. 'Don't say I didn't warn you. That German girl who's trying to get street cred by photographing fried eggs at bad caffs in Limehouse. Meanwhile she was brought up by a nice pair of academics in a farmhouse on the outskirts of Essen.'

She left Conrad to his Saturday night opera and met Rachel at Bar Italia. Rachel arrived fifteen minutes late, and far too casually dressed for an opening. Instead of leopardskin or leather, orange corduroy or patterned tights, she wore a pair of black jeans and a simple shirt.

They perched on stools, their reflections bobbing in the mirror that lined the café.

'We're not going to an opening,' Rachel said.

She put her coffee cup down. 'We're not?'

'I'm sorry to get you out on false pretences,' Rachel confessed, 'but I wanted to talk to you about Conrad.'

'What about Conrad?'

'I want you to keep an eye on him over the next few weeks.'

'Why?'

'You weren't here for his last show, were you?'

Alex shook her head. Conrad's last show was over a year ago. She had still been in hospital.

'Listen, I don't know how to put this.' Rachel fished a cigarette from her pack. She inserted the cigarette into her lips with surgical practice. 'You know, having a show sometimes causes Conrad to go off the rails.'

'I know he gets nervous.'

'Try nervous breakdown.'

'That's just what he wants you to think—'

Rachel cut her off. 'No, I'm serious. His first show caused him to have a nervous breakdown. He had to spend a week in hospital. When he was there he saw a psychiatrist, and they diagnosed him as manic.'

'Manic, as in manic depressive? I know he's energetic—'

'He has been since he was a teenager, apparently,' Rachel said. 'But they failed to diagnose him in the wilds of Canada. They thought he was just hyperactive. Apparently his mother would tie him up, to calm him down.' Rachel exhaled, blowing a thin stream of smoke right into her reflection in the long strip mirror. 'I don't know the extent of it. It might just be a mild form of mania. He might just be a borderline case. He never talks about it.'

'But I've never seen any medication around the house.'

'I doubt he puts it out for display in the medicine cabinet. Especially not with the traffic through your house recently.'

She hadn't realised Rachel knew about Conrad's serial conquests.

'I think he stopped taking it, more than once. He couldn't

bear being dependent on drugs. It made him feel more out of control than being sick did.'

'What happened?'

'He got worse,' Rachel sighed. 'Not right away, but progressively more energetic. You would see him in the studio and he'd be painting all night. He wouldn't have been to bed in three days. We've got a few manic depressives in our family and they always went off like that, if they stopped taking drugs, poof!'

'Maybe it's not a disorder at all. Maybe it's just Conrad being Conrad. He's got such energy.' She could hear the admiration seeping into her voice, and moved to mop it up. She did admire Conrad's energy, the intensity and commitment he employed, simply to shut a door or take milk out of the refrigerator. But were these actual signs of illness? She could never imagine Conrad being unbalanced.

'I'm too sensitive a soul,' she heard Conrad's voice start up in her head. 'I can't take criticism.' He hated to read reviews of his shows. Sometimes a bad review could put him in bed for a day. But in bed for a day was not a mental illness.

'I'm pretty skinless,' he had said, more than once. But then she was skinless too. Artists could be skinless. They were practically required to be.

'I just want you to keep an eye on him,' Rachel was saying.

Outside the café it had begun to rain. She watched water stream down the window. Inside, she felt like that too: liquid was running down her intestines, her lungs.

'Do you think he would hurt himself?'

'He's only done it once, a long time ago. After his degree show at college. The show got reviewed in a few places; it was my degree show too. I've kept the reviews, they weren't that bad. But someone singled out Conrad's work and said not very nice things about it, and he took it badly. He tried to kill himself, actually. Fortunately he didn't try very hard. He took a bunch of pills – lithium, I think – and threw them up. I read somewhere that's usually how women try to kill themselves: minimum risk, maximum cry for help. Men just blow their brains out.'

She stubbed her cigarette out in an already overflowing ashtray, and scowled. The lines around Rachel's eyes gathered like fine puff pastry. She really was beginning to look her age.

'I'm telling you this because he's got a show coming up. I know it's important to him. It's his biggest show since he left art school.'

'I can't believe he's never said anything to me.'

'It's not fashionable to have a mental illness. In the art world you can go around with a beer in your hand and coke dripping from your nose twenty-four hours a day for ten years and no-one says boo, but if you've actually got something wrong with you: instant pariah.'

'I still can't believe he didn't tell me.'

'Well,' Rachel waved her hand, 'I've known Conrad for-ever.'

Forever. How reassuring it must be, she thought, to know someone forever.

Conrad had a previous life he hardly ever spoke of, a life which he had shared with a woman and a golden retriever. This was a place in Canada that had been given the name of one of the English Home Counties: Sussex or Surrey. Conrad had a mailbox with his name painted on it at the end of the drive and a little flag for the postman to leave up when he had mail. Conrad still had a picture of the dog and the mailbox he had left behind, but of the woman there is no trace.

Neither did he have any photographs of his parents, although he had mentioned his mother to her. 'She was a frustrated soccer mom,' Conrad joked. 'I refused to play soccer so she couldn't display her rampant femininity to the other soccer moms.' She was one of those women who made a life-long project out of being the Perfect Mom, he explained. 'She bought the whole story, hook, line and sinker. Romance, finding a Real Man, having children.' It had been important for her to have sons, Conrad had told her. It had confirmed something elemental about herself to herself.

He had shown her a photograph of his brother, Harold. In it

was a thin boy, fifteen or sixteen, two glossy brown eyes in a pale, narrow face – the kind of face she would call *intelligent*. Something was alive behind it, and trying to break through. He was wearing a quilted jacket with a fur-fringed hood called a parka, standing in front of a ridge of dirty snow against a sky the colour of milk.

She peered closer. The dark eyes of his brother stared at her, half-uncertain, half-defiant. What was the name of that expression? she searched for the word. *Hounded*. It was a look she had seen only in paintings, on the faces of Renaissance stags, an expression pitched on a blood frequency, listening for the quiver of dogs.

When Conrad was eighteen Harold jumped off a bridge into a cold April river. After his brother's death the cordon of silence that his mother had erected around the family tightened. His mother never spoke Harold's name again. His father reinforced his characteristic thin, hard mouth, until his face was set in stone.

Somehow, although he was not even twenty, Conrad realised that he had been born into that place and that family quite by chance, and in that place there was no hope for the sensitive. He hatched his escape plan. Instead of going to the nearest city and becoming a waiter he thought of something much more audacious. Someone mentioned that because his mother's father had been British he could live there legally, at least for a few years. He arrived at age twenty. Fifteen years later, he was nearly English in manner and vocabulary, although his accent had hardly softened.

Conrad had something of the crippled survivor, although it was obvious only to Alex and Rachel, and a select few friends. He had endured his upbringing and then his exile only by switching parts of himself down or off as required, like one of those astronauts in the sci-fi movies of his childhood, travelling through the cold corridors of their crippled spaceship, decommissioning areas of it so that the ship could survive.

For most of his adult life he had been resurrecting these shut-down areas of his persona, flipping them on one by one. That was the Conrad she came to know: moving through icy corridors, cold condensing on the walls, dodging the little electric sparks, recovering these used husks, living in them again by putting up first fairy lights, then, as he became more au fait with interior design, concrete tea light holders and naked pine furnishings. By the time she came to live with him, Conrad had developed the rigid self-sufficiency of people who have spent a long time alone in foreign places.

She never considered she knew everything about him, and her lack of interest in secrets meant she never wondered much about his past. In any case, she felt, it was always difficult for someone English like her to imagine being brought up in more elemental places. A near lifetime labouring under the reduced horizons and the little social boxes of England meant she lacked an understanding of what it could be to live in an Arizona trailer park, or work in a Thai brothel, just as she could only gather impressions of Conrad's early life in a place to her that seemed simultaneously punishing and deeply dull.

But she was Conrad's friend, and she should wonder more. She made a resolution to ask him about his past more often.

Although at times she wasn't sure if they really were friends, or just two people who had chosen to incarcerate themselves together in the same space, for the purpose of some cunning symbiosis. She wondered how long it would last. Friendship can surprise you in the same way love does, she knew. For a while, it fills your life. Then one day it might start to leak, like a burst pipe and you think, where has all that friendship gone?

But they go on because, in a sense, they really were each other's only friends. There was something of the siege mentality between them. What it would be like out there, in London, without each other? They were not sailing the family ship into uncertain waters; they weren't surrounded by old school friends; neither of them had any contact with their families, or even a steady lover. They were simply two misfits living in an unforgiving city, without children or parents or a family who would remember them when they were gone. They could disappear without a trace.

*

It is May and it hasn't rained in nearly a month. The temperature is more like July. The windless streets are smoky. The air is laced with diesel burn, and milky sun filters though a smog haze.

She walks to work on these bizarre soggy mornings, the smell of asphalt-boiled urine and mushed vegetables rising from pavements littered with the discarded entrails of flowers in Dover Street market, or blocked by lorries unloading mineral water into the back entrance of The Ivy.

One day in mid-May the temperature rockets to thirty degrees. On the tube people faint, caught in an airless crush of commuters. No-one notices until everyone alights and the unconscious person, so far supported by their indifferent bulk, falls to the floor with a thud.

The city is covered in a thin yellow glaze. At night weather presenters come on and look perplexed. It's just not your usual British spring, they say.

She steps out of their flat in the morning and there it is again: another dazzling day. The sun seems to be angry with her, with everyone. It frowns at them, a single Cyclops eye.

*

Nine or ten o'clock is the time she is most likely to panic. It has been dark for three hours and it would be dark for another seven or more. The night is a distance test, a marathon of will.

The strangers who she had sat next to and who now lay in pieces all around her – a hand, a foot. At first they looked like parts of abused dolls in a child's toybox. Now they were beginning to swell and smell.

Why hadn't she been diced up like this? She knew it was a rule of airplane accidents. When there were survivors, there were few. Out of plane loads of 230 people, twelve survivors. Of seventy-eight people, three. Death had majority rule.

Each of those first days was a waking dream, as she floated along on a cloud of hunger. It seemed obscene, that the body should be hungry so quickly, that the intensity of its hunger should drive her to cry, to try to sleep, to faint, anything to get away from the howling emptiness that had blown in and ransacked her body.

She scoured the forest for food, striking out in larger and larger circles from the wreck. Several hundred metres away she came upon another backpack of the kind American college students carried. It sat primly on a bed of primeval mosses, a streak of mud on its suede backside the only evidence of the violence it had suffered. She imagined its previous life, being carried from class to class across one of those campuses filigreed with ivy, the white classic columns of the buildings like two femurs stalking the entrance. The knapsack's owner, clever and optimistic. Young. Alive.

She ransacks its contents as if it were a treasure chest. Inside are rubies and emeralds: two granola bars, neatly wrapped in foil, one coloured green and one pink. She tears them open. Their woody cereal smell floods her nostrils. She takes a first bite, but before she can swallow, a sick dark wave washes over her. She throws up, spewing the granola bar over the forest floor. Then she passes out.

ten

THE BANALITY OF LOVE

'In all my career as an artist I have *never* queued for an opening before.' Rachel was furious.

'Della Multon.' Alex squinted at the press release. 'It's a strange name.'

'Oh, she made it up. Her real name's Miranda.' Rachel lowered her voice, conscious of who might be in the crowd. 'She wanted to be more authentic, more working-class.' She looked up at the window with apprehension. Heads bobbed in the gallery space above. 'I'm almost dreading what this is going to be.'

'Why?'

'You don't know her work?'

'Not really,' she admitted.

'Well,' Rachel settled in for a long explanation. 'We were friends at art school, Miranda and I. Years ago we used to collaborate together. But then she got too personal for my taste.'

'Like what?'

'Let's see. I always have trouble remembering the sequence. I think her first piece of work was called My Maternal Feelings. She parked a milk float in a large, white room with fluorescent lighting beating down from above. On the back of the float was a crate of glass bottles, all full. Each was labelled Breast Milk. On the audio speakers were the sounds of crying children.

'The next one was the best. It was called My Hypothetical Boyfriend. Imagine a wall of photos, Polaroid shots of men.

She went out into the street and approached random men, asking them if they would be her boyfriend. Then she took Polaroid photos of their faces.'

'What was her point?'

'I think it was something about how men still display disgust when approached directly for sex by a woman. How they still need to give chase. Or maybe it was a comment on the randomness of life, you know, that any man could be your hypothetical boyfriend, but you never meet them so you don't know.'

Rachel paused. 'Every time she goes out there she's got to do something more outrageous than the last time. Now she's ghettoized herself as a wailing harpy. But you have to admire her,' Rachel went on. 'How many women get that kind of attention?' Rachel sounded as if it was something she wanted: attention.

The queue was finally moving. They fought their way up a cold concrete staircase and entered the gallery. There they were confronted by a series of paintings of blurred flowers.

'Bloody hell,' Rachel said, looking from one side to the other, her face blanched. 'What's happened here?'

A cadaverous man standing behind them tapped Rachel on the shoulder. 'She had a kid,' he said.

'I beg your pardon?'

'She became a mum. Read the show notes,' the man pointed to the sheaf of white press releases on the table. 'Bloody shame, isn't it?'

Alex fetched a sheet and they read it together. 'I wanted to do something to celebrate the corporeality of having a child' the text read. 'To join the liminal and the subjective in a re-imaging of desire.'

After the show they sat in a pub on the tattered fringes of Soho.

Rachel stirred her bloody mary absently. 'I'm thinking how amazing it is, how people can change their tune. They spend years railing against something and then, as soon as it happens to them, poof! Wholesale endorsement. People are so up their

87

own arses. Like, oh, I support abortion, but not for me. What ever happened to principle, to *values?*'

'But haven't you ever changed your tune?'

'Not that radically. I mean, not so much as to take the entire sting out. Look at her paintings: they're lovely, but they're contentless.'

'But that's the same criticism you had of her bolshie work.'

'I know, I know. Maybe I'm just thinking of my own work. Maybe it's time for a change.'

Rachel's latest 'happening' was staged at the opening of a good friend of hers in some West End gallery. It was so popular she transferred it to a draughty former dressmaker's space in Stepney for a limited run.

It was tightrope act, even though the rope was suspended just a few feet off the ground. On one side of the rope was a small children's swimming pool filled with mud. On the side of the pool was written DESIRE. On the other side of the rope another pool was titled ABDICATION. She walked the rope in a white dress not unlike a toga. Sometimes she deliberately fell in, sometimes not. Despite her circus training she wasn't a very good tightrope walker. But that was part of the whole show – the unpredictability, the possibility of a messy spectacle.

She had got the idea from reading some book by an American feminist. 'It personified women's predicament in the face of love,' she explained. 'That as a woman you have to abdicate to pursue your desires. That somehow, for women, there's always a pot of mud to fall into – people are waiting for you to fall into it, hovering around you like vultures to watch you make an ass of yourself, even your so-called friends – while men just sail through love and life without so much as a misstep.'

It had backfired slightly, in that while attendance was good, the audience was predominantly men. Women stayed away. A couple of art students even picketed the last show outside, and heckled Rachel as she left the building. 'Reactionary cow,' the twenty year olds yelled. 'Women are in control now, you seventies relic!'

Rachel took a drag of her cigarette and a gulp of her drink. 'To be honest, I'm still bewildered by the women's hostile reaction to the piece. I just wanted a more profound picture of women's dilemmas about love and trust. Maybe I've got it completely wrong. Maybe I've just pandered to the usual concerns. It's tough to look back on your career and see that you've committed that level of misunderstanding.'

'Do you think it was like that with the Banality of Love?'

Rachel gave her a suspicious look. 'Why? Who told you that?'

'No-one. I just heard about it.'

That wasn't strictly true. Conrad had told her about the Banality of Love. In it Rachel, a friend of hers from art school, Helen, and an actor named Jason had acted out being interviewed as a couple. Rachel and Helen changed positions being the interviewer half way through the piece. They were supposed to be from a magazine, and were writing a *Marie Claire*-type feature on how often people have sex. The couple was encouraged to talk about their vision of love.

Jason, the boyfriend character, said: 'I see love as trust mixed with longing.'

'I don't feel any desire for other men, because he really satisfies everything I want in a man,' said Helen.

'We have an open relationship. We talk about our desires for other people. But we don't act on them.' Jason, the man, laughed. 'We don't act on them because we talk about them.'

Helen looked pained. 'I feel cold every time he mentions he saw a pretty girl or says, what a stunner.'

'I found a vibrator in her drawer last month,' Jason said. 'I said, "am I not satisfying you?" '

'Last night I found a stash of *Loaded* under his bed.'

The dialogue went on like that until the couple were in complete disarray. 'They started out so sunny,' Rachel said with a smile. 'So smug. In that couple-smug way that says, we refuse to recognize uncertainty. No-one will ever penetrate our love. Precisely because they know it could happen at any time.'

The piece finished in an uncomfortable, thirty-seconds long stony silence.

'People found it disturbing,' Rachel said, shrugging. 'But we need to be reminded it's not happy out there in couple land. There are people who want your lover. And they're going to try. And anyway, so many relationships are a sham of wishful thinking.'

She was silent for a minute. When she looked up there was a strange raw pain suspended in her eyes. 'Who's going to want me?' Her look was blank, pleading. 'There's a glut of thirty-nine-turning-forty women in this town. It doesn't matter who I am as a person. I'm about to be forty and that's the only detail that matters. I'm going to be thrown on the great biological scrap heap: too old to reproduce.'

'That's a very Darwinian interpretation.'

'Darwinian schminian.' Rachel scowled. She had spent a year and a half in Manhattan and still used the New Yorker's rhyming slang. 'You're ten years younger. You've got time on your side. You can say, oh, I don't really feel like having children. You've still got years of possibility in front of you.' She gave her a warning look. 'But how much longer are you going to have this hair, this skin, this body?'

Her stomach rumbled threateningly. Rachel seemed not to be delivering advice so much as stating one of those punishing statistics she had to contend with at work: *four-fifths of the world lives in abject poverty, one in three children will die before they are three years old.*

Then again, Rachel was right. She knew she was no longer a bona fide young person, and she was under no illusions that she was beautiful. There were so many women who looked like her. She saw them all the time, on the street, in the Tube, shopping for clothes in Jigsaw and French Connection – women who were passably good-looking, who wore black and kept slim. If they were all put together no-one would be able to single her out, say, *that's Alex.*

'Those years go fast,' Rachel was saying. 'All those years you were in the driving seat of your little vehicle, cutting through space. Then all of a sudden, you're not in the driver's seat any more. It's the same car but you've become a passenger. And it's accelerating, until eventually you disappear around that bend you thought looked so far off on the horizon.' Rachel paused. 'I could do a piece based on that, in fact.' She smiled, satisfied with her analogy. 'Want to get some chips?' Rachel took her by the elbow and dragged her into the nearest greasy caff.

eleven

SURVIVAL KIT

'I need to ask your advice.' Erica slid into Alex's cubicle, casting fugitive looks in their wake. Then she leaned toward her and whispered in her ear: 'I think I'm going to have an affair.'

'An affair?' Alex could hear the alarm in her voice. What she meant was: with who?

'Sssh!'

'Why are we whispering?'

'Because it involves someone here.'

She stiffened. Who was there to have an affair with in their office?

'I don't want to say who.' Erica lowered her eyes. 'But I think we're going to do each other a lot of damage.'

'Well then, don't.'

'But don't you see, it's the only interesting thing in life, for me.' There was a pleading look on Erica's face. 'What you might feel for someone, what they might feel for you. What you might say to each other, how you might touch each other.'

'Sex.'

'It's not sex that interests me, really,' Erica shrugged. 'For me sex is in the head. It's the thrill of the interaction, of the feeling.'

'Sounds like an ego trip.'

'I know, but it's so much more than that.'

Part of her thought, well, why not? She's young. People still want her.

'Have you ever felt that?' Erica asked.

'Have I ever felt what?'

'That excitement.'

'Of course I have. Thanks for asking.'

She didn't know why she was so annoyed. Erica was only one or two years younger than her, but she was still shy of reaching that exact point where she had landed, where life did not seem to be offering much that was new, only variations of things she had felt before, old dilemmas in new guises. Hers was not an age for crushes and distractions, but for starting a family, for beginning a process she had heard North Americans call consolidating, sounding as if they were talking about a merger between insurance companies, which in a way she supposed they were.

Erica dropped her eyes. 'I've upset you.'

'No you haven't,' she lied.

'It's just—' Erica paused. 'I don't want to do it, but I feel compelled.'

Alex shrugged. 'Don't do it, then.'

'It's not that easy.'

'What, to deny desire? Of course it is. Most of us have to do it all the time.'

Erica gave her a quizzical look. 'I want to be serious,' she said. 'Be responsible. Have a family.'

'Oh,' she sighed. 'A family.'

'You don't want a family? Don't you worry about being alone?'

'A family is no guarantee that you won't end up alone.'

She thought of the family she had travelled with, a textbook family from one of those Explaining Reproduction manuals from her adolescence: all tall and blond, all so obviously of the same blood and bone and sinew. They had gone to the trouble of having children, of raising them, only for the world to deal them all a black, dizzying blow.

Erica was looking at her strangely. Perhaps she was waiting for an answer. Did she want a family?

To have a family you had to first fall in love. She knew it from novels and films, but couldn't remember it – the pure spasm of falling in love, the thrilling feeling that you are about to get closer to something elemental.

When would she get closer? She wanted to get close to the raw fears, the misdeeds, sharp shafts of delight. She wanted to bask in a changeable, sometimes extreme mountain climate. She was sure there must be someone out there who could offer this cold immersion, followed by a baking sauna, like Turkish baths: a life of hot followed by cold; of density, wild contrast, evaporation.

Erica spoke out of the silence, giving Alex one of her warm, open looks. 'You know, I never talk like this with anyone.'

'Not even your husband?'

'Sometimes. But not with friends. I suppose I don't really have any friends. They've all left me, or I've left them. It's the same as a love affair in that way, isn't it?'

'I don't know.' When she moved to get up from the chair, she realised she had been very tense, holding her back away from the frame and sitting bolt upright.

'Well,' Erica said. 'I'd better get to work.'

After Erica left Alex turned her chair around and stared out the window. Her office was on the top floor; from her window she could see the upper parabola of the London Eye, suspended like a distant trinket above the roofs of Covent Garden. It had appeared on the horizon less than a month before. It really was a giant Eye, revolving slowly over the city, people trapped in its glass pods, watching.

At night she watches survival programmes on television. She had become addicted to a series called *Survival Kit*. It showed how to survive being stranded in the Arctic (develop a taste for raw fish); how to survive an attack by a grizzly in Alaska (don't run, don't play dead, don't climb a tree; running into a frigid ocean and swimming for your life is a good option, though); how to survive in a blistering desert (find water). She took notes through all of this – carry a good knife, string, binding. Remember to leave matches in wilderness huts.

The jungle survival installment was presented by an ex-SAS survival expert who managed the right combination of jaunty optimism and grim attention to reality that television producers seemed to think survival required. 'Water isn't too much of a problem,' he said, standing beside a stream of water of the kind that had given her lifelong amoebic dysentery. 'As long as you have a water filter.'

She heard Conrad come home, banging the door shut in his usual frenzied style. 'I don't know why you insist on watching these bloody programmes,' he complained. 'Especially when the principal piece of survival information you need in this town is what to do when you've been waiting for the 149 for thirty minutes and one streams by without stopping.'

That happened to him only last night, he told her, and a woman at the bus stop had burst into tears.

*

Each new memory is like a blurred postcard sent by an unknown correspondent. The one most recently arrived shows a misted coastline, tall palms tipping like drunkards over grey volcanic sand. It drains the sun of its heat, sizzles the soles of their feet.

Before they went to the mountains they spent a week on the coast in a small cabin loaned to them by a local fisherman. They were still getting used to the heat, to the small details of being in a tropical country, like the louvred windows through which breezes blew like airborne flowers. The smells were of honey and coconut, and something sweet and slightly putrid.

The cabin had a tiled floor. She can still feel its coolness under her hot feet. They were right on the Pacific; outside, breakers collapsed against the shore. At night lightning stalked the sea, rain drummed on the roof and raindrops dripped from the razored edges of tropical plants.

The sand on the beach was grey and lustrous, like a seal's back. The breakers cracked themselves open on it with such ferocity that the entire beach was shrouded in a fine mist.

Vultures hung out on its fringes like undertaker's lackeys, waiting for the sea to divulge one of its periodic corpses. They went for everything, she noticed: a dead turtle, flipping it over quickly and efficiently to get at its soft underbelly. The only thing they avoided was a dead pelagic sea snake washed up on the beach, thin and black like a strip of rubber tubing, with a yellow paddle-shaped tail.

She saw dawn break, the sun rising from behind the

mountains, the morning heat sliding down the side of the extinct volcano. By ten o'clock the mist had nearly dispersed, sinking into the groves of tall fey palms that line the beach and which lean into the wind languorously, their legs flung out like tired horses.

Then they left the coast and ascended to the Highlands, rising through humid forests of sweetgum, giant pines studded with trogons and motmots, whose calls and shrieks filled the empty air. Tiny waterfalls threaded themselves through the highlands, spilling out at the side of the road. Here was land of the Maya; rushing with water, green with floppy-eared corn.

She can remember all these things: the names of trees, the fields of corn, and the misted beach. She remembers someone saying. 'It's too lush.' But there is a smudge where his face should be, as if the grey fluff that covered her optic nerve for a month had always been there.

That's all she knows. She turns the postcard over in her hands, searching for a message written on the other side of memory, but it is blank.

twelve

THE BRUTALIST MOVEMENT

'Pass me the spirit level will you,' Conrad barked.

'Where is it?'

'Christ.' He stomped down from the top rung of the ladder, missed the bottom step, and landed heavily on his feet.

'Look, I'm sorry, I didn't see it—'

'I want you to tell me if I'm hanging this canvas straight, okay?'

Laurence, the gallerist, a small, quick French woman – were French women ever anything but small and quick? – twittered in the background. Her gallery was neither up-market nor 'alternative' nor 'up-coming East' as the listings magazines defined them. Hers was an ex-industrial space on an unlovely road in Clerkenwell. The gallery suited Conrad perfectly, who also wanted to be cool yet respectable. This was a tricky act to pull off, but both he and the French gallerist managed it, in their own way.

'What do you think?' Conrad said, lighting a cigarette. He only smoked when he was angry or hanging his work or both.

She scanned his paintings. They looked frail and vulnerable, stacked against the wall.

Conrad's work was various – he could paint in a number of styles, all without reference to each other, like a clever art forger. But for the past two years his subject had been the same, showing scenes that had been left, a second before: there were exquisitely executed hair baubles, empty baby strollers left in the sunshine, finished cappuccinos, all recently vacated. The colours were intense but at the same time strangely diluted, like the way paint looks on adobe walls. He loved those southwest colours too, indigo blue, Georgia O'Keefe shell pink, cactus green.

She studied the canvasses. His empty objects suggested some hurried departure, but the fume of emotion still curled around his coffee cups, and there was ambiguity in the tussled bed-sheets in an empty bed. Had one person or two slept there? What had happened in that bed? It seemed elated, somehow, the emptiness.

That the ghost of feeling remained in Conrad's paintings stopped them from being mere clever objects, or comments on emptiness or abandonment. Something was left behind, even if it was just the absence of a presence; although she had the feeling that the absence wasn't of the temporary kind, that the invisible people who had left the scene in such a hurry wouldn't be coming back.

Conrad stood in the middle of his paintings, adopting his characteristic elk posture – one of those lean, elegant animals who always looked to be in a state of alert.

'You know, this show represents two years of non-stop work.'

She nodded. 'But what's the title all about?' Conrad had decided to call the show Tolerance.

'Why not?'

She considered backing off. She could see he wasn't in any mood to argue. 'Because tolerance makes me think, I think, of racial tolerance, social tolerance. Allowing other people to live and to be in peace.'

Conrad grunted. 'I haven't got any big social statements to make. You know that.' He sat on the top rung of the ladder, his back against the wall, smoking. Poised there he looked like a work of art himself, on the top of the ladder in a white shirt and dark jeans, smoking an uncharacteristic cigarette. 'I'm thinking of the tolerance required to just let objects exist. To not require them to have any individual story or destiny.'

'You don't think destiny is important?'

He exhaled fiercely, smoke billowing from his nostrils like a steam train. 'What's destiny these days? Taking your holidays in the Loire and bringing back a car clinking like a milk float full of fucking Sancerre. There isn't any destiny in a society where your tough choices and moral quandaries come down to 'should I buy Nigel Slater or the *River Cafe Cookbook*?'

'Okay, okay.' She was familiar with Conrad's rant against the reduced horizons of the upper middle-classes. 'Do you think you could come down from there? You're hurting my neck.'

They packed in the hanging for the night and went to get a curry in Brick Lane, walking through the deserted streets of Clerkenwell, then Shoreditch, then along Great Eastern Street. Silent office buildings, square and rubberised, squatted beside them, refused to divulge the secrets of what happened inside them by day, the office politics, sexual harassment, career disappointment.

This is what she liked best about Conrad's company: that they could walk this way, side by side at night, not speaking, just feeling the streets and the night as they brushed through them, as if they were passing through a different dimension. This was London the aquarium city, watery from the constant rain and the proximity of the river. In other cities the colours of London at midday, in the palm of the afternoon, would be seen only at dawn and dusk. A city of long delicate springs and dedicated plunges into winter. She thought of the droop of damp roses, their petals pummelled from them by the rain, how they litter the ground like confetti thrown at weddings, the saline river, hemmed with an oyster haze, the thin estuarine sky, clouds hurried across it by impatient westerlies.

At night the city never darkened to black but stalled at navy – not just any navy, but that deepest blue of skirts and blazers worn by Home Counties matrons. Soho she saw in red and purple, its jungle of faces; garish expectant faces trapped behind glass in bars and restaurants.

Alex thought in these streaks of angry colour, and she had painted like that, too. Conrad's take on the city would be different. He would paint gutted *Evening Standards* papering the floors of Tube carriages after the nightly commuter run, or the residue of mojitos drunk by slim girls in Cuban-themed bars, or cabs hurling down narrow streets, passengerless.

In the two weeks she was lost to the world and to herself she had thought longingly of London's dark meandering streets, the gulfstream sky. But now that she was back in it, she found it overwhelming, how it deflected meaning and muffled sound, like one of those rubber rooms where they incarcerate schizophrenics.

Beside her, Conrad looked contemplatively at the buildings as they passed, his educated eye scanning them for architectural style, labelling them Gothic, Norman, Neo-classic, Modernist, Post-modern, the Brutalist movement of the generic office building in the tangle of streets between Moorgate and Liverpool Street.

She longed to know what he was thinking, but almost never asked. With Conrad, you had to wait for him to volunteer information. As long as she didn't try to get too close, she knew, Conrad would tell her anything. He was offhand, even careless that way. But if she overstepped that invisible line she would become suffocating, a sponge woman like all the rest. She was getting tired of maintaining this friendly distance, of accommodating his insistence on not being known. She wanted the thrilling possibility of intimacy, of feeling herself deep inside a heart and mind; a pleasant, necessary immersion.

Maybe Conrad took his cue from the city. They both had the same quality of something glimpsed in a mirror from an oblique angle, of a life glanced at sidelong, not particularly deeply felt. Which was more or less how they all lived their lives now, she thought: striding purposefully toward futures tended like gardens, with plans and forecasts and pensions and mortgages, one step away from feeling.

Michael made the announcement in his best Caring Man voice, deep and sloshed by concern. 'I'm pleased to tell you we've won the Polyp account.'

Polyp was a charity that supported victims of one of those diseases where the body began to attack itself, slowly but

101

steadily, over a long time, like a willful subversive. Eventually the victims were paralyzed, then they died. There was no cure.

'It's a big campaign,' Michael started, his face heavy with the seriousness of someone used to stating the obvious. 'No screw-ups this time, team. Not like the Smear campaign. Frankly, mistakes were made.'

Alex leaned toward Erica and whispered in her ear. 'President Reagan-speak.' Erica laughed. When Alex looked back the room had fallen silent. Everyone was staring at them. The grey chairs, mauve carpet, polished pine wood desks – all glowering. She had to resist the urge to cover her mouth and say, 'oops!'

Erica spoke. 'Sorry. We were discussing the targets.'

Michael's neat eyebrows shot up. 'Which targets?'

'The ones that have to be met,' Erica said smoothly. 'Actually, we were saying that one of our ideas might be appropriate for the campaign. We thought we'd do a special appeal pack in three pieces which you fit together like a puzzle, to show a deformed spine. The other side shows a straight spine. We say the difference between one and the other is a flip of the card. Or your contribution. It kind of drives home the fate aspect and how you can correct bad luck by charity.'

The room was silent.

'That's a good idea, Erica,' Michael spoke with vowels coated in honey. 'Really very good.'

'Cool,' the others burbled, as if on cue.

'I just don't understand why you had to share it so immediately with Alex while the rest of us were having a meeting.'

Erica stiffened. 'I'm a creative person. That is why you employ me. To be creative.' She threw a look at Michael, demanding he acknowledge her point. He gave a curt nod. 'Sometimes so-called creative people have ideas which they have to share, quickly,' Erica continued. 'Or the essence of them is lost.'

The room was silent. Everyone hung their heads a little, repentant, as if Erica had just delivered a religious sermon.

After the meeting she approached Erica's cubicle. She was staring at the computer screen and didn't hear her arrive. She reached out and touched her lightly on the shoulder. 'Thanks.'

Erica turned around. She smiled. 'That was good, wasn't it?' There was a triumph on her face, and also a childish delight. Erica could be like that, in isolated moments: a clever child whose intelligence is of the sharp, combustible kind.

'It's a great idea.'

'I think we should get working on it.' Erica's voice tugged at her.

'Yes, sure.'

She wondered again, who in this office was Erica's lover? She tried to resist thinking about it: it was prurient, none of her business, what did she care about who Erica slept with?

There weren't many candidates. Stuart the art director was pleasant looking enough, but Stuart was a follower: he read style magazines and bought the latest uplighter lamp and case of wine recommended in the *Observer* weekend magazine. He had no notion of politics, other than office politics. He had let slip that he had never voted in his life.

Prakesh's imminent departure for India had not provoked any reaction from Erica, nor did the succession of copy-writers and policy advisors who came and went on a freelance basis.

Who was she sufficiently moved by among this crowd to have an affair with, when she was married less than a year? Who could excite her in this affable but largely mediocre bunch of aspirant New Men? There were five or six men in the company who she had only tangential dealings with – they worked in the administration and print-buying departments.

And then there was Michael, of course. But Michael was gay, wasn't he?

'You looked tired in the meeting,' Erica sounded concerned.

'I was up late helping Conrad hang his show. And then we talked until about three in the morning, which isn't that unusual.'

'Do you ever think about him as a lover?' Erica asked.

The word *lover* seemed to leave Erica's mouth in slow motion. It was such a charged word; it carried its own electric current. The tongue against her teeth for the l, the slight widening of her mouth to make way for the o, the lower teeth against the upper lip for the v.

'It's already like having a lover,' Alex conceded. 'Without the sex, of course.'

'It sounds like he makes it difficult for you.'

She shrugged. She wasn't sure what Erica meant by *it*. Her life, perhaps. Or did Erica suspect something? Did Erica think she was in love with Conrad? 'We argue much more passionately than most people who aren't sleeping with each other do, that's all.'

'But he seems to really upset you,' Erica persisted.

'And you'd never allow that, someone who wasn't your lover to affect you.'

'I haven't so far.' Erica gave her a look, both worried and curious, as if Alex were an advance ambassador of such a future state of being. Then Erica's telephone or her telephone rang. Someone needing something, some sudden emergency, things to be dealt with. Another conversation with her was over; another conversation in which she knew less about Erica when it ended than when it had begun.

thirteen

PRIVATE VIEW

On the night before his opening Conrad sat at the table in his habitual reading posture, chin parked in the cups of his hands, his elbows on either side of the newspaper pages.

'What are you reading?'

She went to stand behind him and was surprised to see the property pages of the *Standard*. He was perusing the rose-strewn cottage section. She flinched. She hated the property pages, which seemed to her a kind of pornography for the national cult of home owning.

'Buckinghamshire? Where the hell is that?'

Conrad sat up straight. 'Christ knows. Hey, you're English, you're supposed to know.'

'Okay, I do know. But I've never been.' She drew a breath. 'Are you thinking of moving?'

'Maybe. I think I'd go further afield. Sheep country, maybe Wales or Shropshire.'

'I've never seen you look at the property pages before.'

'Have you noticed the boom in house prices in this town? I could sell this flat and buy a farmhouse somewhere.'

'But what about your work?'

'There's no prohibition on painting outside of Shoreditch, you know. I'll build myself a studio in the country. I'll buy some pretty little cottage in some windswept valley and dessicate happily.'

'Conrad, let's be real. You're not going to live anywhere but London. Outside London you'd be a foreigner. Outside London there's only dark towns filled with football-supporting family units and regional accents you can hardly understand.'

'I could go somewhere posh.'

'Then you'd end up teaching the wives of bankers water-colour painting in Provence.'

'Doesn't sound so bad.'

She couldn't tell if he was serious or not. 'I never thought you'd buy the rural idyll fantasy.'

Conrad looked at her coolly. 'Don't you ever think about what you'd like to do in the future? Don't you ever *dream*?' He folded the newspaper and turned to face her. 'I get the feeling you want us to live in a permanent present.'

'That's not true—'

'Alex, you know that things change, don't you?'

She frowned. 'What things?'

'Me, for one. Have you noticed I haven't had a party in four months? Have you noticed I'm not working as much as I used to? Have you noticed I spend more time on my own? I don't know,' Conrad sighed. 'Maybe it's nothing. All I know is I feel different. Maybe talking about leaving London is just the easiest way to start recognizing it.'

Inside her, anger had been replaced by dread. 'I see.'

'Don't be upset, please.'

'You're not living your life for me. You have no obligation to—' she stumbled.

'I forget sometimes too.' He rustled the newspaper between his fingers. She thought that was the end of the conversation, and turned to move away. But then he spoke again, and his voice was quiet.

'I'm thinking about things I haven't thought about in years. It's almost as if an alarm clock has gone off inside me. But it's not about waking up, it's about memory – not your favourite subject, I know. I'm remembering things I haven't thought about in fifteen years.' In his eyes a small light throbbed. It had the look of fear, or revelation. 'I hope this doesn't mean I'm going to die.'

'Why would it mean that?'

'Because I'm superstitious, that's why.'

A memory is the windy arrival of an image. A windy day on which white sheets are hung out to dry; they don't so much flutter in the breeze as whip back and forth. Images are projected on them, but these too torque and thrash in the wind. If only they would keep still, memory would be readable, like a film, but it is hacked into separate frames.

In those moments which are like folds in fabric, hidden, soft moments between buttering his toast, lurching toward the Tube, Conrad thinks of oranges, of seaweed, of fires. Thaw-water; the mashed leaves, coppery brown, that appeared from under the snow in April. A whole continent waking up from its yearly ice age.

Memory is returning in gusts. His eight-year-old self is there, standing on top of a hill, swathed in the goose down stupor of his snowsuit, looking at winter fields, practising his defiance.

When he thinks of his childhood he doesn't think in memories, exactly, but in snapshots, in discrete objects. Jelly-fish washed up on the shore, vanquished, their entrails splattered over stones and baked by the sun until they were only crusts. The raw tentacles of seaweed, like nerve endings, floating ganglions of the sea. He sees himself waiting for the school bus on his first day of school. Standing in his ridiculous sweater, his leather schoolbag and its smell of saddles.

Now his hands roam a body with an anonymous dexterity. Any body will do, anyone who wouldn't say, hey, aren't you Conrad Emmerich? Wasn't that your brother Harold who jumped off that bridge?

'I don't think he ever had a lover,' he told Alex. 'Harold was only sixteen when he died. Although he did ask me about sex. I think the possibility of it just blew his mind away. I think that's how we all feel, at fifteen, sixteen. But we forget it, or it gets diluted, until you're like me: nearly thirty-five and I can't remember the last time I fell in love.'

He wonders, after all this time, how he ended up on the Hackney Road. Police cars whip up and down it, responding to

107

calls in darkened parks, in the floodlit stairwells of tower blocks.

He could just have gone to Toronto, or to the west coast. At least there were fewer police cars, the air was better, real estate cheaper. He could have lost himself among those cities' suburban populations of internal exiles, people fleeing limited worldviews, claustrophobic regionalism, fathers with alcohol problems, declining cod stocks and disappearing tractor factories and other conditions giving rise to the great unemployment-benefit circus, which, if you weren't careful or lucky, could last for a lifetime.

He could have been a waiter in a restaurant, a teacher in a further education college. As it was, his escape was far more spectacular. In his early thirties he found himself with what was, shockingly, a prime piece of London real estate, some colourful friends, a partially realised career, and enough money to not only feed himself but travel to Europe from time to time. And he had made his dream come true: he was a painter.

Now he was discovering ambitions beyond his miraculous escape. Escape, he had found, especially the kind involving changing country and negotiating immigration rules, could take up the best part of a decade. And then, after the successful break out, what then?

He had lost momentum, somehow. Like so many people, his life had been bouts of struggle punctuated by long periods of indulging in distractions. But an imperceptible change had happened inside him, silent and mysterious as mitosis. This was the lurching, painful nature of some changes: suddenly there were two Conrads, each divided against his former self. Each wanted something different, new; something *more*.

She threaded her way through the crowd, winding through boys – it was impossible to think of them as *men*, even though they were all over twenty-five – dressed in short-sleeved checked Ben Sherman shirts, combat trousers, rucksacks of yellow nylon and black netting hanging, half-empty and half-open, from their backs.

She searched for Rachel's figure among girls in silver lurex mini-dresses worn with Adidas trainers, like track-and-field versions of the *2001: A Space Odyssey* stewardesses. Somewhere beyond the crush of these people Conrad's work hung, mute and unregarded, on the wall.

Finally she saw him. He was standing quiet and astute, apart from the crowd, a pained expression on his face. He looked like he wanted to be left alone, so she went to talk to Alain, a French installation artist and Conrad's friend since art school.

'I wonder why we still call it a private view,' she said, scanning the room. 'There must be a hundred people here.'

'They used to be for private buyers,' Alain explained. 'Now the private has become public. Just like everything else.'

'What do you think of the work?'

'A bit abstract, but good.' Alain said, a little taciturnly, she thought, considering he was Conrad's friend.

A woman swung into the room with a small girl balanced on her square hip. She wore a grey felt dress with a lumpen sixties cut. On her head was a straw sombrero; from it little coloured pom-poms dangled around her face.

She waved at Alain, who returned the gesture. 'That's Johanna, she's a real bohemian. She lived five years in Majorca or on some Greek island and had two children before she was twenty-six.'

'She looks exotic.'

'She's got one of those killer multicultural ancestries: quarter Indian, a quarter South African and half Scottish. Or whatever. It's true, don't you think, mixed-race faces are the most beautiful?'

'What's her work like?'

'Everybody says it's competent but witless. I think she's a good draftsman, actually.' He lowered his voice. 'Really, everybody's terrified of her because she's had kids so young. She's *real*; not just another of those skinny girls on the pill wearing big glasses and flip-flops.'

'I don't see any of the A-list here,' she observed. The A-list were the buyers and West End gallerists like Richard Duvalier or Silke Gürning, who sometimes came to hunt for talent at little East End venues like Laurence's.

Rachel appeared next to them. 'Christ,' she breathed. 'Here comes my bloody younger rival. She's going to finish me off. She's decided she has to do everything like me, have my friends, my lovers, my galleries—'

They watched as Rachel's younger rival threaded her way through the crowd. She wore leather trousers, Nike trainers, a tie-dyed type t-shirt tight across her breasts. On her neck was a choker with a square piece of lapis lazuli in the middle. Her skin was the colour of unrefined sugar. She looked like a human piece of satin.

'She's got a show straight out of art school,' Rachel hissed. 'I was her tutor, which failed to have the usual sabotaging effect. Her work's still fantastic. She's one of those people who are so beautiful it makes you dizzy, sick. You know, that feeling—' Rachel stopped.

'What's it called?' Alex tried not to smile. 'Jealousy?'

Rachel and Alain moved on to get another drink and she was left alone in the crowd. Around her mouths opened and closed, cries of delight or astonishment emanating from them, a seething sea of faces. They smiled so widely she could see the dark mauve folds of their gums.

She caught a glimpse of Conrad talking animatedly to a short man with dark hair and sharp features. They hadn't spoken all evening, in part because she was respecting the artworld code that this occasion was for Conrad to make new contacts and find buyers, rather than talk to old friends.

In the course of the evening the temperature in the gallery had shot up ten degrees. The girls in the sheepskin jackets were wilting. Bottles of beer gathered like conspirators in corners.

It was time to leave. She stood on the pavement gulping the air as if she had been held underwater. Damp London air seeped into her lungs, and the lime sky began to rain.

Memories, she knows, should be crisp, accessible as the fresh hurt of the first heartbreak. But if she tries, instead of an impression or feeling she only hears the sound of water draining away. As if at some point, the plug was pulled in her memory reservoir.

Dreams took on a special significance for her. Those nights she went to bed eager to discover more about her past, the way you would look forward to seeing a good film. She reverted to the routine she had used in her earlier artwork, when she had mined her dreams for ideas.

She set her alarm clock for four-thirty a.m., when she would be in the deepest trough of REM sleep, and recorded what she saw there. Like the teams of scientists in the documentaries she watches on television about the function of sleep, the human brain, the reproductive system, she wanted to dive deeper, to excavate the broken mystery of the self.

In waking life she is required to function in a world of random happenings and inscrutable signals: the missing dog, the bunches of flowers wrapped around lamp posts and bus shelters where people have been murdered or hit by cars, the beggars who ask for change and she's sure she knows them, sure she's seen their face before.

Does this mean they are all connected, she wonders. Like a child reading their first sinister fairy tale, she has to join the dots to discover the ending of this black story? Maybe there are no signs, no signals, no story. Everything that happens is random and unimportant.

No, there's a puzzle she is being asked to solve. She is getting closer to some elementary mystery, she is sure, following clues laid like foil-covered Easter eggs hidden in grass.

*

The gears gnash as the driver shoves the old bus into second. He wears a baseball cap and mirrored aviator sunglasses of the kind last seen on seventies dictators.

He is about twenty-two, she judges by the downy buzz on his upper lip. Even so he has obviously given up all love of life. In his hands they hurtle down valleys at the tipping angle of an amusement park ride, only to turn the bend and have to climb, winch-like, the motor wheezing up the hills.

It's raining. Thick mist weaves in and out of conifers. Beside the road white horses appear out of nowhere, dissolving themselves from cloud.

She wipes the steam from the window. Figures slowly take shape through the zig-zag streaks. She is surprised to see a dozen men and women trudging along the shoulder of the highway in a single file, covered in plastic sheeting. The women's skirts are hemmed with dirt and on their backs they carry odd-shaped bundles smothered in dirty grey tarpaulins. The men's trousers stop at their calves to show blackened feet encased in sandals that look as if they've been made from rubber tyres.

'What is it?' A voice leans over to see.

She hears herself say, 'Returnees.'

'From where?' The face asking the question is familiar; long eyelashes framing discerning eyes, a narrow chin.

'Refugees from the civil war. Displaced people going back to their homes in the Highlands.'

'But the civil war ended years ago.'

112

'Not for them it didn't. The government's just let them go back to their villages. They've walked from Mexico.'

'But that's fifty miles away, at least.'

She puts her face to the window again. Tendrils of mist swirl around the figures like silver scarves. The women's faces are hard and set. Sweat runs from their temples; or perhaps it is just rain.

She sits back in her seat and closes her eyes.

fourteen

THE ATRIUM

There he was the next day, standing in the kitchen doorway, hiding behind a bunch of flowers. He thrust them at her. He had never bought her flowers before.

'Okay, what's going on?'

'You know,' Conrad brushed past her with the flowers, sprinkling her with bright orange pollen. 'I was thinking of going to the Gambia, or Jordan. Maybe Ecuador—'

'So why don't you?'

'Because I went to the Columbia Road instead. Do you think there's some connection – cut flowers come from Colombia, and it's named Columbia road. Except they got the spelling wrong.'

'Of course it's a conspiracy. We love conspiracy theories. But the flowers come from Holland. A peace-loving nation,' she reminded him.

'Full of stone-jawed men who always have to mime talking on the telephone,' Conrad held two fingers to his face and his thumb to his ear. 'Blugh, splugh, fquok,' he spluttered in pastiche-Dutch. '*Peace loving*. That's what they tell you,' he said blackly. 'That's what they want you to believe. Actually the small Dutch town of Erzenblugger is the headquarters for all international conspiracies. They're run by Mrs Smit from behind her lace curtains.'

Conrad looked around the kitchen, his nose patrolling for dirt. He hated dirt. On the weekends he spent at least half a day dousing everything in Dettol.

'So that's where you've been then, Ecuador?'

'What?' He had forgotten already. He never remembered his intention to go anywhere long enough to buy a plane ticket.

'Where have you been, Conrad,' she persisted. 'Last night?'

'Oh—' he rolled his eyes. 'Last night.'

She peered at his pupils. 'Are you on something still?'

'Only the natural stuff. Endorphins, adrenalin.'

She didn't believe him. He was vibrating slightly. She could see it when he picked up the newspaper. The edges rattled in his hands.

'Some light showery activity followed by spells of sunshine.' He threw down the paper in disgust. 'After nearly fifteen years in this country I don't understand how the fuck you can have *spells* of sunshine.'

He shot out of his chair and leapt toward the fridge but halfway there he juddered to a halt and turned around. 'Hey, I'm thinking of having children.'

'What—'

'You know, to address the imbalance.'

'What imbalance?'

'Haven't you noticed that the people who have children are generally the people who don't *think*. The people who think, lets say the well-to-do middle classes, educated people with responsible jobs, they wait longer and longer and have fewer children. Where do you think this is going to leave humanity?'

'Wearing puffa jackets and watching *East Enders*.'

'Exactly.' Conrad nodded so vigorously she could see the blood flooding his face. 'We're terrible snobs.'

She shrugged. 'But what's the alternative?'

Suddenly he looked sad. 'I don't know.' Whatever had been burning in his mind found its balm. When he spoke again, his voice was calm, even mild.

'So how's work?'

She eyed him suspiciously. 'Why do you want to know about work?'

'Why not?'

'You've never asked before.'

'I really want to know.' He sounded hurt.

115

'Well, we've started working on the climate change campaign. We're supposed to explain the destruction of the rainforest by oil companies, the plight of indigenous peoples, and the threat posed to the world by climate change, all in a couple of two-minute adverts.'

'Oh well, but that shouldn't be too difficult.'

She ignored his sarcasm. 'I really don't know why we got the account. We're so small. We don't really have the resources for this kind of work.'

'Will you get to travel?'

'We just develop the idea. Some other lucky sod gets to go and film it.'

'And what's the idea?'

'We don't have one, yet.'

'And whatzername?' he said. 'Are you still friendly?'

'*Erica*. Yes, we talk.'

He narrowed his eyes, squeezing goblets Armagnac from them. She thought he was going to make some joke about *office friendships*.

'We should go to that new Vietnamese restaurant. I hear it's really good. We should go to Vietnam.' He jumped up and raced toward the stereo, threatening it with a CD case. 'Wait till you hear this.'

In a second drumming skipped from the stereo speakers, then wavering male voices began to chant. He was going through another one of his phases, she decided. Once he bought nothing for months except musical renditions of the Persian poet Rumi's verses.

'It's not a phase,' he said.

'I didn't say a thing.'

'It's Qawalhi. From Pakistan. These guys are talking to God.'

'God?'

'God. You know, big guy in the sky.'

'Oh, *God*.'

The enthusiastic gibber-like phrases crescendoed. Conrad sat down in the chair carefully. That was the word that thrust its way into her head without asking permission first: *carefully*. Why was he doing everything so neatly all of a sudden?

'I've met this man.' He said it slow, deliberate.

Another word invaded her head, but she couldn't make it out. She thought, *strange*—

'He's very funny.'

He's very funny. She shook her head.

'What's the matter?'

'Everything you're saying is echoing in my head.'

Conrad's face was shining. At that moment, something small, concentrated, began to throb inside her. The voice fought its way through the throbbing. *Something is different about this man he has met*. And then: *I can't compete with a man*.

'Is that why you've bought me flowers, to break this to me? Are you in love? Do you want me to move out?'

Conrad kept his eyes on the floor. 'No, no. None of that. It's just—'

'Just what?'

'He's like you,' Conrad grinned. 'Does it matter?'

Matter. There it was again, the echo.

Matter. Molecules. And the smaller things, subatomic parts no-one knew for sure existed; what were they called? Quarks, quirks—

'Matter.' She heard the hollowness in her voice. 'Yes, it matters.'

She got up, walked across to the other side of the table, and gave him a slap. Hard. Even though she had always hated that. In films and in soap operas women are always slapping men. Why can't women just punch men in the face, like everybody else?

The palm of her hand stung. She snatched it back.

'Thanks,' Conrad said. 'I needed that.' His voice started out sarcastic, then wobbled. Then he burst into tears.

Conrad is smooth, suave, light. Being with him is like being in the atrium of a skyscraper: all light, angles, praise for modernity. But then there's that revolving door, endless interesting-looking people passing through it. She sees them catch his eye, she feels the cool draft curl around her feet.

Tolerance is as far away from passion as it is possible to be. Conrad tolerates her, she knows, because he doesn't have to think of her as a woman.

fifteen

THEORIES OF FORGETTING

In those summer months she and Erica went out to eat together once a week, leaving the office separately, as if they were going to a clandestine assignation. She didn't know why they become furtive with each other, only that they had colluded in it wordlessly.

She wondered if Erica were doing this with her lover, too: leaving half an hour before and loitering in the Chet Baker wine bar until she experienced the final thrill of seeing his face come through the door.

Erica didn't look up as she walked in; she continued chewing olives and inspecting the grains in the table – the posture of someone used to waiting.

Her face is such a blend of *races*, Alex thought, looking at her, before snatching the word back as inappropriate. Erica's skin was not that dark but her eyes were black and fathomless – so dark she couldn't see where the pupil ended and the iris began.

'I know I'm not beautiful,' Erica said to her once. But she was wrong. Beauty has little to do with the symmetry of a face, the perfection of features, tallness and thinness. Alex thought of it as a kind of inner grace, and, in Erica's case, an energy, a charisma. Erica's wasn't the kind of mystery that swirled around a person like so many translucent grey scarves. Mystery was a stone lodged somewhere in her, like a petrified fruit from an antediluvian forest, preserved in bog. How amazing that Erica should end up in London, and that she should know her. But then in London anything was possible. It was stocked with

Polynesians and Malawians, Ecuadorians and Cherokees. London was the world's transit lounge. Even if Alex spent her entire life here, it would still feel like an airport.

Erica smiled – quick, tinged by a nearly imperceptible guilt. What was she guilty about?

'Hi.'

'Hi.'

Alex sat down. Erica went back to fiddling with olives. She seemed content to sit in the company of her own thoughts.

A strange feeling stole over her, both familiar and remote. What was it? In another second it came to her: it was exactly like being on a date. Erica was making her work, for her approval, her affection. How did she manage that, to suggest, with her gaze, her posture, the clipped way she spoke, that she would be just as happy sitting by herself, letting her own thoughts skitter through her mind?

'Would you rather be somewhere else?'

'No,' Erica said mildly. 'I was just thinking.'

'Okay.' She crossed her arms over her chest. 'Let's continue this sometime when you don't have so much to think about.'

'You're tough.'

'Not as tough as you, evidently.'

They lapsed into silence, but not of the comfortable kind. This silence draped itself around her neck like a boa constrictor, and tightened.

'I don't usually have these problems with friends.'

'Maybe it's because there's more to it than friendship.' As soon as she had said it, Erica dropped her eyes.

'You mean there's a rivalry.'

Erica shrugged. 'I don't know what it is.'

She couldn't classify what she felt about Erica, either. She knew it wasn't exactly the elements that made up rivalry: jealousy, envy.

'I've been thinking about what happened to you,' Erica said, finally. 'I can't quite believe it. It's the kind of thing you read about in detective novels, you know, where someone wakes up with blood all over them and they can't remember a thing.'

120

She had read those stories too, looking for clues to her present condition.

'Retrograde amnesia isn't that uncommon.' She tried to sound sensible and understanding of her own condition. 'I was actually more concerned with being partially blind.'

'Blind?'

'The impact exploded blood vessels in my right eye—' she drew her finger up to her eyeball. 'Fortunately it was all right.'

Erica shook her head. 'The car crash accident rate in my country is terrible. People have no idea how to drive. It's because you buy your license, there's no testing. My uncle—'

'It wasn't a car crash.'

Erica looked up. 'What was it?'

'A plane. A light plane,' she elaborated. 'Two engines.'

'You survived a *plane crash*?' Erica sat back in her chair with a start. She was so amazed that the vaccinating warm quality she felt sure Erica used to reassure, almost anaesthetize people, was absent. In its place was a glassy, uncomprehending stare.

'In the Petén.'

'The *Petén*.' Erica breathed.

'You must have been there.'

Erica shook her head. 'No, never.'

'But it takes up half the territory of the country.'

'Why go there? There's nothing. Just jungle.'

'There's Tikal, for a start.' She named the jungle ruins she assumed everyone would want to see. 'That's your country's past.'

'No, it's the past of the Maya. My country began with the conquistadors, with Alvarado.'

She had read about Alvarado. Pedro de Alvarado, the blond conquistador of Guatemala who the Maya called Toniatuh, 'the Sun'. They had never seen a blond-haired person in their lives, let alone this kind of sunny psychopath. He had massacred nearly all the Maya warriors of the region, including the Maya king, Tecun Uman, who he killed in hand-to-hand combat. He hacked his way into the Highlands and found the abandoned city of Xelajú, also called Xela.

'What happened?'

'I still don't know. The weather was bad. They think it was pilot error; he didn't read his instruments well.'

'How did they find you?' Erica asked.

'I found them.'

'What do you mean?'

'I walked out of the jungle. Well, I walked *around* the jungle. When they showed me on a map I'd made two or three serpentines in the same area. It took me two weeks to get out.'

'The Petén is like. It's like,' Erica paused, 'like a wall.'

'That's why they couldn't find the wreck. Most of it broke up when it hit the canopy and then it just fell into the trees. They just ate it up. It was a week before anyone pinpointed the site, apparently, and even then they had to use radar.'

'Were there other people travelling with you?'

'Nine other passengers.'

'What happened to them?'

She gave Erica a long, silent look before answering. 'They died.'

'Why—' Erica snatched the word back. 'How did you survive?'

Her mouth went dry. She ran her tongue over her teeth and the ridges of her gums carefully, like a wet proboscis sent out to test the acidity of the air. 'The only thing I can think of is that I was sitting at the back of the plane, and the front of the plane bore the brunt of the crash.'

'You must have been terrified.'

'To be honest, I can't remember.'

'You must remember something.'

She shook her head. 'I can't remember the last part of the flight at all. All I have is an impression of trees reaching up to me, all hands and arms, and they were going to catch me. You know, like a net—' she paused. 'I don't know why I thought that. They ripped everyone else to shreds.'

'But you don't remember at all?'

'I remember snatches, when I'm falling asleep or waking up. But if I try to grab hold of them they just dissolve.'

'Maybe there's a good reason you can't remember,' Erica said.

'It's possible. Have you heard of Geoffrey Sonnabend?'

Erica shook her head.

'He was a scientist. One night in the 1930s he was on holiday at Iguazú Falls, on the border between Brazil and Argentina, when he had a brainwave. He stayed up all night to work out his theory. He decided memory was an illusion. He thought we try to make experience live again by infusions of imagination, that memories aren't real, more like a buffer to protect ourselves against our knowledge of how fleeting life is. He devoted his life to writing a book on memory called *Theories of Forgetting*. There's a line he writes: "memory is only the decay of experience".'

'I'd like to think that's not true,' Erica murmured.

'But what worries me is not how faulty memory can be as much as how cavalier. It demands newness, like fashion, it needs to be constantly restoked. You can forget something that was once so meaningful, just because newer memories have been stacked on top of it.' Alex could hear the strident tone in her own voice.

'You mean memory pales beside experience.'

'I mean memory is nothing compared to the raw chemistry of a body.'

They were silent for awhile, chewing the exotic bread the regal waitress brought them arranged in a Moroccan basket in a way that reminded her of paintings of the Last Supper.

Then Erica did something exceptional, something completely unexpected. In full view of the other diners in the restaurant – hand-holding couples all, huddled over candles – Erica reached across the table and took her hand. Alex felt their fingers entwine, and she let it happen. Then, within another second, their fingers unlaced themselves, and the gesture was unwound.

sixteen

LAST DAYS OF THE WEIMAR REPUBLIC

The fish and chip shop in the City was stuffed with hyperactive junior City boys, all identically dressed in financial sector mufti low-grade suits from Marks and Spencer's or Burton's.

'He's been behaving really oddly,' Alex began. 'Yesterday he bought me flowers.'

'Christ,' Rachel breathed.

'He also bought a lot of God music.'

'Hmm.'

'I sold the SEDART option to Tri-Am but RIM was on to it before RTZ got hold of Borneo.' The suits bounced around them, talking in short bursts of the code they used instead of English.

'He says he's met a man. He acts like he's in love.'

Rachel frowned. 'Conrad's in love?'

'There's this strange gleam in his eye. I've never seen it before. He said he was thinking of having children.'

Rachel shook her head. 'With a man? Even Conrad can't pull that one off.'

'Do you think I should talk to him about it?'

Rachel wiped her fingers daintily on a thin white napkin. The grease from the fish melted it instantly to a thin, transparent membrane. 'The last time I tried to ask him whether he was ill or not he wouldn't talk to me for a month.'

'That could be a bit tricky, considering I live with him.'

'You could move out,' Rachel said. 'Then you wouldn't have to deal with it.'

She nodded. 'I could.'

'But you won't.'

'It's not that easy.'

'I know. House prices are going through the roof. You'd never find anywhere like Conrad's place. It's a palace. Good for him that he got in there before the Shoreditch boom.'

She cut Rachel short. 'It's not that.'

'What is it then?'

'It's more than a living arrangement I have with him. It's more like—' she struggled to crush her instinct to tell Rachel.

'Like a family?' Rachel looked skeptical.

'Like a refuge.'

- By 2015 fifty per cent of the currently inhabited islands of the Maldives will be under water.

- By 2030 there will be no glaciers in Glacier National Park in America.

- After the temperature of the water on Canada's Pacific coast soared six degrees in two years the population of the North Pacific salmon has collapsed.

At work she researches facts for the climate change campaign, jotting down frightening statistics. She pores over issues of *New Scientist*, *Scientific American*, specialist reports that talk about climactic modelling and endless websites.

She learns coral reefs are dying and pensioners bake in kiln temperatures of fifty degrees in Athens. Future wars will be fought over access to water and arable land, as environmental refugees are driven from their homes.

She learns about the Coriolis Effect. It makes the wind blow from west to east in the northern hemisphere and the opposite in the south, circulating warm air from the equatorial regions to the cooler north. If there were a simple shift in the Coriolis Effect, everything on earth would wither.

The scientists quoted in the magazines think it is too late to reverse the process of warming. There is nothing to be done:

Polar bears will starve, Bangladesh will be waterlogged, the molar-shaped atolls of the south Pacific will sink below the sea. Warm meltwater from the Arctic will push the cold water of the Atlantic down and the Gulf Stream will shift. Britain will become either Norway or a desert – no-one seems sure which.

Her computer melts into her screensaver, a photograph of earth, taken from the moon on one of the Apollo missions. It hangs there, luminous in the terrifying velvet of space, a gassy jewel.

She thought how, on planes, riding the stratosphere, she could almost see its curve. If she looked out the window, looking up into the heavens, there was no sky any more, only the cold indigo of space. She felt closest to the planet up there, in the same way that we are never closer to anything or anyone than when we are farthest away.

In the hospital they had asked her: 'Where is your home?'

She couldn't really remember. In her delirium she replied, '*el mundo*'. The world is my home.

That night there was a leaving do at work. Prakesh was going to live in India for a year, to 'discover his roots', as he put it, which they all thought was such an American thing to say.

They went to the pub in a posse, walking through Covent Garden against a steady tide of opera-goers. They had just finished renovating the old Covent Garden opera house. Women wearing patent leather shoes and chocolate-coloured fur coats emerged from purring Jaguars; men rushed after them, waving tickets embossed with gold.

In the pub they talked in isolated groups that, once established, proved impossible to penetrate. Every time she looked in Erica's direction she was surrounded by people, by Samantha, by Hattie or Michael. When had Erica become so popular?

There was Michael, his wide, manly face framed against the black and white bathroom tiles crawling up the bar's walls. He was talking to Stuart, his smiles punctuated by serious nods. His face disgusted her, she realized, with its easy acceptance of itself. She thought of him as a fugitive who has taken permanent refuge in a small town where no-one is too knowledgeable about the outside world.

Why did she feel so hostile toward Michael? What had he ever done to her? She interrogated herself. He had given her a job, after all. He let her get on with her work. He wasn't the kind of boss who breathed down your neck.

Erica was there, talking to Michael and Stuart. She wore black trousers and a black silk shirt. Around her neck was a thick silver necklace Alex had never seen before. When she went to the bar or to the loo, she walked lightly, as if she had been born wearing sandals. Maybe this is how people walk when they are in love. Was Conrad walking that way too?

Erica was so emphatically a woman, she thought, as she watched her lift her beer bottle to her lips. She was so feminine she had crossed some invisible line and ended up on the flip side, had become almost masculine. What was the term? *Ephebe*: she remembered it from her classics course at university. It referred to young army recruits from Sparta, drafted into the army at eighteen years old, who still had the girlishness that in some people intertwined itself so effortlessly with boyhood.

She avoided Erica that evening, without really knowing why. It wasn't difficult; neither of them sought each other out. Once Erica brushed past her and she reached out and touched her arm lightly, as if to say, I'm here, but Erica didn't even turn around.

For the rest of the night she drank lethal drinks ferociously and with a scowl on her face, the way she imagined jaded cabaret heroines of the Weimar Republic did, when the country was lost and they didn't give a damn any more. After the fifth consumed this way she left.

*

They come upon a city of wrecked ocean liners in the jungle. Their funnels soar above the trees, themselves forty metres high. Once white, the breath of a million trees and the pummeling rain has oxidised their hulks to black.

This is Palenque, the ancient city dug out of the jungle less than a century before. They must have gone just after dawn, because the temples are covered in mist. Macaws fly from the ramparts. Toucans taunt them from the upper branches of the *Ceiba pantandera*, the giant silkwood.

By ten o'clock the ruins are sizzling. They rummage in temples of the Cross, of the Sun, of the Inscriptions. The stone of the temples has absorbed centuries of solar heat. Like a fire stoked low, they never cool. They smell foetal; something has been gestating there.

Dizzy, claustrophobia rising inside her like a dark cloud, she runs out of the damp bowels of the ruined palaces and emerges squinting into a dazzling curtain of sun.

She sat up and stared blearily out a window lashed by rain. Had it been a memory or a dream? For so long now the boundaries between the two had been dissolved.

As in her dreams, the face that had accompanied her through the hot shipwreck city refused to show itself. It remained only a blur, more indistinct than a dark corner of an ancient palace, or the shadow of a vulture as it streaked across the sun.

128

seventeen

PATTERNS

She came home to find Conrad talking to a man in the kitchen. The man had his back to her, but she already knew who it was.

'Oh, Alex—' Conrad started.

She extended her hand toward a blur in the middle distance and they grasped hands, their nails scratching each other's fingers.

'Sorry.'

'Sorry.'

'This is Fernando,' Conrad said, a beat too late.

When her eyes focused she saw a small man, not any taller than her, with dramatic brown eyes and cheekbones she could have hung the washing from.

'Nice to meet you.'

'Nice to meet you.'

She had to sit down because the kitchen was swirling and who had painted it yellow anyway? She resisted an urge to ask Conrad, and sure enough, in a second it had melted back into its true blue-green.

The small man sat down too. Eventually, through twenty minutes conversation about nothing – the area they lived in, house prices, how long Alex has been in London, why Bethnal Green Tube is a little too far to use for daily commuting – she realized that Conrad's new lover, if in fact that is what he was, was one of those shockingly beautiful people that make you inadvertently hold your breath while you are talking to them. She couldn't maintain eye contact with him for long or an

129

internal meltdown took place, just like how if you stare at the sun for too long you risk burning a hole in your cornea. It wasn't about sex, or attraction, it came from the place in everyone that is instantly moved by symmetry.

She found herself saying pleasant, agreeable things like, 'How did you meet?'

'At Rachel's house. Didn't she tell you?' Conrad said.

'When?'

'Oh, a dinner a couple of weeks ago. Or maybe a month.' He shot a confirming glance at Fernando. 'Just a dinner party. Fernando showed up with a friend of Rachel's.'

'Why wasn't I invited?'

'I don't know, Alex,' Conrad said, a little annoyed. 'I think it was a night when you were out with that married woman from work.'

'That's not fair, Conrad.'

'What's not fair?'

'You know what I mean.'

She watched Fernando's eyes flicker from Conrad and back to her.

'It was a lov-e-ly evening,' Fernando's accent dismembered the word into three syllables. His voice was deep, but tremulous and golden in its upper tones, like a xylophone.

'Fernando walked out of a thunderstorm,' Conrad said.

A vision of the night in question sped through her mind like a sequence from a film: tall nervous candles stalk Rachel's kitchen table. Conrad's fingers hold slices of crusty bread oozing thick pieces of Camembert. The first peal of thunder has just ruptured the sky; rain pummels the roof. Through the open door oblong raindrops leap back from the pavement.

Conrad hears steps coming from outside, then a figure stops in the doorway. He looks up and sees a small man in a wet, dark blue jumper. His hair is plastered to his head, and drops of water fall from his thin, precipitous nose. His eyes have the amphibious look of the newborn. He laughs and towels his hair dry.

'Did you know the optimum places for humans to live on the

130

earth are areas where there is a lot of electrical activity?' Conrad was saying. 'Thunderstorms stimulate brain cells.'

The cinematic Meeting Scene fizzled from her mind. 'No,' she said. 'I didn't know that.' She turned to Fernando. 'What do you do?'

'I am an architect. I came to London to work on the Doom.' He spoke like a diplomat announcing his credentials.

'The Doom?'

'The Millennium Doom.'

'The Dome,' Conrad laughed. 'I love your accent.'

'The light in the building is amazing,' Fernando was saying.

'I haven't been,' Alex admitted. Neither had Conrad, or anyone they knew, although she had seen it from the river. She thought it looked like a crippled spaceship. It had been filled with an ersatz 'experience' exhibit for which people were expected for fork out eighteen pounds per person to ride up and down escalators surrounded by gangs of hyperactive children.

'Light makes me feel electric,' Fernando went on. 'Sometimes I think I can feel it passing right through me. Sometimes I get completely charged.'

'Just from light?'

'No, no, no,' he shook his head mournfully. 'From the way it interacts with space. I do projects based on that.'

'Projects?' she queried.

'I am an artist, too. But mainly I work as an architect.'

She studied him. Until now, his face has been a haze of threat. She thought: This is the man who will take Conrad away from me and install him in a monogamous flat somewhere, a flat full of light and containing only a bed, a tasteful plant, and a couple of objects scattered at feng shui intervals.

His face was unusual. There was something old and finished about him, as if some hand had spent years refining his edges. But it was a curiously ageless face – he could have been twenty-seven or forty – of diametrically opposed elements: wet and dry, serious and frivolous, generous and cruel. Fernando really belonged in another time in history, she decided. She saw him in cities perched on the edges of deserts: Alexandria or

Carthage – ancient cities inhabited by fallen aristocrats and homosexual druids.

She watched him talking with Conrad, Fernando reacting, smiling, listening, laughing. With every movement he made he looked like he was watering flowers. Meanwhile, Conrad was grinning by the stove. They were so obviously delighted with each other. She felt like a black hole, a patch of mould in comparison.

She left them talking in the kitchen, Conrad's censorious why-are- you-being-this-way? look trailing her. She got her coat and left the flat without a word.

Once outside on the street, she found she didn't know where to go. For months now she had experienced a strange paralysis in the face of everyday choices. Should she walk or take a bus? If she walked she might see something crucial to her existence, or it would give her time to have the devastating thought, the single realisation that would change her life. She might meet someone. If she took the bus she would have to concede all those possibilities to the dark side of fate, where all acts and accidents that never happened resided. She got a lot of walking done in those months.

That night she walked from their house to Clerkenwell, then down St John's Street. The streets were smoky with London dust, the sky was the colour of a boiled egg. From time to time she had the strange sensation that something was following her, right at her heels – a dog, or a cat. This had happened more than once lately, when she had gone for a walk, especially at night. It wasn't a menacing feeling, rather that she was being accompanied. The presence was a shadow of a thought, so contingent it was easy to dismiss, even when she heard what sounded like a snuffling, then a scrabbling of paws on the pavement. But every time she turned to look, there was nothing.

She found herself following the path of the Fleet, one of the many underground rivers that used to bubble through the city. She thought of the aboriginal artist's paintings she had seen in a Fitzrovia gallery only the week before. She had gone with

Rachel, who, unlike Conrad or herself, was established enough to be on the mailing list of upmarket commercial galleries.

The paintings showed dotted undulating landscapes, a knitted pattern of ley lines called song lines. These were boundaries of the known universe for the Aboriginals. Her world, meanwhile, was composed of similar boundaries: Old Street and Liverpool Street, Whitechapel and Shoreditch, Clerkenwell and Angel. Under the hand of the aboriginal painter the mashed asphalt of the streets would have become a black snake, and the neat brick houses the flanks of a hot lizard. He turned everything into animals, she remembered; animals were the key to the journey.

She wondered about the journeys they had all made, before they knew each other: Conrad, Fernando, Erica, Ben, her colleagues in the office. She wondered if she could draw a map showing the lines between them, places they had intersected once: an airport, a lift, a Tube carriage. She would do a tracing of the points of intersection, like a giant geometric piece. Perhaps, she thought, if she joined up all the dots, a pattern would emerge.

She swung round and walked up Gray's Inn Road. By this point her feet were stinging and her throat parched with London dust. She dived into a bar near King's Cross. From the street it had looked safe: groups of well-to-do women dressed in black, laughing. She ordered a drink. As she did so she got a better look at the clientele. The women were laughing exaggeratedly, their mouths held open a second too long, displaying the red of their gums. They all seemed excessively beautiful. They all seemed to know each other. She began to wonder if she had crashed a private party.

The music was so loud it was impossible to talk, yet everyone was carrying on conversations effortlessly, mouthing things in each other's ears, drawing back, their swan necks straining so she could see the lithe muscles there, a scandalised expression on their faces. Then a second's stasis before the eruption of the red gum laughter.

She elbowed her way through the women to the bar. The

bartender had three studs in her lower lip and what looked like a chain-link fence embedded in her ear, but her face was actually very sweet.

'Could you get me a Manhattan?'

The chain-link girl nodded and did several things in very rapid sequence that resulted in a drink being parked on the bar within seconds. She took it and tried to find somewhere she could perch inconspicuously, but there was not an inch of bar or table or ledge free. In the end she stood alone in the middle of that room of delighted women, sipping self-consciously and too fast.

It wasn't long before she felt a tap on the shoulder. She turned around to find a tall woman with long brown hair standing there.

'I've seen you here before, haven't I?' The woman mouthed. The music was still very loud. Alex tried to place her face: two large almond-shaped eyes underneath perfectly plucked eyebrows. Her mouth formed the shape of a bow when closed.

'I guess so,' she lied.

'I'm lying,' the woman said, running her hand nervously through her hair. A thin wedding band clutched at her fourth finger. 'I haven't been here before. I've never been to this kind of place before. I'm sorry, I just didn't know what to say.'

It dawned on her. She was in a gay bar – no, she corrected herself, a lesbian bar – and what she had in front of her was one of those bi-curious girls, as they called themselves in personal ads. She had always pictured them sitting across a table, a perpetually curious look on their faces.

'Listen, I think—'

'I know, I know, I don't belong here. But I just wanted to make contact with—' The music drowned out the rest of the girl's words. She moved her mouth to Alex's ear and yelled into it. 'Do you want to go somewhere else, where we can talk?'

If she were Conrad, she would. If she were Conrad, she would take this woman home, just for the hell of it, just to see what happened. There was nothing visibly wrong with her. She was really quite pretty.

But in that moment she took the proper measure of the gulf that separated her from Conrad; it wasn't the gaping yaw between a man and a woman, she understood, but more a crevasse of character. It meant that, for whatever reason and which had been determined long ago, probably before she was even aware of the possibility of sex, she would never be able to sleep with strangers, with someone she met, just like that.

She applied what she hoped was a suitably sympathetic and rueful expression to her face, and shook her head. She left the woman standing at the bar, drink in hand, darting anxious looks into the crowd. She went to get her coat and received a pitying glance from the cloakroom girl. She must see a lot of us, she thought, before opening the door and diving into the night.

*

Volcanoes stud the glistening horizon like barnacles on a whale's back. It is the rainy season and by late morning clouds have gathered on their summits, whispering, forming and reforming.

In the afternoon they regroup and advance, transforming dry mornings into monsoons in less than fifteen minutes. Now she understands why men wanted to appease the gods of nature. In temperate countries the weather seems ambivalent, like a moody child: annoying at times, but still part of you, still your friend. Here the rain is furious. She's stunned at its anger, and takes it personally.

Lightning storms buzz around the mountains. They pass farmers wrapped in sheets of clear plastic and wearing straw hats from which the rain falls in a neat oval curtain. The rain clears by sunset, although the sky is still lightly greased with thin clouds. Sunsets leak through them, pouring a strange nearly neon light onto the land, making the edges of everything glow red. The women of the town come to their doorways to watch the sun go down, pulling thin cardigans around their shoulders as the air fills with smoke from charcoal fires.

They were in a hotel room somewhere. His voice called her over.

'Alex, come look at this.'

'What?'

He held a piece of paper up to the mirror.

'What?'

'Look at the word in the mirror.'

'What? I don't see anything.'

'The word. Xela.'

She looked in the mirror again and read her own name. aleX. The second she saw it, something inside her shifted, like sandbars after a coastal storm.

'We're in a place that's your name spelled backward. Isn't that strange?'

As always, Ben is faceless in her memory, although she has remembered his voice correctly.

He turned his eyes on her, those dark brown eyes in which she could see her face reflected. 'I didn't notice at all, that Xela was Alex spelled backward. Did you?'

No, she hadn't. Although all the time they were in Xela, the town that spelled her name in reverse, she wanted to leave. She looked in travel agent's windows and at the fading airline stickers pasted there – IBERIA, AMERICAN, VARIG – with unbearable longing. She could not shake off the sense of dread that followed her like a stray dog, sniffing at her heels, asking to be fed, given a pat, anything that would confirm it had a life other than the kicked-at, abused, hungry spectre it was.

Dread was seeping into her, like ink. 'I think we should get out of here.'

'Why, what's the matter?'

'I don't know.'

She remembered him saying, at some point during those days, 'You're just fixated by the dark side of things.'

The dark side. Was there really only that, she wondered: a dark side and a bright side, and in between, what? A teetering ledge, always threatening to slip over into one or the other. Perhaps that was the shadowy precipice where she was destined to spend her life, while people like Ben basked in the sun.

eighteen

WHAT DID YOU THINK
WAS GOING TO HAPPEN?

She came home to find Rachel leaning over Conrad in a comforting posture.

'It's so utterly hostile,' Rachel fumed.

'I don't know,' Conrad sighed. 'I'm not the first person to be scewered by Theo Marsden-Smith.'

'Where is it?'

Conrad waved in the direction of the kitchen. The newspaper lay spreadeagled on the table, open to the offending review.

Theo Marsden-Smith was the art critic for a serious newspaper; he was taken even more seriously than the organ he wrote for, if that were possible.

As far as they could tell, in his critical universe there were two possible categories for artists to inhabit: an artist was either an extraordinary visionary, able to ignore the cultural chatter around them and produce something of real, lasting value; or the artist was fundamentally flawed, not just as an artist but as a character, nursing their little obsessions, honing their sublime statements, without character or analytical ability, in hapless thrall to the cultural rubble and lifestyle stupor which made up everyone's (except Marsden-Smith's) life.

If Marsden-Smith decided an artist was Type Two, even on a temporary basis, a single bad review by him could make you feel it had all been a waste of time; not just the adolescent thrill when art was first discovered, nor the expensive art school education, then the wholesale battle to form cliques and aesthetic cabals that came after graduation, but the entire futile procedure of living that had taken you from birth and delivered you to this moment when you held the newspaper in your shaking hands.

She picked up the newspaper and started to read Marsden-Smith's familiar obliterating prose.

Conrad Emmerich's gigantic canvases express the easiest thing possible, and exactly what the media, voracious for novelty, want to see: objects, empty and used. It is dead, devoid of commentary or vivacity. Emmerich should do well, though: his work is in fact the perfect expression of a morally empty, object-obsessed age.

She dropped the page. 'I guess he didn't like it.'

'Very perceptive,' Rachel said.

Conrad was kneading his thighs with his hands, something he did when distressed. 'I'm not sure how seriously to take his stuff. I think he deliberately trashes shows just to up the paper's circulation.'

'Maybe he is out to destroy people,' Rachel said. 'Maybe that's the only explanation.'

'Maybe he's just doing his job,' Alex said. 'Criticizing.'

Conrad gave her an impatient look. 'I don't think it's ever that easy, unfortunately.'

'It's possible to criticize the work without assassinating the character behind it,' Rachel said.

'I can't bear his suave dismantling of my intentions,' Conrad grimaced. 'Even my passions.'

'You always said you didn't have any passions.'

'I think I might finally be developing some. Just in time to have them dismissed as ridiculous. I always said I had lousy timing.'

'This is part of the deal, Conrad' Rachel said. 'Putting yourself out there. You've got to be prepared to take rejection, even ridicule.'

'Sure,' Conrad concurred. 'All's fair in love and criticism. That's why I can't stand either.'

'What's the worst thing that can happen?'

'You mean as a result of the review?' Conrad pursed his lips. 'Not much. A slippage in my stock, in the pecking order.' He put his long, nervous fingers on either side of his head and kneaded his temples. 'God, why didn't I get into selling cars? It's so disorienting, to be in a market where the only value something has is what people are willing to pay.'

'I don't know why you put yourself through this,' she said.

'Through what?'

'The exposure. The hurt.'

Conrad rolled his eyes. 'Because I'm a painter, Alex. Painters paint. Or have you been a retired artist too long already to remember that?'

She swallowed his comment. 'I just don't understand what you want out of all this – this effort.'

'I want respect. Real respect. I want to put my work out in the world and have it be judged and seen to be good.'

Rachel was nodding her assent. 'That's all any artist wants.'

'Anyway,' Conrad stood up. 'It's already happening, the short trip to obscurity. You know the fundraiser for the new Tate? I was supposed to go to that. Plus a party afterward, a big party where there might be buyers interested in my work. But I didn't get an invite. That's a slight.'

'It's only a slight slight.'

'It's not a joke, Alex,' he admonished. 'It might have been, at one point, but I'm thirty-five now. It's serious for me.'

'Do you think they left you out on purpose?'

Conrad rolled his eyes. 'Of course they did. That's the whole point of exclusion: the person has to know they're being excluded. They're just making sure I know my place in the hierarchy.' He looked at her. 'I know you don't want to hear any of this. That's why you stopped making work, isn't it? You couldn't stand the ego circus.'

No, she couldn't. But it was only part of the forest of obstacles to be negotiated, just to get her work seen, just to attempt to communicate something. Although she had tried, for a few years. She had made friends, talked to gallerists, showed

140

some paintings and sold them. Everything was going quite well. Even to plan.

When she tried to go near the memory of her work, the colours, the shape of it, her obsessions at the time – lines and the sea, horizons, sere-blasted landscapes – all she felt was steam rising. She had to snatch her mind away quick, like a hand from boiling water.

Her early paintings stood stacked against the sloping wall of their loft, abstract rushes of colour. Grey and white, predictably, in the case of the Arctic Fox, which she had based on a photograph she had seen of a glacier in Alberta that was being studied by geologists. She loved its dirty striations, the layers of millennial ice, how one year it was hard and transparent, the next the colour of slate. The geologists said they could read the glacier like you would read the life of a tree by its rings.

Arctic Fox would have sat well in the drawing rooms of the bourgeoisie. Louise, her gallerist at the time, had told her so. But it was her first really good painting, and she had refused to part with it. From the beginning she had the possessiveness fatal to an artist: she wanted all her paintings for herself. She couldn't bear the thought that they might spend their lives in some spaceship-like living room in Australia, in California.

In her third year she met Ben, just before her degree show. Ben was a better painter. It was abstract work of a depth and subtlety. He also worked in those greys and whites she had used for her Arctic Fox, and he was better at using them, more moody, more musical.

She left painting on one side and took to constructing strange little works. Like the months she spent taking postcards from scenic, idyllic spots – the poppy fields of Holland, lush Lyme Regis in Dorset – and scrawling interrogating messages over them in white Tipp-Ex: 'Why Compare Myself with Someone Else?' and 'What Did You Think Was Going to Happen?' You could hardly see the postcard any more, only a few flowerbeds and spires peeking from the white rage of the Tipp-Ex messages.

She framed them and took them off to her gallerist.

141

Surprisingly, Louise liked them. She sold them to a few friends of hers happy to have lacerating works in their sitting rooms that would inevitably provoke dinner party one-upmanship. Who's the artist? How much did you pay? After the Tipp-Ex cards, she had the Christmas card show, which Conrad referred to as Messages from the Void.

It was three years now since she had put a brush to canvas, eighteen months since she had made an artwork of any description. She knew what would happen if she tried. She would try to paint the only thing buzzing in her mind: eyelash vipers, heliconias, blackberry-sized bullet ants, katydids. Her work would look like a second-rate Greenpeace poster.

Apart from the rainforest, that place in which she had been lost and then found, there was nothing she wanted to represent. She was so surprised by this that she preferred to simply forget she had ever wanted to be an artist. That was all gone. Now she was left with what she supposed most people had: a life to live.

nineteen

WHAT CONRAD DID THE
DAY PRINCESS DI DIED

An hour later Rachel left. Conrad stayed where he was, on the sofa, staring out into the scorched London sky.

'There are eighteen year olds out there getting better shows than I can get. It's not as if I haven't paid my dues. I can tell you a dozen soul-destroying stories. Which one would you like to hear?'

He didn't wait for her answer. 'How about those small biting moments, rather than the big-time rejection scenarios. The time the gallerist with that dank basement space switched off his mobile phone when he heard me calling about getting a show. Or the time my so-called friends invited me to submit a proposal to their achingly hip little space and then said, "Oh, Conrad. So sorry. It's all full up."

'Or how about the unreturned phone calls, the unanswered letters. The German curators who used me for my contacts and failed to put my work in whatever show they were putting together for some derivative space in their God-awful country.'

'Okay, Conrad, so you've done humiliation. We all have.'

'That's just the thing,' he sighed. 'I don't think I can take it any more. I used to be young and resilient, but there are these cracks in me now. I feel like a badly pinioned wall.'

'Are you well? I mean—'

'What do you mean am I *well?*'

'Rachel told me.'

'Rachel told you what?' Conrad looked at her sharply. 'What did Rachel tell you?'

The room had become eerily silent. There were no airplanes overhead, groaning like exhausted angels as they lowered their landing gear, no police vans whining up the road.

'Rachel told me you had been diagnosed as manic depressive.' She was surprised to find her voice flat and cold with fear.

Conrad pursed his lips. Behind them, he seemed to be chewing on his gums. 'That was a long time ago,' he said, finally.

She let out the breath she had been holding. 'Why didn't you tell me?'

'Because it doesn't matter,' he snapped. 'What does it matter to you that I had to take some pills and see some doctors? I refuse to be stigmatised by an illness. God—' he faltered. 'I hate unbalanced people, I can't bear the thought that I was ever one of them myself.'

'I can't imagine you ever being unbalanced.'

'Oh, no?' He gave her a grim little smile. 'I could tell you some stories.'

'Like what?'

'You don't want to hear them.'

'Yes, I do.'

'I don't want to tell them.'

'Come on, Conrad. I tell you everything.'

He gave her a cool, evaluating look that said: that's a lie. 'All right,' he said. 'But I need a drink first.'

'It feels like falling in love. Lights and noise in your head, like a fun fair has set up inside you and before you know it all the rides are going full tilt and are full of screaming kids. Or it's like that terrific excitement, when you've got a dinner date with this person you are besotted with and the whole thing is rushing toward you like a freight train. You feel like you're God, you feel invincible. The world has just been painted in bright colours. It's better than drugs, better than sex.' He pursed his lips.

'The only problem is, you know there's something wrong. You know you're not in a normal state of mind, but there's nothing you can do about it. It's like being displaced in your own self. You're you, but something is out of kilter.'

'How often have you felt that?'

He thought for a second. 'The actual mania doesn't happen very often. Since I was diagnosed I've really only felt it once or twice, when I stopped taking the pills.'

'Why did you stop?'

'I didn't stop altogether,' he conceded. 'Sometimes I take them, sometimes I don't. It depends how I feel.'

She frowned. 'Is that what the doctor tells you to do?'

'At the moment I'm fine,' he glided over her question. 'There've been times when it's been risky, though, to just stop.'

'Have you been on lithium since I've known you?'

'Of course. Remember when I used to suffer from nausea and I complained I couldn't see straight?'

She did. When she had first moved in with him he seemed to be sick all the time. She had thought he had a delicate stomach.

'Those are side-effects. That's another reason why I don't always take it.'

'What does it do, exactly?'

'They don't know,' Conrad shrugged. 'It's amazing, isn't it: the single most effective drug for an illness and they don't understand how it works. They know it wards off manic episodes, but it doesn't have much effect on depression. They put me on anti-depressants for that. I don't care for them much either. They make me bright, like a piece of chrome.'

'Isn't it risky, not taking the drugs?'

Anger flared in his eyes. 'I'll tell you what I think is risky: not living enough, not feeling. I'm put on drugs because I feel too much, because I feel in the wrong intensities. But how much is too much? Who's got content control on feeling? Everybody's on some kind of drug: lithium, prozac, ecstacy. We're just a drugged generation, anaesthetized against ourselves.'

'We're not *drugged*.'

'You've never taken lithium.'

'Of course I haven't.'

'Well, imagine wrapping yourself in thick gauze. You feel

145

neutral, content, even complacent. Maybe this is what most people feel most of the time. But I tell you, once you've experienced mania, almost everything pales by comparison. Imagine falling in love, then the next day being told to just snap out of it. Go back to your dreary preoccupations. Do your laundry. Buy more litter for your cat. That's what real existence feels like, on drugs, after you've been manic. Like laundry and cat litter, and for your entire future, as far as you can see.'

She tried to absorb what he was telling her. In her worst estimation she had judged Conrad to be the perfect personification of his time: emotionally lazy, driven into a state of anomie by too much experience, too much travel, sex, drugs, clothes. An overdose of sated desire, until, like a jaded restaurant critic, his palate was dulled by too much satisfaction.

That this should turn out not to be the real Conrad – that this was essentially a medically managed version of him – relieved and secretly thrilled her.

'When I'm taking lithium my work's no good,' he went on. 'I'm convinced of it. I need to feel angry, even just a little bit, in order to produce. There has to be an edge. Besides, I don't want to be mechanical.'

'You're not *mechanical*.'

'Pharmaceutical, then. I don't want to be manipulated. I don't want to be controlled. I want to be me, even if that means being edgy, even a little nuts.' He poked his chest with his index finger. 'So I thought, let's see what happens if I stop taking everything, lithium and anti-depressants. Cold turkey.'

'When was that?'

'You remember when Princess Di died?'

'How could anyone forget.'

'Well, the two events just happened to coincide. I turned on the telly. Remember it was Sunday morning? I never watch TV on Sunday. But something told me, out of nowhere, there's a message for you, Conrad. Turn on the TV. She had just been pronounced dead. I didn't hear it, it was obvious from the news anchor's face. What's his name? Quark or something. He looked like his best friend had died.

'My heart started to pound. I mean, *painfully*. I thought I was going to have a heart attack. Then a thought came to me, out of nowhere: she's not really dead. It's a conspiracy by the royal family. I can go and liberate her. They're holding her in the Ritz Carlton hotel, hostage, in room 1066. I didn't even know if there was a room 1066 for Christ's sake, but I reasoned that was the year the Normans conquered Britain, she's a Norman, or the royal family is, I forget my logic. Or lack thereof.' He smiled wryly.

'I thought: the royal family are trying to conquer the hearts and minds of this country by doing away with Diana. I thought, those cynical old Ming dynasty vases of humanity. And I became incensed. I mean, *incensed*. By noon I was down at the Eurostar terminal. But it was the end of August and all the trains were booked up. So I went first class, that was the only way I could go.

'I sat there and refused champagne all the way to Paris. As we skidded across those endless fields of northern France I kept seeing these cows. And these cows would turn to me and say, but wordlessly, just speaking with their eyes, "Conrad, we're with you. You're doing the right thing. We've spoken with the princess and she's waiting for you".'

He paused and looked at her appealingly. 'I know you don't believe this, but it's true. I can show you my discharge note if you want.'

'Your what?'

'I was hospitalized afterward. But that's later.' He took a breath. 'So. I'm on this train in first class, surrounded by business types. Everybody's reading the newspaper and talking about Diana. The woman in the aisle across from me is crying. I'm drinking water to keep myself strong. We're in France now and passing through those empty fields they have there, except for the cows, of course. The French cows are on my side.

'Then we get to Paris. You know how Paris from the train looks like northern Africa? All those narrow courtyards garlanded by washing. The colours, ochre and yellow, the sky. I felt like I was arriving in Morocco. It all looks so old, so dusty.'

Conrad fell silent. He seemed to have gone off on another track, thinking about desert cities, bleached with sand-dust.

She pulled his attention back. 'Then what?'

'Then the train pulls in and after fifteen minutes of studying the map of that fiendish Tube system they have there I'm off to the hospital. I've dispensed with the Ritz fantasy and am being more real. I know she's injured; I know it's bad.

'By this time the adrenalin is really pumping. I can't wait to get there. As soon as I get out of the metro I see the people. *God*,' he whistled at the memory. 'There are people everywhere. Police cordon around the hospital, cars coming and going, all these women wearing sunglasses and crying. You can't see their eyes but you can see the tears hovering above their lips. Just poised on the edge, waiting to drip. The women's sunglasses send me a message that my plan has been detected and the hospital infiltrated. A bunch of photographers try to take my picture – at least this is what I think – and I hit one of them.

'So. I'm arrested. Then let go. They take me to Gare du Nord and make me buy a ticket on the Eurostar. I buy a first class ticket again and drink champagne all the way to London. When I get here I check myself into the hospital. I stayed there for two weeks.'

'Then you had to be medicated.'

He nodded sadly. 'It was just chemicals. I had too much of this, not enough of that. When I was a kid they just said, what can you do? He's hyperactive. My parents used to lock me in the woodshed to calm me down. But there's nothing really wrong with me anymore. That was my last episode of mania. I've stabilised now.'

He went quiet, staring into the middle distance. 'I think of all the people in history who have been like me, who haven't had any diagnosis. They were just that way. People said, he's a character, he's an eccentric. Now we're pathologized and medicated. Just because I feel too much, or not enough.'

'Like Rachel's show: you feel too much.'

'I know for some it frees them to behave like normal people,

148

but the pills didn't allow me to feel much of anything. There were no highs, no lows, just this constant flat plain—' Conrad cut the air with his hand. 'That's why I stopped taking them. Plus they didn't allow me to paint.'

'Why not?'

'Because I wasn't feeling anything. It was like floating on a cushion. When I do my work I feel I'm getting close to the part of myself I've lost, the ill part of me. Where I can remember how it felt, to feel things so acutely I thought I would burst. I thought I would simply explode.'

The refrigerator juddered to a halt, leaving them stranded in a sudden silence.

'I'm worried—' she hesitated. 'About the effect – about your show. The reviews.' She gave up. She couldn't string a sentence together. Conrad looked down at his knees. When he spoke again his voice was quiet. 'I'd like to feel love again, like I used to. That rush. The trouble was, it always made me sick, unbalanced.'

'I didn't have that effect on you, did I?'

'I felt stable with you. I still feel—' he stopped, unsure of where this was taking them. 'I think I'm worried, for the first time in my life, about my future. God, I never believed it would happen for me: a future. And here I am, living it. My present will just become more and more future, until there's no future anymore.' He looked up to see if she was still with him. 'That's what it means, isn't it? Getting old. Time accelerates.'

'What part of your future are you worried about? As a painter or as a person?'

He shrugged. 'They're one and the same.'

She must have felt it once herself, the lack of division or boundary between herself as a character and herself as an artist. Although it was dangerous, she felt instinctively, this blending, something of a provocation to fate. If Conrad didn't succeed as an artist, then he would also fail as a person.

She fell into silence. After knowing him for nearly three years, she was being forced to re-think everything she had thought true about Conrad. Maybe she was a terrible judge of

149

character. Maybe she had been deliberately, wilfully blind to the real meaning of his erratic behaviour. Maybe she had been too caught up in herself.

Once, she recalled, Conrad had told her his vision of a perfect life, a perfect future. He had described it like a film he kept playing just under the surface of his consciousness.

This film was sun-lit, shot in Tuscany or the south of France. There he was, seated at an alfresco dining table studded with bottles of San Pellegrino, laughing with a group of his equally successful friends, a stone farmhouse texturing the background. In this narrative he is forever about thirty years old, surrounded by a halo of infinite promise and his own not inconsiderable beauty.

But lately the film has shifted tone. The initial director has been sacked, and new talent has been brought in to save the project. Unbeknownst to the studio, this new director is edgy, unreliable; he makes films that are much darker and contingent.

In this new film Conrad's life is a parade of lovers he can't trust. He himself can't commit to a country, to a dog, a job, a lover, even a gender. He sees himself becoming a certain type of middle-aged gay/undefined aesthete who can find an expression of beauty only in younger lovers and in paintings done by other people.

His worst fears were not part of the film and its ironic little clips. They sat on the cutting room floor, spliced out by a nervous editor. In his worst fears he saw himself old, unbalanced and derelict. Forgotten.

twenty

THE ENGLISH LANGUAGE

Rachel said to meet in the kind of caff she insisted on frequenting, ones with lime formica tables and last year's Turkish calendars on the wall.

'Did I tell you I've taken up flying trapeze again? The teacher they have now is a Cuban.' She exhaled a stream of energetic smoke. 'He's gorgeous. Gay, though. There's a woman who does it too. She's wild, all scarred. She looks like she's been through the wars. You'll have to come and see me one night.'

Outside, traffic from the Shoreditch one-way system rumbled past. A posse of schoolboys ran by the window in a flock of black trousers, white shirts, the purple crest of a City boys' school on their blazers. It was the hour in London Alex liked least; the pavements full of children travelling like directionless missiles.

'So how's the work going?'

'Actually, I'm thinking of giving up performance pieces and going back to making objects.'

'What?' It was hard to imagine Rachel as a sculptor, a painter.

'It's not really working.'

'What's not working?'

'My career. It hasn't launched me in the way I expected it to. And now I'm getting too old for it. Another year or two and I'll be a joke.'

'What did you expect it to launch you into?'

'Oh, I don't know. I guess I wanted to be an art star.' Rachel took a drag on the cigarette dangling precariously from her lower lip. 'I couldn't act, I couldn't sing, so I decided to become an artist. It was the only way I could be centre of attention.' Rachel laughed. 'None of that is true, you know. That's a line from my show a couple of years ago, You're Nobody Unless You're Famous.'

She stared pointedly at the out-of-date calendar on the wall opposite. In DECEMBER rotund women in headscarves and voluminous skirts laboured in stony fields.

Rachel nodded, penitent. 'I'm sorry. I know I'm 'on' all the time. I'm like a broken television. I'm thirty-eight and I still have no idea how to turn myself off. I don't even know what I want out of life. That's pretty pathetic, isn't it? Other women my age are married and have three kids. I bet they don't even have time to think about what they want. I bet they don't want to think about it.'

'You wanted success and it hasn't really happened,' she said, bluntly.

Rachel gave her a pained look. 'I think it's actually love.'

'Love?'

'A dirty word in the lexicon of Rachel Silcox's art, I know. But let's just imagine the impossible happened, that I fell in love once, just when I wasn't expecting it. We're always told: it happens when you least expect it. Although I can't imagine going around and thinking: gosh, I'm really expecting to fall in love today.'

Rachel lit another cigarette, passing it dextrously, even nervously, through her tentacle fingers. Rachel was a strategic smoker: it was like a silent conversation partner. She exhaled when she wanted to make a point, forcefully; at times of confusion she allowed the smoke to get in her eyes.

'So who did you fall in love with?'

'He started talking to me at a college degree show. Five hours later we were still talking at this bar somewhere in South Kensington. I never know where I am in South Kensington. All those rich people, it's disorienting. Anyway, we had a fling. He was younger than me, but only by a year or two. He was very *smart*.' She winced as she said the word.

152

'He was going to be a critic, or a gallerist. He'd studied art and philosophy at a university in the States. He was the first man in years who I'd had a stimulating, intellectual, proper conversation with. It was just eerie: we used the same words, constructed our sentences the same way. We had similar opinions on almost everything. I got chills just having a conversation with him. I felt like I was talking to myself.'

'What happened?'

'We slept together a few times. Maybe that was the mistake, maybe we should have been friends. *Friends.*' Rachel scowled ferociously. 'What a bloody appalling word. Anyway, he decided he didn't want to – to continue, I think was his word. I think he had other fish to fry.' Rachel stubbed out the remains of her cigarette.

'The thing was, even though I only knew him for about three weeks or so, he really got under my skin. I can still feel him here—' she pinched her forearm between two fuschia nails. 'I think it was the only time I've ever really fallen in love. I don't know how to describe the effect it had on me. It was like entering a quiet church, where all the candles and flowers have been arranged so beautifully . . .' She shook her head. 'I don't know how to describe the feeling: reverential, or humbling. There should be a single word for it, but there isn't.'

'But he didn't want to continue seeing you?'

'No.' Rachel paused and sat up straight, rearranging her posture so quickly she thought she heard a bone crack somewhere in her lanky frame. 'And I didn't take it very well.'

'What did you do?'

'Oh, the usual crazy stuff. I wrote him letters. One of them was twenty-five pages long. I quoted Lacan, Derrida, or Schopenhauer, dissecting his response to me. That's what happens when you've spent half your life being enthralled by theory.'

'Did you send that letter?'

'Of course! I'm not one of those spineless people who write letters for therapy. I send the damn things, thereby making it impossible to ever talk to him again. He'd probably run a mile if he met me now. He'd think: there's that mad woman.' She took a last sip of her coffee. 'It surprised me, how quickly I lost my dignity. Maybe I never had any to begin with.'

Rachel gave her a thin, defeated smile. 'And here's the real horror: I'm still living for him, in a way. Not for *him*, exactly. More like for his approval. I'm someone who needs a witness, someone who is watching what I do. Most people live for the love or the approval of someone they know. Then there are people like me, who live for the disembodied eye, for the approval of someone they don't even know anymore.'

They sat in silence while the juggernauts rolled by outside, rattling the windows. When Rachel looked up again there was pain, still fresh, suspended in her eyes. 'I still imagine him in the arms of other people.'

She nodded. It really was a sad story.

Although what was sadder, she thought, was how Rachel's experience with this man had turned her off love and onto seduction. Seduction was safer, and it meant she always had the upper hand. Now Rachel went through men like water, breast-stroking casually through them as if they were all the same continuous substance. At parties she had seen Rachel swimming at men from an oblique angle, looking at them sideways out of one eye, like a shark. She would make several sorties like this. Then she would sidle up to them, quietly. The men didn't even know she was there. She watched these men go home with Rachel, following her out the door with the resigned posture of captives.

Alex looked at her watch. It was nearly three. 'I have to get back to work.'

'Sure.' Rachel gathered up her cigarettes and lighter in one swift movement.

They parted beside a confusion of traffic. Rachel was poised to dart out into the road but turned back at the last second and touched her forearm in a gesture that surprised her. 'Take care of yourself.' She said it like a warning.

154

- Number of words in the English Language: 67,000.
- Number of words in the average person's vocabulary: 2,000.
- English has 20,000 more words than any other western language.

At the office she trawls through her collection of Facts. She is putting together a leaflet with fascinating statistics designed to pique people's interest, then she would insert the number of people with the disease the organisation Polyp was fighting against, which was 48,000.

She thought about Rachel struggling to describe the feeling of falling in love. For her, she remembered it was like being struck over the head with a heavy object, but pleasant. She walked around for days dizzy and disoriented, feeling hushed and reverential, just as Rachel had said – as if she had entered a cathedral of the self. The air was still and cool and she was simultaneously supplicant and priest, doling out benediction.

What did you call it, that state? So many words in the English language, and still there are none for that feeling.

※

'Oh, English,' the hotel owner in Xela, a soft man of thirty or so, tells her. They are staying in pensions, small hotels in cold old colonial buildings, their walls like the ramparts of fortresses, studded with those flowers the colour of blood.

'It is so hard. I have tried to learn it so many times, but the words are never sounded as they look on a piece of paper.' He shakes his head in a way that suggests he has not quite given up learning yet. 'So hard,' he says again, and smiles.

He takes her to look at the requisite caged bird, a garrulous scarlet macaw. The bird is dishevelled, his wings frayed at the edges, from beating them against the mesh.

'Why don't you let him out?' she asks.

'Oh, he would leave.'

Yes, he would, she thinks, looking in the parrot's yellow eye, which swirls with fantasies of escape.

She makes a promise to herself that night. She will go around all the hotels, posing as a prospective guest, and open the parrots' cages. They will rise above the city, a kaleidoscopic flurry, like a fistful of candy thrown upwards, and fly away.

twenty-one

GALLERIES ARE GREAT
PLACES TO MEET PEOPLE

That weekend she went to the new Tate (as everyone seemed to call it, eschewing it's real name, Tate Modern) for the first time. She followed the flow of tourists down the long ramp and into the cavernous turbine hall. At the end Louise Bourgeois's sculpture of a giant spider stood, poised on the tips of its legs, like a sinister ballerina.

The space reminded her of the lofts Conrad took her to, when they went to parties held by computer twiggers or property developers, all lacerating brick and edgy furniture. The décor said: look how classless we are, how open, without boundaries, but hard, if need be. How rich.

She went to the galleries upstairs in search of something familiar. She found the Rothkos and sat on the bench in the middle of the room, allowing herself to sink into the spell cast by the moody canvases. This new gallery was vast and packed with people who arranged themselves like exhibits, standing in that racehorse posture, one leg thrown wearily behind them.

Galleries are great places to meet people, she can hear Conrad saying. He has done the impossible: met men and women in galleries, and taken them home. *They are the neutral spaces in which we can encounter each other on equal ground*. But as soon as she catches a glimpse of their faces, people turn away from her, as if in disgust.

'What are you doing here?'

She turned around to find Fernando standing behind her, framed against the compelling burgundy of one of the Rothkos.

He was wearing an old blue jumper and dark jeans. On his feet were dusty army boots flecked with paint.

'Just lurking. How about you?'

'This is my first time. I love it,' he said. 'You can still smell the wood, it's so new.'

'What have you been doing with Conrad?'

Fernando frowned. 'I haven't been doing anything with Conrad.'

'He's been away for days on end.'

Fernando kept her fixed with a careful gaze. 'He hasn't been with me.'

'Then where has he been?'

Fernando shrugged. 'I don't know.'

'You're sure?'

'I have not seen him since that day I came to your house,' Fernando insisted. 'There is something I should tell you,' he said, in the stilted foreboding of someone on official business. 'Why don't we go to my studio? It's nearby.'

'You have a studio near here?'

He caught the incredulity in her voice. 'I know, all these luxury apartments. There are only one or two old buildings left. Mine is one of them.'

They walked for ten minutes through the winding cobble-stoned streets of Southwark. At one point they ran into a wall of white catering trucks. 'Oh, dear,' Fernando sighed. 'They are always making films here. It is the only part of London that still looks historical.'

They had to double back through the streets until at last they arrived at a building. They mounted a spiral stone staircase, narrow and winding, like in old council flats. It smelled of the river.

When they reached the fifth floor he inserted a key, a cigarette dangling from his other hand. The door opened with a clank. He ushered her into a large square space. At the end light fell across the floor through a line of enormous semi-circular windows. Dust danced in its broad shafts. It was like entering a derelict cathedral.

'The light—'

'It's incredible, isn't it? I was so lucky, I still can't believe it.'

'How long have you had it?'

'About two years. They will evict me soon, though. It will be turned into lofts.'

She went to the end of the room, to where the windows looked out onto the river. In front of the window was a row of large glass balls, about the size of melons, suspended on an array of nearly invisible wires. They looked like a curtain of metal rain.

'It's meant to be about suspension,' Fernando said. 'I made it for a friend of mine.' He went to a table and dusted off a part of it, reached underneath and pulled out a large book, like a photo album. He opened it and leafed through the pages.

'This is a book of photographs from my first exhibition.' The photographs showed a large darkened room. On its walls were projected luminous, nearly fluorescent clouds. 'I had a cello player in the room. He was hidden behind a screen. He would play fragments – Beethoven, Mahler. He would scratch the strings on purpose sometimes, scrape the instrument. And then there were these—' he lifted his hands into the air, fluttered them around his head '—these ions in the room.'

'Ions?'

'That's what the thunder machine was for. It created negative and positive ions, just like electrical storms do. That's why the air smells burnt after a thunderstorm. It crackles, it's alive.'

She struggled to keep up. 'So you created a thunderstorm in this room.'

'Exactly.' He said, his eyes shining. She wondered if he showed his work to everyone who came to his studio in this way, eager, almost hungry for response, more like a student than an architect-artist. 'My town was famous for its thunderstorms. I wanted to create a thunderstorm in this room to remind me what it was like, otherwise I will never remember.'

'Do you need to be reminded in order to remember?'

His liquid brown eyes flickered across her face, back and

forth, like a scanning machine. 'You know, that's a very good question.'

He began to tell her, then, in a tangled anecdotal way, about long red afternoons, working in laterite fields all day, riding horses up mountains, tending cattle, making cheese. How clouds the shape of small countries would steamroller across the sky.

'For awhile I lived on a farm belonging to an uncle. It was all heat, horses and blood,' the last word slid off his lips with distaste. 'They told me I was useless on the farm. What they meant was useless as a man. They always found me lying on my back in the grass, looking up at the sky. My father and my uncle would say, "What are you looking at?" I said "clouds" of course. What did they think I was looking at? "The way you go on, I'd think you were looking at the angels." My uncle said. He had never stopped to look at clouds in his life.

'He thought I was stupid. When I was a child I was severely dyslexic. I could barely write. For years I was lost somewhere between the word and the meaning. I just couldn't figure it out, couldn't make the connection. I just got bounced back and forth, back and forth.' With his hands he made a parabolic movement, like one of his metal balls swinging on invisible strings at the end of the room. 'I was actually vibrating in the middle, caught. I was thinking, where is the meaning? And there was no meaning.' When he looked at her his eyes were full of a laughter in which she could see the empty shadow of a void.

Something had come to rescue him from that place. She could see it coming again, coming back. It could be promising or sinister, and like an old carnival mask lifted out of a dark trunk it was slow to show its face.

'I did not expect to live past thirty,' he said. 'When I was young, I really burned. I really did not think there would be anything left.'

The end of his cigarette burned orange as he inhaled. She watched the filaments of tobacco ignite and disappear within a second. Behind the cigarette his face seemed to glow, but steadily, as if he was lit from the inside.

'What did you want to tell me about Conrad?'

'I'm afraid I had to disappoint him. Unlike many men I am not afraid of close friendships with other men. But I do not want anything more.' He scowled through cigarette smoke. 'I can never see myself living my life with another man. I respect that way of life, but it is not for me.'

'Are you sure Conrad wanted to live his life with you?' she tried not to smile. 'Maybe he only wanted sex.'

'I will not do that either. I don't know why. I don't think he was very pleased. I think what he needs is something else,' Fernando said. 'I think he needs something steady. Possibly even a woman—'

'Conrad doesn't see people as *men* and *women*. He doesn't even distinguish between them.'

'That is part of his fantasy.' Fernando said it easily, as if he made these kinds of judgement every day. 'It's just his way of explaining to himself why he doesn't distinguish between individuals.'

For a second she was angry. She thought: how conventional. Then, within another second, she considered the possibility that Fernando might be right, that Conrad's bisexuality might be just a way to stave off intimacy.

They sat there in Fernando's studio, not noticing the coming night until the dusk sparrows started to sing. Fernando talked to her in oddly constructed phrases, telling her of winds full of the discarded buds of cotton plants. When he opened his mouth to the air he choked on them. Of the strange small parrots that had lived in the trees; of summer cicadas and cutting winter winds.

Evening fell outside his window, its crumbling frame and soot-smeared pane looking out onto the Thames. She saw water birds skimming its surface, flying against an ermine sky.

They talked together there until the river had absorbed the dark of the sky. Eventually they could not even see each other's faces. Everything faded into reflections and silence but for the water lapping against the building and the quiet, deliberate sound of his voice.

161

*

The stream is so shallow she can't tell which way its trickle leads. Her only hope is to follow it downstream. She knew people lived by rivers in the lowlands. But if she judges wrongly she will hike up into the mountains, where no-one lives, and die there.

She squats beside the stream and throws leaves, twigs, dead bugs on the surface, anything which might reveal the direction of its flow. But the pool stays stubbornly still, its peat waters darkening with the day.

She walks for an hour or so in the direction she thinks, judging from the position of the sun, is due east, following the stream, to see if it would swell and mould itself into a river. As she goes she twists the tender branches of tree ferns and rips threads from her already shredded trousers, tying them, in case she needs to find her way back. She knows the thread will disintegrate in a couple of days.

After two hours of walking the creek remains a stubborn trickle. She moves away from the water to find a place to sit out the night; streams in the rainforest at night are dangerous places. Someone told her that the fer-de-lance – one of the most aggressive, tenacious snakes, the pit bull of vipers – frequented water, especially at night.

Darkness gathers around her in small pools that grow until she is submerged. She will sit on her damp fallen tree for eight hours, until what she calculates is four-thirty a.m., one hour before dawn, when she will begin to move again, each step a new and infinitely detailed agony as she walks on a broken ankle.

Without paper, without a torch, she has only her eyes and mind to get her through the night. She makes a mental list:

Things I will buy when I get out of here:

- A good watch, a proper watch. One that doesn't stop working after a plane crash.

- Perfume: Christian Dior la Dolce Vita, sweet and aromatic. It makes her think of expensive women at the Opera, jewels lying like sharp-toothed animals on alabaster throats.

- Eyeliner in greyish blue. Not one of those cheap chalky ones. An expensive eyeliner. Clinique.

- That Miles Davis CD she has always meant to buy – a classic. The one he recorded in four hours or something. What's the name again?

The recitation of innocent commodities helps calm her nerves. For three days now she has teetered between hope and panic, until she is unable to distinguish between them.

twenty-two

CLIMATE CHANGE

'I'm sick of people always doing things. Going to management trainee workshops, travelling to Tibet undercover to expose the real story behind the Chinese government's clampdown, buying houses, seeing their voice coach, selling companies, making their own wooden toys for children from scraps of DIY—' Conrad twirled around the kitchen like a deranged ballet star.

'They're just hustlers. Tarting their intellects about. As if I've got time to be fucking impressed. I'm tired of reading novels where characters go to Uzbekistan, or talk about metaphysics, polar exploration, theories of navigation. I mean, we all know our intelligence is under-utilized by everyday life. I don't need some smartass writer peddling this ephemeral metaphoric crap to tell me.'

She had to lean against the wall. She felt its coolness seep into the small of her back. 'Conrad, what's the matter?'

'What?'

'Conrad?' There was a tremor in her voice.

'Don't say my name like that. You think I'm nuts.' His eyes were hectic.

She took a breath. 'I don't.'

He sat down quickly, causing the sofa to groan. He pouted and crossed his arms over his chest, like a child. 'I always get this way in winter.'

'But it's August.'

He scowled. 'Have you noticed it's fucking freezing out there? I had to wear my gloves today. It's always winter in this miserable country. Winter is no time for release. Who has ever been set free in winter?' He didn't wait for a reply. 'Winter is when I see it most clearly, this society we're living in: cruel, empty, sporting in that way that Imperial Rome was, getting a thrill out of other people's misfortunes. Falsely benign.

'Listen, try this little exercise. Write down what you think are the most significant experiences of your life. I bet you'll only come up with three or four, apart from birth, death, marriage. Imagine, all this living we do, just for three or four key experiences. All that living, only to have it condensed down to practically nothing.'

'What's wrong? Is it because Fernando told you he wasn't interested?'

He gave her a sharp look. 'How do you know?'

'I guessed,' she backtracked.

'He said he didn't want a man.'

'You can't argue with that.'

Conrad shook his head. 'You sure can't. Although I never think about it that way, *men* and *women*. God, I'd love to be gay and think of nothing else but backsides. But I'm not gay in that way of being oriented toward men. It's more of a protest vote.' He looked at her, to see if she was still listening.

'You know I was brought up in a family where my parents hadn't had sex for about twenty years and that was fine with them, because sex was for procreative purposes only. My parents were too busy fulfilling their biological destiny and perfecting a lifelong performance of the roles of Mom and Dad. I have no idea who my parents are, individually, as people. They never let me see them.

'What's ironic, if not tragic,' Conrad went on, 'is that for all their family-orientedness, for all their patio furniture and bible-reading, my parents have no family. My brother jumped off a bridge. They haven't heard from me in years. They wouldn't even know where to find me.'

When he looked up, his eyes were rimmed with tears. 'For the first time in my life I feel that this might be my fault, *our* fault, my brother and me, and not theirs.'

'I don't know, Conrad. From the little you've told me, your family don't sound like very sensitive people.'

'But they were all I had. They were *my* people. Imagine their shock, having two sons who turned out to be essentially gay. Or at least sexually and emotionally complex beyond their understanding. They just couldn't understand how they had produced such weirdos.'

It was hard to believe Conrad had come from a part of the world whose concerns were so basic. By the time she knew him, Conrad bought the best balsamic vinegar, and at dinner parties he hotly debated the merits of first cold-pressed Tuscan olive oil against organic Kalamata. Maybe Fernando was right, she considered, that Conrad had only roped in his sexuality as part of a larger rebellion, another way of constructing an idea of himself that allowed no connection with the place he had come from.

'Maybe I wouldn't have left if we hadn't lived in one of those smug small towns. You know, filled with local bores who know everything about the type of salmon running in the river and the insignificant local historical figures, putting up recreation centres, pruning their roses, campaigning for the local hospital. Trying to convince themselves they all have something in common, that they are building a community. But if something like Bosnia happened they'd slit each other's throats.' He paused for breath.

'I hate a lie,' Conrad said. 'But most of all lies that are meant to comfort. That is the worst category of lie.'

'I chose art over life because it has a more demanding eye,' is another thing she would remember him saying that night. 'It won't spare anyone.'

Conrad's first memory is of a cold, invigorating, harsh world. When Conrad was only three months old, his mother would put him out on the veranda, covered in a heap of blankets, to sleep in minus twenty temperatures. This was a family tradition of 'toughening up' newborns by exposing them to the elements.

He remembered nothing of these December and January

afternoons, exactly, but something of the pleasing sensation of being in physical extremity stayed inside him, beneath the current of memory, and this was probably why he would come to seek it out in adulthood. It was part of him, compositionally, that glass world in which he had to screw-drill down through four feet of ice on a frozen river, just to get a fishing hole.

He went fishing with his father every winter. His silent father – he could still see them there, squatted around the ice hole he had made on the Miramichi river. Conrad perched sitting beside his father, knees frozen, dead fish scattered around them like discarded Christmas paper.

When he reached puberty his father decided to initiate him into knowledge of the natural world, hauling him out into the woodlot on minus-fifteen days to mumble names of trees at him – *spruce, elm, tamarack, birch, maple, sumach, hawthorn*. His father told him about the insects that fed on their leaves, the birds that perched on their branches, then volleyed staccato observations on the next snowfall, the shortness of the summer, the severity of the ice storm. Together they sat for hours in the woods, a strange satisfied silence, staring hard into the amber slab of winter sun.

In those months everything hardened: the sky turned to glass, the trees to icy scarecrows, the sea became a grey mirror. Conrad skated on lakes frozen four feet deep. The surface of the ice was rippled with air bubbles and he skidded over them, giddy, listening as his blades popped the corpuscles of air.

There he is, three months old on the veranda, suspended in his cold universe, his life stretching ahead of him like one of those new highways that transverse empty landscapes – desert or tundra.

Unlike most people, who live their lives in the flashback of memory and delayed realization, collecting memories and impressions long forgotten as if they were stones, Conrad lived in futureflash: he still thought of himself as that baby, satisfied with his incompleteness. He still wondered how his life would be at thirty, at thirty-five – except he had passed thirty some time ago.

Now the future had vanished, and along with it the thrust that had propelled him so far away from those winter afternoons on the veranda, his pale infant's eyes drinking in his white new world, which he took for granted was his and his alone. A winter-born child, river stones for eyes. Adrift in life.

twenty-three

DARK AND LIGHT

Everyone knew about Arthaus. Even Alex had heard of it. It was run by two young Englishmen with round faces and square glasses. *Time Out* had just done a piece on them – 'Art Warriors' – and they had swanned around London for the whole of that week, secretly hurt when they were not recognized on the street.

'They want writers and artists for live installations in Paris, Berlin, New York. They call it a cattle call.' Rachel put down the magazine. 'I hate that term. Do you know where it came from?' Rachel peered at her accusingly, as if she were the one who had made it up. 'Hitchcock. He said, "Actors are like cattle". I'd like to see him try to make his fucking misogynist films with a herd of Herefords.'

The scene of the mass audition was a disused building somewhere behind the South Bank. Amassed inside were muscled trapeze artists and other circus types, next to serious writers in long black leather coats and baby girl artists wearing platform trainers and their hair knotted on top of their heads like Bjork. Everyone had distinct, hard faces, faces which looked like they expected to be remembered. The Art Warriors were in the far corner, seated behind two miniature desks that looked like they'd been stolen from a primary school, looking bewildered at the carnival they had sparked.

She found Rachel sitting in the queue. At one point, three hours earlier, people had been standing, but like Rachel they had given up and sat in individual pools on the floor.

'I feel like I should start filing my nails or something.' Rachel cast furious glances around her. 'This is ridiculous.' She stood up. 'I've had enough. Let's go. They can take their British Council grant and shove it up their arse.'

They were about to leave the auditorium when she saw Fernando. He was not in any queue, but sat smoking by himself in the corner.

'Are you here for the trapeze call?' Rachel asked.

He looked up at them, unsmiling. 'I'm here because they wanted artists. I am an artist.' He said each 'a' very carefully, separating it from the rest of the word.

'Well, it seems to be taking awhile.'

He stood up, dusted off his trousers. 'I will come with you.' He said it so seriously it came out like a threat.

Rachel laughed. 'All right. Let's stage a walk-out.'

They left the auditorium, followed by three of the Bjork girls and a growing trickle of malcontents, and headed to a café next to the disused warehouse.

Fernando sat down opposite her. As he lowered himself into his chair Alex watched the people next to him fade slightly, as if their own fires were stoking themselves slightly lower to make way for the superior heat he threw.

'I hate for my life to be dependent upon the whims of others,' he said.

She mumbled an agreement. Rachel arrived with the coffees, which she plunked down in front of them.

'Well, glad that's over,' she said, her voice bright. 'I haven't been so humiliated since I went to my first audition and I won't tell you how long ago that was.'

'They are just not very organized. They have all the attention but no practicality. They are not professionals.' Fernando gave his assessment with the impassive but serious air of a pathologist. He left soon after. 'You will excuse me, I have work to do.'

'Right.' Alex stiffened. She found herself listening for any note of regret in his voice, but there was none. He hadn't referred to their conversation in his studio, nor betrayed any intimacy with her.

She and Rachel went for a walk along the riverfront. It was a warm evening and they walked against a steady stream of cyclists and rollerbladers.

'God, Fernando can be heavy,' Rachel sighed. 'Like a Russian, or an East European. Weighed down by melancholy.'

'He wasn't like that at all when I talked to him in his studio.'

'You went to his studio?'

'I ran into him at the Tate, in the Rothko room. His studio's nearby. He invited me to look at his work.'

'Isn't Conrad interested in him?'

'But he's not interested in Conrad.'

'I wonder what does interest Fernando.' Rachel scowled. 'He's a strange case.'

'He seems older.'

'I know what you mean. He has that worldly air of disappointment.'

They stopped just after Waterloo Bridge and leant over the railing. Beneath them the river lapped against the bulwark. The light had faded to a moody mauve.

'But you haven't ever—?' she stopped.

'What, slept with him?' Rachel laughed. 'He doesn't seem to want anyone. He's very gentle, very discreet, in his rebuffs. I think that's the word for him: particular.'

Rachel looked out onto the water, now garlanded with the city's light. 'Such a beautiful man,' she said, her voice wistful. 'I wonder. I really do.'

That night he was in her dreams. They were in a changing room, in front of a mirror. He was trying on a new shirt.

As he took off the shirt he was wearing she saw a small lithe torso emerge. He put on the new white shirt. It reflected in his eyes, where two pools of white formed. Instantly his face lightened.

Centuries ago, his family were Venetians. They came from a water city, she was sure, they would be just that: penetrating, labyrinthine, opulent. Once a year the men would dress in black and white, a duochrome carnival. The contrast lived on in

171

Fernando; if he wore white his face became light, transparent. But framed by black, his eyes darkened, the angle of his nose sharpened, lines deepened on his face until he looked serious, even dangerous.

'What do you think?' he asked her, turning from side to side. 'Should I buy it?'

The shop assistants were outside the cubicle, squawking at them to hurry up. They didn't have much time to choose. There were so many other people who wanted the shirt.

She turned back to the mirror. On his face was a considering, discerning expression. His right eye sat very slightly higher on his face, as if, during the process of sculpting, it had been swept up there by a careless finger. It gave his face a thrilling asymmetry, holding his expression in a constant waver between seriousness and euphoria. She saw herself in the mirror, next to this man turning his face this way and that, his face drifting out of darkness, then into light.

Strange things were happening at work. People in suits were seen entering and exiting Michael's office. He went out to drink with them. Sometimes, she noticed, Erica did too.

Monday morning. Erica arrived, looking exhausted. 'I've spent the whole weekend thinking,' she said.

'Thinking about what?'

'I don't know what to do. I don't want to tell him. I don't want to give him up.'

Erica was loved by two people, two people who wanted her, and she had to choose. Alex didn't really want to be involved in her surfeit-of-love problem. Erica was a walking reminder of the fundamental unfairness in life, that some people starve in the desert while others are fed ripe figs in oases.

'Why don't you just tell the truth?'

'Tell who the truth?'

'Your lover. Your husband. Tell them both the truth. Whatever it is that you actually feel, tell them.'

Erica stared at her, genuine astonishment on her face. 'But what good would that do?'

'It's the only way to be clear. To stop living a lie, to end the discomfort you're in.'

'Oh,' she waved away the suggestion. 'I don't think the truth is going to help anybody in this situation. I don't really even know what it is, the truth. I don't even like the sound of the word. Tr-uth,' she stretched the word to two syllables. 'So Anglo-Saxon, upright.'

Alex walked away. She knew this was rude, transparent, that Erica would think she was judging her on moral grounds and this was fine, as long as it cloaked the real reason for her reaction, which was jealousy.

Erica had a capacity she would never have: she was able to divide her life into compartments. Her life was a train and she went from one coach to the other, taking whatever delights she found in each. She had no need to knock down the walls and create one of those breezy, open-plan spaces people their age aspired to live in, everything on display, no boundaries.

She sat at her desk for the rest of the morning, clicking in and out of web universes. She even paid a desultory visit to diagnoseyourself.com. Over the past year frequent visits to the site had nurtured an electronic fascination with illness, but now she found she didn't have the heart for hypochondria anymore. She had to face the stark truth: she was perfectly healthy. She was probably going to live for years.

Erica sat at her desk, too, studiously not looking in Alex's direction, which was difficult in such a small office. She went to the water cooler, she went out to get a sandwich, she came back. She betrayed no loss of composure, but neither did she smile that day, or speak to anyone else.

Alex's hands tingled (repetitive strain, advised diagnoseyourself.com). Her tongue felt dry (anything from jaundice to diabetes to hypothyroid).

After she left diagnoseyourself.com she didn't know where to go. Perhaps she could find a website that would tell her about friendship, about why she found it so difficult to be friends with Erica, about why she wanted the kind of love everyone hoped to find in friendship but she found it impossible to sustain: either she fell in love with her friends or she got bored with them.

She really didn't know what she wanted; to be in love or to find a friend. Most people didn't get the two mixed up: there was the love of friendship, and then there was desire, both distinct and separate.

She typed KINDS OF LOVE into a search engine and received 40,302 matches. She clicked on number 22, something called Categories of Love in Greek Thought. The web address was at a classics department of a university somewhere in Canada.

A short list appeared on the screen, under the title The Greek Loves. It began with *agape*, altruistic love; then *pragma*, the understanding that exists between a long established married couple. *Ludus* was the playful affection of children and between casual lovers; *storge* the love between siblings or people who have gone through much together. Then, nearly at the bottom of the list, *eros*, or sexual passion. The last was *mania*, also known as obsession.

It is August and some parts of the country are flooded under two feet of water, while others are parched. Amphibians' skins are rasping for water, and otters and birds are buried in sand.

Every night weather presenters come on, unstable-looking young women in yellow suits, and try to explain why the weather is so erratic – dry, wet, hot, cold, but mostly hot.

Without rain the country seems brittle and defensive. At night she lights candles, as if holding some private vigil. She sees her reflection in the mirror, just above the flame, seeing how the light turns her face to wood. The candlelight erases the small lines that have begun to gather in the corners of her eyes like conspirators.

On these bone-dry nights she thinks how things should happen in the rain – people should be kissed, taken to bed. In England the rain has the dreary eroticism as the smashed pomegranates and melted marzipan in the Turkish shops that line the streets of their area.

But there was no rain that August. She felt exposed, as if she were living her life under a floodlight. At the fruit stand grapes and peaches withered in a day, even though they were under shade. When she drank coffee her stomach broke into a sweat. The heat seemed foreign, as if it had been manufactured on some other latitude and then shipped north to London.

After a certain point her memory of that summer becomes hazy. She sees them all going to pubs, bars, sitting there in tiny shirts while the sun stalks the streets outside. Talking, drinking. Ashtrays overflowing. Eighteen-year-old barmaids in platform shoes coming to wipe down the table with a sponge. Lights going on at eleven and illuminating their sallow pub faces.

She remembers them all arguing about the importance of recognition, and heated discussions about being intimate with life, rather than treating it as a ladder they had to climb.

'It's taken me nearly twenty years to figure it out,' she remembers Rachel saying. 'But that's what I want: to just *live.*'

She spends a day hiking next to the sodden ridges of the stream, but it refuses to turn into something bigger. The sticks and leaves she throws tells her it has a current, and that she is moving in its direction. But then streams could take a hundred kilometres to turn into a river, and by a hundred kilometres she would be dead.

That night her wish list refuses to recite itself in her head, nor will singing the remnants of jazz tunes or seventies songs she knows reassure her.

She can already see her bones, picked clean by the gnawing animals that rummage on the forest floor: the agouti, a cross between a squirrel and a rat, the coatimundi, a scavenger. Her eyes are quails eggs for vultures. She understands now how having an imagination is detrimental to survival. Her ability to imagine her own death makes her only an open wound for which there is no balm.

Her future – she can see the rim of it, its luxurious horizon, far off in the distance. It is populated by future lovers, maybe a family. She had never even thought of having a family. But look, she can even see the faces of her children . . .

Suddenly time was being reeled in like a fishing line. It was happening so fast. There might not be any more time. Who was taking it away? Who held all her future time in his hands? Was it God? Where did he keep all that stolen time, snatched from people who had lives to live?

Panic sloshes through her insides. She will fight. She will not be a victim of any tyrant logician, either the God with time in his hands, or the rainforest, the natural world.

She goes crashing through a thousand barriers to her existence. Lianas swiping her face. Thick moss, intent on muffling her screams. She becomes, for those minutes, a prehistoric creature, bellowing in the undergrowth, running headlong into nothing, intent only on destroying the universe around her, just to show it she still can.

twenty-four

FÊTE WORSE THAN DEATH

As they approached they could hear unidentifiable noise blaring from a sound system. Shiny children's balloons floated into the trees, the sun glinting off their foil.

The Fête Worse than Death was an annual event that took place in a scruffy square near Conrad's flat. It was modelled on the village fêtes usually held in June or July in churchyards up and down the country, where people did silly things to make a bit of money.

'Hey, isn't that . . .' she pointed to the first stall, a small raised stage where a man stood in front of a microphone dressed in a gold lamé dress.

'Yep, that's Graham,' Conrad nodded.

She had only ever seen Graham Moor, the post-pop painter, at private views, his blond hair shaved close to his head. In his droopy grey fleeces he looked more like a van delivery driver than one of the most successful artists of his generation.

Now Graham stood on stage, dressed in drag, apparently lip-synching to a Polish cover version of some seventies rock classic.

'Cool,' Conrad said.

Next to Graham was a stall draped in Tarot-card reader decor, purple curtains obscuring a dark interior. The sign outside read DEATH PREDICTOR. A Bergman-like Death, complete with scythe, stood beside them. The Death Predictor invited punters to answer a series of questions about date of birth, weight, health, accident history. These were fed into a computer program which calculated an expected date of death.

178

'Hey, Zilla, Zara, how's it going?'

Conrad stopped to talk to the Z sisters. She had heard of them; they were upper-class girls who hung out in the art world in the hope of meeting Jarvis Cocker. She waited to one side, observing them as they talked animatedly with Conrad, thinking how you could always tell rich women by their feet and their hair: tanned narrow feet stuffed in butter-soft leather shoes, and thin hair expensively cut to look casual, even lank; their flowery laughs.

She surveyed the fête: there was a Paint Your Way Into Oblivion stall, dedicated to simultaneous marathon-painting and drinking. Shoot The Art Star offered people to take up pellet guns and shoot at targets superimposed with pictures of the current generation of hot young artists: among them she recognised Grant Mahler, a savagely abstract painter; Steve Goodlife, a video artist whose work was always set in airport departure lounges; Hilda Wiczwicki, the installation artist who did gigantic pools of oil and grease.

'This is such a lark,' Conrad said.

In the centre of the square adults jumped in a bouncy castle while their children frowned from the sidelines.

Conrad poked her. 'Hey, do you want to do the Death Predictor?'

'No.'

'Well, I'm going to.' He lurched off, ice cream dripping down his fingers. In the distance, Graham started up his rock star routine again.

She sat down on a patch of dishevelled grass. The sultry heat was like being trapped inside a launderette. People walked along the pavements in a desultory shuffle, the occasional non-artist resident launching scandalised looks in the direction of the fête.

A few minutes later Conrad emerged from the Death Predictor, a piece of paper fluttering in his fingers.

'What's the big day?'

'Good news,' he grinned. 'It's passed.'

It was getting too hot and crowded, so they went home.

179

Conrad plunked himself on a kitchen stool and fixed her with that look of his, the one that sometimes reminded her he was five years her senior. 'What's the matter with you?'

'Nothing.'

'You didn't enjoy the fête.'

'I did. I just thought—'

'I'll tell you what you thought: enough of this grubby subversive aesthetic. You thought, what a bunch of adults behaving like children.'

'Okay,' she conceded. 'I did.'

'Do you think adults can't be silly? Do you think once we hit thirty we have an obligation to be serious for the rest of our lives.'

'No—'

'Well why can't you fucking enjoy yourself then?'

'Don't browbeat me into enjoying myself.'

'I'm sorry. I just want you to be happy.'

'You make a great show of having a good time, but do you really enjoy yourself?'

'At least I try, despite the obvious obstacles.'

She decided to ask the question that had been rumbling around her mind that day, as she watched Conrad go from one fête attraction to the other with the enthusiasm of a seven year old. 'You don't ever just stop being manic depressive, do you? There are no spontaneous cures?'

He paused before answering. 'Not that I know of.'

'So it could recur.'

'I suppose.'

'Tell me what it would look like.'

'Do you remember last October and November? When I wouldn't answer the door?'

She vaguely remembered how, six months back, Conrad had thought people were shouting at him. He wouldn't answer the door or the telephone. He went to the movies and came back four hours later, having watched them twice in a row. Some mornings he got up far too early – four-thirty or five – blaming his insomnia on terrible headaches. When he was tense his hands would go into cramp and he couldn't paint.

180

She had taken these things as examples of the random complaints that assail everyone. Apart from that, there had been only the unspecified pressure she had often felt coming from him: an urge to act, to experience, to discover things.

'I never suspected that they were signs of any illness.'

'You were too busy thinking about yourself.' There was no reprimand in his voice. 'Besides, I'm very good at appearing as though these twitches I have are just part of my personality.'

Yes, she supposed. Conrad had the natural cunning of the smart person burdened with an unlucky illness. It wasn't that his symptoms were innocuous, but that he made sure people did not suspect.

'You need to tell me what it feels like for you, so I'll understand.'

'Okay,' he said. 'Deep breath.'

'What?'

'Take a deep breath. And don't contradict me until I'm finished. Right,' Conrad began. 'If I come home and say, today I'm going to achieve world peace, that's a giveaway. I'll start to tell you how I will solve the world's most pressing problems, I will neutralise wars, inspire peace. For example, I will go to the former Yugoslavia and have a word or two with the main actors, your basic regional-power-mongers-slash-psychopaths: Milosevic and Karadzic. I might make a speech on the radio exhorting all Serbs to peace. Harmony will be restored, people will love each other. All they needed was me.'

He peered at her. 'You're not laughing, are you? I mean, inwardly.'

'No.' She definitely wasn't laughing.

'Or there's a plot,' he went on. 'Some are in on it. Others aren't. Codes are sent to me in the numbers on five pound notes. License plates corroborate these codes, tell me of elaborate plans to kill you using red Ford Escorts. Or actually I'm David Bowie's best friend and I'm spending next week at his place in Switzerland. I'm ringing his assistant on his mobile phone to get her to pick me up at the airport in Geneva.'

He paused while something inside him shifted gear. 'Then

there's depression. It starts as a tickle in the back of my neck. Then – I don't know how to explain it. Normal perception evaporates. Just, poof!' He threw his hands up. 'All I have is the dark, and this urgent feeling that everything is not as it seems. There's threat everywhere and I need talismans to guard against the invincible danger. I think about things like creatures that are half-men, half-wolves. They are going to shred me with their nails. There they are, lined up around my bed. Children are thrown into wells alive. They never see the sun again. They go blind before they finally die.' A painful gleam shone through his eyes. It gave his already invincible eyes new urgency. Conrad was even more beautiful when in distress, if that were possible.

'These things actually happen in the world. In Algeria, for example, women and children were thrown into wells by fundamentalist zealots and left to die there. The threat is everywhere. It's inside you and it's out there.'

'How long ago was it you last felt that?'

'Oh, ages. The last time I had a depression like that the London telephone code was 071.'

They sat in silence for a minute. Outside the world seemed to have gone quiet too. For several seconds there was no traffic, no sirens.

'I don't want to feel any of this,' he said, after awhile. 'You might think it makes a good story, like my jaunt to France to save Lady Di, but I tell you, it's not funny.'

'I don't think it's funny,' she said. 'I don't think anything about you is *funny*, in that dismissive way.'

'You think I'm frivolous, that I can't get too close to things. But I have to fight to deal with the world as it is. Maybe that's why I became a painter; I can put something between me and the world, like a negotiating tool. A buffer zone.'

When he looked at her again his eyes were glossed, as if covered with a fine film of tears. 'I'm getting better, though. Soon I'm going to stop taking this medication. I feel like I'm getting younger, not older. I feel like I'm moving away from death, rather than toward it. Can you understand that?'

'I'm not sure.'

'You wouldn't believe the place I come from, Alex, unless you saw it for yourself. There's nothing. No art, no museums, no theatre, no galleries, no *life of the mind*. It was like a living death.

'I don't know—' He turned his palms open on the table and stared at them, as if he could read the lines on his own hands. 'I can't explain how I feel, how lucky. Like I've escaped from prison. I still feel this, even after ten years. But I'm still afraid, like one false move and I'll be back there, forced to play hockey and to hang out in shopping malls. And when Harold killed himself—' he shuddered.

Like hitting a buffer, he couldn't get past saying his brother's name. His brother who jumped off a bridge into a cold April river, the ice barely melted. The rusted girders, the river water the colour of peat, dyed by the copper and cadmium that oozed from the fissures of the land. His leap witnessed only by a solitary startled heron, just returned from a Florida marsh.

For years after his brother's leap, Conrad couldn't jump into a pool, not even from the side. He had to lower himself gingerly into the deep end, allowing the water to wash over him gradually. Even so, he heard the water, the rush and clog of it as it closed off Harold's hearing. He felt the attraction of breaking the surface of a river; the water's dark alluring gaze, the mossy smell, liquid ice flooding his lungs.

It was the preferred method of suicide among young men from their part of the world: hurling yourself into one of the province's many fast-moving rivers, preferably from a great height. If it wasn't the initial shock or height that killed you, the treacherous-whirlpool currents that curled around the bridge stanchions would. Or you could tank up with beer and whisky at the local bar after showing your fake ID attesting to the fact that you were nineteen, then get in your father's pickup and drive it, full-speed, into an innocent tree.

He was free of the memory now. There was nothing in Britain to remind him of his brother: his brother had never been here, there were few rusted old bridges over cold rivers, Harold had probably never even thought the word 'Britain' in all his short time on the planet.

He had moved to a new country to escape. Simultaneously the abandoner and the abandoned, Conrad was doomed to repeat the cycle of escape and abandonment over and over again, because he knew nothing else.

But slowly, with a creeping sideways certainty, he was beginning to want to see something familiar: the thin April ice that knitted river rocks together, the shivering pussy willows in early November. He couldn't decide to go back or to keep running, because he had spent his whole life tracing that thin line, the one between freedom and abandonment.

'I need a break from painting,' Conrad said. 'I want to try different media, give myself a chance to dream.'

In those months after his Tolerance show Conrad's work shifted away from painting to photography. He showed her his first batch of pictures. They were standing in the darkroom he'd made out of the bathroom. Every time she went to brush her teeth she got high on fixer fumes.

He was taking photographs and reversing them, presenting them as diptychs, using a mirror to create a kind of rotational centre, so you saw the image and simultaneously its reverse.

'Why mirrors?' she asked.

'Did you know that before the war there were no buildings made of that reflective glass. Can you think of New York or Chicago without reflections?'

She nodded, although for her mirrors were tricksters. She never saw in them what she expected to. When she looks in the mirror it is someone else who stares back, either an unrecognisable self or a stranger – a man once familiar, but whose face she cannot place. He is trapped in that mirror dimension, beyond her. Behind him she can see birds flying against a sky turning to night.

She can smell her own blood, warm and mineral. Biology, the dumb, lumbering machine with which she is saddled, notices nothing. Shock and trauma don't even faze it.

She has nothing to stop the blood, so she lets it drip down her leg. She hasn't had to do this since she was twelve and she got her period for the first time. White painter's trousers had been in style, and she had just badgered her mother to buy her a pair. She wore them proudly to school.

In English class, just after lunch, she rose from her desk and noticed a warm, sticky, wet substance on the seat of her desk. She did the worst thing possible: she screamed. Her classmates hadn't noticed, but they did then. She was sent home to change her clothes, followed by the shrieks of the girls: 'Alexandra's got her period, and she doesn't even know what it is.'

She went home and threw her new trousers in the rubbish. She lay in wait, like a crouching puma, for her mother to come home. When she opened the door she flew at her.

'Why didn't you tell me?' she screeched.

Her mother looked at her in horror. 'Tell you what?'

She retrieved the trousers from the kitchen garbage. They were covered with coffee stains and apple rinds. She tore them open to reveal the crotch, her shimmering red blood now turning to an ugly brown.

'This?' she screeched, before bursting into tears. 'Why didn't you tell me?'

'I gave you those books,' her mother recoiled. 'Didn't you read them?'

Yes, she had given her books. Books which showed pictures of developing foetuses, which explained in diagrams and charts the life cycle of the human being, and which showed embarrassing pictures of naked men and women lined up, as if for inspection.

Her mother gave her books for everything, handing them to her silently, wrapped in a paper bag, like contraband.

'I needed you to tell me,' she sobbed.

Her mother backed away, into her book-lined study. She went out and returned five minutes later. Wordlessly her mother handed her a package in a bag bearing the chemist's green cross.

Now here she was, an injured remnant of a person, death's afterthought. Broken ribs catapulting shocks of pain through her chest, bones ruined by walking on their shattered ends, her lips puffed and burnt, an eye exploded.

Where were those girls from English class now, who had ridiculed her so thoroughly? Married with children, probably, or maybe not: maybe they had exciting, challenging jobs which took them to Tanzania and Morocco on a regular basis.

She had always wanted this kind of life. Her life would be wild, eventful. When she told the story of her life at its end, it wouldn't seem real. Isn't this what she wanted?

Above her the clouds coagulated into different shapes. She tried to focus her exploded eye. One was a sickle, she thought, like the symbol that used to grace the Soviet flag. The next one was the ragged shape of Scotland. Another had the profile of a commedia dell'arte puppet – what were those characters names? Petronio? Petruccio? She had only seen them once, when her parents had taken her to a children's puppet theatre in Verona and she had clapped and laughed with all the Italian children, despite not understanding a word.

She watched as the cloud with the hooked nose and disparaging lips condensed, ruffled, then finally drifted out of sight.

twenty-five

PORTRAIT OF A MARRIAGE

She ran into Rachel in the café on Curtain Road. They hadn't seen each other since the Arthaus debâcle.

'Where did all these furniture design showrooms come from?' Rachel squinted across the road to where the usual unforgiving furniture sat gleaming in the window.

'The same place the Century 21 Estate Agents came from. From South Kensington, smelling money.'

'Did you hear Desmond and Charity are being chucked out of their studio? The same bloody developers who bought the whole road got hold of the lease. Simon and Haroun are being evicted too. They've been in their studio since they finished art school.'

All around them, rents were skyrocketing, leases weren't being renewed, developers were ethnically cleansing artists from the draughty cold-water studios in which they had laboured for ten years. The artists who pioneered the area were being shoved out to Leytonstone and Plaistow. Creatives were being replaced by consumers, or by pseudo-creatives: people like her, who rented their expensive art school educations out to design or advertising or multimedia companies.

The people who bought former studios and renegade galleries were odd types, Alex thought. They wandered around with large bunches of exotic flowers in one hand, laptops slung over their shoulder, looking deliberately in windows, ostensibly to keep their eye on estate agent's prices for property in the area but also to look at their own reflections.

Rachel invited her for a quick coffee. They sat down at long wooden tables surrounded by young people wearing square-framed glasses reading *Art Monthly*.

'I saw Conrad the other day,' Rachel began. 'He seemed nervy. He wouldn't settle down, kept jumping from one subject to another. The worst thing was, he didn't seem to be aware that he was doing it.'

'I know. When I came home the other day he was going on about all sorts of things – I couldn't really follow him. It frightened me. He was so *angry*.' Alex took another gulp of espresso. As she lifted the coffee cup to her lips she noticed her hands were shaking, if only slightly. 'I can't believe he kept it – secret. That's the only word I can think of.'

'Everybody has secrets,' Rachel shrugged. 'Although there's nothing I don't know about Conrad.'

She had heard this before, from other friends – Conrad was someone people claimed to know intimately, even competed over who knew him best. It was undignified, she felt, this playground game among adults. Yet she couldn't resist playing it.

'So you know everything about him.' It was less a question than a statement.

'Everything that's worth knowing.'

'Then you'll know he's married.'

'Who?' Rachel said.

'Conrad.'

Rachel opened her mouth and laughed in that exaggerated way she had. 'That's a good one. Conrad married.' Then, poised to laugh again, mouth open, she saw Alex's face and hit the pause button. 'You're not winding me up are you? Wait, I know—' her face folded itself back into seriousness. 'This is one of Conrad's delusions: he's married.'

'No,' she said. 'We really are married.'

'We?'

'Conrad and I.'

'I don't understand.'

She could only repeat herself. 'We're married.'

For once, Rachel had nothing to say. She saw Rachel registering her shock, fingering it.

'You said you knew all Conrad's secrets, and I'm telling you, you don't.' She looked down at the table. 'It wasn't love, don't worry.' She caught the bitter twist in her voice.

'When?'

'Just under a year ago.'

'It was for tax or property reasons, right?'

She wondered, not for the first time, if Rachel were in love with Conrad – they were contemporaries, after all, they had gone to art school together. Or maybe she merely needed her friends to be within her orbit, revolving around her, anticipating her needs, telling funny anecdotes about her flakiness, her perfect art pedigree. Any defection, like getting married, having children, was an unpardonable betrayal.

'When?'

'A year ago. It was a few months after I came back. Just after I moved into Conrad's flat. We didn't see much of each other—' the key, she felt, to so many harmonious flat-mate relationships '—Conrad went to the studio, I went to my job. We only saw each other to watch telly in the evening.'

One of those nights she felt him settle into the sofa. She was watching a nature documentary about birds of paradise in Papua New Guinea.

'*Alex.*'

The way he said her name, so weighted – was that *dread* she heard in his voice? – actually made the hairs stand up on the back of her neck.

'I might have to ask for your help with . . . with a problem I've got.'

She switched the television off.

'It's . . .' Conrad ran his hand quickly through his hair. 'It's about my being here.'

'The flat?' Did he want to move out? Did he want her to move out?

'No, here, in Britain. In this country.'

'Oh.' She frowned. He was thinking of leaving, of going back to Canada.

'You know I told you I came here because my grandfather was British? Well, that's true, and when I came they gave me ten years.'

'Gave you ten years?' she laughed. 'Like a prison sentence?'

' "Leave to remain" as they call it, as the descendent of someone British. What I didn't know, or what I forgot, is that I had to apply for permanent residence when they were up. I—' he foundered and tossed her a conciliatory little smile. It sat, grotesque and leering, on his usually defiant face. 'I forgot to apply for permanent residence.'

'You *forgot?*'

'I thought it would be no big deal. But then I went to a lawyer and he told me I'd missed my chance. It was impossible to restart the process. Some law they'd just passed to keep white trash members of the former Commonwealth like myself from settling permanently in Britain. I was back to being a tourist, with only six months leave to remain.'

'When was that?'

'Two years ago.'

'But what have you been doing? Are you illegal?'

'Not so much illegal as pushing my luck. I've been in an immigration limbo, I guess that's how you describe it. You know I go to Europe a couple of times a year?'

She nodded. Conrad was always going to Rome for the weekend, or to Lisbon.

'I've been doing that so I could exit the country every six months.'

'Exit the country?'

'That's immigration-speak for leave. I mean, I've been leaving, and then returning as a tourist.'

He stood up abruptly and began to pace the room. 'It's mad, I know. I own property here, I have a career. The only reason why I can get away with it is because I don't have a job. I'm self-employed, so I'm not on the system. But now I want to "regularise my situation" as they say. I can't keep going on like this.'

Despite his accent, she had forgotten that Conrad wasn't British. It seemed absurd that he should have to live anywhere else. She could imagine how lost he would be, without the London art ghetto of which he was indisputably a resident, without the giant new gallery spaces and the freedom he seemed to find there, treading their squeaky new floorboards every weekend.

On his face was a waiting look.

'What?'

Conrad swallowed. 'You could help—' he gulped. He seemed to be having difficulty talking. '—me.' His face had turned floury.

'But how can I help?'

'By marrying me.'

She nearly choked. 'Sorry?'

'By getting married.'

In her mind, the word 'No' was growing bigger and bigger, like a balloon, until it filled all the space there: NO.

'No.'

'What do you mean, no? You're not going to even consider it?'

'They'll never believe us.'

'Yes, they will. We have a history. We met through Ben. You can tell them what happened to Ben. You can tell them what happened to you. They'll be sympathetic—'

She stood up. 'There's no way I'm using what happened to me as a way to get you into this country.'

Conrad put his hand on her elbow. His touch was light but insistence. 'Please? Just hear me out.'

She sat back down.

'Okay, that was crass. I'm sorry. Never mind Ben. We can just explain that we met before, but only got together after you came back. We've been living together for four months.'

'I've been *living in your flat* for four months. It's different from living together.'

'But they don't know that.'

'I can't, Conrad. I just can't.'

'I know. I know it's too much to ask.' His tongue was lapping percussively at his words. His mouth must have dried out. 'It's too much to ask of anyone. It's just, I'm so scared.'

He began to talk in a low voice, almost to himself. 'For a year now I've been having to avoid Heathrow and Gatwick. They're so much tougher there. Last year I flew into bloody Cardiff and had to take the train, then I came on the ferry into Dover. The Eurostar is the easiest of all. But the last time they looked at my passport – I've "lost" my passport three times now – so they can't see all the entry and exit stamps. But then the Canadian passport office were on to me and they told me they wouldn't replace it again.'

He seemed to be compelled to tell the story, as if he had been waiting for months for someone to tell it to, like a guilty criminal.

'So they saw four entry stamps, each at six-month intervals, and the guy knew what I was doing. He looked me straight in the eye and he said, "Mr Emmerich, do you intend to go home at some point?" I almost said, "This is my home, you bastard". I didn't know what to say. I was shaking so hard I thought I would wet myself. I thought he was going to send me to a detention centre near Gatwick where I'd be with a bunch of de-commissioned Bosnians with Kalashnikov faces and then they'd put me on the next Air Transat charter flight back to Canada; me with my knees up to my chin next to the vacationing family units, returning to their four-wheel drive outdoor activity paradise—'

'But he let you in.'

'He let me in, yes. But he made it clear it could be the last time.'

Conrad splayed his hands on the table, fingers down and spread out, as if he needed to keep his balance.

'All right.'

He looked up, sharp, hopeful. She could see the panic evaporating like a pixelated image, dot by dot, from his eyes.

'All right what?'

'I'll make inquiries. I'll go to see a lawyer. I know someone.'

That dry-mouthed, preternatural sound again. 'You're serious?'

'I'll ask. That's all I can promise.'

She looked straight at Rachel. 'I never wanted to be married.' No, that was wrong, she corrected herself; she had never *aspired* to be married.

Rachel pursed her lips. 'I can't believe he didn't tell me.'

'We didn't tell anyone. We didn't even really tell ourselves.'

'So you're really married?' Rachel said the word with a scowl.

'I guess so.'

'Where's your ring, then?'

'We only wore them around the time the Marriage Fraud Squad visited us.'

'We share a flat together anyway. It'll be convenient,' Conrad said, in the days when they were still figuring it out, discussing the pros and cons of the arrangement.

'Convenient?' Her knowledge of marriage was limited to her famished teenage reading of the entire Virago Modern Classics series. If there was one thing the unhappy and constrained women who lived in those green spines had taught her, it was that marriage had never been *convenient*, at least from the woman's point of view.

'There are things like married couple's allowance,' he explained. 'They *want* you to be married.'

'Listen, I didn't have the good luck to be a woman living at this point in history only to voluntarily enter into the social and biological slavery that women have had to submit to for most of humanity.'

'Don't think of it as marriage. Think of it as a mortgage. I'll give you half the value of the flat.'

'Okay,' she said.

They went through with it, visits to Lunar House in Croydon included, where they sat on blue plastic chairs, self-consciously holding hands among a riot of Iranian dissenters, Japanese students, Indian women, regal-faced Ecuadoreans. They, and the odd Antipodean marrying a Brit stuck out like so many storks.

They had their papers and passports taken away. Then, soon after their wedding, such as it was, the Marriage Fraud Squad visited them. She remembered how a neatly-but-casually dressed couple – one male, one female – of immigration officers had turned up, unannounced, on their doorstep, not once but twice during the first three months.

Of course, they were prepared. They knew to sleep together, intertwine their underwear, have his and hers toothbrushes in the same cup. They used her bedroom as a studio. The strange thing was, they liked sleeping in the same bed.

'It's nice to have company,' Conrad said, at the time. And it was: they would read to each other in bed. Occasionally their toes would intertwine, or they would throw an arm around each other. 'We're like an old married couple,' Conrad joked. 'Just waiting for the Marriage Fraud Squad to burst in the door any second to check that we sleep naked and I wake in the morning with an erection.'

Eventually the Marriage Fraud Squad left them alone and she went back to her room. For most of those months they socialised separately: Conrad went to his art world parties or birthdays or pub nights and she went to her lonely repertory films in far-flung corners of London: in Hampstead, in Hammersmith.

If they ever bumped into each other at private views – both of them subtly or overtly looking for love – they avoided each other. They were embarrassed about being married, and wanted to keep as far apart as possible, as if someone would guess.

But at home and alone together, they were absurdly happy. Things that would drive real couples to distraction only made them laugh: they would burn each other's toast and giggle, or bicker good-naturedly about who last cleaned the windows. They took turns putting the rubbish out.

'We are really insanely compatible.' She smiled.

'But you were never in love?' Rachel said.

'In love?'

'I'm just wondering.' Rachel exhaled smoke in two thin streams.

This was the point at which she usually stopped telling the story to herself. It ended there, as a whimsical tale of a bisexual man and a shy straight woman setting up house together, giving each other companionship and a certain kind of refuge from the vagaries of real love lives, never mind immigration hell.

But it was precisely at this point that the truth began to exist. The real truth, such as it was, began to exist one night when they actually went to a party together.

Seated around the dinner table, someone – an unknown man, a friend of Jake's, one of Conrad's 'friends' – asked, 'Are you an item?'

They had looked at each other, both thinking: an item. Didn't they say that in the 1950s?

Then he surprised her. 'We're married,' Conrad said. 'Alex is my wife.'

She felt a peculiar thrill travel up her spine. She was shocked. Was she responding to some atavistic code, some female programming that meant she should quiver at the phrase, *she's my wife.*

They tottered home together that night, leaning on each other. They had taken to pretending that they were in a Victorian marriage of convenience.

'Dear Husband,' she said. 'Step from the curb with care. You poofs can't walk straight.'

'Darling Wife. How practical you are. Now we can go home and smoke opium and I can have my under-age boys and you can have your—'

'My embroidery.'

'That's right, your *embroidery.*'

They arrived at the door, still laughing. They managed to get the key in and stumbled upstairs. On the landing Conrad paused before hitting the timed light on the staircase. Then he twirled around in that deft balletic way he had.

'What—'

His mouth was on hers, his palm cupped the small of her back. He prised her lips open; she tried to laugh but something turned over inside her. Her body settled into a peculiar seriousness. He bent her backwards and she registered teeth, a tongue that tasted of champagne and cigarettes.

The next day they sat in the kitchen. A marching band stomped around her head, all wailing bagpipes and crashing cymbals. Judging from his bloodshot eyes, Conrad felt the same. She and the marching band watched him break open two eggs and whip them to shreds.

'I was drunk,' he said.

'And I was the nearest chunk of flesh. If I hadn't been there then presumably you would have kissed the bannister.'

He chuckled. 'The *bannister*.'

She was amazed to find there were tears in her eyes.

'Hey—' he started to move toward her, a spatula dotted with globules of fried egg in his hand.

She sprang out of the chair. 'I'm going out for the day.'

For the next few days they avoided each other. Things went back to normal, or almost normal. But they did not joke in the same way, or argue over who would go out and buy more tomatoes.

As for Conrad, he had a subtle, almost imperceptible air of guilt. She could see it in how he held himself perhaps just half an inch lower than his normal height, ducking his head to avoid imaginary objects.

She decided to confront him. 'Look. Conrad. I feel vulnerable—'

'Vul—' he gurgled.

'Because our year of probation isn't up. If this doesn't work out—'

'If what—'

'Our marriage.' Horrified by the garishness of the word, she corrected herself. 'Our friendship.'

The next week they made a Friendship Date.

'We're going to go out as friends,' Conrad said. 'We're going to have a good time doing what friends do. We're going to the movies.'

'Great. Popcorn. Don't let me have any butter on it.'

They went to see a film about a group of thirty-something Londoners in which two peripheral characters who had been friends and flatmates for five years fell in love, much to their surprise and the surprise of all their friends.

'I didn't know—' Conrad protested as they walked home. 'Honestly.'

She stared at the pavement. 'It's the domesticity of it I find disturbing. It's like they fall in love with each other simply because they're there, in the same house. It's so unimaginative and also tribal, like those men who need any woman in their household, their wife, their daughters, the au pair, to be in their sexual orbit.'

'Hey, there was nothing about incest.'

She stopped and grabbed Conrad by the elbow, forcing him to grind to a halt. 'But it's the same principle. It's not going beyond what's familiar, what's right there, what's connected to you. That's the definition of incestuous. We should be adventurous. We should be seekers.'

He took her by the shoulders. He even shook her a little. 'Alex. What's this about? Really? Is it about this?' Before she could answer, he kissed her again.

That night they went past the landing and into bed. Conrad fell asleep quickly, muffled in that curious post-ejaculatory stupor. Her body was still singing. She ran her fingertips over his lips, thin and dry like two pieces of kindling. Then she fell asleep, her hands in his hair.

In the morning she got up before him and prepared a giant breakfast. She was in the middle of scrambling eggs when he came into the kitchen.

'Hi,' he said.

'Hi.'

'Well.'

'Well.'

He sat down at the table. 'I'm starving.'

'So am I.'

Between mouthfuls of egg Conrad asked, 'So what are you doing today?'

'I thought I'd take the day off.'

'Why, are you sick?'

'No. To celebrate.'

She saw him fumble for a second. At least he was smart enough not to say, *celebrate what?*

She put down her fork. It rattled tinnily on the table.

'Don't look at me like that,' he said.

'Like what.'

'Like I'm a rat that's just got into the house. Can't we still be friends?'

'Friends?' The word sounded dreadful. Worse than *enemy*, than *hate*, than *violence*.

'Why are you getting so emotional?'

She was crying again. She hadn't cried in a year, now she was crying every day. 'Because this is serious.'

Conrad went to the studio, she went to her job. All day she tried without success to expunge the image of Conrad's face above hers, hovering in the dark, serious, intent.

She spent the entire day staring at the stickies she had posted to herself on her Mac. She had no idea what they said. Not since the accident had she felt so simultaneously outside life and in it. Her mind was blurry, distracted, but also buzzingly alive.

She decided to visit Conrad in the studio after work, as a surprise.

When she arrived he was leaning into a canvas on the wall. She saw the oily surface of a river taking place. He told her he was trying to paint the Thames. 'I'm going to become the new Turner. All those greasy skies.' In the painting the sky was full of shadowy birds in full flight; some were drawn in black outline. This was what he was doing, tracing them with a thin brush, when she burst in the door.

There he was, draped over the canvas at a lazy, athletic angle, the length of his limbs falling into his oily river. She stopped short of the door and stood still. Something had taken her heart in its grip and was squeezing it. Some terrible charge, almost electric, whipped through her. The weight of his lips on hers, the insistence of his fingertips, the hairs at the nape of his neck: small details of his body she hadn't even known existed.

She had to sit down; she felt faint, her breathing was laboured. The weight of his fingers was on her heart and his mouth had blocked everything from her eyes. His mouth had assumed a new shape, his lips grown thicker, bow-shaped, askew, like a sluttish cupid.

He turned around and saw her. He had begun to sway.

'Why are you swaying?'

'Are you okay? Alex?' He reached out to her, solicitous, absurdly gentle. So different from how he had reached for her body the night before. 'Do you want to sit down?'

'I am sitting down.'

'Oh, right.' He gave her a helpless look.

The sudden descent of love was like a heavy veil thrown over her head. She couldn't see through it, she couldn't breathe.

'I sound like I'm drunk. Maybe I am drunk—'

'What?'

'No. No.' She pushed him away. This was all such a mistake. 'I was just passing.'

'I'll see you at home,' Conrad called behind her. Then he added, helplessly, 'Thanks for dropping by.'

Thanks for dropping by. Is that something your lover says to you, the day after they have slept with you for the first time? Is that something someone says to you if they are in love with you?

She flicked through television channels, then the CD player, then the video. At some point she had three remote control panels in her hands. She settled on listening to Nina Simone's 'Nobody's Fault but Mine'.

If I die and my soul be lost. If I die and my soul be lost now.

She remembered going with him for his HIV test, his first. He was shaking. She held his hand in the doctor's waiting room, and she held his hand as the verdict was read out: negative. She held him as he shook against her in front of the hospital, underneath the tall London plane trees, bursting forth with spring leaves. Life all around them, and the shadow of death safely where it belonged, at bay.

She tried to remember the exact moment her feelings for him had changed, but there was no pivotal moment, no crashing realisation. It was simply time: both time spent together and age. As he got older Conrad was becoming more thoughtful, serious, subtle. As long as he had been light, flippant, indiscriminate, she had never wanted him. But now he was ageing like good wine. To her surprise, she found she wanted to sip from him, to have that blackberry taste on her tongue.

But would he want her? He had taken some decision along the line not to think seriously about men and women. He was looking for individuals, he said.

She knew the kind of man he liked: fiery, small, difficult to convince. Like her. He had said that once, even, when she first returned and they started living together. 'If you were a man you'd be my type.' She had gone around for days with another of those tinny echoes in her head: *If you were a man. If you were a man*. She had forgotten to say, 'but Conrad, you like women too. Am I only your type as a potential man?'

It was nine o'clock when she finally heard the key turn in the door.

Conrad threw his keys on the table. 'What are you doing there sitting in the dark?'

'I couldn't bear it if you slept with anyone else, male or female.'

Conrad stood, speechless.

'I won't compete with a man for you. It would finish me off.' Her voice sounded so faint, like the sound of a sheep bleating in the distance, eaten by the mountain air. 'You'll have to want me.'

Conrad sat down and looked at her levelly. 'You're telling me I can never sleep with anyone again, or look at men, if I'm going to love you. Are you sure that's love?'

She saw him saying this. She saw his mouth open and close,

open and close. She saw his gums and saliva. A word grew bigger and bigger in her mind until she had said it. Obscene.

He frowned. 'What's obscene?'

'It's not such an outrageous demand. It's true, I don't have any claims on you.'

'What's it about then?'

She wanted to say passion, but it was too garish. Passion was for Easter, the body of Christ and the blood and the wine. Passion was the kind of hate that executed people.

She picked the nearest word she knew. 'It's about survival.'

At the beginning, before the marriage, they had gone to dinner parties together, to private views, birthdays, openings. They had always behaved like conspirators, seated at opposite ends of the table, their eyes finding each other's, usually to mock someone's dress sense, or engage in a thousand other thoughtless dinner party cruelties. Such a close friendship, everyone said, admiringly. *It's so good to see men and women can actually be friends.*

It was true: they were friends. Although she wondered if their friendship was so strong because it had been born out of sadness. Before she went travelling with Ben, she hadn't known Conrad well. He had been Ben's friend from art school, a character on the outskirts of her life. Underneath their friendship ran a swift current of death and loss. They could hear it sometimes, humming and gurgling. Their shared loss gave them a resonance as friends which few of the people they knew understood. It was strange, she thought, how relationships built on sadness could be the most tenacious, the most rewarding.

Only eight months before they had stood at the Registry Office, surrounded by couples who seemed to be mostly from Ghana. The women wore spectacular bolts of cloth. The men looked ravishing. She was dressed in a white linen dress she had bought at a French Connection sale. Conrad wore a suit he had borrowed from a friend.

She couldn't help thinking how good he looked, Conrad and his wavy, gravity-defying hair sailing above the white of his shirt. He could have been a model. He was pretty in an otherworldly way, like those men in Armani Occhiali eyewear ads.

The Registrar, a bald man with square NHS glasses, stopped speaking. They both looked at him expectantly, their lips parted.

'You're married now,' he said.

She said, 'I guess I was waiting for "You can kiss the bride."'

'That's in church. Next!' He called to the couple in the queue behind them. 'Don't forget to pick up your certificate on the way out.'

Just as they were about to turn away the Registrar had leaned toward them, so close they could smell the mint-tobacco scent of his breath. 'It's such a pleasure to marry a couple who can actually remember each other's first name.'

He grinned. They grinned too. Although they hoped it was a joke. Then she kissed him. They kissed on the lips and she could taste the glass of champagne they had drunk before the ceremony to steel their nerves.

That night they danced together at an Italian Cultural Centre in East London, just them, no friends. They'd told no-one about the wedding, anyway. Around them men and women in their fifties twirled to accordion waltzes. The couples staggered themselves at intervals, as in a film scene which required stately and dignified ballroom dancing. They must have looked so out of place among the fifty year olds. Still the staff said *che bella. Bellisima*.

That night they got into bed together, still wearing their wedding clothes.

'That was so much more fun than I ever thought it would be,' Conrad said. 'Everyone should get married.' They fell asleep together, absurd liquor-smudged smiles on their faces.

'How can it be about survival?' Conrad repeated.

She wondered the same thing. She thought of her two-week sojourn in the prison of green, trying to find a way out of that spiky rainforest, singing bits of songs to herself as she thrashed through the undergrowth, the phrase inflating in her head until there was room for no other thought: *if I survive this.*

Conrad dropped down until he was sitting on the floor beside the sofa, his feet tucked underneath him. 'I'm sorry about last night. I don't want it to damage our friendship.'

'I can't imagine what sex has to do with friendship.'

'That's another difference between us, then.'

'Why did you start it? Why did you kiss me?'

He looked helpless. 'I wanted to.'

'Do you always do what you want? Do you just act? Do you not *think*?' She flung her hands open on her lap. They flapped about there like asphyxiating fish on a trawler's deck. 'Why is it, that men always do what they want? Why don't men – *queers* especially—' she gave him a savage look, 'why can't queers learn to contain their precious fucking desires. Everybody else has to.'

He gave her a stern look. 'I'm not queer.'

'What are you then?'

He shrugged. 'I'm nothing. I'm me.' He shook his head.

'Why do men have to be so short-term, so bloody promiscuous?'

'I really didn't think you'd react this way.'

She staggered back a little, drew a shallow breath. 'What did you expect? Did you expect me to get up in the morning and say, Oh, nice fuck last night. Not bad at all, for a fag. Surprised you could find the right orifice. By the way, we're out of coffee.'

'Alex.' His voice was heavy. 'You know me.'

It was true: she knew him. Or thought she did.

But what amazed her was how almost overnight Conrad had gone from being Conrad, a friend, although a friend she was slightly wary of, who she thought superficial, even disapproved of, to being this creature she looked at and thought, of course I want you. How could she not have seen it before?

And in the same moment in which she discovered she wanted him, she learned she couldn't have him.

She would become Conrad's worst fear. He had said to her

once, soon after they had first met: 'To be honest, I find women too hysterical. Their emotionalism can be overwhelming. It's like living on the lip of a volcano. I don't understand why they just can't take things more lightly. I just don't understand that incendiary mentality.'

Incendiary: to burn. Conrad did not want to be burnt, nor did he want to burn.

In their kitchen that night he put his head in his hands. 'I'm sorry.' At least he was intelligent enough not to say, 'let's just go back to the way we were before.'

'It's just. It's just—' she paused. 'I think I'm in love with you. And no-one's going to believe it. Because we're *married*.'

They laughed. It really was very funny.

When they stopped laughing she said, 'Do you love me?'

'I love you because you make me laugh.' As if to illustrate the point he laughed again, but is was a strangled sound, and his eyes were stricken.

She said, 'I'm so tired.'

Stranded together in the moment in their flat, they rose from the late night city silence which is never quite total, and went to bed.

*

Time curdles until it is only clumps of pain, thirst, sunburn. Walking along streams leaves her exposed to the sun in an otherwise shadowed forest. She tries to shade her face with a giant leaf from the plant they call *sombrilla de pobre*, poor man's umbrella, but the sun still lances her skin.

At night dreams percolate through her. She can't tell if these are fugitive memories, lost in the folds of her mind, or fabulous constructions, frescoes of faces of people she has never met.

There is a man she has dreamt of more than once since she has been in the forest. He has dark hair and wears glasses. He tastes of vanilla. Other times she can taste the salt residue of his sweat.

She is fingering the triangle of muscle on his stomach, her tongue searching, wetting the fine hairs on the inside of his ear. She runs her palms over the flat plain of his lower back. Muffled within the fabric of the dream, she hears herself think: I wish I could grow more hands, just so I could place them on his body.

Her tongue sloughs his cells. He hovers above her like a cloud about to burst, this unknown man, his face like a disintegrating archangel. He is speaking in abrupt code-words. In the dream she is trying to turn toward him, to get close enough to hear the turquoise roar of his heart.

twenty-six

SUSPENSION

She and Erica ate lunch together once or twice a week, ostensibly to discuss work, but they always ended up on more personal terrain. Alex felt almost guilty, having lunch together, as if they were breaking some code they had signed up to when they joined Michael's company. She always looked over their shoulder in whatever café they were in, just to make sure Stuart or Samantha wasn't sitting behind them.

They sat on high stools in front of the curved window of Pret-a-Manger in St Martin's Lane. A thick stream of people flowed past outside: a posse of Japanese teenage girls; a blond woman who had just slipped over the threshold of youth; a curly-haired, olive-skinned man with startling green eyes.

'This is what I love about London,' Erica said, between bites of her tuna nicoise wrap. 'Just watching people go by. I think there's more sheer variety in people here than anywhere else – their faces, the way they dress.'

'It seems recent, though. I can still remember the days when everyone in London seemed to be dressed in pinstripe navy and looked miserable.'

'Why did you come to London in the first place?'

'To go to art school, mainly.'

'I don't think I ever asked you,' Erica said, 'but why did you want to be an artist?'

'It was the only thing that interested me. Everything else I learned at school was about rules and interpretation. Art seemed pure, somehow.'

'I only know what I read in the newspapers,' Erica said. 'All those feature articles on artists in the East End and the Turner Prize.'

'That's recent. A few years ago you hardly ever saw press about artists. People are more fascinated by what art costs rather than what it means. It's a lifestyle thing. All those articles are about personalities; only the reviews of shows and exhibitions comment seriously on the art.'

'What's it like, being in the art world?'

'I'm not really part of the art world.' Here Alex smiled to show she didn't care to be. 'It's tough. There's a lot of people competing for few resources.'

'You get that in any profession, though.' Erica said.

'But when you're an artist, your work is yourself,' she explained. 'In the end it's not down to how well you've grasped the cannon of law or your experience dispensing aid in Angola, it's down to you, your sensibility. That creates certain pressures.'

'Was it hard to give up, being an artist?'

'What I miss most is having that buffer zone between me and the world. Objects that I could say were my response to reality. I miss the healing aspect of it.'

'Healing?' Erica frowned.

'The way art stimulates and heals; heals not only it's maker, but also its audience. If anyone I know heard me saying that they'd think, what a sad romantic. But it's true; that's why everyone does it. There's a huge power in being able to make things of real, lasting value.'

Alex was leaving out much of what she really felt. With Erica, she usually felt she could be open. She didn't know why she was holding back. When she had been in art school, the whole project of becoming an artist, then actually being one, had seemed infinitely exciting. She had dived into the pool of the art world imagining she would find herself there, that it would hold up a mirror to her life and all her questions about identity and meaning would be answered.

She wasn't sure if everyone who went to art school actually believed in the basic integrity of art, that it was the only

207

legitimate way to be a sentient being in the world. But she had, and so her disillusionment was more profound. Experience had taught her that most artists were not driven by a burning vision, or caught in the helpless grip of an obsession. It might have been like that at the beginning, but in time what drove them to create was a flinty self-obsession, fuelled by a savvy understanding of the art market.

Ten years after graduating from art school, the art world seemed to her more and more a cruel lottery, a baroque collage of personal ticks, rivalries, projections. Like a religion of which she had once been an unquestioning devotee, it had lost its ability to give her meaning and direction in life.

'The best thing about being an artist,' Alex found herself saying, 'is that your tools are what is distinctly yours. You're not hiring out your blood and soul and skills for someone else's purpose.'

'Is that what you think we're doing here?' Erica inclined her head in the direction of the office.

'More or less. Although it could be worse.'

'I really enjoy working,' Erica said. 'I know it's not fashionable to say that. But it gives me meaning. It gives a structure to my life. I meet people like you.'

Erica smiled. Alex smiled back. She wanted to say, 'Thank you', but felt embarrassed. Maybe Erica could make this kind of bald, unguarded statement because she had been brought up partly in the States. Whatever it was, Alex liked it, as a quality. And it was the nicest thing anyone had said to her in some time.

Fernando's voice purred through the telephone. 'I want you to come and see me fly.'

'Fly?'

'My trapeze class. I do flying trapeze.'

'Oh, like Rachel.' It looked like she was the only person in London who hadn't signed up for bloody circus school.

The catcher's voice rings through the upper vaults of the abandoned power station: One. Two. Three – Fly!

His body leaves the bar.

There is always a part of a second, a piece of time which has no name, in which he wonders if his partner is going to drop him. But she can hold him easily; compared to him, his partner is a giantess, nearly six feet tall, her body as muscled as a woman's can be. When she is on the bar she vibrates like a cat. He struggles to keep up with this solid stutter of her motion, the steely capacity she has to shatter into motion at any moment.

But after that moment of uncertainty his hands always snap into hers like a tool, an enclosure. He can feel the elongated muscles on either side of his ribcage, the ones that serpentine smoothly around his stomach. The cartilage in his wrists stretches.

She is hanging from the bar by her ankles. His ankles have developed to a point where he can do it too, although not for as long as she can. When he makes love he sometimes pins women down this way, placing his feet over theirs and turning their legs outward, gripping them with his ankles. They try to escape, laughing and flailing upward like fishes. He likes having strength in unexpected parts of his body.

They are flying through the hot, stale air of the upper reaches of an abandoned power station. The bar is suspended ten metres from the ground. He never notices the net beneath them, but he knows it is there. He wonders what it would be like to perform without it. His partner has done all these exercises without a net to catch her.

Two drops of sweat hang on his skin, shining like mercury. He is vaulted and begins to travel through the air. He torques himself into a jackknife on the downswing; the upswing launches him from her hands into a somersault.

They tried to be lovers once. It didn't work; they couldn't recreate the physical chemistry in bed. On the ground they became heavy with each other, lost their kinetic, buoyant connection.

There was nothing he could do about it. But he knows she blames him and this is why, in the midst of the grapple and the tumble he has just taken, launching himself from the outer reaches of her body, his hands searching through the air for her fingers, amid the fear and the risk of the moment, he thinks one day she will drop him.

When they are on the ground she wipes her hands on a towel, looks at him with that lop-sided expression caused by a light scar running the length of her cheek.

'It's too hot,' his partner says. She wipes her hands again. Her arms are covered in a thin sheen of sweat. 'I can't get a good grip. We'd better stop until it cools down.'

When Fernando had showered and dressed they went for a drink in the market café. Seeing him again in daylight he looked thin and taut, like a violin bow strung slightly too tight.

If in doubt, look at the eyes and the hands. This was a strange counsel someone – maybe Conrad – once gave her. If you like the hands and the eyes you will like the man. Or the woman, she supposed.

His eyes were light brown, lit with flecks of yellow, the irises ringed by caramel. If she licked them she was sure she would taste something creamy and vaguely bitter, like coffee or dark ale.

Since she had seen him last, his skin had lost the luminous brown of summer. Without it he seemed transparent; she could see the architecture of his veins, his muscles, just beneath his skin. Everything about him seemed dangerously close to the surface.

'What do you want from a man?'

'From a man?' She could hear the disbelief in her voice. He had caught her off guard. 'I don't want anything from a man.'

'What do you want from a person, then?'

She looked at him, his abrupt nose, his eyes dark and mirrored. He was all angles and sharpnesses. Next to him other men looked waxy and uncertain: their noses were too wide, their lips too thick, their eyes floating in their faces like jellyfish.

'I want someone who hasn't taken the usual package tour of life, I suppose. The school-university-gap-year-job-flat-mortgage-holiday experience. I want to be independent, but close. I don't want to have to struggle to be understood. I want to feel close enough to be able to get inside him. We will be close, like brothers. Like brothers we will never say: "I won't hurt you". Because we know we will.'

He frowned. 'You want to be the brother of your lover?'

'That's the closest I can get to the feeling. Like brothers, but in love, sexual.'

'Is that what your relationship with Conrad is like?'

'I think it has more to do with my first boyfriend.'

'And where is he now?'

'He's dead.'

Fernando frowned. He turned to stare out the window. She could see the reflection of rain clouds in his eyes, gasping and flailing in the sky like big silver fish. His eyes were flitting over the faces passing outside like a supermarket scanner reading bar codes. For a moment she thought he was ignoring her.

'You have to let him go.'

For a second she thought he was talking about Ben, but she had told him nothing. 'Let who go?'

'Conrad.'

'Conrad doesn't have to seek my permission to love or to leave the flat or to go to Thailand or whatever the hell it is he wants to do.'

'Do you love him?'

'Yes, I love him. Of course. Like a friend.' Her voice was stiff.

'There's nothing more?'

What did he suspect? Did he know, she wondered. Had Conrad told him?

'You can't imagine the two of you making love?' Fernando pressed on.

An image forced itself into her mind, but she dodged it effortlessly, from long experience. 'No, I can imagine it.'

'Everybody wonders about you and Conrad.'

'Who's everybody?'

'Everyone in the art world.'

'Oh, Christ, the art world—' she waved her hand.

'Please don't mistake me.' A note of apology chimed in his voice. 'I don't gossip. But everyone thinks you have a strange relationship, because you live together and you are good friends, but you don't have lovers.'

She sat back. 'How do they know we don't have lovers?'

'I don't know anything. I'm just telling you what people say.'

She had always known that she and Conrad would be discussed, at dinner parties, at private views, in coffee shops. She had been privy to such discussions, although about other people. Still, she felt exposed.

Fernando said, 'Conrad will never be there for you.'

'I wonder, though, if that's realistic. That someone should be there for you.'

The amber ring around his irises widened. 'Do you always ask of people only what you think they can give?'

'I suppose I hedge my bets, calculate emotional risk.'

'I don't really understand it, that kind of caution. The only thing we have to offer is intimacy, and the only freedom we have is to walk away.'

She absorbed his comment. It was typical of him to say such weighty, un-ironic things. It reinforced her impression that there was something not quite modern about Fernando. He was a figure from those old stories; the Prince escaping through chaos on a night-black steed, or his shrewd messenger. With his luminous melancholy dignity, he would have once belonged to the era of princes and castle plotters. He would be the wise but exiled figure, keeping his counsel, passing silent judgement on the depravity of his times.

She thought of him like El Greco in Toledo, where the great painter lived for many years, a foreigner, sociable but also solitary. He learned to resist gravity there and in other desert cities with large Jewish quarters in which he came and went, as welcome as any inhabitant. Everyone in its bars and ateliers thought him a bon vivant, but actually he was transfixed by an interior horizon.

She walked home thinking of Fernando, past the strip of bad Turkish cafés that lined their street, baclava dripping stale honey in the windows, thin pieces of rubbish whipped up by the hot convection currents of the London streets. Crisp packets, newspaper pages thin and transparent like parchment, or pieces of skin.

twenty-seven

THE BORDERLAND

She came home to find Conrad sitting in a darkened living room lit only by the reflective gleam of the City towers.

'It looks like a submarine in here.' She went to flick the switch. 'What are you doing sitting by yourself in the dark?'

'Where have you been?'

'Why do you want to know?'

'Because I don't think I'm going to like the answer.'

She sat on the edge of the sofa. 'All right. I was with Fernando. I ran into him at the new Tate last week and we arranged to meet for a drink.'

Conrad snorted. 'I've heard that five times already this week: I ran into him at the new Tate. How did we ever meet anybody before they built that monstrosity?'

'I thought you liked it.'

'I do like it. You didn't sleep with him, did you?'

'No.'

'But you might.'

'Conrad, I've just met him. I'm not like you, I can't jump into bed with people I've just met. Besides, he told you he wasn't interested. Is that what this is all about?'

For a long time – it must have been only a minute but it seemed endless – Conrad did not speak. She expected him to say, 'That's okay, Alex. There's plenty more fish in the sea for me.' But he said nothing. She feared this silence more than she had ever feared his outbursts.

'I'm thinking of stopping my medication again.'

'What?'

'It's just – I think I can live well now. I think I can be well. I think I can balance myself—'

'What do you mean *balance*?'

'I just want to get as far as I can from all this cultural chatter we live in. I can't think here.'

She struggled to keep up. 'What do you want to think about?'

'I don't know. Review my life. Do a post-mortem on the years I've spent here. You know how, in a time of crisis and uncertainty, you review your life, and things become horribly, grotesquely obvious? Well, that's what happened. I've looked at it and determined my whole life has been a cliché.'

She frowned. 'That's not true.'

'No, listen,' he said with the grim enthusiasm of someone who had just discovered the formula to the end of the world. 'I realized that going to art school had been the most reasonable expression of rebelliousness I could think of at the time. I didn't go because I loved art. I went to get away from the shag carpets and the station wagons and the ritual killing of moose every winter. The horse races my father bet on and my mother's shopping trips to the discount factory mall.

'I came here. I went to art school. I took drugs. I lived through the last part of the Thatcher years and the early nineties recession. I went to summer shows, to degree shows, to openings in Mayfair, to umpteen zillion private views in Clerkenwell. I bought things. I bought trousers and trainers and CDs and magazines. I got my hair cut every six weeks and took holidays three or four times a year. I went out to restaurants. And now I've arrived at some stage where all of that looks, in retrospect, unpleasant. Even dangerous. Like chaos.'

'And I'm part of that chaos.'

'I just want to find my true self.'

'What do you mean, true self?' She thought they had been in agreement on that subject, that there was no such thing as a true self; there were only versions of the self that came to the foreground through accident: what you experienced, who you loved, who loved you back.

215

'I mean I want to find out who I am now, without medication. Besides, my work will be better.'

'I don't see why you can't paint and take medication at the same time.'

'I just don't trust my instinct on drugs. If I do a painting while I'm taking lithium, I look at it and think, now that's a nice painting. Perfectly serviceable. Who did that? It looks just like a painting done on a mild dose of lithium. No challenge, no emotion in it. A painting that looks just like life, like everyday life. There's no art in it, no real distinction.' He ran his hands through the wheat-field of his hair, making it stand up on end. 'Maybe this is what Marsden-Smith saw in my work: a weak purpose, the lack of emotional tension.'

'Did you paint those while you were on medication?'

'Some yes, some no.' He paused. 'I'm scared, Alex.'

'Of what.'

'Of it not working out for me, as a painter. This is all I have to offer the world. If it doesn't work then I have nothing to give.' He sighed. 'Although sometimes I wonder if it matters any more, really.'

'If what matters?'

But Conrad wasn't listening. He stared out the window and into the wedge of night sky. Planes flitted back and forth across it like fireflies.

'I don't think I was properly sick until Harold died. I remember waking up one day and realising I needed to be living two lives: my own and my brother's. I should be living the things he hadn't experienced. I felt like his envoy. In a strange way it gave me the courage to come here. I always thought I was running away, but now I see I was trying to live fully, to realise my dream, because Harold couldn't.

'The problem was, I didn't have enough time and nothing was ever enough. No feeling was ever intense enough for two people: no sex, no satisfaction, no joy. I think that's when I become manic, when I realise most experience isn't enough, at least not for me. I want so much more.'

She was trying to absorb the meaning of his words. If she

understood him, Conrad's giddy intensity came from a need to live both his own and his brother's lost life by proxy.

'I want to go away.'

She sat up with a jolt. 'Away where?'

'Travel. I don't know,' Conrad sighed. 'Somewhere I can do nothing.'

'But it isn't possible to do nothing.'

'I'm going to try. I'll get as close to nothing as I can.'

'Why do you want to go travelling all of a sudden?'

'I guess I think if I get out now then everyone will think I'm one step ahead of the game.'

He had lost her again. 'What game?'

'The art game. The property game, the progeny game. Life is just a series of games; there's winners and losers and it's all far too simplistic. I don't want to be alive only to triumph or to sink into failure. That's the grand narrative of our lives and it's more tiring than a Victorian bourgeois comedy.'

'I never realised you thought like that.'

'You mean you never realised I was capable of thinking like that.' Conrad didn't sound defiant, as he usually did when they bickered, but deflated. 'You thought I was just another hyperactive male. You don't give me much credit, Alex.'

Maybe she hasn't. Maybe she hasn't properly perceived the people around her. Does she think of them as scenery in her life? Why had she disapproved of Conrad for so long, disapproved of his obvious taste for pleasure?

This is all I have to offer the world. If it doesn't work then I have nothing to give.

She is familiar with this desperation: to make yourself heard, to do something meaningful, to present the only thing you have to offer and to have it valued. She had once felt this herself, she supposed.

She can almost taste Conrad's distress. That night she tries to soothe his fear, saying, 'but there are many things you can do. Besides, you haven't given up yet.'

But she knows Conrad is right: if his painting doesn't work

out, then there is nothing. He slips away into the crowd, the mass of voices and bodies to buy Lancôme face cream, Camper shoes. This is part of who they are, they tell themselves. *I am the whimsical health-freak kind of person who buys Camper shoes.*

Conrad is afraid of being just another consumer, just another flat-buyer, holiday-maker, reproducer. Of course, there are worse fates. She is aware that his particular fear is a luxurious one, built on the good fortune to be alive at this particular point in history, when war, famine, disease are more abstract concepts found in history books and the foreign pages of newspapers than an actual threat.

Conrad also fears an absence of feeling, of not being engaged with life. She's afraid of this too, she realises. The understanding comes upon her like a wind blowing straight through her body. She is afraid, suddenly, for him, for herself, for all of them, her whole generation, if she could call it that. We want so much from experience, she thinks. Our expectations are so high.

Conrad went into the kitchen to make a late night stir-fry. He didn't invite her to chop the onions, as he normally did ('I love to see you cry') so she remained in the floodlit living room.

She watched him as he cooked, his beautifully strung face lit only by the blue leaking from the gas flame. Wasn't this intimacy? Talking together, cooking together, listening to the nameless tunes someone hummed in your presence?

If he went travelling, they might not know each other. She suspected Conrad was not very good at friendship from afar. He would go to Laos, to Cambodia, to smoke dope with backpackers fifteen years his junior. He might write her one letter, then dissolve into the continuous frieze of faces in the world.

She felt suddenly claustrophobic. She had to get out of the flat. She left him cooking and went for a walk.

She closed the door quietly behind her and started up the Kingsland Road, past the lonely ex-warehouses and grocers with their grilles pulled down. She stopped and craned her neck to the sky. It was empty, except for planes flickering, on some nocturnal landing track for Heathrow. She pictured the view of London from low-flying planes: the city orange and infinitely dispersed, like a burnt quasar, the floodlit barges in the Thames only pieces of candy scattered across black velvet, the thin veins of motorways branching into the night.

As she came to the curb she had that sensation again, that there was someone or something following her, right at her heels. She looked behind, but there was nothing, of course. Just the empty oblong paving stones, slightly slick with the night's humidity.

She went to cross the street, stepping out onto a pedestrian crossing, looking first to see if anything was coming. Most drivers simply didn't stop any more; you had to make sure they were going to let you cross.

She had got less than halfway across when she felt a violent whoosh of air only inches from her body. She caught a fraction of a blur, then a metal wind brushed her skin. Ribbons of siren sound, travelling fast, unravelled in her ear.

She stood stock still for a second, barely able to register what had happened. She looked in the direction of the gust and saw a police car, siren on, travelling at what she guessed was ninety miles an hour. It had come over to the wrong side of the road in order to pass a car in the other lane. She had looked before crossing all right, but the police car had come on the wrong side of the road, and she had just avoided death by two or three inches.

She hadn't heard – no, she had *failed to hear*; this was the language used in police reports, in obituaries – the siren. London was full of sirens, they screamed up and down the streets every day. Like all those other screeches, she simply blocked it out. The driver had managed to position himself between her body and the bollard. For a second she admired his precision, then she started to shake.

She turned around and went home. Conrad was already in bed. As she switched on the light she considered calling out to the ghost, asking, are you there? Maybe he would understand. Then again, maybe the ghost that would appear would be hers.

She ran her hands down her arms, her legs, around her torso, as if to check if they were all there. She felt insubstantial, like a walking shadow of herself. The feeling was all too familiar – she had spent a month living in that borderland between the living and the dead, after the accident. She had never wanted to return, but there she was again, like a truant child carted back to school by the collar.

She poured herself a glass of wine, even though it was after midnight, swishing its currant velvet across her tongue. She sat down at Conrad's desk, opposite the long mirror on the wall, and stared at her reflection. Sure enough, someone stared back, but she didn't know who it was, exactly. Her doppelgänger, maybe, or merely the Alex other people saw, the version of her that would live on in their memories, when she was dead.

*

Her torn nails bit through skin and sunk into flesh the consistency of roasted walnut. She put it to her lips to test for signs of an allergic reaction. She popped it in her mouth and chewed carefully. It was so sour it made her face pucker.

This hard green nut-fruit became her main diet, along with a spiked, hairy fruit that looked like a sea anemone and came in two livid colours: banana-yellow and blood red. When she opened up the skin she found a lychee inside. Perfumed sweetness flooded her senses. She hadn't tasted anything sweet since the day of the accident, when she demolished a chocolate bar that fell from a tree.

She hadn't uttered a word in two weeks. She couldn't imagine what words had last come out of her mouth and travelled into someone else's ear. Presumably she had ex-changed noises of fear with the other passsengers, maybe even screams. *Oh my God, Oh my God.*

She wasn't sure she wanted to hear her own voice; it might be like hearing a ghost. She always found the voices of the dead more disturbing than seeing their image on film or television. She remembered listening to a recording of Sylvia Plath reading her poems. She could still hear the voice perfectly, its attractive tone, zest tugging at its edges, those long Massachusetts vowels swamping the 'r's and stretching the 'a's on a torture rack. It was the voice of a bitter, grave, ecstatic young woman, even though the voice had been dead for thirty years.

She tried speaking aloud. Her lips were puffed and bleeding.

Opening her mouth so wide cracked the skin. Blood trickled onto her teeth.

'I am lost. Please help me.'

Pleased, she sat back, huddled under the shadow of her sombrilla de pobre leaf. She decided to experiment with emphasis. 'I am LOST. Please HELP me.'

Three toucans shot out of the trees above her.

'I AM lost. PLEASE help me.'

The forest went silent.

Diarrhoea cramps wracked her stomach. She was going to lose all her fluid again.

'I AM LOST,' she shouted, her voice strangled by internal vines. 'PLEASE HELP ME.'

twenty-eight

RETROSPECTIVE

She spent the morning after her almost-accident immersed in sudden silences. She would stop what she was doing – making coffee, writing a letter – to clutch at one of her limbs, as if to verify it was still there. She felt trapped in a separate dimension, guarded by a perspex shield, walking slightly apart from the rest of humanity. It felt like being wound in a bolt of felt, insulated against feeling.

She wondered what form her absence would take. She pictured her bedroom, the sheets still askew from where her body had wound them into ropes the night before. Her morning coffee cup with a little coffee left in the bottom, the cherry imprint of her lipsticked lips on its side. A bank statement attesting to her financial chaos, a pound coin, the discarded hairs that litter the floor of the bathroom and which Conrad was always complaining she never swept up.

There was a knock on her flimsy partition wall. She turned around to find Erica hovering uncertainly in the gap.

'Are you all right? You look like you've just seen a ghost.'

'Maybe I have.' She stared back out the window, where clouds were being hurried across the skies. 'I came an inch away from being run over by a police car last night.'

'That's been in the news lately; police cars killing people when they're answering calls. They're never prosecuted.'

'It's odd, isn't it, that when a person kills someone by beating them or shooting them they call it murder, but when you get hit by a piece of metal being driven by a person they call it an accident.'

Erica leaned against the partition. 'Why don't you come home with me tonight? I'll make you dinner.'

'I don't think I'm very good company at the moment.'

'That doesn't matter. You don't have to talk. We can just have a quiet evening.'

'Won't your husband mind?'

'He's away.'

They got off at Archway and walked for nearly ten minutes in the direction of Tufnell Park. They stopped in front of a big-boned terraced house.

'Here it is.' Erica fished a key from her pocket. Erica's flat smelled reassuring. Alex realised that every time she put the key in her own lock she expected to be confronted by that block of air, the condensed breath that drifted through their flat and the pungent muddy smell that travelled on its back.

'How long is your husband away for?'

'A couple of days. He goes away for work now and then. I think he's in Brussels.'

She found it strange that Erica didn't know where he was. If she were really married, she would want to know where her husband's body was, every night. There were so many nights when she had no idea where Conrad's body lay – in whose bed, in whose arms.

She stood in front of the fireplace. The flat had generic young professional couple décor; bunches of dried flowers, watery Portuguese tiles propped up on mantelpiece, posters of Rothko.

She scanned the photographs on the mantelpiece, looking for her husband, but they were all of Erica. In each she wore large pieces of silver jewellery. In one she sat dressed in black, stunningly offset by an enormous silver necklace. She looked like an Inca princess, sitting at a boozy alfresco table scattered with ransacked bottles of Sauvignon.

'Where's this? It looks like Tuscany.'

'Guatemala. At my uncle's house.'

224

She looked closely at the picture. The chairs had iron stalks for backs; the wooden table was peeling paint. In the corner of the photo she saw the razored leaves of a heliconia, the tropical plant which dangled its thick red flowers in a single woven rope.

'That's about a year and a half ago. I went back for my uncle's fiftieth birthday. He looks good, doesn't he, for fifty?'

She followed Erica's finger to her uncle. He was fair-skinned, with penetrating blue eyes.

'He doesn't look very—'

'Latin. No, he doesn't. But then he's Catalan, or his father was. My grandfather came from somewhere near Girona. He was a tough Catalan with flint-blue eyes, descended from a hundred generations of Cathars.'

That explained Erica's fair colouring, the mixture of Northern and Latin in her face.

'Why did he go to Guatemala?'

'To seek his fortune.'

'Did he find it?'

Erica smiled wryly. 'Thirty years after he emigrated he owned the biggest bottling factory in the country, the local branch of a multinational, several farms. He owned half the country, essentially.' Erica put the photo back on the mantelpiece. 'Let's have some supper.'

Erica lit four candles on a gothic candelabra. Outside, two London plane trees threw filigreed shadows on the walls.

'Wine?' Erica held up a bottle.

'Not so sure. I drank a whole bottle last night.'

'Well, you don't have to be frightened tonight.'

'I wasn't frightened.'

Erica gave her a steady look. 'You aren't scared by being almost killed? You know what I think: I think you're in shock, still.'

It was true: she hadn't allowed herself to register the fear she felt, after the police car incident. She really did feel safe there in Erica's flat. She was back in the land of the living, those who had supper cooked for them and could taste wine.

She watched Erica go about things she probably did every night: boil water, open bag of pasta, stir sauce. How was it that with some people, everything they do is a kind of revelation: look at those deft strokes of the knife; the way she hauls the hunk of parmesan down the grater. Erica would never bloody her knuckles, as she did.

'You've never told me which part of England you're from.' Erica said.

'Nowhere, really. When I was small we lived in France and Germany.'

'So you speak French and German?'

'I did. But it evaporated as soon as we came back to Britain. My parents both got jobs teaching in Brighton. Well, one at the University of Sussex and the other at the Polytechnic, as it was known then.'

'You don't talk much about your childhood.'

She shrugged. 'It's not that interesting.'

Erica flashed her a critical look. 'Everyone's upbringing is interesting.'

What could she tell Erica? She thought of the uneventful blur of her years in Brighton. She had been a day student at a private school for girls poised on a hill above the Channel. In the winter the wind battered the windows and doors incessantly. At some point they got double glazing and she remembered how silent it seemed, without the chattering of the wind off the Channel.

There is her fourteen-year old self, on her way home from school, swinging her flute case in her hand. Seagulls loiter above her like delinquents, horizon-awed clouds travel double-time across dingy skies. Her most vivid memory of that time was not of friends or dances or gymkhanas, but of walking by the sea at night in summer, the groynes built to stop the incessant erosion reaching like dark fingers into the sea, watching the cargo ships and oil tankers melt into the horizon.

'I've only been to Brighton once,' Erica said. 'It was awful. The wind was blowing and hurling pebbles up from the sea. I spent the afternoon in the cinema.' She rested her chin carefully in the cup of her palm. 'I hope you don't take this the wrong way, but you don't seem very English.'

'I don't feel very English,' she admitted. 'But then I don't feel very anything.'

They finished dinner. She watched Erica clear away the plates, her long fingers curling themselves around the crockery.

'What did your parents do when they heard about your accident?'

'They thought I was dead. They didn't fly out. I suppose they were just going to wait for Federal Express to bring my body back to Britain.'

'They must have been amazed when they heard you were alive.'

'They didn't seem all that relieved, or even surprised. Then, they're not the kind of people who would show surprise.'

She had always been an intrusion in her parents' lives. She had felt it even when she was very small. She would walk into a room and they would be sitting there, reading or listening to music with their eyes closed, as if revelling in something. Their eyes would flip open with a start at her arrival. They looked at her as if someone had inserted her there, in their lives, but they couldn't remember who.

Alex had always wished she had a brother or sister. They would have been conspiratorial, trading confidences about the capriciousness of their fate: *can you believe how boring our parents are?* To fill the long silent hours of her childhood she began to draw, and found she was good at it. More importantly, it gave shape to the silence that was beginning to swirl inside her, and which she feared would one day take her over. She kept herself under surveillance for signs of her parents' strange serenity. Maybe it was hereditary, she considered. Could you inherit silence?

'I knew the first time I met you you'd had a hard life,' Erica said, frowning. 'That something strange had happened to you.'

'I'm making it sound worse than it is. I feel angry, of course, that they didn't try harder. My parents were afraid of me. I think it's something to do with how you can be so close to death that

227

you're tainted by it. The living become afraid of you, like you're infectious. If they don't watch out, they'll catch death from you. And they refused to believe I couldn't remember Ben.'

'Who's Ben?'

'My boyfriend at the time. He was one of the people killed. Although I can't remember him. That's another reason why my parents don't want to know me. They can't accept it.'

'What do you mean, you can't remember him?'

She had never told her story beyond this point to anyone, other than Conrad. She wasn't sure she wanted to tell Erica. Could she trust her not to treat her as a victim? She had no interest in raking in the limp prizes that were a victim's due – a shocked, slightly self-conscious sympathy, often accompanied by a nasty prurient fascination.

'I know about him, of course,' she went on. 'He was a friend of Conrad's, I have photographs, a few memories of him from before we went travelling.'

Erica sat down and stared at her. 'You really don't remember anything about your boyfriend?'

'You know how we remember by thinking, and then I did this, and then that? Well, all I have are islands of recollection, but there's no context. I remember certain things from when we were in Mexico – we went there first – but even then, when I recall what we did it's as if he'd already started to fade out of the picture. I can't see his face properly. It's like a face I dreamed once, that my mind made up all by itself, and never saw again.'

'But you travelled together?'

'As far as I'm concerned I was travelling alone. It's as if my mind cut him out, like taking scissors to a photograph and excising someone. There's dead space where he used to be. Just a hole filled with confusion.'

'But you remember meeting him, knowing him—'

'I remember more now than last year. Some things are fading back in.' Alex put her hands on the table between them, palms up, like a sigh, a plea for pardon.

'I couldn't go to his funeral. The one time I saw his parents, after I got out of hospital, they looked at me as if I'd killed him. As if it was *me*. I'll never understand that. I stayed in their house, I was their son's girlfriend. They will never speak to me or try to contact me again. Maybe they think I could have done something to save him, or maybe even that I left him to die in order to save myself.' She swept her hand across the table, sweeping crumbs and granules of salt onto the floor. 'People don't trust sole survivors.'

Erica was staring at her, her face closed, intent. 'But you've been to see doctors?'

She saw herself being slowly inserted into a darkened tube, images of her head blooming in cool blue, alarming yellow, fire orange, her brain lit up on the screen like a miniature cosmos.

'There's nothing wrong with my mind *architecturally*, as the doctors say. I had a bad concussion, but that's not enough to produce the effects I have. My therapist has a theory. She thinks I must have seen Ben die, or at least I saw him dead. The shock wiped all memory of him from my mind. I remember seeing other people, parts of bodies, but I don't remember anything of his death. The only way to find out is to be hypnotised, but I won't let them.'

'Why not?'

'I'm afraid. I don't want to go into the twilight zone – it's too—' she searched for the word. 'Too *spooky*. I'm afraid of what I might experience. Maybe I'd see the whole thing over again and be back to square one. I just want to be normal. I just want to live in the now.'

I am living in the present. She had to remind herself that the now was now. If she didn't, the present would slip immediately into that waiting lounge where it cooled its heels before becoming memory.

She wanted to be in the middle of that current of the now, the continuous stream of becoming. Other people did too, judging by the manifestos bandied around by film-makers and writers: no flashbacks, no easy but apocryphal set pieces, like amnesia. No retrospective.

Although she went to see retrospectives all the time: Conrad took her to the Antonio Tapiès in Barcelona, the Wolfgang Tilmanns in Frankfurt, the Bridget Riley retrospective in London, in all of them canvases and photographs lined up like years on the walls.

Was it lost time, she wondered, those days when she had existed only in the present moment, when she had been only eyes fizzing to life in the morning like a television switched on, shorn of past or future, buzzing in the now? When she drank in the tapestry of leaves underneath her feet, the muddy squelch, the hours of warm rain.

She had fought the uncaring face of fate and she had won. Now she was back in her city, the place she belonged. She was back in the present; the God who had taken her future away had miraculously handed it back to her, intact.

She looked at her watch. Eleven-thirty.

'I should go. The tube—'

Erica caught her wrist, covering her watch with her hand. 'Why don't you stay?'

She coughed. Her wrist was buzzing.

Erica let go. She placed her hand beside hers, close enough to touch, if she wanted to.

Erica was one of those people who promised hidden rewards. She had the impression she was being handed a gift and asked to unwrap it. Was Erica promising to let her into that interior courtyard she guarded so carefully? She wondered what it would be like there. Yellow adobe walls; above them a blue wedge of sky. Oleander and bougainvillea, a jar of lemonade made with lemons from her own trees on a mosaic table.

A creeping awareness of what might happen stole over her like a blanket put around her shoulders by an unseen hand. She coughed again.

'Let me get you some water.'

She waved her toward the kitchen, spluttering. Outside moonlit trees swayed in the wind.

'Here.' She looked down to see a glass of water gripped by

Erica's slender brown fingers. They were wet where the tap had splashed them.

'Thanks.'

She noticed the fridge was leaning toward her. Maybe Erica and her husband had subsidence too. But then shards of sky were loose in the kitchen, posing at crazy angles by the refrigerator. The trees were flimsy, like kelp underwater they waved their arms about helplessly. It was like being in that surrealist painting by Dorothea Tanning or Leonora Carrington. She half expected a sunflower to come slinking up the stairs or unicorns to march through the door.

She knew how Conrad would handle this: he would be seductive, with his drinkable eyes he would convey his thrilling mix of vulnerability and prowess. He would take control of the situation, rather than choking and gasping like a dying fish.

She's a woman, she reminds herself. The phrase leers. She finds it means nothing to her. Erica is Erica.

It is a simple accident, that Erica comes from the country where she has had such a central experience, but which she can share with no-one. She can imagine Erica growing up there, toucans in the garden, sub-tropical pines standing guard around her house. She sees in Erica's long brown fingers the twigs she snapped behind her, trying to trace her route through the forest, in case she had to return. That she should find her working in her charity-advertising firm office in London seems uncanny. A gift, or an invitation. She can take it, or leave it.

'I'm not sure what your invitation is, exactly.'

'To stay here,' Erica said. Neither her voice nor her gaze wavered. 'With me.'

'What about your husband?'

'My relationship with my husband is my business.'

'Don't you ever think about betrayal?'

'I have a theory about betrayal,' Erica's face was serious, intent. 'Although I don't think most people would agree with it. I see betrayal as the best way to get close to someone. You're never closer to someone than you are to the person you betray.'

'I don't see how you get that.'

'When you betray someone you get closer to them, like putting your face up against a mirror and seeing them looking back at you. The person you're doing the betraying with is just the mirror.'

'I'm not sure I want to be your mirror.'

Now that it is closer to happening – she can taste Erica's skin, see the way her hair parts on her scalp, the length of her fingers, the roundness of her girlish teeth – she hesitates. Reality was about to puncture the uneasy truce they had established between them, both happy to inhabit that transit lounge between friendship and desire, before taking planes to different destinations.

Now they would have to struggle to be friends. She had never understood how people could sleep with each other, then say: let's be friends. If her experience with Conrad had taught her anything, it was that sex could be so many things, but friendly wasn't one of them.

The journey from the kitchen table to the bedroom is full of sudden silences and shynesses and negotiations. 'No, it won't be a problem, don't worry about the toothbrush'. 'What time do you want the alarm set for?'

A switch is thrown inside her, and it is as if one creature lies down and another morphs into being. This other self takes Erica and handles her deftly, smoothly. For a second, her hand on her waist, her mouth near her neck, she feels a rush of power. She didn't know she could be this searching, this hard. Now she knows for certain there are other selves within her, stacked against her walls like a dozen folding chairs, some of them maybe never to be opened.

That night they make love in the bed where Erica and her husband sleep. There is an underwater quality to it, as if they are trying to save each other from drowning. Their kisses are bottomless and searching. She can see the thin muscles in Erica's neck. She runs her hands through her hair.

She knows, with a terrible clarity, that this isn't love. She has the sensation that she is not sleeping with Erica at all, but with someone else, or their shadow. Then again, perhaps that was all there was to be seen, in sex: a shadow, a side shown for display. An elusive fish in the slipstream of identity.

Afterwards she couldn't get to sleep. She lay awake, her eyes patrolling the unfamiliar darkness of the room. Beside her Erica's breath came in regular, deep scoops. The trees outside the window waved in the wind, spilling liquid shadows onto the bare floorboards. In the distance she heard the whee-whee sirens of emergency vehicles racing up and down the Holloway Road.

In those stranded moments between sirens she thinks how she likes the lessons contained in the velvet folds of night, in elongated minutes, or hours that rush by like ambulances. They tell her that the lover is the mystery of another life, and a reminder of its fragility. A hot, slippery mouth, the shudder of a heartbeat. The wiry hairs, a body and the puppeteer's magic it contains, a neck that swivels in surprise, dexterous fingers meant for exploring hollows. The dreaminess of eyes, like the misty approach of a squall. The parchment of skin. How these details are magnified by memory until they are each enormous, pixelated. Until she is living a Delacroix life, dreamy and intense. Grainy.

*

The storm lasts for two days and two nights. The rain is insistent, violent. She understands now why people in the tropics refer to it in the plural: the rains.

A lightning storm clutches at the fabric of the sky. In the sudden wind the tall canopy trees wave like Furies. Charges seem to rise up each tree and shoot into the sky. She wishes a bolt would travel right through her and jolt her upward until she is flying over the canopy, beyond the ramparts of her luscious prison.

But no bolt vaporises her. Instead she has to endure their illuminations, the sharp ragged pictures she watches, like a jump-cut film, as the forest is bathed in metallic light. She is sure that with the next bolt, the next slash, she will see the jaguar there, or the fer-de-lance, or some unnamed forest monster, a remnant from the days when men were apes.

Controlling her fear has become a full-time occupation. Previously immune, it even invades the daylight.

In the days she steps through the stream forever, bitten by new flotillas of mosquitoes, drinking the parasite stew that is its water. Then, without being aware of the change in state, she is floating. Her eyes are full of sky. A current is taking her. The weight is off her crushed ankle and the water cools her head.

In the morning she drifts downstream, looking into a giant face that hovers against the sky; the face of someone she knew, not so long ago, but who?

She can't play her things-I'm-going-to-buy-when-I-get-out-of-here game any longer. She can't remember where home is, where she is even headed to now.

Out of the corner of her eye she sees a long green ribbon of a snake swimming beside her, only two or three feet away. *Lora*, she catalogues it. Their guide at Tikal had pointed it out; they had come across it sunning itself on a tree stump. Highly venomous. It will wrap itself around her, a bow on a birthday present.

But the snake ignores her, whipping efficiently through the water, its head held up like a periscope, preoccupied with some other business, like a City broker striding through the crowd at Blackfriars.

Her mouth is bleeding, her fingernails shorn. A fuzz covers her teeth. Her hair sticks to her head with dried blood and sweat. The balance of perception is tipping in hallucination's favour. She is being dismantled, peeled apart layer by layer. That was all she was ever, anyway: fog, breath. Two jelly orbs for eyes. Stringy hair, braided with leaves.

She remembered reading somewhere that, for every individual, death comes in the guise of what they love most. For some men it looks like a beautiful woman; for women it might have the trusting face of their child.

Death has the sick audacity of the enchantress, but it will have a hard time taking on the shape of what she longs for most. Because for her, what she values most, she is only beginning to realise, is at once abstract and everything: consciousness, perception, emotion.

It is fading now, as if it had all been a gilded promise, a delightful dream. She sees the world, a jewel floating in black space, whipped by wind currents. The planet was a lovely idea, but so improbable, really. Just like the faces she couldn't see, smudged by her own fear.

Her parents are there, waving goodbye. Bye-bye, darling. They were sending her to camp in France, to stay with relatives. They were always sending her away and then going without her on ancient history trips to Syria or trekking holidays to Ladakh, bringing her back oily weavings of yak's hair as a consolation prize.

They stare down at her from the forest canopy with their well-educated, cautious faces.

Bye-bye, darling. Have a nice time.

twenty-nine

YOU DON'T KNOW WHAT IT MEANS TO BE ALONE

Fernando wasn't just ten or fifteen minutes late for their meetings, but the full Latin half hour. This was one of so many things about him that were unfamiliar to her – the way he obviously didn't care how he looked; he would open the door of his studio to her wearing pink and red Peruvian slippers and shorts that reached his knees, some brown Chinese herbal substance – a remedy for shaving cuts – smeared across his face. He spat into gutters and smiled at passing strangers. He smelled pleasantly fresh and astringent, like grapefruit. In public situations he was quiet, at home he could be hyperactive.

They arranged to meet in a restaurant. As she waited she toyed with the idea of telling him about Erica. What did it mean, what had happened? She tried to get close to the question, but some part of her kept brushing it away.

She knew she lacked the hard veneer of the one night stand veteran. She simply hadn't had to deal with streams of people wanting to sleep with her. She had never been chic and knowing, a woman who attracted admirers. She was too thoughtful, too analytical to be one of those instantly attractive people. Naturally introspective, even entropic, she fed off the energy of other, more dynamic people, like Conrad.

But in spite of her thoughtfulness, her intellect, she left some parts of her life curiously unexamined: she had no idea, for example, why her friends liked her, or valued her company. She never thought very deeply about why she had failed to

237

build an understanding with her parents. Although she could dismember details of everyday life, the larger mysteries in her life, the crucial questions, lay untouched.

She couldn't admit to herself that she was genuinely shocked by what happened with Erica, by how experience could turn around and bite you, like an untrustworthy dog, as if to say: wake up. Notice things.

Should she confide in Conrad? Should she tell Fernando? But it dawned on her: she was an adult, finally, and adults had secrets.

'What is the matter?'

She looked up to find Fernando hovering above her. He asked the question in that formal way of his. He never used contractions and he pronounced every syllable of a word as if it were a distinct experience.

He gave her a canny evaluating look. 'Something has changed.'

She shook her head. 'No, nothing.'

'People tell me I am very sen-si-tive,' he said, his accent dismembering the word.

'Really? Why?'

'I suppose it is because I have met many people.'

She smiled to cover up her natural suspicion of individuals who claimed to have known lots of people. 'How's that?'

'Just all the crazy things I have done in my life, or which have happened to me. I was a very early starter. I developed quickly. When I was still a teenager I was already a businessman, buying and selling expensive French clothing,' he explained. 'Then I had worked as a chef, founded a travel agency for students in my early twenties. Although none of that ever interfered with my art.'

'I never did anything like that,' she conceded. She knew she had done less living than some people. She had always been too preoccupied with her own loneliness, with trying to work out what might be her essential uniqueness. She never even tried experience on to fit, as Fernando had done.

He was looking at her attentively, his head angled to one

238

side, in the way he might look at a slightly defective work of art.

'You don't know what it means, to be alone.'

She sat there for a few seconds, in a strange kind of shocked silence in which she forgot Fernando was actually there.

There she was, crossing the silent kiln-baked plazas of a town on the Central American coast, a drunken fisherman approaching and trying to sell her a day-old catch of crayfish. She saw the seaside winters of her childhood. She heard the weepy music her mother played day after day: Vivaldi, Corelli, Berlioz. She saw herself on that pedestrian crossing two nights before, walking toward her inch-removed appointment with death.

Why should Fernando think she didn't know about loneliness?

Less than a second or two after the sentence had departed his lips and she heard it again, like an echo, a reverberation. Travelling on the back of the echo was a whole train, each carriage full of forgotten things. This time it was running inside her own head: *You don't know what it means to be alone.*

*

Some places are colonised by dark and light in equal measure. Like the way the days begin and end in the tropics: the sun bounding over the horizon, then crashing back into darkness as if it were relieved to go. There is none of the elongated silk of the northern evening, that blue meridian between life and sleep.

They travelled for three weeks through that land of sudden nights, in southern Mexico and northern Guatemala, before arriving in Xela. She liked the name, Xela, the way it was said 'Hela', but with an aspiration on the 'h'. It sounded like a mythical kingdom and for awhile it was.

Xela, officially Quetzaltenango, lies west of Lago de Atitlán, the mirrored lake in which upside-down volcanoes appear. To the west the Highlands rise until they are a corrugated ridge, topped by razored lines of pines. On the other side of these steep stony ridges lies the Quetzaltenango basin.

The conquistador Pedro Alvarado had been here, hacking his way through the Maya to get to the plain. The city he founded was Quetzaltenango, called Xela by the locals, after Xelajú, the old name of the city abandoned by the Maya which had stood on the same site. It was a cold mountain city, not unlike San Cristóbal de las Casas over the border in Mexico, which was where she and Ben set out from that spring.

Xela was part of the administrative department of el Quiché. In the 1980s, at the height of the civil war, it was the scene of some of the worst massacres. The Army called it 'pacification'. For years tourists could not go there. Then, slowly, they began to come again to the Highlands, to watch the market scenes, enter into centuries-old colonial churches, to photograph the women and their head-dresses, a jacob's ladder of blankets folded and piled on their skulls.

She thought the women more beautiful even than the landscape, admiring them although they looked straight through her. She had the impression they were willing her not to exist. After a few days of this she began to feel like a ghost walking the streets, an invisible spirit from the past, possibly five hundred years old, when the Indians first found it necessary to look through Europeans.

Xela itself was not a lovely city. Most days a grey sky lowered over it and Diesel-powered buses lumbered through its thin streets, belching fumes. But all through the town she could hear the sound of running water, trickling down from the mountains in innumerable rivers, brooks, streams.

She didn't know if it was the thinness of the air, or the echo chamber the mountains created, but behind all these sounds – the trickling water, the cries of the osprey eagles patrolling the mountain-tops, the choke of diesel engines of trucks, she heard a curious silence, less like silence than a wall of choked sound. She wondered if this condensed silence were the sound of oppression and fear. They knew the government had waged a genocidal campaign against the Indians for nearly forty years, but beyond that they understood very little.

They spent a week in Xela before deciding to head out to the surrounding villages. They wanted to see more authentic, more untouched, scenes of Indian market life.

'Why do you want to go there, *mi amor*?' The farmer said when she asked around in the town for a ride. 'There's only *caciques*' – he used the local term for a powerful landowner – 'and the Indians. Both hating each other.'

He took them anyway in his truck, jumping over jagged rock after jagged rock. She had to grip on to Ben to keep from bouncing out of the back. Through the cab window she could see the gnarled hands of the farmer on the wheel. Dusty cacti sprouted by the roadside next to ragged pine trees. In stumped fields black-clad men gathered maize into conical piles.

After an hour of the roller-coaster road they arrived in the town, passing farmers battering their loose-axled trucks over the cobblestone streets, tailgates hanging open. They tumbled out of the truck in front of the town's plaza, no more than a broad tiled square, empty except for four limp palm trees and a woman standing behind a cart.

'Well, we'd better find somewhere to stay.' She excavated the guidebook from her pack. 'There's one place, Pensión Paraíso. But it doesn't say where. That's not much help, is it?' She squinted into the noon sun.

'Maybe you should ask that woman.' He pointed to a woman standing on the corner.

She approached the woman with a smile. Smiling was obviously for imbeciles, because the woman gave her a tight-jawed look of appraisal in return.

'*Señora, ¿sabe Usted*—?'

The woman listened, expressionless, as she talked. Then she began to gesticulate jabbingly up the hill. 'Pensión. Pensión,' she said, shouting, as if she were talking to a child. Then she turned and walked quickly away.

They found the pensión and went to sleep that night, exhausted.

The next morning Ben appeared at the bedroom door. 'Shit.'

'What's the matter?'

'There's no water. And the toilet's kind of exploded.'

They knocked on the door of the house. The owner turned out to be a small, soft-featured *ladino* in his thirties. He came to the door wearing nylon running shorts and a blue t-shirt. Even though it was nearly thirty degrees he clutched a musty blanket around his shoulders. He was sweating and his eyes were yellow.

'*Fiebre*,' the owner smiled a chattering smile, then put his arms around himself. Fever.

'Well,' Ben hesitated. 'There's no water.'

'Ah, hah,' the owner said, as if this was to be expected. He gave them another chattering smile. 'Use ours.' He gestured toward a door inside the house.

They went in, their washing bags hanging hopefully from their fingers. They opened the bathroom door to find that everything, including the sink, was pink.

The taps gurgled and spit a few flecks of brownish liquid. They trooped out. 'You've got no water either,' Ben told the owner.

'Oh, the pipes. We need a new motor for the pipes,' he shivered gleefully.

'How do you expect us to wash?' She was becoming angry.

The man shrugged. 'I brush my teeth in Coca-Cola.'

'Poor bloke,' Ben said. 'We'll give him another day and then we'll move, okay? The guy's ill.'

The three sluggish girls who cleaned their room did nothing about the exploded toilet and the next day there was still no water. She went to confront the shivering man again. His eyes had changed colour; now they were amber. She left him alone. Then, travelling down another hallway, she discovered the communal toilets. They were working fine.

'Why didn't anyone tell us?' she complained to Ben. 'They let us suffer. Maybe that's the point.'

'They probably didn't know. Anyway,' he shook his head, 'he's ill.'

'I feel edgy,' she complained. ' I think I'll go for a walk.'

'Sure. Whatever.'

'What are you going to do?'

He yawned. 'Read a book, probably. Maybe sleep.'

She left the pensión and walked the streets of the town, ducking in and out of cool wedges of shade. There was no-one on the street; most of the houses had their shutters closed. Even the dogs were silent. When she arrived in the central plaza it too was empty except for small shapes underneath one of the plaza's scruffy palms. Two of these shapes approached her.

The smaller boy, his face scowling under a straw hat, held out his hand. '*Chicle*,' he said, demanding gum. The other

243

thrust his tiny, dirt-streaked palm into her face. '*Tengo hambre.*' I'm hungry. She gave them money, which they took wordlessly, inspecting it carefully in the centre of their palms. Then they walked away.

'There's nobody around,' she told Ben when she arrived back at the pensión. 'It's like everyone's gone away. Just these kids begging. I gave them both money and they didn't even thank me.'

'Maybe it's a religious holiday. I was just reading that some towns still use the Maya calendar.'

In the late afternoon they went out together. They passed by a doorway where a little girl sat, staring blank-faced at her fingers. They had seen the little girl several times. She was about five or six and wore a filthy pink dress of frilly nylon.

'Hello,' Ben said, as they passed.

The girl gave him a terrified look, scrambled to her feet, and ran away.

'Another example of my staggering charm.'

They found the museum in an unsigned dark adobe house. At the entrance a tiny old man who looked as if he were fused to his rocking chair accepted their contribution in his bird's-claw hand.

They entered into the gloom. It was cool and dark inside. A life-size man, sculpted in what looked like wax, stood near the entrance, clothed in a suit of rusting armour. On his head was a stalk of white hair made from corn floss.

She stooped to read the card beside the figure.

Toniatuh means Sun God and also 'blondie'. This was the Maya name for Pedro de Alvarado. He was the conqueror of the country, and burned many people alive, or roasted them over spits. Alvarado is thought to be literally the father of the nation, for the number of Indian women he himself raped.

'Another inspiring story about our ancestors.'

'Not our ancestors,' Ben corrected. 'Unless you've got Spanish blood somewhere.'

'You think our ancestors behaved differently?'

They moved on to a drawing, framed in a dusty square of dark wood. It showed an Indian man, naked, tied down, his feet and hands bound. His genitalia lay like a sleeping animal against his thigh.

As she looked at the picture she began to sway. The world coagulated into bunches of black berries. Between the berries she could just make out Ben's face.

'What's the matter?'

'I'm dizzy. Could we get out of here?'

'But it's really interesting.'

'It's horrible.'

'Come on,' Ben sounded as if he might laugh. 'It's not that bad. We're just seeing the negative things. The kindnesses never get recorded.'

He must have taken a better look at her face, which by then was the shape and hue of a blanched almond. 'Come on,' Ben put his arm through hers. 'We'd better get you outside.'

She always read the paper more than him. In Guatemala she bought three every day. Each put car accidents on the front page, complete with close-ups of mangled bodies. The rest of the news was about armed hold-ups and kidnappings.

On page five she found a story about a group of students from some college in the Midwest. Their tour bus had been stopped by a gang of armed men. They were all taken off the bus. The men were robbed, the women taken away and raped. The students all went straight home to receive counselling.

Why isn't this on the front page? she wondered. She turned there and found the story that a Free Trade Agreement had been struck with the United States. 'From now on we are going to have to think service,' the President of the country was quoted. 'We must diversify if we are going to prosper.'

Next was a long article about so-called adoption orphanages. A lawyer alleged that children were being stolen from their families in the countryside and taken to the city orphanages to be sold to Americans and Europeans, making fortunes for the

245

adoption brokers. The whistle-blowing lawyer had just survived an attempt on his life. She put down the paper, picturing children wrenched from their mother's arms, hopeful parents swooping down from the north on silver American Airlines planes, arriving at night, clutching pictures of dark-skinned babies.

The article quoted a woman who had been arrested for selling children: 'It's the easiest thing in the world, having babies. I don't know why these white people can't do it. I'm giving them something,' she said. 'I'm providing a service.'

New travellers arrived in the hostel, backpackers like themselves. The two girls were from Michigan, or was it Minnesota? The girls wore their limp blonde hair pulled back in ponytails. On their legs were loose Indian trousers. Surfer sandals clasped their pudgy babies' feet.

While Ben chatted easily with these girls in the hostel kitchen, about sea turtles, beach towns, cheap restaurants and which border crossings to avoid, she did the laundry. The pensión had a roof sink and a washing line. She washed their clothes by hand, using a green soap that gave off an industrial smell and left her hands lined and dry. She hung the clothes up to dry, watching as they fluttered in the convection currents that bounced off the mountains. The sky was an insolent cloudless indigo. The sharpness of the light made everything look as if it had been trimmed by scissors.

In the late afternoon they went out to get something to eat. Ben touched her arm. 'Look at the kids. They have such incredible faces. I hope they'll let me take some pictures.'

The kids stood on the street corner in a ragged group. They wore miniature versions of their parents' costumes; the boys in brown tunics of a rough wiry wool that looked as if it came from camels or yaks; around their waists were black belts and machetes. The girls were dressed in a technicolour jumble of turquoise, maroon and white.

The kids stared at them with rheumy eyes. The boys – they were nine or ten, she judged – already had the faces of men,

246

even looked at her as men did. She found it creepy, that hostile, hungry stare coming from little boys.

'The kids,' Ben said, again. 'They're so beautiful.'

That night she lit the candle and placed it on the table beside the thin bed, watching as flames climbed the walls of the room slowly, painting them with caramel strokes. They carried candles everywhere as protection against electricity cuts, which were frequent. A wind from the mountains blew through the window.

'I want to go,' she said.

'What's the matter?'

'Ever since you showed me that it spells my name in the mirror, something's been bothering me. I can't put my finger on it.'

'All right,' Ben said, his voice tight. 'We'll go. Tomorrow.'

'I'm sorry. It's just – I'm afraid. I don't know why I'm like this.'

He sighed. 'Everywhere you go you see atrocity waiting to happen. You just see ugliness.'

'That's just the problem: Everywhere we go you're delighted with. Don't you realize how it offends me, how easy it is to delight you?'

He seemed to be considering this. He started to undress. Then he stopped, and turned toward her, standing in the vibrating half-light of the candle. It heightened the impression she had had the first time she had met him, that he was one of those in-between beings; between man and boy, man and woman, guilty and innocent.

'You have to work at it, don't you understand? I know it's such a cliché,' he said, 'but beauty really is in the eye of the beholder.'

The next morning is dazzling, like all the mornings since they have come to the mountains.

Their packs sit on the bed, stuffed and ready.

Memory is a strip of film. Someone has taken scissors and

hacked at it, so that only individual images remained, stunned into freeze-frames:

Farmers riding around in pick-up trucks, a cargo of Indians in the flatbed. The way, in other countries, people transport cattle.

The black, waxy hair of the girls who work in the hotels. The men have the faces of ancient statues.

The shallow lakes and estuaries. Birds frequent them, white ibis and the Jabirú stork, wading through the water with their sprinter's warm-up steps.

A Maya family walking in single file with a quick, skipping gait, the father followed by the mother and two barefoot children. They disappear around the sun-lit corner of an adobe building, their spindly shadows cavorting behind them.

A dark-eyed man, thin and tall, waiting beside her on an airstrip. Staring uncertainly into mountains, standing in the morning rain.

They are going to the airstrip. A plane will take them back to the capital. Unusually, it is raining in the morning. The sky is knitted shut.

They would never have taken the plane if she hadn't complained, if she hadn't wanted to leave right away. The rainy season storms had washed out the roads, and they wouldn't be clear for another day or two.

She didn't like flying, especially in the tiny Cessnas or Britten-Norman Islanders that buzzed like hummingbirds around the country. But the mud and scree that covered the only road out made flying an attractive option: forty minutes in the air as opposed to ten uncertain hours in a bus that might at any point have to turn back.

The passengers amassed in an untidy group at one end of the tarmac in the morning drizzle. The pilot shouted to someone, gesticulating at his watch. They had to get airborne early, to avoid the charged thunderclouds.

The pilot looked incredibly young, even in this country of young people. She put him at no more than twenty-three or twenty-four. Even though she was only six years older, she didn't like the idea of entrusting her life to a twenty-three year old.

She barely had time to look at her fellow passengers before climbing into the tiny cabin. There were about ten of them, a prosperous-looking group which looked to be a family – two tall parents with even taller children, about sixteen or seventeen. Then an older couple. Next to them was a dark-skinned, rather European-looking man, and an American woman talking to the pilot in perfect Spanish – a resident, she reckoned.

They settled into seats whose worn plush was grey streaked with blue ribbons, the kinds of seats she had more often seen on buses than planes. The elderly couple sat beside her and rustled magazines. The tall family patriarch a few rows ahead kept hitting his head on the ceiling. His two children buried themselves in their Walkmans.

The plane bumped down the runway and then, like the lightest piece of paper, it snagged on an updraft and lurched into the air.

thirty

ARCHAEOLOGY

She saw very little of Erica that week. She didn't know where she was keeping herself, if she was simply avoiding her. Eventually, on Friday, Erica slipped into her cubicle.

'Hi,' she whispered.

'Why are you whispering?'

'I don't know. I feel furtive.'

'I can't imagine why, with two lovers in the same office. Now, if you had three, that would be something to worry about.'

Erica nodded. 'I thought you might be angry with me.'

'I'm not,' she lied.

'Do you still want me to come to the market on Sunday?'

They had arranged to go to Spitalfields, so that Erica could meet Fernando, or the other way around – she wasn't certain. She told herself she wanted them to meet. They had something in common after all; they both spoke Spanish. She ignored the possibility that she was trying to choose between them, even though she had no assurances that either would want her.

She took a breath. 'Of course.' She stared at her computer screen, that blank void where she was busy depositing the best years of her life, her best work.

'You look unhappy.'

'I just wish—' Alex wondered what she really felt. She decided to chance it. 'I just wish you weren't sleeping with someone else. If it were just your husband, then that would be easier. It would still be tawdry, but at least I've never met him. Don't you realise every time I walk down the corridor in this office I think, I wonder if that's who I'm sharing Erica's body with?'

'You're not sharing my body. My body is mine. That was one night. It doesn't have to happen again.'

'The problem is, once you make love everything changes, whether you like it or not.'

Erica stared at her. 'Does it?'

'Who else are you having a relationship with in this office? That's all I want to know.'

Two red dots appeared on Erica's cheeks. 'Who *else*? Do you think we are having a relationship, just because we've slept together?'

'Of course not,' she said wearily. She felt like smacking her forehead. How could she step into that old trap, after thirty years on the planet? She heard echoes of ten-year-old impassioned conversations about open relationships, about sharing, about the essentially indiscriminate and unfair nature of attraction.

'I knew I'd told you too much.' Hurt bit at the edges of Erica's voice.

She turned to face her. 'You haven't told me anything. You haven't told me what's so wrong with your relationship with your husband that you feel compelled to seduce people—'

'I didn't *seduce* you—'

'You haven't told me whether you'd ever slept with women before, or whether that was even something that you were interested in—'

'I'm not *interested* in women. I went to bed with you, not with the entire gender.'

'You haven't shared anything with me. You insist on keeping yourself hidden somewhere. I don't know what you find in that place that's more comforting than intimacy.'

'I am *intimate*.' The red dots had spread. Now Erica's whole face was flushed.

'You're trying to get closer to something. I don't know what it is, but it's not me. At least I'm sure it's not whoever else you're sleeping with, either.'

She lapsed into silence, suddenly exhausted. She looked at the floor as she spoke. 'I've never met anyone who was so loved. Your husband loves you, your other lover in this office – whoever he is – probably feels the same. You act like you never asked for this but it was you who stood up with your husband and said, "I do". It was you who said, "I'll love you forever". It was you who pursued whatever affair it is you're having. I would kill to have a lover, to be loved—' she stabbed her chest with her own finger '—here, for who I am. I don't have that, and you do. And you don't understand what a luxury it is.'

'I see.' Erica nodded curtly. She opened her mouth to speak, but something – a telephone call, a message – took her away.

They met that weekend in the dark streets of the City. Fernando took her hand to run across Bishopsgate, dodging buses, passing in and out of the shadows of bullying bank towers, the same ones that only a few years ago had been bombed by the IRA, turning the streets into rivers of glass.

'What does that mean, that symbol?' Fernando pointed to the fleur-de-lys that huddled in the corner of the street signs of Spitalfields: Quaker, Crispin, Fashion, Fournier, Fleur-de-Lis.

'That's the symbol of France. The Huguenots used to live here.'

'The who?'

'Huguenots. They were French Protestants. They came to London to escape the Catholics. They used to weave silk. Almost all the silk in England came from here, for a while, even the dresses the Queen wore.'

They looked into the brooding interiors of the Shaker-simple houses that lined the streets, imagining them filled with giant looms, balls of silk, deft women's fingers.

Fernando bounded ahead to a roped-off area at the back end of the market. When he reached the boarded-up hoarding he stopped in front of a sign: MUSEUM OF LONDON. 'They are digging,' Fernando said. 'They are doing – how do you say it? *Archeologia?*'

'Archaeology.'

The sign explained how, during the excavations, before building more glass stalks for international banks, construction engineers kept finding crypts, burial grounds underneath medieval foundations. Not long before, archaeologists discovered the tomb of what was thought a high-born man. Rubies were still attached to the bony fingers, and a solid cross of gold lay around the neck. The body had been buried in cloth of green and purple. The surprise came when the palaeontologists examined the pelvis and found that the high-born nobleman was, in fact, a woman.

Behind the hoarding was her tomb. She had been trapped there for seven centuries beneath Spitalfields market, keeping vigil. Then finally, discovered on the eve of the twenty-first century. On top of her, the City is changing, it is finding its curve into the future. Skyscrapers have sprouted like glass-stemmed flowers from her stomach.

She looked at her watch. 'We'd better go.'

Erica stood outside the market at the appointed time. They all kissed on the cheek and entered the market, where they wandered, or tried to wander, in the crush, looking at gold-trimmed handbags, organic vegetables, bottles of hempseed oil, soaps, candelabras. When the crowd coagulated to a point where movement became impossible, they retreated to a café.

Erica turned to Fernando. 'How long have you been in London?'

'Tem years.' Fernando always pronounced it 'tem' instead of 'ten'.

'Oh really? It's just, your English—'

'I know, I have a very strong accent. It is definitely my second language.' Fernando spooned froth from his coffee into his mouth. 'When did you come here?'

'About two years ago.'

'What brought you to London?'

'My husband, he's English.'

'And do you like it?'

'I do, it's something about the English gentility, their fair play. Which as we know is just really a clever mask for their ferocious ambition.' Erica smiled.

'We're working together on this project,' Alex explained. 'It's about oil exploration in the rainforest.'

Fernando nodded absently.

'Environmental degradation,' she added, to push the point home.

'Oh, yes.' Fernando's eyes widened. 'Nature. It is very important to protect nature. Who is destroying it this time?'

'Multinationals. They're taking land away from the Indians.'

'And they are doing nothing to stop them?'

Erica cut in. 'Westerners are doing the work, really. The Indians know they are under threat but they don't know how to handle the situation.'

Fernando took a bite of cake. 'And how do you handle the situation?'

'With politics, advertising, press coverage. A certain amount of media exposure. Diplomacy,' Erica sounded as if she were reciting a complex theory she had worked out without any difficulty.

Fernando put down his coffee cup. 'I do not know much about politics.'

'That's what the oil companies want,' Alex jumped in. 'To get the Indians to give up their land. They'll accomplish it through terror or through force. For them the Indians are only an obstacle.'

'They know the Indians' lives are ruled by superstition and fear.' Erica shrugged. 'So they play on that.'

Something in her head vibrated, like a wire that had just picked up a signal.

It was Fernando who spoke. 'Is that really what you think, that Indians' lives are about superstition and fear?'

'I grew up with them, I should know.' Erica attempted a sweet shrug, as if to say, it's my experience. I'm allowed to present it as fact.

Fernando was looking at her intently. 'I think the fear they

254

might feel is probably to do less with superstition than with the genocide that has been their experience for hundreds of years.'

Erica retaliated by changing the subject. 'I understand you're an artist. What's your work about?'

'Space. I make things that contain energy and light.'

'You make "things"?'

'Installations. I make objects. Temporary experiences.'

'You don't paint?'

'That is what everyone thinks,' Fernando sighed. 'That the only kind of art is painting. My kind of work has no place in living rooms.'

'So you don't sell it then?'

'Only to museums,' Fernando replied. 'Or private collectors, very occasionally.'

'It must be hard to make a living.'

'Not as hard as you might think.'

Listening to Fernando, she felt a new kind of respect for him. He knew exactly what Erica was doing – trying to put him down, although very subtly. He perceived, as she did, that Erica was threatened by something about him. She was hiding something, trying to deflect attention from herself by being slightly condescending, hoping Fernando would be angered by this, and lose interest in whatever he had picked up about her.

But he stuck in there, teasing her. 'But Erica, you cannot be happy in this terrible city! There is no bougainvillea and the sun never shines!'

'I like that the weather is dull. It's such a relief from twenty-five years of blazing sunshine. Or the kind of heat we had in Virginia. In the summers you can't even breathe.'

Fernando frowned. She could see he was trying to place Virginia.

A few minutes later they parted outside the café. As she watched Erica walk up Commercial Street she felt a great weight spring off her. She had the feeling she had just witnessed a complex silent choreography. Fernando and Erica had been communicating in codes that were inaccessible to her. She knew what words had been spoken, but what had actually been said?

'What is the nature of your relationship?'

She turned, startled. 'You sound like a detective. We're colleagues. We work together.'

He gave her a long transparent look. 'You wanted me to like her. Usually that means a friendship.'

'Well then, we're friends,' she shrugged.

Friends. The word sat, heavy and leering, on her. Her mouth, dark and howling, her hands grappling for control. She couldn't remember whether sex had always been like that, like entering a wind tunnel, sucked in by a vibrating force she hadn't known was hers. The sudden rise of a stranger passion shooting to the surface, like a submarine running low on oxygen, its crew gasping as they opened the hatch into the salty air.

On their way out they passed the archaeological site again, the sunken sarcophagus of the woman and her ruby-studded fingers. What had been her passions? Alex wondered. That ancient woman had lived in the same city, recognisably London. She had seen models and artist's impressions of Londinium. The place they stood right now had once been a gate to the walled city.

Did she have a lust for power? Did her fingers stray into hollows, imprinting their rubies on other skins? She would have been a knowledgeable, deft woman, she was sure, vibrating with unknown inner tensions.

Now she lived again, if only as a bag of bones and dust. She was back in life, poised between the past and the future, overexposed in the harsh light of the now.

*

The magazine the elderly couple seated across the aisle were reading was called *Brown Gold*. On the cover was a group photograph of indigenous people dressed in western clothes. Behind them stood two tall white men clutching spears.

The man turned to her. He had eyeballs like those watery skinned onions bartenders used to put in proper martinis.

'Where you going, honey?'

The whirr of the engines obliged them to shout. 'Back to the capital,' she yelled. 'Isn't that where we're all going?'

'This flight has two more stops. These puddle jumpers always put down a couple of times just when you're not expecting it,' the man laughed.

'Are you on holiday?'

'Hey?' He cupped his ear.

'HOLIDAY?'

'Vacation? No. We're working with the Indians in the Petén. It's a wonderful place, the mission. So quiet in the morning, you'd think you'd woke in Eden itself.'

'You're missionaries?'

He nodded, a satisfied expression on his face.

'What part of the States are you from?'

'From CANADA.' He pointed to the miniature Canadian flag pinned on his lapel, in case she didn't understand English, she supposed. She noted how the little flags somehow said, don't hurt me.

'Do you know they don't clear gardens or fields?' His wife looked at her appealingly. She spoke in questions, her voice

257

tipping up at the end of each sentence. 'They just plant their corn or whatever right in the jungle, on little areas they've cleared away? Can you imagine? Planting like that? It makes no sense?'

'Did the villagers invite you?' She kept her voice innocent, inquiring, even though she guessed there was no such invitation.

'The government wants us there,' the woman said, nodding double time. 'They even give us transportation?'

The man's eyes swam toward her. 'What's your name, honey?'

'Alexandra.'

'That's a pretty name. Where are you from?'

'England.'

'Oh,' the woman laughed loudly. 'I told Rog here I had you marked for Australian.'

The conversation petered out. She turned to look out the window. They were flying about 12,000 feet, she judged, quite low. She saw lazy, snaking rivers that laid themselves like velvet scarves across the plains, glinting silver when the sun caught the nap of their backs.

They flew into a sudden wedge of cloud, and the land beneath vanished.

What happened in the minutes between her conversation with the missionaries, the wedge of cloud, and the second she regains consciousness will always be shattered. Like a triptych they will stand apart, separate panels of time.

This will be her final, necessary, island of forgetfulness. She will never be able to approach it, that grassy mound studded with lush threatening creatures – the boa, the puma – dividing the river of her life in two tributaries, as long as she lives.

She is spiralling. Something has already broken apart, either inside or outside her. The whoosh in her stomach feels just like when she was a child and she bounced on a big trampoline. She had fallen on the iron railing and cracked her head.

Whump. Her wheeze as the air is sieved out of her. It is just like those dreams she has always had in which she is shot in the back.

A strange noiselessness before darkness. She feels protective of herself. She wants to treat herself like a mother tucking a child into bed.

Silence shredded by the screech of birds. Leaves sprinkle down from the trees in a confetti burst, covering her body.

thirty-one

REVOLVING DOOR

'I would like to talk to you.'

It was Fernando on the telephone, speaking in his customary Interpol-calling-you manner.

She gulped. 'All right.'

They met in a bar at the end of Charlotte Road. Fernando went to get the drinks, leaving her at a tiny table, the last free one, by the window. As he fought his way through artists to the crowded bar she eavesdropped on the conversation at the neighbouring table. A group of girls sat wearing skirts and trainers, a combination she found inimitably unsexy, like a man naked except for baggy socks.

'He's an actor, right. He's away on tour,' a girl in a vintage denim suit said. 'So I phone him in this hotel room in Leeds and another woman answers. I hang right up. And do you know what, the bastard doesn't even call me back to explain? I guess he knows what's good for him.' A hum of commiseration rose from the other women.

She looked for Fernando, plastered against the bar, trying to charm the gay barman into a free packet of crisps. She felt sure she would never phone Fernando in Leeds and get another woman's voice.

Really, he was unique. He couldn't sing a note: if he tried he only managed a metallic hum. His writing was pictogrammic, like broken hieroglyphs. He didn't know the telephone number of his closest friend. He got the days of the week mixed up, as well as confusing Christmas with Easter. And his geography was terrible.

'I have never paid much attention to details.' Fernando shrugged, when she mentioned this to him.

'They're not *details*. They're important.'

'I prefer to concentrate on other things.'

'Everyone would rather concentrate on other things. But they can't. Because they know it's important, to be able to distinguish Christmas from Easter.'

'How important can it be? They both happen once a year. The rest of the time we do not think about them.'

He returned with their drinks and sat down. Fernando gave his Guinness a contemplative look. 'The woman I met the other day. What is her name?' He couldn't remember names either.

'Erica.'

'*Erica.*' He digested the name. 'There is something in her story that does not add up. I asked her when her family had to leave, and she wouldn't tell me. She would never be a refugee. She comes from the upper class, and not from the intelligentsia upper class. Her values are fundamentally conservative.'

'How can you tell?'

'Oh, it is not difficult. Just her confidence, her attitude. Most of all from what she said about the Indians. Anyone from a liberal family would never say that. They might think it, but they would never admit it out loud.

'I think she is an ambiguous character. I am just thinking of my own story. When you have had to leave your own country it is really not an easy experience. The way she talks about it, there is no trauma, no regret. She seems glad to be gone. I think that is possible when you have left out of choice, but not when you have been compelled to leave.'

'Is that what happened to you?'

'We had to leave, but I was too young to understand. My mother and father were in their early thirties, and they had entire lives to leave behind. You know, there are parts of your life that are lodged inside you like splinters, or fragments of glass. You would touch them more often if it didn't hurt so much. Nothing can pluck them out.'

261

They sat in the bar for hours that night, while Fernando told her his story, the candle flickering between them.

The town where Fernando grew up was set in a cleft between two hills. A river wound its lazy course through; at sunset it turned red, then orange, like a livid snake. It was a prosperous town; timber trade, minerals, livestock, education, the sort of town which produced many of the country's liberals, and therefore casualties.

Fernando grew up in this town with no unhappy memories, until the day his parents left.

'We're going on holiday, to see your grandmother,' his father told him. Fernando knew, with the terrifying instinct of children, that he was being told a lie. He went to live with his grandparents in the city and didn't hear from his father for another five weeks.

Then a telephone call in the evening. In Europe it was midnight.

'Your life depends on it.' His father's voice was barely audible through crackles and buzzes – the sound of the deep Atlantic, where the telephone cables that connected them to Europe lay. Fernando imagined whales' whiskers, as thick as the small branches of trees, nudging their words.

His father could not say it directly, but he knew what he was being told: tell no-one you are leaving. His family was already in Europe 'on holiday' – they had also told the transparent lie to colleagues and relatives they did not entirely trust.

Even so, everyone knew they were not coming back. No-one went on holiday to Europe, not at a time of interim military rule with imposed curfews and identity checks everywhere. It was a time when the international airport was full of the casually pained faces of people who could not openly display distress.

That night he was to board a plane for a Europe he had never seen. He went to school, as usual, putting his rucksack – the same red and black rucksack in which ten hours later he would put his plane ticket – on his back, now full of schoolbooks and homework.

His friend asked him over after school to play. He gave the excuse that he had to help his grandparents, with whom he was staying while his family were in Europe, 'on holiday' he said, carefully adding the phrase he had been given to say. It was a new experience for him, lying to his friends.

Then, what everyone had been waiting for happened. Fernando realised he had been living for months in an odd, drained silence, like the sound before a bomb explodes, when the air has been sieved of noise. The military coup came. Sombre marches replaced tango on the radio. The air turned as grey as the officers' uniforms. Even the leaves on the plane trees sagged.

Soldiers lined the streets and tanks rumbled through, followed by queues of buses full of silent commuters. At school, soldiers sat on the roof, looking for signs of subversion. The younger children played hesitantly in the schoolyard; the older students exchanged furtive glances.

The international airport was still open, although it wasn't certain citizens would be allowed to leave.

His grandparents decided to risk it. That night Fernando's grandfather put him in the car, still wearing his school uniform, and drove him in the opposite direction to the airport. Five kilometres down the road, when he was sure they were not being followed, his grandfather swung the car around and headed south-west, toward the airport. His grandfather had been in the mafia. He was well-schooled in deception; no lower-class military thug was about to outwit him.

He had left his wife at home making dinner for the three of them, for when they returned. Anyone who might come to the house to inquire about them would be given biscuits and maté, then shown to Fernando's room, still full of his clothes, his homework book open on the desk, an unfinished mathematical equation waiting for him to return and solve it.

At the airport there were military checks. No, his grandfather told the soldiers, he did not have his passport on him. He was not leaving the country, after all. The boy was going to Europe on holiday, although what a date, eh, to have a plane ticket on.

Then again, how could everyday people know what was going to happen? His grandfather smiled.

The soldier had the long mournful face produced by generations of immigrants from Calabria. He poked his head in the car window and peered at the boy. But it's the middle of term, he said, and pointed to Fernando. He still has his school clothes on.

His grandfather lit a cigarette, very casually. He offered one to the soldier, who accepted. As he brought the flame close to the soldier's face Fernando heard his grandfather say, in a tone that was unfamiliar and chilling, as if strips of metal had been nailed all over it, 'His grandmother in Spain is ill,' this metal voice explained. 'He is very close to her. He is going to see her before she dies. In a week's time he will be back in class.'

The soldier stepped back as if he had been bitten, and they passed into the airport. Years later, Fernando would wonder if his grandfather had spoken in some old mafiosi code, telling the soldier: you don't know who I am, but I can find out who you are.

In the departures terminal was a board with names of places Fernando had learned with the aid of school maps. Frankfurt was written next to Lufthansa; New York was followed by Pan Am. Other names were of nearer places, but cities he had never visited nonetheless – Santiago, Rio de Janeiro, Caracas. Then his destination, Madrid.

It was autumn in the airport; in Europe it would be spring. Some travellers had slung fur coats casually over a forearm. Fur coats were unnecessary in a European spring, but they could be sold, in an emergency. Everyone had the look of sleepwalkers: their faces intent, their movements mechanical. No-one seemed to be travelling with much luggage. At the departure gate there were no tearful goodbyes, or even hugs. As he went down the escalator with his grandfather to the place where they would have to part, Fernando had the feeling he was part of a silent cadre of voyagers, all of them aware they might be making a one-way trip.

In the plane he looked at the city below him. It didn't shrink so much as rise up, a black carpet studded with dots of orange sodium, as if it were angry and trying to snatch him back. The plane banked and flew over the broad river. He could see the lights of ships moving up and down its inky darkness. And then the giant country disappeared behind him, swallowed by the southern hemisphere night.

He awoke in the light. For a moment he thought it was a dream, and waited for the crucifix and the pale blue of his room in his grandfather's house to materialize.

He looked out the window and saw a desert blooming beneath the plane; russets, reds dotted by the brown and green forms of what looked like shrubs. We are flying over Africa, he thought, excited. But it wasn't Morocco, or Tunisia; it was the landscape of the country that would be his home for years to come.

Half an hour later the plane touched down in Madrid. His father was there to greet him. He had not seen his father in five weeks and at first he did not quite recognize him; he seemed so much paler, less substantial than he remembered. After they had embraced each other his father lit a cigarette. As he watched him bring the lit match up to his face Fernando saw that his father's hands were shaking.

They reached the city centre in a taxi. There were tanks and soldiers in this city too. The closer they got to the centre, the more the streets were full of shouting people. Placards held messages he could not quite see; underneath them were faces with indeterminate expressions. He could not tell if they were really angry, or if it were some kind of game, a street theatre.

'Franco is dead,' his father said, casting a glance at the taxi driver. 'That's why there are these demonstrations. People are waking up from a long sleep.'

Fernando thought of the sleepwalkers in the airport.

A tank blocked the road and no traffic could get through. On all sides were young people of a type Fernando had not seen at home in months, they had long hair, wore t-shirts openly in the street, seemed underdressed. At home such men had been forced to shave their beards and cut their hair, to avoid random detention.

'Why are they angry?' he asked his father.

'They're not. They're protesting.' His father tapped the taxi driver on the shoulder. 'We have to get out now.' He grabbed Fernando's arm.

Out on the street they found themselves in the middle of a throng. It was ten o'clock in the morning. Cafés had closed for the demonstration, fearing vandalism. Someone said there were tanks coming up from the south, to break up the demonstration and to clear the streets.

His father dragged him toward a hotel. They entered, negotiating the suspicious gaze of the doorman, through a revolving door. Its panels were made of wood and it squeaked slightly as it turned on its circular hinge.

Fernando had never seen a revolving door before. He got in the partition behind his father and then, once he was in, couldn't find the way out. They went round and round, Fernando wide-eyed, staring at the people shouting in the street, the hotel reception staff, each whipping around in separate panels of the door, kept in separate dimensions. The world was spinning. His father was in the next partition, saying something he could not quite hear, pointing to the hotel lobby, mouthing, get out, get out.

But how? He thought of the biscuits his grandmother was baking on the other side of the Atlantic. They would be done now. Still warm, waiting for his mouth.

'Get me out of this place,' he yelled at his father through the glass partition that separated them. 'I want to go home.' Fernando put his hands on the glass, pushed at the door so that it spun even faster.

He saw his father's agonized expression, his face slightly distorted through the glass and the reflection of the demonstrators. They went round and round in the door like that for a few seconds, neither of them able to leave.

*

Twelve years after being let out of the revolving door, Fernando arrived in London without speaking a word of English. Within three weeks he could say *cigarettes, Underground, please, thank you, cake,* and *piss off*. Over the coming years these words would form the cornerstone not just of his vocabulary but of his whole understanding of life in England.

It was the obvious place for someone like him, someone essentially countryless, to end up. The city teemed with other people who had been nudged by the capricious desires of fate onto England's shores.

Even so, many things were strange to him: the creeping, sideways cold, the diluted northern light, the lack of animation in the faces, the fact that people did not seem to talk for the simple pleasure of talking – they seemed to feel they needed to have something to say.

He found himself gravitating toward other foreigners, striking conversations up indiscriminately and meaninglessly with a Brazilian waiter, Spanish shop assistants, Italian fruit sellers. Even the Danes and the Germans would happily chat in the street, knowing that the interaction was going nowhere and comfortable with the thought that they would walk away and never see each other again. But the English were wary of talking to him. At the first sound of his accent he could see them thinking: what do you want from me?

By the end of his first two years in London the only English people Fernando knew were his fellow students at university. He told himself this was enough, but still he couldn't explain where he had gone wrong: he had certainly tried to meet people, through random interactions in cafés, in clubs, on Sunday visits to art galleries. These struck-up conversations sometimes led to short-term friendships, but for the most part they had been marred by that question hanging in the other person's mind: where is this taking me?

Where exactly did these English people want to go? Did they want to board a plane and arrive in a more exciting land? He doubted it; in so many Londoners, especially young ones, he saw bricklayers, builders. They were constructing houses for themselves; the plans were set, the furniture un-rearrangeable. No unplanned events or accidents would take place inside their walls. There were smoke alarms and burglar alarms, even a garden, high-walled and private, into which guests were rarely admitted on the pretext of the weather being bad.

After eight years Fernando was surprised to find himself still in London. He couldn't imagine what was keeping him there. He did love London, he reminded himself: its battleship architecture, the necklace of lights reflected on the river at night from the Hungerford footbridge. Each time he thought of these things he renewed his commitment to the city, as if he were thinking of the best traits in a lover whom he had secretly many times thought of leaving.

Of the lovers themselves, they had come and gone. Most of them were like him, foreigners in London for a specific reason, to work or to study, then to return to more organised or sunny countries. But he had stayed. It was not until he entered the third year of his thirties, two years after the last of these loves had departed, that he perceived he was lonely.

thirty-two

RETURN TO DELIGHT

It began as the usual kind of conversation they had late at night, when Conrad had come home from another frustrating day in the studio spent honing his technique. After days like these, days that every artist endures, when they are convinced they are getting nowhere, Conrad felt a need to reaffirm his commitment to painting.

'What I love about the individual object is that it doesn't need to tell a story,' he told her, his voice full of hard rapture. 'I'm sick of stories. Sometimes I feel I'm choking on them.'

'What do you mean, stories?'

'I mean you read the *Evening Standard*, say, and someone's been stabbed by a maniac out of community care on day leave. There's a story behind the whole story: the negligent official, the tragic story of the maniac, the woman's mother, the pain of her kids, the woman who will be forever disfigured. Then you go to see a film. Another bloody story. People telling their life stories on talk shows. Really I'm just sick of this cause and effect, which is only accidents after all, strung together to make a convincing narrative so we can all feel a little bit better about existing.'

He drew a breath. 'Painting allows me to concentrate on the object. It has a clean independence. I want my life to be like that ideally: not something you read and think, oh then and then and then. I don't want to explain my life to anyone.'

When Conrad spoke again the hard, invincible tone in which he was speaking had dissolved, and it was like an old man had taken up residence inside his voice. 'I need to believe in escape, in the possibility of escape. Otherwise I'm nothing, not as an artist, not as a person.'

Fernando had told her something similar. He had escaped certain death, or his family had. 'Sometimes I feel I'm moving backwards through life. I'm travelling away from death, not toward it.'

She wondered if she were on that same journey: a reverse life, where everything is becoming more urgent and pungent with each day lived. Perhaps that journey was the preserve of people who were haunted by their pasts, by some sudden rupture which had torn them forever from their present and hurtled them, unwillingly, into an uncertain future. They spend the rest of their lives skating back into childhood; a journey back into innocence, a return to delight.

As for Conrad, it was clear he was changing. He seemed haunted, although not by the ghost she sometimes felt in their flat. He was being haunted by a smell, the fume of old wooden houses, by the way light fell, filtered through a net of oak tree leaves, covering the floorboards of the old house in a filigree pattern.

He was haunted by the tufts of pussywillows and ducks sliding across iced rivers and the startled deer at the edge of their field. By his brother Harold's red snowsuit, the one embroidered at the hem of the jacket with Inuit figures, men swathed in seal fur, spearing fish.

He remembered watching his brother's twelve-year-old face growing longer by the day, his jaw stiffening, his eyes darkening. Watching his brother become the man he would never live to be.

At thirty-five memories were coming to the surface, as if sunk in a wreck where they have been kept pristine by cold and pressure. Crazy Carpets, submerged for twenty years, were bubbling up: the way they would never stay rolled, how they used to take them out in November, before there was really any snow, and slide over the frosted tufts of field grass. Or clouds of blackflies in August and the way the lake turned the colour of red wine as the sun went down.

He remembers the grandfather clock that stood sentinel in the living room, marking the hours that passed like frozen sap in that house. Conrad realized he had never really tasted the pine-bitter sweetness of those elongated hours. For so long he was poised, like an animal sat back on its haunches, to spring out of the grip of family, of time, of winter. He spent every year of his life in that position, coiled in the posture of an angry penitent, waiting for release.

The day he left he watched his father walk away from him and into the blue afternoon, silent and a little bent from years of chopping and chainsawing.

He wouldn't come to the airport, so Conrad went by himself and sat in the small terminal waiting for his plane, surrounded by families: the fathers wearing John Deere baseball caps, the women dangling keys to muddy pick-up trucks, anxious-looking children there to welcome Grandma or Grandpa. Even then he knew he would never be one of these family men, waiting in a small provincial airport for planes that came from distant glass cities, like messengers from the Gods.

He was two hours early, so he went to the window and watched the occasional jet land on a runway carved from bog and pine trees. That afternoon he took one of these planes. It arced over a green mat of conifers, a waterlogged province of thin lakes and corrugated bare rock so that from the air it looked like a skinned fish. And somewhere on the back of that fish, looking into the sky to catch the arrowed thrust of the plane, was his father, a shadowed forest spectator, his eyes squeezed shut by the sun.

'What's the matter, Alex? Why are you so angry with me? You've been furious with me for months.'

She was silent, ransacking herself for an answer she thought Conrad would tolerate. She couldn't find one, so she said the first thing that came to mind.

'I keep feeling that you want to be let off the hook.'

He frowned. 'What hook?'

'When you talk about painting you're so committed, so certain, and still you can't commit to the most basic things.'

His lips dipped down in an expression of exquisite disapproval, like an ancient prince. 'What kind of commitment are you thinking of?'

She shrugged. 'A relationship, for instance. A real relationship, where you might have to confront unpleasant things about yourself.'

'You think you have a right to lecture me on commitment, just because your boyfriend was killed.'

'That's not fair.'

'No it's not,' he shook his head. 'But that's how it is. And another thing: if Ben hadn't been killed you would have found some other way to be so dark, so judgemental, so fixated on your inner life. You're so dark, obsessed with the validity of your own bloody experience. You're eating yourself alive.' He shivered.

'*Dark.*' Oh, yes, she was one of a legion of so many darkened women. She marched with them in a single black column, a female troupe of gladiators. Too-heavy women burdened with the notion of themselves, whose internal dramas were not just about love and reproduction. She was restless, obsessed with her inner narrative. But at the same time she wanted to slash through the obscenely lush territory of the self, to get somewhere prowled by horizons, somewhere beyond the usual story of women's lives: beyond love, beyond sex, family, progeny.

'*Alex.*'

The way he said her name, it had the ring of death. When she looked at him he seemed to be expanding and contracting, but imperceptibly, like an idol or a ghoul.

'What?'

'I've been wanting to tell you this for some time. I think you should move out.'

'Move out?'

'I mean, not right away. But I think you should start thinking about having a place of your own.'

272

'That's the only power you have over me and you're using it just to make your point.'

'No, I'm not. Really.' He sounded tired. 'You've been jealous when I don't come home. I'm becoming afraid to introduce people to you. Look how you treated Fernando.'

'I was perfectly polite to Fernando.'

'Polite? You had your claws out. I thought I was going to have to take one of us to Casualty.'

'You think what I feel is *jealousy*?' She stretched the last word to within an inch of its life.

'Yep,' he nodded. 'I do.'

'When I've gone through hell, really hell—' she stopped to gather breath. 'When we were married, and then suddenly you didn't want to be with me—'

'We were never married, not in that way.'

'We slept together. All that time, when you were bringing your Rent-a-Redheads home, I put up with them traipsing through this place, your one-night conquests, your ego-assuaging sex partners, your consumption of people. I learned to live with it by telling myself: Conrad is my friend. And then I find someone I really like, someone you wanted, but who made it clear he didn't want you, and you throw me out.'

'You're only interested in him because you think I wanted him,' Conrad parried. 'You can't get really excited about someone unless you think they're claimed by someone else. That way you don't have to contemplate real risk. Look at that woman you work with – she's got a husband and a lover in the office. Bonanza.'

She felt her face grow hot. 'That's not sexual.'

'Maybe it isn't,' he agreed. 'But the result is the same. Anyway, I'm not throwing you out,' he paused. 'Or if I am, it's not because of Fernando.'

'Yes you are, and it makes us worse than little children in a playground. It makes a mockery of our lives as adults.'

'I know you're perfectly capable of taking care of yourself,' he countered.

'I don't live here because I'm an emotional invalid, but

273

because I *want to*,' she shouted. 'Because I want your company. I want to be with you. I had to live here, until recently, under the law. The law. Remember.'

'And now that's all solved,' Conrad said smoothly. 'I think it's time to make a clean break, strike out on your own. You'll feel better—'

'—*you'll* feel better—'

'Our *friendship*,' he seemed to say the word as a last minute stand in for relationship. 'Our friendship will improve.'

'We don't have a friendship.' Her voice was dull. 'It's all been the most incredible sham.' She paused. 'I'm so tired of evasive people. I'm tired of you, of everyone.'

Conrad folded his arms on his chest and stared at her. '*Evasive*.' He bit on his lower lip, pinning the word there. 'You know, Alex, you're the one who's evasive. You've done nothing but evade since you came back. You gave up making work just like that—' Conrad clicked his fingers '—saying, Oh, the inspiration has left me, the desire. Well I have news for you. Art is hard work. Nobody ever said the inspiration would be there, day after day. You get through those inspirationless days on tenacity. But you won't do the slog, not in your professional life, not in your personal life. You think I'm the one who's taken the giant opt-out clause offered to us. That I'm the eternal child, wallowing in a life of emotional irresponsibility and moral mediocrity.'

His voice was taut with a strange anger.

'This isn't about art, is it?' she said. 'It's about Ben.'

'When you first came back I thought, okay, she doesn't remember. Who am I to judge her? I've never been in a bloody plane crash. I've never had anything like that happen. But it's over a year later now and I find it increasingly hard to believe—'

'You think I'm making it up, that I don't remember.'

'I think you're not trying hard enough. Ben was my friend. I think you owe it to him to try harder.'

'It's not about *trying*. If someone has an illness, a disease, do you ever say: oh, they could get better, they're not trying hard

274

enough. I should say, Oh Conrad, he doesn't have a mental illness. He's just trying to draw attention to himself. If he tried harder he could control his moods. He must want to be a medication junkie—'

'There's no comparison. What's wrong with me is organic.' He tapped his temple. 'Too much chemicals. Not enough.'

'That's not what I've heard. Manic depression isn't just biological. It's about the architecture of your feelings, how you learn to feel.'

'Well, you've obviously been reading *The Lancet* or whatever, but as far as I'm concerned I don't have a choice.'

He drew a breath. 'You need to feel you're caught up in big dramas, major passions. You hold your own consciousness in your lap like a soft animal and stroke it. I can see you doing it: standing up there on the landing at night, looking at God knows what, walking around London, nursing your little thoughts, thinking: I wonder if I'll remember something today. But it's all up here,' he tapped his head. 'You *do* remember. It's right there, accessible to you. All you have to do is find the courage to look at it.'

Her lungs felt hollow, as if they'd been scooped out. She opened her mouth to say something, then closed it.

What did an evasion look like? An animal disappearing around the corner, only its tail visible. Tendrils of thought, half-formed, never to be articulated.

'Now you're thinking: I always knew Conrad had a cruel streak, but I never thought he could be so mean. I'm just doing for you what I wished my parents had done for me, all those years ago: to be straight with me, say, Look, Conrad. We're taking you to the doctor. You're too speedy, disoriented. We need to sort you out.'

'You were my friend.'

'Go ahead. Put it in the past tense. Keep dodging the truth.'

'That's why you want me to move out. You're angry with me for everything that happened. For Ben's death, because I don't talk about him more, because I can't—' she faltered. 'I thought you were different from all those people who blamed me.'

275

'I don't blame you. I know we've never spoken about this, not really. But for nearly two years I saw you with Ben at openings, I went with you to dinners, we went to films together. And now you stand in front of me and you say you can't remember him. That dislocates everything I've thought of as real. That's my problem with you: you're unreal. What happened to you was unreal. It's too much for me. I've tried really hard to understand. I wish I were more robust, but I'm not. I'm sorry.'

'All right.' Her voice sounded hard.

Ahead of her she saw a dreary short-term future of *Loot*, of the *Guardian* Flatshare, of notice boards and telephone calls. Veg Household. Gay Flatshare. Must like Cats. No smokers. No DHSS.

'I'll start looking tomorrow,' she said. 'I'll be out within a month.'

*

She spent the final two days in a delirium, drifting downstream, rolling her face into the water from side to side to cool it. Diarrhoea exited her in a steady stream, into the water. If she had more strength she would have laughed at the irony of it: she was surrounded by water, she was enveloped in it, and yet she was dying of dehydration.

She would not remember when she first saw him, but he told her later he thought she was a corpse of the kind that used to drift down the river from the massacres in the mountains, although that hadn't happened for ten years. Except this one had white skin – so white, to his eyes, the sun glinted off her edges as if she were a piece of metal.

Trino was in his mid-forties or possibly fifties – he was so weathered it was hard to say, and when she asked him later she found he himself didn't know the year he was born. Nearly his entire family had been killed in the civil war, and he had come to the edge of the great rainforest to get away from the patrols: the Army, the Civil Defense, the guerillas. They all killed indiscriminately. He still didn't know which one had murdered his sister and raped and killed his daughter.

When, days later, she eventually shook his spiny, toughened hand she thought how years of work could bend and shape you and turn you into Trino, a spindly wrought iron lamp. It was a miracle anyone could work that land. His farm was a sod-grass area littered by the stumps of rainforest trees that had once grown to a height of twenty metres or more.

The thin topsoil peeled off like a layer of powdered icing to

277

reveal the livid red of rainforest soil, which was effective for growing trees but not crops, or pasture.

Trino fished her out of the water and laid her on the wooden deck of his house. He gave her clean water, spread aloe on her burnt face. He tried to get her to eat. At night he put her in his hammock and slept on the floor. When she woke up screaming he woke up too, and sat with her until her eyes folded back into sleep.

He had a macaw and a toucan for pets, although not in cages. Unlike in the town hostels, his birds stayed with him of their own free will. He hunted tepezcuintle and peccaries. Otherwise he lived on fish, and corn. When she could walk again, he took her to his maize patch and she watched him tend the stalks lovingly, shearing away a stray leaf, a weed.

On the fourth day she was with him she found him by the river, holding what looked like a baby crocodile. She swivelled her head and peered at it through her good eye to see that it was actually a trussed-up caiman. She had seen many like it, sunning themselves on tree trunks by the river, whipping away at the first sight of her.

The caiman's snout was clamped shut, his body bent back, as in a convulsion. Three of his tiny legs were tied with rope. It turned his yellow eyes on her and gave her an accusing look, as if she were responsible for his present situation.

'I just snatched this out of the hands of a trapper,' he explained in his soft, slightly lisping Spanish which she some-times found hard to understand. 'I gave him a bit of money for it. More than he'd get for selling the hide. I just can't stand to see them killed.'

They told her she was in Trino's care for seven days, but it seemed like a month. She couldn't tell him who she was, or where she had come from. Only that she had fallen from the sky. 'You must be an angel, then.' He laughed to show he wasn't serious. Her burnt lips and injured eye were not the trappings of angels.

On the other hand, he didn't seem much bothered where she had come from. He had no family, no people living near by. He accepted her unconditionally, knitting her into the fabric of his silent life.

His house had screened windows that were papered with the corpses of moths. The only decorations were a picture of the Pope torn from a magazine and tacked haphazardly on the wall, and disintegrating boxes lined a single shelf of sagging wood. She took a closer look and found they were full of bullets.

She stayed up long into the night, staring into the darkness, waiting to see something – she wasn't sure what. But the darkness only stared back, implacable. She was amazed how safe it felt, on Trino's small porch, a roof over their heads, lanterns with candles which he hung on the corners of the raised porch. It was luxury, the most coddled she had ever felt, to be off the ground, sleeping with light and with another person's breath beside her.

On one of those days he told her he was going to take a trip in his canoe, which was made from a hollowed out log. He called it a *panga*. He would go downriver and pick up some supplies: flour, oil, batteries for his tiny radio.

'Don't leave me here.'

He could see the terror in her eye, so he took her with him. They stopped at the *muelle*, the dock of the closest town. There, he took her to the Rural Guard, which was just a hut at the end of a scraggly street. The boy in charge of the station couldn't have been more than twenty. He looked at her as if she were a ghost.

'The crash? They found the wreck two weeks ago. No-one was missing.'

She shook her head. 'I was missing.' Startled into realisation, she changed her tense. 'I am missing.'

thirty-three

EXPOSURE

Rachel sat perfectly immobile on their sofa. Conrad rose in one deft movement and intercepted Alex as she came through the door.

'Her father died last night,' he whispered. 'Some drunk aristocrat drove his sports car into him just as he was pruning his orange trees. The worst thing is, the drunk guy's their neighbour. He's threatening to kill himself. His wife has to keep him in a straitjacket while she dumps all the coke in the house down the toilet. Big Tuscan soap opera.'

'What do we do?'

'She won't talk but she doesn't want to be alone.'

So began a strange watery afternoon of sitting in their living room, Conrad perched on the overstuffed hessian chairs, Rachel on the leather couch, dipping in and out of pools of silences.

Rachel spoke in fits and starts, beginning sentences only to sputter and fail, drift off into nothing. She seemed not to be talking to them so much as to herself.

'I only ever used my father. Or resented his name, his fame. And now he's gone. Same old story.'

She wanted to say, same old story as what? But Conrad intercepted her with a warning look.

'Now I'm the one who's crying. It's funny: an Angry Young Man or Angry Young Woman is interesting. An Angry Middle-Aged Woman is just ridiculous.' She gave Conrad an appealing look. 'I've got to come to some sort of emotional amnesty with myself. I don't want to end in anger. Or worse, in delusion.'

'Like Basia.' She said it without thinking.

'Exactly.' Rachel grimaced. 'Like Basia. At least Basia's got a child. For years I wanted to be pregnant. I've almost given up now. I think there's something wrong with me. I blame it on the water. All the oestrogen they dump—' She drifted off.

'It could still happen.'

'It could,' Rachel looked out the window. 'I'm going to Italy. I'm going to live in my parents' house. It might be too late, but I'll do it for my father.'

Conrad kneaded her shoulders. 'Rachel—'

'No, I know what I'm doing. I'm going to grow a little wine. Tend a few olive groves. Buy fresh rabbit in the village market. I'm going to read all the books I meant to read. I'm going to learn Italian.'

Alex looked out the window. She saw the empty offices of old engineering firms, about to be turned into brash cafés; the park with one abandoned can of Tennant's lager; the minicab drivers racing over the cobblestones.

'I've done my time here.' Rachel's voice was simple, less strident than usual. 'I'll still make work in Italy, although I don't know what I'll do, exactly. Maybe photography. Or painting. Or textiles.' Rachel looked up at them, dry-eyed, unsmiling. 'I can do anything.'

She wouldn't be able to remember much about those last two weeks, the last ones they lived together, whether she saw Conrad or not. She had been so wrapped up in her own concerns – work being so strange, Fernando – that she failed to notice Conrad's increasing absences.

Then again, in London people could go for months without seeing friends. Meanwhile one could be thrown into the canal, or thumped by a police car. Even then the friends only think, she's busy; maybe she's gone abroad. Anything could happen in this city and no-one would notice. Suddenly she found this terrifying.

Conrad didn't go to his studio much in those last weeks. This man who had been a painter's painter, working doggedly every day, almost obsessively, frequently covered in paint, stray flecks nestling among his eyelashes, simply stopped.

Then he wasn't there at all. It took her twenty-four hours to notice. It wasn't unusual for him not to come home in a day, so she let one more pass.

Then another. No insertions of his key in the lock, no turning of the door handle, no humming as he opened the refrigerator door, as he kicked off his shoes. She hadn't realised how much these sounds had filled her life, until they were gone. In the days while she waited, sound made that hissing noise, like the end of a tape, when the music is over.

She tried to remember from cop shows she had seen on television how long the police required someone to be missing before they would investigate. Finally, she rang them up. They invited her to come to the station to give a statement. She passed through the hands of surprisingly sympathetic police officers until she ended up in a small windowless room. Children's stuffed toys were scattered on the floor. There was a smell of stale piss.

'Now, what about his sexual history?' the officer said, midway through her statement.

She walked out of the station telling them she would think about it – she was sure he would show up any minute – and call them back. Conrad would kill her if she started up a police file on him for no good reason. Plus it would take her at least six hours to recount his sexual history.

It was only the second time in her life that she genuinely did not know what to do. She lived for a week on what she had heard people term a knife's edge. Any way she moved, or thought, she felt the blade.

Each time the phone rang she expected to pick it up and hear Conrad's voice saying, 'I decided to go home, just for a while, just to see if my family still think I'm the Antichrist.'

She would laugh. Then she would scream at him.

But the phone call never comes. She goes rummaging in his filing cabinet and finds that his passport is gone. She looks some more and finds a half-empty shoebox. In it are little brown plastic bottles filled with round white pills. She looks at the label: Lithium carbonate, 300mg, then a smaller cluster of different sized bottles are labelled Tegretol. She wonders if this is his future stash of the drug, or if he has stopped taking it.

At night she paces the floors of their flat, feeling the cool Norwegian pine Conrad had laid at great expense underneath her hot soles. She begins to break out into sweats. She can't eat. If she does she feels nauseous.

When the phone does ring she lunges for it like a spurned girlfriend. It is Rachel, or Fernando, saying, 'Any news yet'. But they don't ask it, like a question, rather it is a statement. She wonders if this is because, like her, they suspect the worst.

At last it rains and rains. The rain at night in London feels huddled, interior. It cascades in oblique angles instead of drumming as it does in the tropics, drilling a hole through a tin roof, through the *sombrilla de pobre* leaf that covered her on those nights.

It has the sound of memory, it encourages her to think of people left behind but not much regretted, of her careless past. It promises that tomorrow will be time, and time will be the tomorrow after that, that the waking dream that is her life and all our lives will continue uninterrupted.

She begins to inhabit a place that feels exactly like one of those international transit lounges where there's only a vending machine that accepts a currency you don't possess and men in flowered shirts trying to flog last-minute duty free. She desperately wants to get on her flight, the one that will take her either home or away from it. It doesn't really matter where.

Sometime during that strange week she is walking across London Bridge. The sun is low and pearly in the sky. Overhead, flotillas of birds hold a voluble conference about wind patterns and coordinates. They are about to migrate south, to the swamps of the Camargue.

She reaches the middle of the bridge when suddenly she can't move. Dread has been thrown over her like a blanket. Her heart pounds so hard she thinks it will leap out of her chest.

She grips onto the stone edge of the bridge and thinks: don't look down. If she looks down she will throw up. Nausea blossoms like a dozen perfumed roses in her stomach.

She stands there on London Bridge at dusk, looking down-river to the place past Tower Bridge where the river widens out, the wharf houses converted into loft apartments, the bijoux river enclaves.

Only a week before she had walked along this part of the river with Fernando, peering into apartments where people lived suspended over the river as if on glass platforms and you could see everything.

'They are exhibiting their wealth,' Fernando had said, 'and themselves,' and they had laughed at how people would want to live that way: so exposed, permeated, vulnerable.

The phone rings. It is Laurence, Conrad's dealer. 'Is zere any news?' she says, her voice soft and slightly lisping. 'Zis is really very annoying. I have a buyer interested in Empty Stroller and I need to agree a price. You know, Conrad, he can be very fickle.'

'It's you who's fickle. You and the entire art world. Your collective fickleness has worn him down. You don't give a shit about Conrad. All you care about is your percentage.' She put the phone down.

She begins to imagine herself organising Conrad's funeral. She doesn't know how to get in touch with his family. No-one does. For all purposes he might never have had one.

She can imagine Conrad's friends dressing up for the funeral, thinking, this Matthew Williamson skirt will inject a little bit of colour into the undifferentiated sea of black; or, thank God for Karen Millen and her power suits. For them, it would be just another art event. Just another private view. SOMEONE IS DEAD.

Conrad would enjoy his own funeral, being the star of the evening, standing apart from the crowd just as he did at his openings, observing the mourners filing away into the drizzle; thin people, like glistening black matchsticks, a flare of red at the top – the broken capillaries in the cheeks of the drinkers.

There is Alain on the periphery, talking to a girl in a white fake-fur jacket, predictably trying to remain stoic, above it all. He even tells jokes and laughs. Soon he is joined by the ever so slightly uncomfortable laughter of the girl. Later he will congratulate himself on having made the girl lighten up. At a funeral. What talent. What levity.

This was the kitsch of funerals: that beyond the sorrow, the loss, is the social event, the chatter, the alcohol, the people at whose attendance the dead person would have been surprised.

She feels a heavy, sudden certainty, as if large pieces of furniture are falling through her body. It feels like everything will be exhausted, pre-scripted, pure kitsch from now on. In fact, she herself is pure kitsch: the secretly married, the plane crash survivor, the woman with impaired memory, the woman who doesn't know who or what she loves.

Rachel had known this all along. Her performances and installations had sought to ruthlessly expose the kitsch at the heart of so many people's lives. She began to think she hadn't given Rachel enough credit.

She wondered if, in the months and years to come, she would have to erect barbed wire around these weeks, just as she had to do with the accident, and Ben. She wondered if her memory will be made up of no-go zones, each surrounded by a cordon of landmines.

She wondered if Conrad's voice will roam around her head as Ben's does. She may have forgotten details of Ben's face, the feel of his skin, the way he ate a meal or drank a bottle of beer, but he still talks to her in his voice. It's not a particularly unique or memorable voice, rather generic male, wavering somewhere between low- and medium-pitched, but pleasant. Sometimes she talks to him, in her head. How strange, she thinks, that the voice should be what endures.

＊

From her hospital bed she watched sudden torrents cascade down the window. The days are gelatinous; each of them is built from the same substance and there are no boundaries between day and night. Smudged contact lenses are stuck in her eyes. Any words, whether Spanish or English, have to be sieved through a fog.

There is a policeman. Later, an Embassy official, and a woman doctor who probes between her legs. The woman doctor, a forty-ish figure with large square spectacles and a thin face, comes into her room and stands by her bed.

She wants to talk to her but can't bear, for some reason, to even open her mouth. Slowly, they tell her how she was found. Although she knows, or thinks she does. She remembers waking up on Trino's porch.

'You were severely dehydrated,' they tell her, in Spanish. 'Giardia bacterium. Dysentery. Sunburn. Hypothermia.'

'Hypothermia? In the tropics?'

She was in water at night, all night, and her body temperature had dropped. In the day she was burnt by the sun until she was feverish. She bobbed up and down, nudging the extremes of the body temperature scale.

Over the days to come people come to tell her things. The words she will remember are body, parents, repatriation, embassy. Then there are words she won't remember at all. She learns how shock wields a haphazard eraser, like a drunken teacher wiping the blackboard of her mind.

'Your friend's parents have been notified.'

'What friend?'

'Our records say you were travelling together. Benjamin Salkey.' She pronounced the name 'salkigh'.

'I don't know anyone called that.'

'Yes,' the doctor insisted. 'Your airline tickets receipts were recovered from the plane. They show both your names. Then your insurance—'

'I don't believe you.'

'Oh, well.' The doctor shrugs, as if to say, there's nothing I can do about that. She puts her chart back on the hook at the bottom of the bed. She turns to leave the room, but at the last minute, by the door, turns around and says to her, her voice very low. 'You've had an enormous shock.'

'Have I?' What has happened, exactly? She can't remember any shock.

She closes her eyes and falls into a consuming sleep, barren of dreams.

The next thing she remembers is the plane scudding along the runway. She has been drugged for the journey home, to quell her fear. She feels like she is sitting on a thousand downy cushions. A truck is parked on top of her heart, to stop it from running away.

Then they are aloft and she looks down to see black squares of net tarpaulins, glistening with rain. These are the nurseries for tropical flowers, now the country's third biggest export, after coffee and bananas. Underneath them azaleas and heliconias brew. As the plane gains altitude they form a patchwork quilt with pockets of green matted squares – the hacked-at remnants of tropical forests.

The plane banks and heads toward the coast and soon they are flying over curlicued lagoons. In the distance she sees the hooked finger of Cabo Gracias a Dios – Cape Thank God – pointing into the Caribbean. Then the isthmus slips away behind her.

Somewhere over the Caribbean she falls into a heavy chemical sleep and she is back on the lonely beach where they stayed in the cabin, walking along a sleek shore. The first streaks of a pink dawn are lain like ribbons across the horizon. The ocean fizzes at her feet. Silver waves cascade legions of sea turtles onto the sands. They are wet and smooth, like outsize stones of polished jade.

She shades her eyes against the rising sun. In the distance she sees a figure walking toward her from a long way down the beach. She can tell it's him from the peculiar square way he walks, swinging his arms by his side. He is wearing a checked shirt and jeans, the clothes he wore the first day she met him.

Her fingertips begin to hum with the anticipation of touching him. Any second now she will be able to see the detail of his face, to run her hands along his arms. But even though he seems to be coming toward her, he remains a small figure on the horizon.

She realizes there is an object in her hand. She brings it up to her eyes and turns it round and round. It is made of glass.

The sun comes charging up above the horizon. She watches as it spreads itself through the glass object in her hand, separating into cool orange, mint blue, red, orchid-violet, green. She turns the prism round and round, watching as the bars of colour fall upon the sand, transforming its grey lustre into a kaleidoscope.

When she wakes into the muffled roar of the airplane's engines she remembers the dream. She recognizes it as a fragment of meaning she will never be able to place within her. So she will hold it in her hand, a prism she will occasionally put to the light, to test the depth and density of the colours of life as they pass through its demanding eye.

thirty-four

UNDERWATER LIFE

Around her the usual crowd of snifflers and hypochondriacs sat on orange plastic chairs. Ripped children's books were splayed across the floor and the walls lined with threatening leaflets about safe sex and how not to contract hepatitis B while on holiday. All the other leaflets seemed to be directed at pregnant women. A Samaritans poster screamed: DEPRESSED? SUICI-DAL? LONELY?

The police had advised her to get an appointment with Conrad's GP. She would talk to him first, then ask for the name of Conrad's psychiatrist or whatever medical doctor had prescribed him the pills.

She had brought a serious book on the belief systems of indigenous peoples to read, but it seemed a poor match for the jelly-like NHS hours she was sure she would have to wait.

She picked up a magazine. 'Aran sweaters need no longer be reserved for wearing with jeans at the weekend,' said *Company*. She put it down and picked up her serious book. 'Forgetfulness would appear as a true category of mythical thought. A certain intimacy exists between them.'

A certain intimacy. Nearly two years before, Conrad approached her at a private view, in full view of the art crowd. She had been back two months and everyone avoided her, darting little salamander looks from the corners of their eyes: did you hear she's lost all memory of Ben?

'If you need a place to live, Alex, I'm looking for a flatmate.' He squeezed her hand in a silent gesture of sympathy. No-one, not even her parents, had done that for her. He had none of the

289

fear, the disapproval she had felt emanating from other people. They were afraid to come near her, as if it would rub off on them, as if she carried it on her skin.

And then, when Conrad had found someone he really liked, she had taken him. She understood how, even if the person you love or are attracted to rejects you, somehow they are still yours, they are a kind of lover. And if your friend then takes that person, snatches them away from underneath your nose, in fact, albeit without meaning to—

She remembered Conrad talking about how he felt going out into the world after having spent days in his studio, painting. 'Even just walking down the street, on the bus, I felt so exposed, observed. I felt I needed to be protected.'

She sees the habitual flecks of paint on the edge of his hairline. He always managed to get paint in his hair. The faint whiff of turpentine on him, his ravaged nails.

The doctor called her in.

'I can't tell you anything, I'm afraid,' the doctor said. 'I haven't seen Mr Emmerich in nearly two years.'

'Did he ever discuss depression with you, or manic depression?'

'I'm afraid I can't really discuss that.'

'But I'm his wife,' she says the word, dragging it out of the box inside her where it lived, for the first time in a year. It is her trump card.

'He's missing. He's been missing for a week now. I need to speak to his psychiatrist, or whoever prescribes his medication. I think he stopped taking it a month ago. I found all these bottles of lithium.'

'I'm sorry, but we can't release health records to spouses, at least, not in this circumstance. Now, if your husband is located and the police—'

'If he's found dead, you mean.'

The doctor sighed. 'Well, then, that's another story.'

'So what do I do?'

'If you file a missing person's report, then we can liaise with the police. I'll look up his record and talk to the consultant psychiatrist. He must have been referred to the Homerton.'

'Right.' She rose.

The flat is eerie. She has to keep the television on, for company. When she goes to sleep she leaves the radio on. It murmurs classical music all night.

Without Conrad's presence, she can feel him more. Although what are ghosts? A projection, the shadow of a soul. Only their rage or their disappointment gives them shape. That is the force of anger, she thinks: it can last for centuries. Meanwhile, love evaporates.

Yes, he is there. She can hear him pacing back and forth in the living room when she is lying in bed. He's a nail-biter, a worrier, the anxious father she never had.

On television she watches a documentary about the discovery of volcanoes on the ocean floor. It is about basalt heat vents in the Juan de Fuca strait. The scientists talk about chemoreactive amino acids and black smokers. They are struggling to bring columns of lava-like rock up from the ocean floor. This is where all life began, first as single-celled organisms, then feeding on nitrogen and oxygen, dividing and reproducing. We are close to discovering the origins of life, the scientists say.

But when brought to the surface these black smokers look like no more than debris, piles of ash or burnt rubber. The scientists seem unfazed by this: they are dedicated and have glamorous names like Veronique. They seem quite sane for people who have lived half their lives underwater, in diving suits, in submarines.

She catches a glimpse of herself reflected in Conrad's wall mirror. There she is, sitting alone in a flat lit only by the blue flickering light of the television and the reflected gleam of the City.

They are each manning their own submersibles, she understands, trapped in a cold capsule of self. All underwater explorers, bumping along in the permanent night of the depths, glimpsing fantastical things: transparent fish, giant sea-

291

worms, squid and manta rays, those winged angels of the deep. Looking to spark the chemical reaction that will bind them to someone else, and finally call a halt to these lonely underwater missions.

The next two days are like brushing up against pine trees. She feels itchy, serrated. By this point she has gone to the police and given them all the details. Manic depressive, although controlled. Supposedly on medication. She holds back on the sexual history.

The police nod sympathetically. They must be trained to do this. At night, at home in the empty flat, she practises this in the mirror. Up her head goes, sympathy cascading off her forehead. Down.

thirty-five

CAMERA OBSCURA

She is standing in front of the mirror in the living room, practising her sympathetic nod, when she feels it.

At first it is like a cool hand at her back, near her kidneys. She looks in the mirror, but there's nothing. Only her face and its expression of fear, blaring on and off like a car alarm.

She whips around. He is there, standing by the non-existent pillar. His brilliant brown eyes stare at her out of the darkness. River-smell floods her nostrils.

He is not transparent at all, but amazingly solid, like a wax figure escaped from one of London's many dungeon museums. His shoes have heels and pointed fronts. For some reason they make her think of Quakers.

She hears herself say, I don't believe in ghosts. Although she has said it out loud, her voice echoes weirdly in her head.

If she believed in ghosts, then Ben was out there somewhere, looking for her. He would be angry; he would yank her into that realm the burning-eyed man in front of her inhabited. At that thought, she went cold with fear.

My wife and children, all dead. His eyes shimmer with tears. I was put in prison, on the order of the King.

What did you do?

My beliefs. I refused the Oath.

A Quaker, she thinks. She had learned in History class how they had been persecuted, from the mid 1600s, for being non-conformists.

I had a dog, a whippet—

Two fireplaces erupt from behind the brick walls. Or rather, the image comes from that camera obscura in her mind, and projects itself upside down onto her retina. Flames crackle in the fireplaces, sending a bitter fume of charcoal into the room. For a second she is thrilled to smell the unreal past.

Now he is sitting at a desk, a thick blanket thrown over his knees, writing. She hears the strange scratch of quill on parchment. It has the sound of thinking.

Behind him flames crawl up ancient brickwork. Two brooding paintings appear and hang themselves on a vanished wall. A dog curls itself in the shape of a question mark at the man's feet. A mild expression takes hold of the man's face. He looks far less ravaged. In fact, he looks content.

What are you doing in my house?

The man looks up from his desk. He says something, but without moving his mouth. His words drift into her mind like clouds, then vaporise.

Can you tell me where Conrad is?

She doesn't know why she has said this. In the strangeness of the moment, it is all she wants to know.

He gives her a disappointed look, like a schoolmaster. Then his face shuts down, the fires extinguish themselves and the paintings melt. She waits until only a whiff of mud and sludge is left.

She brings her shaking hands up to her face. The downy hairs on her arms stand bolt upright.

Within a second a cloud of depression forces her onto the couch. There she assumes the brace posture recommended on airplane safety announcements. She had once sat like this for three long minutes, waiting for the rip and jolt.

The ghost reminds her of hallucinations she had in the forest: quite real, but obviously out of kilter. Ghosts have no scientific basis, she tells herself. Maybe she was caught on a trembling frequency between reason and fantasy. It was part of her larger failure to distinguish properly between fantasy and reality, love and desire, possibility and impossibility.

'You try to close yourself off from experience, but instinctively you're an open person.' Conrad had said this to her, more than once. He was trying to make sense of the change in her, after she came back. He witnessed her struggle to try to be in life, really inside it, to live without fear that it would be snatched away from her any second.

Yes, she was open. She saw her edges flapping. Letting people in, then out again. Like gills, or osmosis, the permeable boundaries of amoebas, which is how life began in the first place, the scientists on the underwater documentary said.

Maybe what Conrad had meant was *vulnerable*. Death had done that, made her permeable, over-aware of how delicate her boundaries actually were, over-knowledgeable of how it will one day end.

It would be a relief, in fact, to read recipes, to buy garden furniture, to pore over pension options. But she has been fingered by that brand of loneliness, the kind Conrad also knew, like a lion or some powerful and potentially malevolent creature might brush the face of its prey, lick it even, before devouring it.

But she had been let go. She would never be able to find solace in everyday things; in gardening, children, buying furniture. For her, as for Conrad, those miniature refuges from the inevitable could only be fought for with great valour, while the rest of humanity accepted them as their earned due.

The telephone rang.

'I have been trying to get hold of you.' It was Fernando.

'I haven't heard from him.'

'But what about you? Are you all right?'

'I need to get out of here.'

'Come to my studio.'

They drink on the terrace of a riverside pub, watching a greasy London sunset, then walk along the river, passing the Design Museum, where a wedding party spews out shivering women in thin dresses and delicate sandals.

It's dark by the time they return to his studio, picking from a conical packet of chips held between them like a trophy. They fall asleep recklessly, mixed up in each other's limbs.

*

To retrieve the moment of their meeting she has to open a towering filing cabinet on the other side of her retina. Once she has the image between her fingers she inserts it in the camera and projects it, upside down, through a small point of light.

The flipped image lands on the darkened wall of the past. It has the thinner, less coherent look of distant time. Look at Ben, look at her: they are blurred, hazy; two people who haven't yet become themselves.

She is in the university library, one of those suitably dusty and ancient buildings prowled by a prickly librarian. She is vaguely aware of another figure browsing the same shelf of books. She has seen him around before, but never took much notice. He is unremarkable looking, brown eyes obscured behind too-big glasses. His hair is unkempt and his nose a bit squashed.

A shaft of sunlight breaks through the tight ranks of the English clouds. It beams itself through the library window, cutting a path through the dust and the years accumulated in that dark room.

The shaft of light lands in the aisle and comes to rest on Ben. He stands surrounded by dancing dust mites, his dark hair licked amber by the sun.

'It's great to see the sun,' he says.

She looks up. 'Yes, it is.'

'I'm trying to start writing my essay on German expressionism but I'm getting nowhere.'

'Me neither,' she admits.

She looks again at his face and finds it neither handsome nor plain. 'Your glasses are too big.'

He seems nonplussed. 'I know. I've had these since I was in school.'

They went to the pub together. She has forgotten what they talked about, except that they spoke for about five hours and found they used the same words, the same ideas, had the same (being arrogant students at the time) 'approach to the world'.

What is it about being so suddenly in love? How can it happen? One day he is just another figure roaming the library shelves. The next day he is necessary to her existence.

In the weeks to come they ran into each other often. If she had to brush his shoulder her heart pounded, fuelled by adrenalin. She felt she was touching a silent altar. The air between them crackled and buzzed with a kind of threat. A silver streamer strung itself between them, a thin ribbon of fear and delight.

She stared at him for weeks, horrified. Is this love? When she saw him she felt truly nauseous. Yes, that's it, she told herself. You're sick.

Ben did get new glasses. Then he got contacts and stopped wearing glasses at all. The best thing he had ever done was to liberate those obsidian eyes; serious, intelligent, unfathomable. She liked the way they seemed to scan her intentions, their wary friendliness that for her was the key to his attractiveness.

They got a flat together. She wouldn't appreciate for years how easy it had all been: you meet someone in the library, fall in love, go through university together, decide to cohabit. She didn't know it then, but love would never be so simple again.

Ben was embarrassing; he cycled everywhere; he would arrive with half his shirt hanging out of his trousers and one sock rolled up over a trouser leg. He carried his helmet and his bike seat with him. She cringed at the memory of how she had moved away from him at parties, seminars, private views. Ben sweaty and hot from battling with London taxicabs and White Van Man, entering a room of people she knew or wanted to know. He didn't give a damn how he looked. Sometimes he forgot to cut his hair and it hung in his eyes.

He was always thin, his skin smooth, and he tanned easily. People were always thinking he was French, or Spanish, and they always underestimated his age. If there was anything childish about him it was more that he had retained a capacity for delight, rather than naïveté, or a child's wild trust. She was coming to realise that she would only be able to love people in whom a remnant of the child they had once been survived. Sometimes it was in the face, or the casual proprietorial way they splayed their limbs over chairs, tables.

Ben's death had torn a gash in the fabric of his family's well-ordered lives. It took six weeks for his body to be brought back to England. By that time she was back in London, staying – temporarily, she thought – with Conrad. He had gone to the funeral, but she stayed away. She would be a stranger to Ben's family, just as he was a stranger to her memory. She never asked Conrad what the funeral was like, what elegies were read, what was said about her.

She wonders if even then, on that day in the library, dust mites dancing in swords of sun, if dark forces were already circling them.

Dark forces. She had never believed such things existed outside of lushly menacing children's books, with wicked princes and corrupt queens who ate children and kept pet hawks.

But there they were: faces seen on the other side of steamed-up windows, caught for a moment, indistinct and blurred. She can see them even now, their sharp-featured faces and dishevelled hair, like blackbirds in the rain.

thirty-six

THE SCAPEGOAT

They met in the corridor, brushed by colleagues in a hurry to photocopy, answer calls. They hadn't seen each other in a week or more.

'You're not a political exile.'

Erica scowled. 'Is that what Fernando told you?'

'Why say you are, if you aren't?'

'I am. We had to leave the country.'

'Why?'

Erica gave her a long defiant look. 'Because my father, who was a very good man, was in the military. He was accused of killing some Indians. Union leaders.'

'Did he?'

'He didn't. But troops under his command did. Human rights organizations made a big stink of it, and the Army decided my father would be a – a, what do you call it, when someone is singled out to take the blame so that others don't have to?'

'A scapegoat.'

'That's it. A scape goat.' Erica said it as two separate words. 'There is always one, isn't there? You've even got one in the art and design section. That funny animal you built. You think it's such a good joke. A scapegoat. My father faced twenty years in jail.'

'But the Army never indicts its own officers.'

'How do you know so much about the internal affairs of our country?' It was the first time Erica had called it that: our country. 'I'm afraid it's more complicated than that.' She walked away.

*

At home those nights after Conrad disappeared, she drank nearly a bottle of wine. She sat back in one of Conrad's soft leather chairs. They were from Denmark; she remembered going to buy them with him in a second-hand furniture shop off Brick Lane. He had sat in every chair in the shop, throwing his long legs over their arms, waiting for her to nod her approval.

Conrad's absence buzzed around her like a real thing, more like a presence than a lack of it. With Ben it had felt different: somewhere in her mind, she had known what had happened to him. She knew where his body was.

She was legally married to Conrad. She felt close to him, to his body, thought she knew all its details and the story they told – the curve of his eyelashes, his hipless gait, the grainy semolina feel of the skin on his waist. The scar on his neck where he was hit by a bullet from an airgun when he was twelve; his slightly crooked left index finger, which he broke in a fall from a ladder while hanging his degree show at art college. His peculiarly lithe knuckles; the first grey hairs which congregated in a patch on the left side of his head.

Was Conrad still out there? At that very moment was he in another time zone, lowering sunglasses over his eyes, cowering under an awning against a typhoon, drinking a café au lait?

She went to stand by the window, as she had done so many nights, listening to Conrad move around below, the floorboards groaning under his feet, humming to himself, popping open a bottle of wine. She thought of the ghost, writing at his desk behind her, trapped in some parallel dimension. His dog sealed there too, with the fires.

She stared at the skyline, felt it spinning around her. There it was again, the breathless quality of London, of a life lived at speed. She had the impression she was speeding through life, skimming along very fast on surfaces. Where was this all taking her? How had she arrived here, alone in a flat in an old part of London, waiting for a friend who has disappeared, just like that? Where were the other, possible lives, the lives never lived?

Her life as an artist, in a flat shared with Ben. Both of them in their thirties, maybe being successful painters. Or the life she would have lived with the German boy she loved when she was sixteen; he would become an anthropology professor and she would be living in an attic flat in Freiburg, looking out onto a Gothic cathedral. She sees herself making gingerbread and Christmas ornaments for her children.

Her life with Conrad, if he had really loved her. She sees them travelling in off-the-beaten-track places: Malawi, Bhutan. There they are, dusty with savannah grass, heaving sweaty backpacks into the sunset. The soundtrack of their life together is laughter.

Where did these other lives live? She imagined them stored on a dark shelf of possibility. She wished she could take them out and try them on, one by one, like a jumper. One life wasn't enough, she was certain, would never be enough, just as this world would never be enough. She felt cheated by this one life of hers, by its random design. Maybe that's why their ghost stuck around, to try to live the life he himself had been so cruelly denied, to get a second chance.

That night, he is in her dreams. This hasn't happened for so long. Muffled in the fabric of her dream, she can feel her surprise.

His black hair drips with rain.

You're wet, she says.

What? This? He puts his long fingers to his hair. They come away covered with blood.

She can see his fear and it rips her apart.

Don't be afraid.

His voice is faint now, but accusing. Why did you leave me?

I didn't.

I've gone to live in Brazil, he says.

Ben—

Saying his name has the effect of switching on one of those abandoned spaces, like in Conrad's space station. Lights lurch to life. Machines hum.

She reaches out to him but he gives her a suspicious look and shies away deftly, like a cat.

Then he is gone and she is cocooned in a deep sleep and it is quite different from any sleep she has ever known: a time-gobbling sleep, utterly unlike the regular velvet bolt of fatigue that hides dreams in its folds.

In her sleep she hears the rasp of waves coming from somewhere inside her. She tries to see the gauzy sky, thinned by a cheesecloth of mist, but the gauze has knitted itself tight and dark.

It is dawn on a hot Pacific beach and light, gas-blue, leaks from the horizon. It is the day after Ben's death, a day emptied of another body, the first day in twenty-nine years without him in the world. For Ben it is the beginning of that terrifying empty time people called Eternity, but which she suspected was as close to nothing as it was possible to be.

But she's alive. This is what divides her most sharply from Ben, who she had slept with the night before, whose shoulder she had touched only a minute before they came crashing down to earth.

It is her first morning in the rainforest and she is dreaming of the beach where they spent a week in the cabin, before heading into the Highlands. The palm trees just visible in the spray, the charcoal sands, painted wooden fishing boats riding the breakers. On the beach women are selling *agua pipa*, coconut water.

These dreams welcome her back to life. Waking from them, disoriented and confused, for some minutes this is all she knows. The sum total of her person, her humanity is reduced to those three words: *I am alive.*

thirty-seven

STATIC

Rachel stood by a distant pillar, sandwiched in a group of friends, all established artists of Rachel's age. It was her farewell show, to celebrate her leaving for Italy. She called it Nobody Loves Me.

She went to stand in the group. Rachel's eye brushed over her, but she did not acknowledge her arrival.

Rachel was explaining her concept. 'That's what happens to women over thirty-five. Inevitably, they're disappointed in love. Look at me. No-one will take me because I'm "difficult". I "feel too much." It just goes to show you, men want an inert sex doll. They can't deal with a real person.'

She turned to Alex. No, that's not right. She turned on her.

'You're implicated in this too. You're not young any more; you're going to find out.' Rachel darted across the little circle she had formed with her friends and grabbed her sleeve. She was swaying slightly. Rachel was staring at her with glassy eyes. Alex realized she was very drunk.

Her voice turned savage. Tears seeped from her eyes. 'What have you done with Conrad? What did you do to him? I love Conrad. You've killed him.'

She tore her sleeve from her grip and lurched away. In her haste she bumped into a young man with Asian features who was stabbing at the air with a Gauloise. The lank-haired girl beside him opened her mouth wide, as if in a huge gesture of laughter, but no sound came.

She staggered out of the gallery. Only once she was out on the street did she realise her breath was coming in great gulps.

She went in the Bagel Shop on Brick Lane to get one of their scalding coffees. As the woman filled her cup with steaming water she caught sight of herself in the mirror: a woman of indeterminate age, neither young nor old, blowing on her coffee, her mouth puckered. She thought of the places they had been together, this woman and her: rooms filled with lime light, wandering through glacial airports stranded in the middle of continents – Denver, Chicago – taking breezy walks on footpaths, straying too near the tall white cliffs that stalk the south coast of England.

From now on, there were going to be two people, she realised. Her ghost had caught up with her. It had walked all the way from the rainforest to be with her in Brick Lane. Maybe it had slowed her step that night, ever so slightly, as she stepped out onto the pedestrian crossing.

In that moment she saw these two selves in the mirror, herself hand in hand with this doppelgänger, walking with their heads down, eyes closed against the sun, as if into a desert.

On Friday the telephone rang. She picked it up and heard a hiss. Then a thin, nearly unrecognizable voice, surfacing through static.

'Alex, is that you or is it the bloody answerphone?'

It was a second before she could answer. Dizziness washed over her. 'They've been trawling the canals of London for you.'

'Yuck. You know I'd never do that. I can't stand dirt. Even if I've ended up here in Bacteria City.'

'Where are you?'

'Madagascar. I can't pronounce the name of the place I'm in, but they're chopping down the rainforest here. Are you still working on that campaign at work? They're mining the crap out of the place too. Zinc, uranium, or is it nickel?'

'—'

'Alex? Did you say something? The static's terrible on this line.'

She opened her mouth again to try to speak. Her voice came out weirdly hoarse. 'Have you any idea of the distress you've caused me? Not only me, but Rachel, all your friends, the police.'

'Didn't they check international departures?'

'It didn't turn up anything. No-one had your name on their passenger list.'

'That's—' His voice fizzed away for a second. '—took the Eurostar to Paris and got the flight from Charles de Gaulle. Much cheaper from there. Gotta love that globalization.'

A streak of pain slashed her lungs. 'I don't think I can talk to you right now.'

A tinny hissing came into his voice, but it did not come from the line. 'Alex, I had to leave. We can't live together. It's not healthy. We're both so guilty. We're both survivors. We both saw someone die—'

'You didn't see your brother die.'

'Yes I did, every night in my dreams.'

'That's why you left? You couldn't bear to be around me? Even though I saved you from being chucked out of this country—'

'I left because I don't want to be sick.'

'You're not sick.'

'Nobody's not loved me before. Nobody's not fallen in love with me—'

She didn't know what he was talking about. Conrad's voice was unravelling, until only tiny threads of sound swirled around her head. Black dots were gathering in front of her eyes. They became thicker until they blotted out the world.

'I just want to siphon this out of me,' he was saying. 'If I could wring it out of my cells and bones I would. I don't even know what kind of substance it would be. Liquid turmoil. Quivering—'

The black dots congealed into a heavy, hard substance. Something brushed against her leg. She looked down to see a thin dog rubbing itself against her.

She managed to put the phone back on the receiver. Then

305

she passed out. As she fell to the floor she felt herself knock over Conrad's prized lamp.

She must have lain there for at least an hour. At one point she dreamt a dog was licking her face. When she regained consciousness it was dark, and the lamp was standing upright.

thirty-eight

RELATIVE MERCY

On Monday she went to work as usual. Walking by Erica's partition, she had a sudden urge to look in. Her desk was clean. More than clean, it was empty.

'Is Erica not in today?' she asked Stuart.

'She left.'

'Left?'

'She's left the company. Friday was her last day.'

'What?'

Stuart sighed. 'Alex? How could you have missed it?'

'Missed what?'

'What was going on.'

Samantha turned around from her computer screen. 'She's been having an affair with Michael.'

'Who?'

'Erica.'

She sat down. She felt like she had been hit. 'What was so obvious about it?'

'The fact she spent half the day in his office. The fact he briefed her on things he wouldn't tell the rest of us. You were her friend. You must have known something was up.' Stuart looked at her accusingly. She was older: they had expected her to know these things.

What she felt was not anger, or shock, but disappointment. Like how you would be disappointed in the behaviour of your child.

Of course she knew it was Michael, on some submerged level. Who else was there? But she had always thought Michael a flimsy character. She thought him unworthy of Erica.

'There's something else,' Stuart said. 'Something really big is going down. We're on a gag order. We can't talk to the press.'

'About what?'

'About the campaign, about anything—' Hattie said.

'Some guy came in last week, when you were sick.' In Stuart's voice was the faintest hint that he didn't believe in her illness. That was the day she had taken off to go to the police station and file a missing persons report. 'A lawyer.'

'But what's going on?'

'We have no idea,' Hattie shrugged. 'Just that Erica resigned, and they've been taking files out of Michael's office all day. Last night they took away his computer. He hasn't got email any more – can you imagine, no email?' Hattie rolled her eyes in horror.

'But who is *they*?'

'We don't know,' Stuart shrugged.

She walked to the water cooler and got a drink. For two hours she tried to work, but there was no work to be done. At lunch she went home.

As she walked she wondered if Erica would get in touch with her somehow: send her an email, a note. Then she realized Erica didn't know her home telephone, or her address. She had never been to the flat she shared with Conrad, she had never introduced them.

It was never a deliberate decision, but she hadn't wanted them to meet. Had she feared Conrad's judgement of Erica, or was it the other way around? She roamed her intentions for possible answers, but none presented itself, except that she had wanted to keep a part of her life separate from Conrad, beyond his reach.

In that moment she knew she would never hear from Erica again. It was sad, but also governed by that firecracker rule in life which dictated that sometimes the people with whom we have the most intense interactions will not be part of our larger lives; we will fizz brightly and burn together for awhile, then extinguish ourselves. The fact that they would never speak again was a relative mercy; it would allow her to remember

Erica as someone who had taken her into confidence, revealed her peculiar and interesting views, mysterious and intense, who had allowed Alex into her life for the equivalent of a moment, when set against a lifetime.

She stopped at some lost corner of Clerkenwell to get some cash. She was overdrawn, the cashpoint bossily informed her. It swallowed her card twice, then angrily spat it out, just like the tongue of the Komodo dragon she saw on a BBC nature documentary the night before.

The dragon's tongue was forked and it went in and out constantly, like it was on automatic. In a nearby river a water buffalo lay sick and dying. It had half buried itself in mud and water to keep cool. Then it couldn't get out; the camera had drawn slowly back to show all the monitor lizards getting into the water and swimming over to the buffalo. They licked the animal with their tongues like they were trying to take care of it. Then they bit off little pieces of the water buffalo and soon it was a feeding frenzy. They ate it alive.

TRAVELLING

He must be in Zanzibar now. She calculates his movements from the intentions scrawled on his last postcard. His writing is unsteady, oxygen deprived; it has the mark of a postcard written on a plane.

She has a vision of Conrad, out there in the untamed world, travelling around Africa on his Barclaycard. He will make five-minute friendships with backpacking nurses from California and easy-come, easy-go Australians. He will thumb lifts from truck drivers, the ones accused of spreading AIDS by using roadside prostitutes, staring hard at Lake Victoria as it is consumed by giant weeds.

She has darker suspicions. In these he is thinning, living his days like grappling up and down ropes. Sitting on misted beaches, perhaps becoming increasingly grandiose and addled.

He has schemes to save Tanzania or Malawi; he offers to teach art to entire communities, to instruct the children in painting and drawing. At first people are kind to him, then, on that visceral frequency people use to detect madness, they move away. The villagers will talk about him, later: the tall Englishman or American or Canadian who came and stayed in the village, who drew birds flying against the sky.

She hopes he will be able to take the same journey she made, and come back to where he belongs. Beyond that, there is nothing she can do for him anymore. We all have to be our own heroes, she understood, our own saviours.

It is her last week at work. The agency is being shut down. Michael is being investigated for something called collusion.

He has been secretly informing the oil lobby of the campaign for Rainbow. He gave them everything: the advertising plan, the details of the lobbying effort Rainbow was exerting on the government. For this he was paid a large sum of money. Apparently he was building a house in Spain and needed some cash to finish it. The firm has been taken over by receivers. These receivers are serious types, rather presumptuous, typically, for people given to receiving and not giving.

Stuart, Hattie and Samantha all find work within five minutes with an internet start-up in fashion retailing or travel, she can't remember which. No-one seems that upset. She supposes it's because London is booming. The newspaper headlines confirm this: BOOM TOWN. LONDON HOUSE PRICES UP 400%. Stockbrokers and estate agents in yellow shirts tumble from packed Friday night pubs, loft dwellers buy hyperinflated wine, and for the price of a one bedroom flat she could buy a farm in Iowa or a spa in the Czech Republic.

London is booming. They all repeat it to themselves, like a mantra, noting the weird combination of fear and satisfaction it inspires. How it seems sinister, even, the way the boom looks set to continue forever.

She wonders, are they living in the present, or has the present been converted, instantaneously and before their eyes, into the future? Everything that happens in life happens in an instant, then it's over. She wants things to last, for there to be some truce between experience and memory. She wants to slow down the now, so it is forced to hover – a hummingbird, a butterfly – above the vibrating face of life.

She has shaken off the feeling she has had for the past year, that death was her accompanier, like a shadowy accomplice following her everywhere, dogging her heels. It was gone, although from time to time she feels the presence of something friendlier. It's not Ben, or Conrad who is walking beside her. Maybe it is memory, and possibly love, the only possible weapons against the universe's indifference as to our ultimate fates.

She knew there was a decision which must be taken sooner

or later: to be in life, to be really there, inside it, or to stand on the outside, her nose pressed to the window pane, looking in. It wasn't enough to just live in life: you had to embrace it, before it slipped away.

She would never speak to Rachel again, although she heard through the artvine that she moved into her parents' pile in Italy and planted a plum tree where her father died.

Of course Rachel could afford to be so lacerating, so adventurous in her work. She had always known she had the safety valve of orange groves and Peccorino cheese and risible television waiting for her at the end of the curved drive that would take her to her father's house. Rachel's dilemmas would always be no more serious than the Nobody Loves Me variety. There was no dark tiger pacing the path ahead of her, daring her to continue walking.

As for Alex, she has already played the cruel landlord and rented their place for an outrageous sum to a pair of internet juveniles. She doubts they'll be around for very long. Within a few months they'll be buying their own Clerkenwell loft. Either that or the ghost will scare them off. She feels strangely sad to leave the ghost with shallow juveniles who wouldn't understand his rueful dignity. But she has a life to live; she can't spend any more time with the dead than she already has.

Next month she will travel with Fernando to Spain. They are going to drive the country from top to bottom. She has never been to the south of Spain. She imagines red plateaux, bleached towns perched on them. Names like Alicante and Cadiz canter through her mind, along with snow-capped mountains, their slopes the purple of bruises. Razored fortresses propped on precipices. Cool patios, wood fires.

They will be in the sun and she will be light, empty, muscular. They will scramble over pine-covered hills together until they are both brown and she will watch his eyes deepen with the night. People will drift into and out of their orbit on the strength of his pull. In the sky will be a grape sun, in their mouths the astringency of olives.

They will go further, beyond England, further than Ben, beyond memory, beyond Conrad, everyone. She sees them driving to the edge of Europe. Moving, travelling. Then further, crossing over to Africa.

And then where will they be?

Fran 29
Ranie Louw

15 Northwold Rd
N16 7DG

7245.0128